The Alien
Chronicles

STORY SYNOPSES

Guests of the Chitterer Liberation Force *(Blair S. Babylon)*

It's just a bar story, one of those wild tales of action and adventure that you tell a bunch of your fellow drunks at a college party. No one could survive being captured and held hostage by an alien terrorist group like the brutal Chitterer Liberation Force. Yet when Blake tells it, it's charming, it's hysterical, and for Wellington Smyth, it's familiar.

Uncle Allen *(Will Swardstrom)*

When twentysomething Rachel visits her Grandma Naomi and Uncle Allen for a week, all she's planning to do is clean out the attic. But between the odd behavior of her senile grandmother and the strange diary page she uncovers in the cluttered attic, Rachel may have uncovered a family secret bigger than she could have possibly imagined.

The Kholorian Conspiracy *(Geoffrey Wakeling)*

Professor Serelah Delekin is accustomed to uncovering the secrets of alien artifacts. But when one of her co-workers is killed while researching their latest find, she soon realizes that this particular artifact is protecting far more than ancient secrets—it harbors a conspiracy that will soon put her own life at risk.

318 *(Autumn Kalquist)*

Test subject 318 is next in line for experimentation. One doctor assigned to the case will face the consequences.

Crawlies *(Annie Bellet)*

Sadie's short life on a backwater space station has never been easy. But when she accidentally stows away on an alien trading vessel, it will take all the youthful charm and courage she possesses to deal with the danger that awaits.

The Insect Requirement *(B. V. Larson)*

An exploratory mission discovers the first non-Earth planet truly compatible with human life. But for the planet's first colonists, certain sacrifices will be required.

Hanging with Humans *(Patrice Fitzgerald)*

It's time for *The Zeldar Show*, where the audience tunes in every day to watch host Trazil Krang, the "Funnest Guy in the Galaxy," send someone down to an alien planet at the edge of the universe. Today's contestant is Glendorp Freundzap, a nice young Zeldarian who puts his pants on one leg at a time—all twelve of them. Glendorp is thrilled to be headed for an exotic little planet called Earth. There he'll enjoy a classic human ritual known as the high school prom...

Emily May *(Moira Katson)*

Harry has a stable job, a tolerable boss, and a regular crew on the freighter *Emily May,* the namesake, alas, of an infamous ghost ship from the early days of space travel. Everything seems to be smooth sailing—until the *Emily May* picks up an unusual piece of cargo, and all of Harry's calculations go to hell…

Remember Valeria *(W.J. Davies)*
The leaders of the Valerian rebellion intended only to liberate the Freya, an enslaved race of cyber sapient beings, by granting them free will. But something goes wrong, and instead of simply attaining freedom, the awakened Freya lash out against their flesh-and-blood masters, causing untold devastation. Now it is up to one rebel soldier to salvage what is left of the rebellion—and rescue the Freya from complete annihilation.

Alien Space Tentacle Porn *(Peter Cawdron)*
A 1950s hospital. Temporary amnesia. A naked man running through Central Park yelling about alien space tentacles. Tinfoil, duct tape, and bananas. These are the ingredients for a spectacular romp through a world you never thought possible.

Trials *(Nicolas Wilson)*
When the *Nexus* shifts to one-man missions to make first contact, the security division's second-in-command accepts a challenging assignment to negotiate with the most dangerous planet yet. Where reason does not persuade this alien species, militaristic skill *might*. If he lives through the trials.

Vessel *(Samuel Peralta)*

In suspended animation, on the long journey home from an ice moon orbiting a gaseous planet, she sleeps, unaware that she carries in her dreams something more than she imagined.

The Grove *(Jennifer Foehner Wells)*

An ancient and lonely child wants to discover the universe—but she meets another lonely child who needs a savior.

Life *(Daniel Arenson)*

For years, the Agency has kept its vast field of satellite dishes pointed to the heavens, seeking even a glimpse of extra-terrestrial life. Now, at last, the long-awaited day has come: the day when their telescopes capture an actual photo of a distant alien.

Second Suicide *(Hugh Howey)*

Eight days to planetfall, and I'm being transferred to Gunner. My tentacles slime in disgust. Or is it fear? If this is the last planet we ever conquer, I'll be glad. Be nice to settle down somewhere, get off this ship, own a square of land, learn to love all that open sky. Eight more days before planetfall. Eight days before we reach planet Earth.

CONTENTS

Foreword

by Stefan Bolz

"You're an interesting species. An interesting mix. You're capable of such beautiful dreams, and such horrible nightmares. You feel so lost, so cut off, so alone, only you're not. See, in all our searching, the only thing we've found that makes the emptiness bearable, is each other."

– Carl Sagan, *Contact*

When Ellie Arroway first discovered a message from the stars in Carl Sagan's masterpiece *Contact*, the world was, suddenly and unmistakably, confronted with a powerful truth: *We are not alone.*

In *Contact*, the alien species was technologically advanced, highly intelligent, and benign. It used a universal language we all could understand. We'd studied that language in schools and universities; we'd found its presence in snowflakes and in the leaves of a tree. That language of communication was mathematics. And because the language was mathematics, we could not deny it. We could not twist it into something other than it was. We had to believe it.

Carl Sagan's book gave us a highly plausible scenario in which an alien race would make first contact—albeit with a completely unprepared Earth.

On the other end of the spectrum stands the most frightening, unsettling, and nightmarish vision of alien life there is to date. The phrase "In space, no one can hear you scream" is still one of the most widely known tag lines for any movie. The sentence came out of Dan O'Bannon and Ronald Shusett's script for *Alien*. The screenplay was pitched to studios as "*Jaws* in space"—a fitting short description for a movie that merged the horror genre with science fiction.

Where *Contact* gives us hope, *Alien* destroys it. Where *Contact* touches on the spiritual, religious, economic, and social consequences of our first encounter with an extraterrestrial species, *Alien* makes us dread that very same first encounter, hoping against hope that we are not going to have to defend ourselves against a highly evolved organism that has acid for blood and lays eggs inside our body. But there is a middle ground. Between a light touch and extinction, there is room for visionary ideas—ideas that push the imagination to previously unimagined heights.

The Alien Chronicles—an anthology of such ideas—has been crafted by some of the most visionary science fiction authors writing today, and has the potential to make your mind soar high above the Earth, break through the exosphere and reach into vast space, where nothing is impossible, where science and fiction fuse together, and where the question *Are we alone in the universe?* is answered in unique, exciting, and deeply moving ways.

In June of 2013, the Huffington Post conducted a poll on whether or not the American people believed in intelligent extraterrestrial life. Thirty-eight percent thought it possible. Twenty-two percent did not believe it, and the other forty-one percent weren't sure.

I read through the entire article and discovered something very interesting. Nobody asked the follow-up question. I caught myself thinking that we have no problem with not being alone in the universe. We might even embrace the possibility. It's thrilling to think that we might have neighbors. But the question whether or not we are alone isn't the real question, is it? I think it is safe to assume that somewhere within the one hundred billion galaxies that span the known universe, there is intelligent life besides ours. But there is a second question. It arises after we have pondered the first one for a while. This one is far more unsettling, for it probes to the core of what it means to be human in all its aspects, to be "capable of such beautiful dreams, and such horrible nightmares," as Carl Sagan predicted.

The question is this: *Are we ready?*

Are we ready for our very own close encounter with an alien race? Are we prepared? I don't mean do we have a plan of action to defend ourselves. I'm sure our military has a response to hundreds of scenarios. But are we ready? Us. You. Me. All of us humans? We have not eradicated apartheid in the world, have not even begun to let our belief systems stand side by side with those of others. The gap between rich and poor, between black, brown, white, and yellow, seems more prevalent than ever. Are we ready to add green as an additional color and maybe welcome a race that has one eye instead of two? (Perhaps those of us who watch *Futurama* will have adapted already.)

And as I considered these questions, I was suddenly terrified. Not so much of an alien race invading and taking over our planet, but of our reaction to a benign species trying to make first contact. Would we be able to lay our preconceived notions aside and meet this new species with respect, honor, and an open mind? Given the history of our planet, I would say no.

Is that one possible explanation why it hasn't yet happened?

Visionary writers have always told the truth. Not only have they "invented" things that were to come to pass hundreds of years later—from Jules Verne's submarine in *Twenty Thousand Leagues Under the Sea* to the communicator on board *Star Trek*'s starship *Enterprise*—they also spoke the truth about the human condition, that frail sense of superiority that could screw everything up, big time.

The stories collected here ask the question *what if* in many different ways. What if there is life on other planets? What if an alien species wants to make contact with us? What if we have been watched for thousands of years already, and the prime directive of the other species simply does not allow for them to engage us?

Who knows, there might be, on the other end of the galaxy, a group of writers who are about to publish their stories, about to open the minds and hearts of their readers to the possibility of alien life. They might be talking about us—the two-eyed people, the ones with the two arms and two legs. And maybe, hopefully, one day in the not so distant future, we will exchange our *Alien Chronicles* with each other, gather around, and smile in glad astonishment that we are much more alike than we are different.

Guests of the
Chitterer Liberation Force
by Blair S. Babylon

DON'T MIND ME. I'm not the important one here. Blake is the one with the story to tell.

Blake, lovely Blake. I had been watching her since she arrived at the party, just out of the corner of my eye as I chatted up the women, trying to edge out the other guys and clutching my jacket around myself. My heart palpitated just being around her, like I was having a subliminal panic attack, not that I had those. Blake's hair was the pale amber of the light beer she held in her thin hand. Her eyes were the delicate gray of Earth's cold skies and nothing like the sun. Her skin was whiter than the gleaming alabaster columns and slabs on the floor, so pale that it looked like she had been living underground for a year or more.

Everyone else's skin was the crispy brown of repeated radiation burns. Everyone's except mine. I burn easily, even for a guy, so I slather on the radblock and stay on the university's station. Most radiation damage occurs on shuttle flights. A sunburnt tan means you're well traveled, which means you're rich.

The party was at my buddy Victoria's apartment, far above the clouds of Jupiter on one of the more posh orbiting stations. The apartment had windows, real windows, not just vid screens. Standing next to the immense panes of diamond would have freaked me out if I hadn't been so wasted. The vast iciness of space penetrated all the planetary orbital stations, drying me out so that I shivered constantly, but the smoke and boiling-blood atmosphere were right *there*, right *outside*, centimeters from my where my fingertips pressed on the crystal window. That damned red spot was coming around again.

Victoria's concentrated alcoholic punch, ripe with artificial, reconstituted strawberry puree and ethanol, absorbed through my tongue and dampened my brain enough so that I could, well, not exactly *enjoy*, but *appreciate* the view, rather than cringe by the back wall. Agoraphobia is common among people who have spent a lot of time in enclosed, windowless environments like space stations and whatnot. It's not weird.

We were standing around, drunk off our butts already, we men eyeing the women with more rivalry than intent, when that dork Boris piped up above the general din: "Hey! People! Let's everybody tell a story about the most interesting thing that's ever happened to us!"

Yeah, right. That sounded like a great way to ensure that none of us would ever get laid again. Let's put our very best story right out there, spill all the garbanzo beans. That way, everything we say will be all downhill after that.

Great plan, Einstein.

Besides, I had zilch. I've never raised baby kittens with an eyedropper. I've never been outside the solar system. I've never won anything bigger than a club swimming heat. My sheltered Earthbound life had given me no stories to tell.

Well, it wasn't like I was going to make the beast with two backs with some pretty girl that night, anyway. Compared to all the cosmetically enhanced spacer men in the room, my face looked like it had been taken apart and put back together with an ice cream scoop. Some of the spacers were replicas of movie stars. Some had shimmering variegated coloration. One guy had a hologram on his cheek that displayed his up-to-the-second net worth. We Old-Money Earthlings still thought plastic surgery and enhancement doodads were nouveau-riche gauche. My parents would have shuddered with disdain if I had ever undergone the knife for pretty special effects.

"Come on!" Boris said. "Everybody has something interesting that's happened to them!"

Nope, not me.

I turned away with a negating hand flap of derision, but Victoria caught my arm. "Come on, Wellington. Tell us anything. Just play along."

My hand holding my glass shook and sloshed punch on my pale skin, soaking a fuchsia stain into the white sleeve. Victoria's punch was so strong that it might dye my wiry, black arm hairs pink or eat my skin off.

Blake was quietly tipsy, lounging in an overstuffed chair and talking to a redheaded guy who was practically draped over the arm of his own chair and shouting, "Oh my gods!" at everything she said.

Lovely Blake. I shied away, inching toward the diamond windows that separated me from the hurricanes and gravity well of Jupiter.

I'd met Blake in a sophomore sociology class a few years ago. She got the highest grade. I had the second-highest.

I was Mr. Second: second in my graduating class of five thousand, second in a planetary-wide poetry contest, first alternate for my district's science competition, and runner-up in an all-state drum competition. My disgusted parents said that I had a mental block that kept me from winning.

Blake laughed uproariously in her chair, slapping her thin thigh, and waved her beer, nearly spilling it, as she started talking again and waving her hands. She wasn't *perky*. No, that word doesn't convey the depths of her complex sunniness. She was *effervescent*. Her shimmering bubbles of laughter sparkled.

She saw me looking at her and smiled. On another woman, such a secret-sharing smile would have been coy. On her, the universe focused on the kind curve of her lips.

Even from across the small room and on the other side of the circle, I swore that I could smell her. She smelled like herbs, maybe rosemary, clean and succulent among the musty spacers on a station where water was heavily taxed.

"I'll tell my best story!" one Asian-ish jock announced. His lush black mustache must have been growing since he was two.

"I'll go! I won my high school chess tournament by tricking the first seed into opening a check!"

Precious, a scrawny black woman who was too nerdy to be at this party, said, "I'm an Interplanetary Merit Scholar."

Everyone groaned. Precious was such a grind.

Georgie, who had flashing LED tattoos on his face and up both arms, said, "I climbed the Eiffel Tower, on the outside, wearing nothing but a harness."

Everyone laughed. We had all heard Georgie's extreme streaking stories. It was rumored that he'd uploaded pictures of them with his college application and that's how he snuck into the University of Jupiter, which is very highly selective. Acceptance includes a bus ticket off the cold, slimy sponge of Earth. You either need a stellar GPA and scores or a great story: a sob story or an inspirational tale. Or you need a whole hell of a lot of money.

The University of Jupiter had been my second choice when they accepted my whole hell of a lot of money. Harvard didn't want me.

From outside the circle, Blake piped up, "I hung out with the Chitterers' Liberation Force for a couple months."

Her voice was sunny, like that was a huge joke, like she was talking about riding roller coasters or living in a dolphins' commune.

Everyone near enough to hear her inhaled like they'd had nitrogen ice dropped down their spines—everyone except me. I couldn't breathe. The windows seemed to crack and suck the air out into infinite space. No one thought it was funny.

If you have tears, prepare to shed them now.

Chess Jock said, "What do you mean, you 'hung out' with the CLF?"

Blake said, "We went spelunking in the Chitterers' caves, and we kind of dropped in on them, and we stayed as their guests for a while."

Everyone around us was quiet. Certainly no one offered any more of their piddly little stories about chess or grades or not quite falling off the Eiffel Tower.

Precious swallowed hard and said in a cold voice, "The CLF killed my cousin Leena. She was sampling on Titan, and they dragged her into one of their caves, held her hostage for a week, and then tossed her out an airlock, in pieces."

A woman behind me asked, "Why didn't they kill you?"

Blake shrugged, almost spilling her drink from her scrawny fingers. "I have no idea."

Chess Jock asked, "Why would you hang out with terrorists?"

The pale skin around Blake's eyes crinkled softly as she smiled. "Well, they insisted that we stay. It really wasn't our idea."

That's when we realized that this wasn't a drunken debauchery story. Blake was telling us a hostage and survival story, but she was telling it like the best of bar stories: a rollicking, drunken good time had by all.

Because that's who she was, and that's how she dealt with it.

"We?" I asked. My voice was tight in my throat. "Who is we?"

"Me and Ellis," she said, her voice as bright as the marigold light streaming off the planet below.

The CLF were a renegade ethnic group of Chitterers. We—meaning we humans, not we at the party—had discovered the Chitterers while they were mining silicates and hydrocarbon ice on Titan when we landed there the first time. They looked like giant ladybugs. Their air is about thirty-five percent oxygen, like on Earth during the Carboniferous period, when two-meter-long scorpions stung things to death. I guess we were lucky that the Chitterers were merely beetle-like.

After the scientists finally set up a Rosetta application to translate their clicky language, the first official statement from the Chitterers—our very first contact with an extraterrestrial star-faring sentient alien species—was:

"Well, this is awkward."

Seems that they had checked on us about three hundred years ago, just as we were entering our steampunk phase of the Industrial Revolution, so they'd cheerfully strip-mined a couple of the moons on our outer planets, like Britain was doing to India at the time, thinking we probably wouldn't mind. They had been meaning to observe us again, but things were just so busy in the mines, what with the hydrofracking and tunnel-mining and, well, they hadn't even been up to the surface in over a century, let alone taken a look at Earth.

So they'd been caught poaching elements in someone else's solar system.

Oops.

Awkward.

So our first official conversation with our First Contact Alien Species was filled with long, embarrassed pauses, self-justification, and blame-passing.

We could have just tossed them out of our solar system on their exoskeletal butts and reverse-engineered their FTL drives, but saner heads prevailed after much discussion about how the discovered savages usually got the short end of the electric cattle prod—and humans were definitely the bead-wearing primitives here. So instead, we negotiated with them and signed treaties, allowing them to mine some more. We got access to their wikipedia.

The problem was: we negotiated with *some* of them.

We didn't realize that they had all sorts of NGOs that were also mining oxides and silicates on Titan. We also didn't realize that the Chitterers squabbled like, well, *us*.

Like Burma, ever since it declared independence centuries ago in 1948.

Like the Israelis and the PLO, Hamas, the Palestinian Islamic Jihad, the Army of Islam, and the rest of them.

Like most of Africa with their insurgent rebel armies.

When the Chitterers said they were busy, we didn't realize that they were busy fighting each other in a free-for-all civil war.

And we walked right into the middle of it.

So we covered our collective human eyes and wished them all away. We said, in effect, "All you giant ladybugs look alike to us. We negotiated. You accepted. We're done. Deal with this yourselves."

So the Chitterers went back to killing each other as if we humans didn't exist, just as long as we stayed out of their creepy, crawly way.

And we tried to stay out of the Chitterers' way. We had police departments, liaisons, and embassies.

We had borders, fences, airlocks, checkpoints, and maps.

And we had language barriers.

Blake said, "Ellis and I went down to the Chitterers' consulate on Ganymede and showed them our planned spelunking route on Titan, and we asked them if that was"— her eyes widened and she waggled her hands in a Great Gesture of Imprecision—"*okay.*"

Evidently, the Chitterers' consulate thought Blake and Ellis were asking if it was *legal* to spelunk in those particular caves.

Blake said, "So the Chitterers clicked through their Babel app. 'Sure, it is okay. Go ahead.' We were actually asking if it was advisable, or a good idea, or *safe.*" She laughed. "If we had used those words, the Chitterer Policia probably would have vibrated their wings in Righteous Laughter and told us to spelunk on Earth because no one in his right mind went into the caves wherein lurked the Chitternistas, Al Chitterda, and the Chitterer Liberation Force.

"We packed up our spelunking gear, took passage to Titan, found an airlock, and started rappelling into one of the big chimneys that the Chitterers had drilled through Titan's ice crust. They had sunk containments through the liquid layer and the high-pressure ice layers to get to the rocky layers below, and that's where we wanted to go." Blake noted, "I rappelled down Australian-style, head-first."

Of course she did, because she's fun like that.

I was probably reading a book when Blake and Ellis dropped their ropes down the huge icy chasm in the side of Titan. Probably non-fiction.

Blake spread her hands wide. "So we walked down the side of that ice cliff, down into the darkness. We paused to click on our headlamps and place our carabiner clips."

They did all that other cave-exploring stuff that Blake knows but that I wouldn't if I hadn't read a book on it.

My mouth was dry just thinking about the height they must have rappelled. Sometimes those entry passages tunnel through the layers of ammoniated liquid water and gas ices for miles before they ever reach an airlock. I sipped Victoria's potent punch to moisten my panicky mouth.

Chess Jock elbowed me in my skinny ribs, saying, "Back up, Wellys. You're crowding me. Leave me some personal space, eh?"

Blake passed around a picture on her phone of her and Ellis. Both had the lanky, muscular physiques of vegan triathletes. Behind them, striped sandstone jutted toward Earth's monochrome, clouded sky. Blake's arm was snaked around Ellis's wiry waist. Ellis had dark hair and a tapered black beard that was pointy, almost Mephistophelian, and clear blue eyes. She wore a halter; he was shirtless and hairy. They were both shiny with sweat. They were evidently doing something outdoorsy and strenuous.

I glanced around the party at the thirty or so people now clustered around the photo. No one who looked like Ellis was there. Most people were soft and floppy from extended stays in low gravity, skin drooping on flaccid muscles. The white people among us were crispy brown, and people who were naturally brown or black were really dark, except for Blake.

Pale Blake shimmered like moonlight.

"Is this after you guys got away?" Precious asked.

"No," Blake said. "This is on Earth, about six months before we went in. After we came home from our stay with the CLF, we were *really* skinny, but back to the story."

They descended for hours, she said, until the icy shaft leveled out and diverged into roads.

Chitterers carve their houses and towns when their mine tunnels have played out, like Coober Pedy on Earth. Their streets wander and follow the veins of minerals. When a mine has progressed far enough from a settlement that the scuttling commute becomes onerous, everyone packs up and blasts out a new town farther down the mine shaft.

Blake and Ellis tramped along the abandoned streets of the Chitterer ghost towns, hiding in the empty, icy dugout rooms and jumping out at each other, playing like stoned kittens.

They found three ghost towns in a row, carved out of the flaky rock like giant hamster habitats. Circles of light from their headlamps revealed holes and ledges on the dark cliffs. A normal person would have seen enough and turned around, but these two went on. They had two months to kill.

"And by then," Blake admitted, laughing, "we were hammered. We were so wasted, because the oxygen content of their air mix is so much higher than Earth-normal, like thirty-five percent, that you can drink all the time and never get a hangover.

"That was our whole plan," Blake said, "a two-month drunken love party with no hangovers. We hauled hoversleds with food and lots of alcohol, which was pretty easy in Titan's one-half-ish Earth-relative gravity. We also planned to write poetry, because that's what you do when you're constantly buzzed and scruffing like mad minks.

"We poked around the stone houses, looking at the garbage that the Chitterers had left behind when they moved: broken gadgets with those multi-vid-screens for their compound eyes, pieces of carapace that the kids had shed, cooking stuff, broken mining tools, and guns.

"But you know, we never thought we'd meet any Chitterers. They're all supposed to be so far down the mines after three centuries of blasting out the tunnels that, supposedly, you would have to walk and rappel for months to even get close. Ellis and I had only been exploring for about two weeks when we found a little side tunnel that we crawled down and—you won't believe this—we literally, seriously literally, *fell* into their camp."

The side tunnel was just big enough to crawl through side by side, dragging their hoversleds tethered to their ankles. They were joshing their way down the tunnel, throwing rubble at each other in a drunken game of bonk tag, when the rocky floor gave way.

"The hoversleds didn't fit through the hole," Blake said to us at the college party overlooking the monstrous, glowering eye of Jupiter. "So there we were, the two of us, hanging from one ankle each, swinging about thirty meters above the ground, with big O-mouths on our surprised faces. The light beams from our headlamps slithered over the dark cavern's walls like air raid searchlights. From below, we must have looked like a Soft-Shell chandelier!"

At the party, Blake laughed. They all laughed with her, but softer, nervously.

Later, when were alone and she told me the story again, her laugh was more hollow, studied. "That's when they swarmed us." A shiver ran through her pale, wiry body.

Other than that, she never did lose her sense of humor about being taken prisoner. I saw her tell that story so many more times, each time more hilarious than the last, because that's how she copes with things: she's funny and beautiful and shining with good humor.

At the party, she continued: "When we fell through the ceiling, the Chitterers stampeded up the walls. With these wicked rock-nipping scissors, they cut the carbon-fiber cables that dangled us. We fell, and we could see the rocks flying up at us in our headlamps' beams. The gravity was light, so I just sprained my ankle, but Ellis landed with his hands straight out and he broke one of his arms. Then he landed on his face."

She flinched. "You should have seen the blood, red on his face and shining on the rocks. Broke his nose. He didn't even yell. Seriously, he just sat up and said, 'Ouch.' Just like that. With a period. 'Ouch.' He never talked about how terrible it was or how much they hurt him. He just shoved it all down inside and said, 'Ouch.' He was that tough. And maybe that drunk. Yeah, probably that drunk."

Everybody at the party laughed.

"Then they were all around us." Blake held her arms out, undulating, and showed us how the bugs swarmed them. "I was like, 'Whoa. We come in peace, kemosabe.' They chittered at us, and I was just dialing up my Babel app, even though I didn't think my gadget had Chitterer-English translation on it, because, you know, when do you ever need a Chitterer translator? It's not like they can breathe our air or walk around our stations."

At the party, we were all crowded around her like the Chitterer rebels had clustered around her and Ellis, rapt, listening to her tell the tale. Someone shoved me from behind, trying to get closer to her, and said, "'Scuse me, Wellys."

Blake continued, "The Chitterers lit a chemical flare, plastering us with cold, green light. The cavern was another dug-out town-cave with black holes in the walls that led to more caves and more holes. Luckily, the Chitterers had a Babel app. A big, black Chitterer spoke into his gadget for a second, then turned it toward us."

Blake said to the party in a raspy, staccato voice, like an evil bug, "'Get on ground and perform religious rites.' And Ellis and I were like, 'Holy crap!' Which was not our religious rite, we told them, despite the word 'holy' in there.

"Ellis told them he was Catholic and a priest had to say his Last Rites, or it didn't count. They all buzzed back and forth, because they respect our religious notions even if they don't understand them at all.

"The big black one asked me if I was Catholic, too, and I said, 'Oh, hell, yeah. As Catholic as the Pope,' even though I was raised slapdash Buddhist. They all buzzed back and forth again. I think they looked it up while they tried to figure out what to do with us. I'd gotten my app working by that time, even though—wouldn't you know it—our phone systems aren't compatible with theirs so I couldn't call the cops, but I could listen to them.

"Another big black ladybug said, 'We can't kill them if don't have religious rites. It is wrong thing.'

"And an orange one said, 'We can't shove them back up hole. Whole bug-a-bug national army come down on us.'

"That's when Ellis and I figured out they were rebels, and he was all like, 'Whoa, dudes. We're wasted as Macbeth on a pub crawl though Inverness. We don't even know where we are, and we won't tell anybody we saw you.'

"And the orange one turned his whole head at us, all those hundreds of black eyes glittering in the sparking light of the flare, and said"—Blake's voice dropped to the most menacing rasp yet—"'So, Soft-Shells, no one knows where you are.'

"I was all, 'Um, we're cool, ya know? We're on your side. Screw the government.'

"The orange Chitterer was smarter than the other ones. He just stared at us with those multi-faceted eyes like brilliant-cut black diamonds. They don't blink, ever. He just watched us, like he was looking for a mark on us or something.

"I said, 'We're just college students, on a bender during a vacation.'

"'You Soft-Shells go to government university?' Orange Bug asked.

"'No, heck no!' Ellis said, even though his face was mashed and his eyes were turning purple and swelling shut. 'Private college. No, we don't have any truck with the government. We hate those guys.'

"Orange Bug shined a flashlight beam at the hole we had fallen through. 'What up there?'

"'Sleds,' I said. 'Food. Water. Libations.'

"Orange Bug stared at the ceiling, thinking, then he pointed his big, long, pointy stick that was obviously a gun at us.

"'Whoa! Dude! Sir! You don't have to shoot us!' I said." Blake raised her hands to mime warding off the guns, all vulnerable palms and pale fingers. "'We're on your side.'

"'Move,' Orange Bug said." Blake mimicked his terrible hacking voice again. "'Over there.'

"Ellis cradled his broken arm, and we scooted like drunk crabs over to some rocks about fifty meters away.

"Orange Bug pointed his gun at the hole we fell through. A bayonet shot out of the end, but there was no bang or whiff of gunpowder. They don't use anything that's hot or on fire, you know, because of the hydrogen and oxygen mix of their air. Remember first-year chemistry? Oxygen supports combustion, but hydrogen is combustible. If you add fire, *poot!* It explodes.

"That bayonet, I don't know what it was made of, but it dipped through the rock and scooped out a chunk like the ceiling was soup.

"And then our sleds fell through the bigger hole. *WHOMP!*"

At the party, telling the story, Blake slammed her palm flat on the table beside her. Four drinks on it jumped. One tipped and was going over toward her, but I grabbed it.

22

"Thanks," she said to me. "Quick hands, there."

"Yeah," I said, wanting to fade back into the crowd, away from her luminescent gaze.

Blake turned away from me and continued, "And the fall popped all our liquor pouches like water balloons. The booze spilled all over the floor. Black Bug yelled, 'It's flammable!' and they all skittered back.

"We were like, '*Dudes*, or *Bugs*, or whatever, that hooch was supposed to last for two months.'

"They all looked at us. If bugs had eyebrows, they would have been all frowny and pointy." Blake pantomimed angry eyebrows on her pale forehead. "And then Big Black Bug loped over to us and stuck a scoopy gun right in my face. I thought he was going to cut my head off right there, and I was all, 'It's fine. It's okay. Rots your liver anyway. I've been meaning to cut down.'

"Big Black Bug was all, 'Why you bring bombs into our camp?'

"And I was all, 'Peace, friend. That's not bombs. That's beverage.'

"Behind Big Black Bug, some of the other Chitterers moved in and started to clean it up. That's when we figured out that the ethanol would volatilize in their lower air pressure and become a flammable vapor in their air that already has some hydrogen in it. Like a fricking fuel-air bomb. Okay, so we knew not to take anything into the caves that had to be smoked because of the hydrogen, but I suppose we should have just taken LSD with us instead of ethanol.

"Then Big Black Bug says, 'Why you dig that tunnel? How long you spy?'"

I clutched my glass of Victoria's poisonous red punch and held my chest, my lungs hurting. My face burned with horror at Big Black Bug's accusation.

Blake said to the party, crowded around her and silent, "No kidding, they thought we were *spies*. Can you imagine, me and Ellis, both of us as wasted as pigs, *spies?* We would have been, like, the worst spies ever. So I was all, 'No way, kemosabe. We not spies. Just drunk college students. Not spies.'"

I held on to my drink and the drink that I'd rescued from the table. My knuckles hurt from clenching both of them so hard, like I was hanging on a rock wall. *Damn bugs.*

"'Who you work for?' Big Black Bug yelled. 'Bug-a-Bug Army? Soft-Shells?'

"'No one. Just exploring some caves for fun.'

"Black Bug reared up and shook his first set of arms and shouted at us, 'You think I stupid? Soft-Shells never go in caves! You get lost in tunnels! Can't even bore through rock without explosives!'"

Shouting?

Chitterers' speech—and we've all heard it on the media whenever they give a statement about something else stupid that we humans are doing—is an inflectionless string of, well, *chittering.* It sounds like walking and dragging a stick across corrugated steel. Their volume and cadence never vary.

My tongue was a useless hank of dry insulation, filling my mouth and muffling sound. I slammed a drink into my mouth, burning my raw throat. I was already feeling the effects of just a few drinks. My legs were rubbery. I was such a lightweight. My liver was crap. I asked her, "How did you know he was shouting?"

Blake cocked her head to the right. "His third and fifth legs made an imperative sign. Black Bug signaled 'Anger,' or Ellis would say that he performed The Grand Jeté of Scorn. The Chitterers are pretty interesting, once you get to know them. Their sign language is really evocative. Since I've been back, it seems like we Soft-Shells sing when we talk, but Chitterers dance."

"So the app translates the dance language, too," Chess Jock said.

"No, none of the apps do. I haven't found any publications on it since I've been back. I'm going to write my thesis on it." Blake shrugged. "It took us a while to figure it out, maybe six months or so. Later, I figured out that those Chitterers at the consulate, the ones who told us that it was 'okay' to go into the caves, were doing The Bee-Bopping Finger Puppets of Equivocation and The Irish Step Dance in the Presence of Insanity. I just thought they had to pee."

"No one else has lived with the Chitterers for any length of time," I said. "The official delegations don't allow prolonged interaction, and the rebel groups either ransom and release people within a few days or else kill them."

Precious nodded and said, "And the CLF is the worst."

I remembered about her cousin and felt like crap.

Blake turned her palms up and shrugged good-naturedly. "I don't know why they didn't shoot us with the scoopy gun or boot us out the airlock right away, especially since they thought we were spies, other than a bizarre inclination to make sure we got Last Rites. And I don't know why they didn't get tired of us a few weeks later and just shoot us then. Ellis and I hung out with them for months before they finally let us leave."

Over a year.

"So, anyway, Big Black Bug reared up and did the Port de Bras in Third Position of Fear and Loathing. 'You are spies!' he yelled. 'How you contact your masters? Who are they?'

"'No, sir, Big Black Bug,' I said to him. 'We not spies. We just exploring caves.' I flipped over my phone and swiped open pictures of us outside on Earth's moon, rappelling through Venus's cities, and riding an interplanetary freighter bareback. 'Soft-Shells do all kinds of stupid things.'

"He seemed to consider *that*. It's kind of insulting that the 'As a species, we're too stupid to be spies' argument was the one he listened to.

"Pretty Blue Bug, who was a great guy when we got to know him later, scuttled up to Big Black Bug and said, 'If they spies, we should them kill. Dump bodies in the no-air. Soft-Shells not ask questions about CLF killing two Soft-Shells.'

"Orange Bug came up to us with the other Chitterers. 'No,' he said. 'If they are spies, and we kill them, Soft-Shells' government may side more fully with Chitterer government.'

"And that's how we became guests of the Chitterer Liberation Force," Blake said.

Precious and Chess Jock sat at Blake's feet. I stood behind them. Even though I knew that this story must end well—for Blake was here at the party, drinking cheap college hooch with us in Victoria's apartment floating high above Jupiter's rioting orange clouds—she had been missing for a year: a year of mistreatment and living with only Ellis and insectoid aliens.

Blake talked about it like it was a pub-crawling adventure.

I knew that we weren't hearing the whole story, that she and Ellis had been terrified and bored, and that the Chitterers had nearly killed them several times. I must have seen a report on the news somewhere.

I leaned in closer, examining Blake's slim body and face, trying to remember the show I'd seen. It was more than just that sociology class, I knew. I'd heard her talk about her imprisonment before, in these same mocking, cheery tones. Maybe more than once.

Damn it, my memory was crap these days.

Blake said, "Some of them went up and plastered over the hole we fell through, because their warm air was leaking out. Then they tied us to rocks."

Chess Jock's horrified eyes widened. Precious fanned herself, sweating.

My hands shook. I *had* heard this somewhere before. I knew it. News broadcast? Another party, when I was halfway to blackout drunk? Wouldn't be the first time.

Blake said, "When the Chitterers scoop out their rooms, they leave support columns so that, you know, *their roofs won't cave in.*" She laughed. They laughed with her because they were afraid to break her breezy recitation. "They wrapped a cable around my waist and tied me so that I was sitting up, with my back to the pillar.

"Ellis had tried to grab one of their scoopy guns when we made a run for it when we first fell through, so they tied him to the column like he was hugging it. There were hundreds of those columns. It was like being in a petrified forest, where the branches interlocked and calcified into a stone canopy, shutting out the sun."

Blake didn't mention at the party that she had spent *three months* chained to that rock. That's why I'm telling the story, too: to fill in the terrible parts that sunny, jokey Blake won't.

"So Orange Bug saved you," I said.

"Oh, yeah. We were lucky there!" Blake laughed.

Her pale skin whitened a shade. I even heard her stomach growl.

When adrenaline kicks in and your body goes into fight-or-flight mode, blood flows inward, even speeds up digestion. Blake was in the middle of a full-bore panic attack and was laughing it off.

I hated those insurrectionist bugs that would tie such a gentle soul as Blake to a stone pillar with a steel cord; I hated that they would threaten this effervescent life. I was falling in love with her, in a Desdemona-crying-over-Othello's-war-wounds kind of way.

"And then what?" Chess Jock asked.

Blake said, "We sat there, waiting for them to figure out what they were going to do with us. Eventually, after a couple days of freaking out, we got bored.

"So we started telling each other the plots of books and movies. Ellis, he's an Earth Lit major, so he recited the titles and plots to all forty-two of De Vere-slash-Shakespeare's plays, plus his eight poems and a hundred fifty-four sonnets, in first-published order. I did films, lots of films. It was so dark most of the time. The Chitterers had lights, so we could see beams of light scuttling around the darkness, but we couldn't see each other or ourselves. So a while later…"

Three months later.

"… Some Head Honcho Chitterer comes crawling into camp, and all those bugs jumped *straight up!*" Blake leapt out of her chair, lanky arms and legs spread-eagle. "They lit about a thousand of those cold flares, and the whole cavern was squinty-bright. The Chitterers were all doing The Arabesque in the Presence of Authority. By this time, some of the Chitterers were hanging out with us at our rocks. Pretty Blue Bug sat with us a lot. We weren't just a chore by then. We were more like pets. Luckily, I'm cute."

Blake sat back down in her chair, carefully, like her hips hurt. "So Head Honcho Bug strolls in and the Chitterers all jump, and we sat there because we were tied to those clammy, hot rocks.

"The dark had seemed to stretch on forever, but with the lights, the cavern looked small, like a couple of regular rooms stacked together, and it was round like a big hole in the ground, and the columns stood sentry around us.

"Head Honcho Bug, Orange Bug, and Big Black Bug sat around a table and conferred. Pretty Blue Bug said to us, 'Hey, Soft-Shells, turn off your translators,' so we pretended to, but I kept mine on text mode. They were talking Chitterer politics. Like Soft-Shell politics, it's interesting at first, and then it devolves into nitpicking and a pissing contest.

"So I was barely watching the screen when the translator read, 'What are those two Soft-Shells doing over there?'

"I slugged Ellis and pointed at my phone.

"Orange Bug said, 'They found us. We don't know if they're spies or idiots.'

"Ellis whispered to me, 'Are those our only two choices?'

"Head Honcho Bug asked, 'Why they tied to rocks?'

"Orange Bug answered, 'They might escape.'

"'Have they tried?'

"'Not since the first day.'

"'Nearest Soft-Shells are hundreds of klicks away.' Head Honcho Bug looked over at us. 'Hey Soft-Shells!'

"We looked oblivious," Blake did her best impression of good-natured oblivion, the Head Bobble of Minding One's Own Business, "because, you know, our translators were supposed to be *off*.

"Pretty Blue Bug kicked me and performed The Swan Dive of Indication at my phone.

"So, after I pretended to turn my translator app on, Head Honcho said, "Hey, Soft-Shells! You not try to escape, right?'

"And we were all, 'No, sir, Mr. Bug, sir. We not escape. Why would we try to escape?'

"Head Honcho swiveled back to Big Black Bug and Orange Bug and said, 'Untie them.'

"So the Chitterers untied us, and that's how we got to walk around the camp.

"So that was exciting for exactly five minutes, which how long it took to walk the whole way around the camp, because we'd pretty much seen everything from the middle that there was to see. We were still reciting books and movies to each other, just to have something to talk about. At least they gave us some glowsticks, so we could see each other. It was always like midnight around a campfire, though.

"So we started helping out in the kitchen. Our food from the sleds had run out a while before that. They steal most of their food on raids, but it still has to be prepared, even though they don't cook because they can't light a fire or else: *poot!* So they grind and dry grains to make kind-of-like tortillas, or they soak and sprout some, and they grind some other stuff to make pudding.

"Lowest bugs on the flystrip cooked, and Ellis and I were surely the lowest forms of life in that camp.

"We were still suffering from ennui, though, so we liberated a few big cans from the kitchen and washed them out. I commandeered some wire and made a kind of steel guitar. Ellis made bongos.

"Evidently, both Ellis and I have tin ears, because we thought we sounded pretty good.

"But the Chitterers *hated* our instruments. Every day, after lunch, when we pulled them out for band practice, the Chitterers would all do The Grand Jeté of Scorn or The Port de Bras in First Position of Wanting to Run Away.

"Finally, after about a month, Orange Bug came to us, bowing in the Namaste of Ulterior Motive, and said, 'Look, we will give better sleeping accommodations if you let us destroy infernal noisemakers.'

"So the Soft-Shell Band broke up and went the way of all supergroups, due to artistic differences.

"They really *destroyed* our instruments, too. They had some sort of a gambling thing, like a lottery. Brown June Bug won, or we assume so because he performed The Autistic Hand-Flapping of Joy. Then he took a scoopy gun and carved our guitar and bongos into a thousand tiny pieces. They all stood around in The King Tut Posture of Rapt Attention, punctuated by more Autistic Hand-Flapping of Joy. It was funny as all hell to watch. Pooooooooose, flap-flap-flap! Pooooooooose, flap-flap-flap!

"We thought *we* were bored, but destroying our instruments was the most fun those Chitterers had the whole time we were there, except for raids.

"So that's how we got our sleeping bags, and then we slept a lot better, considering that those caves are made of tons of high-pressure gas ices under a thin shell of sprayed-on plasticky stuff, even though the air was sultry and hot like a dry lightning storm in August."

The party was at a standstill, listening. The music was off. No one even refreshed drinks. Thirty people huddled close, like around a campfire in the cold. Precious's fingers were clamped on my skinny arm, bruising, and she finally noticed. "Sorry, Wellington."

"It's all right," I said, still watching Blake's supple body move as she spoke.

"It was a little while later…" Blake continued.

Eight months after they were captured.

"… that I started going on raids with them."

My chest clenched and I damn near dropped my drink. This beautiful girl, going on those raids, helping her enemy, was just damn evil. She might have been shot by the army or any one of the other rebel groups.

A general murmur broke out.

Precious asked, "With the CLF? How *could* you?"

"Not big raids," she said. "Just food and equipment raids. Stuff like that. They didn't give me a scoopy gun. I was just muscle to carry stuff. Ellis wouldn't go on the raids. He's more moral than I am. They knocked him around for it, but he wouldn't go."

"So they forced you to," Chess Jock said.

Blake said, "I was trying to find us some human food, too. The Chitterers need different concentrations of nutrients than we do. Ellis and I got pretty skinny eating their tortillas and puddings. There was just something missing in their food, like an essential amino acid or a vitamin, and we ate all we could and yet we still lost weight. I've gained twenty pounds since I got back. I was *skeletal* those last few weeks. Seriously, we looked like we were on one of those hunger artist game shows."

"Could you have gotten away?" Precious asked.

Blake puckered her face in intense concentration. Her hands fluttered in The Fingers Like Butterflies Alight Upon a New Idea.

"No, I don't think so," Blake said. "I wouldn't have left Ellis there alone. And we only raided government installations and opposing rebel camps. There are seventy-three Chitterer factions in mutual civil war. If we had left our CLF cell, another group probably would have scooped us for being with the CLF."

At the party, I pictured hunks of Blake's body carved away by the Chitterers' force field guns, and I shuddered, ill. My skin shivered. The tremor grew in my body. Even my teeth knocked together. "How did you finally get away?"

"A government guy came to negotiate a truce," Blake said. "There was a temporary cease-fire, one of many between the CLF and the Chitterer government. The government guy was a squirrelly little yellow bug who perpetually did The Chitterbug Jitterbug of Nervous Nellies.

"Again, they lit up the camp like we were standing in the middle of a cold emerald bonfire. Squirrelly Yellow Bug talked with Orange Bug and Big Black Bug forever. They pushed tablets at each other, then talked some more. The negotiations were falling into the black hole of useless windbaggery at light speed.

"Ellis and I finally stopped listening through the translator apps because even that excitement finally wore off, so we made more tortillas.

"Orange Bug sat in The Attacking Kitten of Righteous Defiance Stance the whole time. Squirrelly Yellow Bug couldn't even get Orange Bug to agree that the civil war was a problem.

"Ellis turned to me and said…"

Blake paused and looked at me.

Her sad gray eyes broke my heart. Damn those bugs for introducing such an exuberant soul to such sadness. The sadness felt familiar, felt normal.

I said, "We're going to die in this hole."

Blake's smile softened. She performed The Exhalation of Existential Relief. "Yes."

The circle at the party became an oval around Blake and me. A bubble of orange Jovian gas belched past the crystalline windows, tinting everyone at the party tangerine.

I shuddered again. Words spoke themselves in my mouth. "This civil war is never going to end. They're never going to let us go. We're going to die here in this cave, miles underground. Either we'll starve to death or the bugs will eventually rupture something when they beat us."

Blake's body stilled in the Pause of Silent and Gentle Expectation.

I didn't move. I couldn't move. This wasn't a Chitterer Dance Language maneuver. My own fear had reared up and dragged me to that place where I couldn't move, where I could remember nothing, where the pain dulled.

Blake said, "Squirrelly Yellow Bug asked, like they all eventually did, 'Who those two Soft-Shells over there?' Orange Bug told Squirrelly Yellow Bug about how we dropped into their camp.

"'What you feeding them?' asked Squirrelly Yellow Bug.

"Orange Bug stomped in irritation. 'What we eat.'

"'Their shells look dull. You feeding them enough?'

"'They eat like they're molting.'

"Ellis walked over to Squirrelly Yellow Bug, who was doing The Frond-Waving Palm Trees of Endless Exasperation, and Orange Bug, who was still in The Attacking Kitten of Righteous Defiance Stance.

"All the Chitterers around us stopped pretending they weren't listening and stood in the The King Tut Posture of Rapt Attention.

"Ellis stood in front of both of the Chitterers and assumed the Bad Shakespearean Actor's Pose of Endless Oration. He said, 'Hey, Orange Bug. You could release us to the Government Agent as an act of good will.'

"I couldn't breathe," Blake said, and she stared right at me. The party froze around us. "I thought he was committing suicide, barging in on the negotiations like that. They'd beaten the snot out of us for far less, like looking at them when they didn't like it. I thought Orange Bug would cut Ellis's head off for daring to speak to them or just to show Squirrelly Yellow Bug that he killed for no reason, to scare him. If I had known that Ellis was going to walk over there, I would have tackled him, dragged him away, begged him not to."

She said, "He was so brave, and he showed none of the fear that must have been killing him. He pushed it all down inside where it wouldn't show. My heart would have burst if they had killed him."

It wasn't bravery. It was desperation. Blake was melting away. She would have died.

Blake said, "Orange Bug performed The Shimmy of Whateverness and said, 'Sure. You take them.'

"So we left with Squirrelly Yellow Bug, went back to their embassy, and caught the first freighter back to Ganymede."

I took a deep breath. The human-balanced air slid easily into my bruised lungs. I said, "At the embassy, the Chitterer staff all danced The Waltz of I-Told-You-So."

"Yes," Blake said.

No one at that party could read the Chitterers' Dance Language. With a lift of my chin and rolling my arms outward, I performed, for Blake, The Opening to Hideous Truths.

Her pale, thin hand turned upward in a very human gesture that beckoned me to her. "Ellis," she said.

Fear of dying in a hot, clammy hole full of crawling bugs caught me. "No. I'm not Ellis. I'm not *your* Ellis. I'm Wellington Smyth, the Eighth."

Blake blinked her lovely gray eyes. Her pale cheeks flushed soft peach. "Ellis, come back to me."

I performed a four-legged Soft-Shell version of The Deflation of Crushing Despair.

Blake grabbed my hands. "No, Ellis. I love you. We went through all that together, and I still love you. Come back to me."

We all handle trauma in different ways. Blake picked up a mild case of Stockholm Syndrome, and her ebullient personality turned being held prisoner by terrorists into a great bar story.

I am Wellington Smyth.

Wellys, for short.

Ellis, between lovers.

I couldn't joke about it. I'd been beaten nearly every day and had a year of my life stolen. I'd had twelve surgeries since I'd returned to try to put my body back together. I looked nothing like the carefree, handsome youth in Blake's photo from Earth.

When I went over to Squirrely Yellow Bug, Big Black Bug had shoved one of those scoopy guns past my broken teeth and pulled the trigger. When it turned out that the gun wasn't charged and I was still alive, they all did the Paso Doble of Unbounded Mirth.

Blake screamed every bit of that foul and filthy air out of her lungs when she thought they had cut off my head.

I stumbled, falling against Blake, and she caught me. If the memory destroyed me, at least I would die in her arms.

A Word from Blair S. Babylon

Like many college stories, this story begins with alcohol.

It was the weekend in graduate school that I went three rounds with Cthulhu in the bottom of a vodka bottle. The next day, I was *destroyed*. I was lying on the couch, shaking with a skull-splitting headache like I had never had before and whining about how my viruses were going to eat all my cells and two weeks' worth of research was going to die and I was too sick to go to the lab to feed my pets. My roommate, who was a medical student, took pity on me, or maybe she got tired of listening to my whining. She dragged me to the hospital, hooked me up with a unit of Ringer's lactate solution, and stuffed an oxygen cannula up my nose, gently instructing me to "Breathe deeply and quit moaning about it." In half an hour, I was *fine*. Really *fine*. It's an old doctor's trick to beat a hangover, and it works way better than tomato juice or the hair of the dog.

A couple of weekends later, I was watching something on PBS about the Carboniferous Period, a time when two-meter-long scorpions roamed the Earth, and how insects don't grow that big now because the oxygen concentration of the air was so much higher back then. The Carboniferous Period would have been a really good time to party.

That idea, two-meter-long scorpions roaming an oxygen-rich atmosphere that would cure a hangover, stayed with me for years, until this story came about.

In addition to science fiction, I write in several different genres. My urban fantasy series, some of which are based in the world of SM Reine, are available on my website.

If you like thrillers about police snipers vs. terrorists, you might like to check out *The Angel of Death* (Police Snipers and Hostage Negotiators, An Angel Day Novel). If you like a lot of romance with your death-defying thriller action, you might want to check out the list of my several long series on my website.

I also plan to publish a couple new science fiction and urban fantasy stories in the next year. If you'd like to get a quick email when they come out, please sign up for my mailing list. You get four free Blair Babylon ebooks as a gift to you immediately just for signing up!

I love to chat with readers. Please feel free to email me or hang out with me on Facebook or Google Plus. Thanks for reading.

Uncle Allen
by Will Swardstrom

THE AIR WAS CRISP and clear, a little off kilter for a late August day in the bottoms of rural Southern Illinois. The soybeans were almost waist-high and the corn still clung to all the green it could, but the advancement of fall was evident by the drying of the plants. A few fields still held the vestiges of farm life from the early part of the twentieth century—crumbling silos, dilapidated barns, and hog houses virtually undone by the ravages of time and nature.

The slight chill made Rachel wish she'd brought more than just a few long-sleeved shirts to Grandma Naomi's house. Actually, the twenty-seven-year-old wished she wasn't heading to her grandmother's homestead at all—the past few years hadn't been kind to Grandma Naomi. A fractured collarbone, a urinary tract infection, dementia, and all sorts of issues in between... lately it seemed as though if it wasn't one thing, it was another.

Rachel absentmindedly turned on the radio. Not a lot of choices on her dial. There were perhaps ten to twelve stations

41

that were at least mildly free of static, but nine of them played country, and the rest were hit or miss depending on the weather. Luckily, Rachel always made sure her phone was stocked with some decent music for trips like this—her own personal jukebox.

Just as she synced her car's sound system to her phone, her phone chirped. She fumbled with the volume on the dash for a moment before answering.

"Hello?"

"Rachel?"

Rachel recognized the voice immediately. "Hello, Uncle Allen. Yes, this is Rachel. I'm on my way, if that's what you're checking." Her tone contained a touch of sarcasm.

"Of course I wasn't checking," Uncle Allen responded. "I was just calling to see how my favorite niece was doing."

"Allen?"

"Yeah?"

"I'm your only niece," Rachel said, a grin creeping onto her face.

"That doesn't make it less true," Allen chided. "But since you brought it up, what time do you expect to be here tonight? I'll see about having dinner on the table when you do."

Rachel glanced down at the clock on her now-silent radio and mentally plotted out the remainder of her trip. "Oh, I'd say about seven o'clock? Maybe later if I get caught in a traffic jam."

Uncle Allen guffawed. If there was anything more unlikely in Southern Illinois than a traffic jam, it was a skyscraper, or perhaps Godzilla. "Okay. Sounds good. I'll tell your grandma. She's really looking forward to seeing you."

Rachel felt a pit in her stomach. "She'll see me, but will she remember me? Will she even know I'm there?"

Allen went quiet, and Rachel realized she should have been more sensitive. She knew that Uncle Allen felt personally responsible for his mother's health—after all, he was the one who lived close by, and he was in charge of her care. Yet most days Allen was needed in the field, so he'd had to rely on a cobbled-together series of nurses, family members, and friends to come by and watch over her while he worked.

This week, it was Rachel's turn to help. And in addition to keeping an eye on her grandmother, Rachel had also promised to purge the clutter in Grandma Naomi's attic. It seemed that Grandma had never forgotten Rachel's long-ago promise to clear out the mess—even though there was no guarantee that Grandma would even remember Rachel's name when she pulled in the driveway.

Rachel was almost sure her call had dropped when Allen finally spoke again. "You know she loves you. She can't help it, and whether or not she remembers, it'll be good for you to be here."

Rachel nodded, even though Allen couldn't see her. "I guess you're right. I better get off the phone and focus on the road then. I'll see you in a couple hours. Love you, Uncle Allen."

"Love you, Rach."

* * *

The trip took a bit longer than she'd estimated, but at last Rachel pulled onto the road leading to what had been her favorite place to visit as a little girl. It had been several years since Rachel's last visit here; after college, she had moved up to Indianapolis, a land full of metal and noise. Now, just turning onto the gravel road gave her goose bumps, reminding her of all the memories she'd shared with her cousins at the farm.

Her sports car kicking up dust behind her, Rachel maneuvered down the gravel road and then up the long driveway belonging to Grandma Naomi. Surrounded on three sides by a thick grove of trees, her grandmother's house was typical of early twentieth-century farmhouses in the Midwest: four bedrooms on the top floor, a large living room and dining room attached to the kitchen on the main floor, and a basement that followed the same basic floor plan of the house. The only difference in the basement's layout was that it lacked the additional bathroom that Naomi and Grandpa Henry had added to the main floor back in the late 1950s, when they were first lucky enough to get running water. Rachel's mom still talked about using the outhouse in the winter when she was a child.

From the outside, the house looked almost like a big cardboard box with the flaps slightly open to form the roof. A hailstorm had devastated the area the year before, and the aging shingles showed the evidence of it. Uncle Allen had promised to take on the repairs, but farming took him away from the task nearly every chance he had. Still, the roof was in decent shape, and everyone knew Allen would fix it immediately if it ever leaked anywhere in the house. Uncle

Allen was busy, but he took care of his family. In fact, he was the kind of guy who was everyone's favorite, whether he was your favorite uncle, brother, friend, or farmer. He just had a certain magnetic personality that kept people entertained.

As Rachel parked, she saw her grandmother out in front of the house, watering her small flower garden. Rachel wouldn't say Grandma was a hoarder, but the years she spent living in the Great Depression had taught her never to be wasteful. That was particularly true with clothes: if there was *any* use to be gotten out of an old item, she would squirrel it away for a rainy day. Her clothing, therefore, was a mix of styles gathered from across decades. Today her top bore a definite resemblance to the homemaker blouses Rachel had seen in a few reruns of *Leave it to Beaver*, while her slacks were 1970s polyester through and through.

"Hello, Rachel!" Grandma Naomi called out as Rachel stepped out of the car. "We've been waiting for you to get here."

Whew. At least she remembers my name.

"We?" Rachel asked, hoisting her suitcase out of the back seat.

"Oh, yes. Me and your Uncle Allen, of course."

"Of course."

"We had more visitors, too, but they left just a minute or two before you got here," Grandma Naomi said. "Funny-looking. Kinda glad they didn't decide to stay."

That stopped Rachel. She knew she'd been all alone on the gravel road coming into the farm. And while the road continued on past the driveway, it was rarely used, and Rachel hadn't seen any dust kicked up. Well, she *had* been distracted listening to the music on her phone. Perhaps she'd simply missed them.

"Really? What were they here for?"

"Hmm… now that you ask me, I can't quite remember. I'm sure they were here for your Uncle Allen, though. They always are," Naomi said, putting her watering can down next to a row of marigolds. She bent down—an amazing feat considering her advanced age—to pluck off a few dead flower heads.

Rachel was still concerned about these visitors to the farm. "Who were they, Grandma? You say they've been here before?"

"Oh, yes," her grandmother replied. "Those men have been coming here for a long time. I wish they would just go away, but they won't leave me and Henry alone. They just feel… off. Like they're here, but not here at the same time. Strange clothing. And their accents… I'm not even sure they're from this country. Could be spies. You know: the Soviets."

And there it was. Her grandma was combining fact, fiction, and history. She may have recognized and greeted her granddaughter by the correct name, but she was also somewhere in her own past, and apparently reliving some political thriller at the same time.

Just then Uncle Allen popped his head out of the side door of the garage, saving Rachel from an uncomfortable situation. "Supper is ready. Glad to see you, Rachel."

After allowing herself another sideways glance at her grandmother, Rachel grabbed the handle of her suitcase and headed toward the garage. As she passed by Uncle Allen, she made eye contact with him for a brief moment. And in that split second, she saw something... strange. Allen had always been so jovial and vibrant. Even in the face of his mother's illnesses and maladies, he'd always kept up appearances. He'd always put on a brave face.

But this time... his eyes told a different story.

Uncle Allen was afraid.

* * *

After a late meal and then getting Grandma Naomi settled into her chair to watch *The Tonight Show* (the "Johnny Carson show," Naomi insisted), Rachel and Uncle Allen reconnected over a small makeshift brush fire near the driveway. The bright colors of Grandma Naomi's flowers were subdued and dim under the curtain of darkness, and the night sky was like oil covering the landscape.

A few stories from her uncle brought laughs from Rachel, but eventually the stories wore out and the laughter did as well. Rachel sat in silence for a few moments, gazing up at the stars, light years away.

"I miss her," she said.

Silence followed from the other side of the fire. Finally, after a few moments, Uncle Allen replied.

"Yeah. I know, kid. I miss her, too. Growing up, it seemed at times like she was the only one who really got me," he said. "Like Mom and Dad loved me, but kept their distance a little. Your mom was the best sister I could've asked for. Your other aunts were just too old by the time I came around."

Rachel felt a slight chill in the air, but being with Uncle Allen was warming her soul. She nodded toward the starry expanse. "You think she's looking down on us? That there's someone out there that cares what happens down here?"

Allen cocked his head and took in the Milky Way and the countless stars that shone down. "Up there? I don't know. I do know I'll never forget her. In that way, maybe your mother will keep on living, you know?"

"Yeah. I know."

With nothing else to be said, Rachel stood, walked around the fire, sat down next to Uncle Allen, and put her head on his shoulder, both of them remembering her mother.

* * *

The next morning, Rachel woke to light streaming in the windows of her mother's childhood room. The house had been built long before mini-blinds had been invented, and the bedrooms had been vacated before window shades would become the norm in homes across the country. The sun illuminated the entire room, chasing away any darkness still lingering.

Unable to sleep any longer, Rachel slid out of bed and dragged herself down the stairs, only to find Grandma Naomi already up and baking. The scent of sugar and cinnamon filled the small kitchen. Rachel pulled a chair out from the table and sat, rubbing the sleep from her eyes.

"Good morning, Melissa!" Naomi said, turning around. Her face showed a brief moment of confusion. Rachel waited a moment before responding, to see if Grandma would realize her mistake. She didn't.

"Good morning, Grandma. I'm Rachel. Melissa is my mom, but she couldn't be here today," Rachel said, a small tear beginning a slow slide down her cheek. One of the worst parts in coming to her grandmother's house was reliving the painful memories of Mom. It'd been three years, but Rachel wondered nearly every day what would have happened if her mom had only gotten that mammogram earlier. What if she had gotten to the doctor even just a few months earlier? Would she still be here?

But her mother was gone, and now Rachel felt compelled to help take care of Grandma Naomi, to take her mom's spot in the family rotation.

"Of course you are. I said Rachel, didn't I?" Naomi didn't wait for an answer, probably because she already knew her mistake. "What do you say we get up in that attic after the rolls come out of the oven? I haven't been up there in probably ten years."

Just then the timer went off, and Rachel hopped up, grabbed an oven mitt, and took the steaming sweet rolls from the oven. As she set them on the counter to cool, she glanced out the window above the kitchen sink to see if Uncle Allen's truck was there. Gone. Rachel was alone with her grandmother. Well, no time like the present to clear out years of dust and memories from a hundred-year-old house.

"Yeah, Grandma. Sounds good. First though, let's eat."

* * *

The attic was foreboding on many levels, and the neglect was tangible. Spider webs and dust covered everything. Boxes were stacked to the joists along the walls, and dated Christmas decorations were scattered haphazardly around.

As Rachel began to inspect the boxes, she noticed many were damp. The leaky roof had affected Grandma's attic after all. Books that had been boxed up, perhaps in the hopes of storing them on a bookshelf again at some point, were now ruined, their pages warped and wilted by the constant moisture coming in from above.

"Grandma, these books are no good," Rachel called out across the large attic space. She'd situated the elderly matriarch in a folding chair as soon as they'd come up to the attic.

"What do you mean, dear? Those books were perfectly fine when I boxed them up last week."

Not again.

Rachel grabbed a book and made her way back to her grandmother, maneuvering carefully around a stack of cardboard cutouts that appeared to be from Naomi's days as a Sunday School teacher at the local Methodist Church.

"Grandma, look at this book," Rachel said, handing her a paperback copy of H.G. Wells's *The War of the Worlds*.

"Oh, yes, this was your grandfather's favorite. All the suspense and the beings from another world. Too much for my taste," Naomi said. "But it's all wet. What did you do to it?"

Rachel sighed. Perhaps she would have to take on this task without Grandma's consent. It wasn't like she was going to remember what Rachel did or didn't do anyway. She took the book back.

"The attic is too moist for books," Rachel said. "They're all this way, Grandma."

"Oh. Well, I don't need to keep damaged books. You just take care of them, Rachel. I'll stay here and look through these boxes." In front of Naomi's folding chair were a couple of small boxes.

"What's in there?"

"Oh, just a few of the kids' favorite toys. As they outgrew them, I'd put them away up here. I always meant to give them back to them, but they've all gone now. Gone or moved away," Naomi said.

"Not all of them, Grandma," Rachel reminded her. "Uncle Allen still lives down the road. Remember? He comes by every day to check up on you."

Naomi's eyes clouded for a nanosecond and then cleared. "Oh, yes. You're right, honey."

Peering into the box on Naomi's lap, Rachel saw many familiar shapes: a toy gun, a teddy bear, a baby doll. Each had special meaning for her mother, her uncle, or one of her aunts. She wondered which items belonged to her own mother when she was growing up in this very house—what special toy her mom had loved and cherished until it was a forgotten object, a mere memory of carefree days.

Then something caught her eye. Reaching down, Rachel plucked a key from the box. It didn't appear old—in fact, it still shined as if it were brand-new. Impossible—Grandma Naomi herself had said she hadn't been in the attic in years.

But Grandma isn't exactly a reliable witness. Rachel had to admit that although Grandma Naomi believed herself to be truthful, her mind could jump not only between decades but between fact and fiction.

"What's this?"

"That's Allen's toy key. I remember he held on to that key until he turned seven years old. Each and every day, you'd walk into a room and find him holding and playing with that thing. Never really knew where it came from—one day he was just holding it. I suppose today I might've gotten turned into the Department of Child and Family Services for letting him play with keys," Naomi said, with a smirk on her face.

"Maybe," Rachel said, twirling the key before her eyes. The small key wasn't aluminum or silver or any metal she recognized; it had an iridescent sheen to it, appearing slightly different from every angle. She'd never seen anything like it.

Grandma Naomi made a motion to put the box down, so Rachel volunteered to find a place for it, and to organize its contents and find homes for the various toys. She absentmindedly stuck the key in her pocket as she moved the box over to the other side of the attic.

"You girls up here?" Uncle Allen called up from the base of the stairs.

"Come on up," Naomi answered.

"Nah. I don't need to see any of that old stuff. Don't want to get stuck doing your job anyway. Just wanted to swing by and check on you two."

"We're doing okay," Rachel answered. She toyed with the key in her pocket, but for some reason resisted the urge to show it to Allen.

"All right, then. I gotta get back to it. I'll come by later for dinner," Allen said, his voice trailing off as he headed back down the stairs and out of the house.

"I do hope that boy is careful. I'd hate for him to run into our visitors from yesterday. They said they'd be back, you know," Grandma Naomi said. Rachel peered over the boxes to find Grandma going through a basket full of *Good Housekeeping* magazines from the mid-eighties.

Rachel worked by herself for the next few minutes before peeking back to check on her grandmother's progress. Grandma's head was down, a magazine drooping on her lap. *Asleep.* At least, Rachel hoped she was asleep. She crept over and double-checked that Grandma was still breathing, then headed back to her work—pitching junk and saving memories.

Another box of books: trash.

A box of greeting cards: mostly trash. Rachel salvaged a few she knew Grandma Naomi would want and tossed the rest into the wastebasket.

Digging out a box labeled "Dates," Rachel found a complete set of wall calendars from the 1970s. She just shook her head and moved on to a box she'd found virtually hidden, stuffed in the back corner. This box wasn't cardboard like the others, but was instead a wooden crate made up of small slats. Hardly watertight, so Rachel was tempted to chuck the entire mess before she even perused it, but something caught her eye.

Inside the box was a stack of small lined pieces of notebook paper that appeared to have been ripped out of a journal or diary. The top page was labeled Oct. 19, 1959.

Rachel probably wouldn't have given it another thought except for one thing: it was the day Uncle Allen was born.

Bending down and folding herself into a seated position, Rachel carefully extracted the loose sheets of paper, noting that some had been damaged by the moisture. The pages were brittle where they weren't damp. Peeling them apart, Rachel set them down on the wooden floorboards.

The pages ran to the end of the year—definitely pages from a diary—but unfortunately, they were all blank except for the first one. And even that page was a mess of seemingly random words interrupted by water stains. Rachel took her cell phone out of her pocket, and selected the flashlight app. Immediately the attic lit up, casting shadows all around. Rachel pointed the light at the page below.

Dec. 19, 1959

The baby (unintelligible) 8 lbs., 5 oz. (unintelligible) healthy. (unintelligible) concerned.

Visitors (unintelligible) hospital. Never (unintelligible). I refused (unintelligible). Naomi wasn't so (unintelligible). Just concerned about (unintelligible). They will be (unintelligible) threats, but (unintelligible) ready.

Rachel was confused. It definitely wasn't Grandma Naomi's handwriting; it had a more masculine tilt to it, and Rachel had seen her grandmother's handwriting dozens of times on birthday and Christmas cards over the years. It must be her grandfather's journal.

She looked at the rest of the pages, confirming they were all blank. And apart from the occasional smudge, they were. There was only that one page that had been used. Given the date and the baby's measurements, it was clearly about her uncle's birth. But what was this about threats?

Should she go to Uncle Allen and ask him? Would Grandma Naomi remember the events of fifty years ago?

Rachel rifled through the rest of the box but found no other papers or important documents. So she snuck down the attic stairs and put the diary pages in the dresser drawer in her bedroom. She'd think about it more later, perhaps that night as she went to bed.

As Rachel re-entered the attic, Grandma Naomi was waking back up.

"Oh, hello," Naomi said, looking around her, confused by her surroundings. "Are you here to take me to the hospital?"

"No, Grandma," Rachel said. "Let's head back downstairs. I imagine you could use a trip to the powder room."

"Oh, I guess you're right," Naomi said. "I feel like I've been up here for hours, but that's impossible. I was just watching M*A*S*H with Henry. Speaking of... I wonder where Henry is."

Rachel didn't want to fight that battle right now, so she just went along with it. "I think he may have gone out with Allen to work in the fields."

"Oh, yes. What a good boy, that Allen. Always staying home to help take care of me. I do hope we get him back one of these days."

* * *

After a nap, Grandma Naomi was in a better state of mind. A late-afternoon rain shower forced Allen to call it a day early, and so the three relatives found themselves eating pork chops around the table just before the prime time TV schedule got going.

"How was your day?" Naomi asked Allen.

"Fine. Had a little trouble with the sprayer out in the field past Wither's Corner, but I got it sorted out," Allen said between bites.

Rachel sat at the table, finding herself staring at her food because she couldn't bring herself to look Uncle Allen in the eye. Finally, she worked up the courage to ask an apparently innocuous question.

"Uncle Allen, what was life like when you were young? I mean… I don't have my mom to ask about her childhood anymore, so I guess you're the next best thing."

Her mind was stuck on the pages of the diary she'd found from earlier in the afternoon. What was so special about Uncle Allen's birth? Why did Grandpa Henry—or whoever—write about it and then tear those pages out of his diary? Where was the rest of the diary, from before that day? She'd scoured the attic the rest of the afternoon after helping Grandma Naomi into bed, but to no avail.

"Life? Like here on the farm?" Allen asked. "Boy, I don't know. Pretty standard, I imagine. Dad always had work for us to do. Your mom always tried to get out of working outside, though. She was usually working with Mom here in the kitchen."

"Oh, yes," Grandma Naomi piped up. "Your mother was the best cook to ever work in this kitchen. I'd like to say I taught her everything she knew, but that just wouldn't be true. She came up with some wonderful recipes I'd never dreamt of."

It was great to hear her grandma talk about her mother—and better still to hear her talk in a coherent manner—but Rachel's mind was racing about her Uncle Allen. She tried to shift the focus back to him.

"What did you do for births back when you had children, Grandma?" Rachel asked. "You don't hear much about women having babies at home these days, but you had all of your kids at home, right?"

"I did. Even my last, my boy Allen right here," she said, reaching over to pat Allen on the arm. "It wasn't easy, but there's nothing like it. I couldn't imagine going to a strange hospital room when you have everything you know and love at your own home. Wouldn't you rather have a baby in a familiar place than some cold, sterile room?"

Rachel knew exactly where she would like to have kids one day, and it wasn't at home, but she wasn't about to tell

Grandma Naomi that. She simply nodded, shoving a forkful of pork into her mouth.

"Did you have any problems then?"

"Me? No, can't say I did. All my kids were healthy," Naomi said, but then furrowed her brow. "Well, there were a few problems with Allen. But I was so exhausted after I had him that by the time I felt better, he was completely better as well."

"Really?" Allen said, stopping his meal mid-bite. "I never knew that. What was wrong?"

"Oh, wow. It's hard for me to remember. Henry was always better with those things. We were actually going to name you Henry, Jr., but we changed our minds after you came along. What was wrong? Something about your lungs. Doctors didn't share as much back then. They did have to show me you were breathing when you were first born," Naomi said. "I thought you were dead at first. A stillbirth."

While Naomi worked on cutting her pork chop, Rachel and Allen looked at each other. Neither one had heard any of this before.

"Mom, you never told me any of that before," Uncle Allen said.

"Family's got to have some secrets," Grandma Naomi said curtly, signaling to both her son and granddaughter that she was done with this particular line of questioning.

The rest of the meal was spent talking about the weather forecast and how the crops were doing. But by the time Grandma Naomi was serving up a slice of rhubarb pie for dessert, any hint of her earlier clarity and lucidity had vanished.

"Rachel, my dear, you were careful today in the attic, weren't you?"

"Of course I was, Grandma. You saw what I threw out and what I didn't," Rachel answered. She worried for a moment Naomi knew about the diary pages she had squirreled away in her mom's childhood bedroom. "Did I do something wrong?"

"You? Oh, no, you were fine. I was just concerned about the men up in the attic with us today. You know who they are—they look like us, but they aren't us."

… And Grandma Naomi is gone again.

"Uh, Grandma? I don't remember seeing any men in the attic today."

"Of course you don't. They're clever. They wouldn't want you to see them. They're very good at hiding, after all. They're best, though, when they hide in plain sight."

"Mom," Allen said, "You're scaring Rachel. There weren't any men in the attic. I stopped by, too. I would have seen them if they were really there."

Rachel took a bite of her pie, but suddenly wasn't hungry anymore. Between the diary pages, the mysterious key, and her grandma's crazy talk, it was a bit much for her. "Maybe you're thinking of a different day, Grandma," Rachel offered. "I don't remember seeing them, but I guess that doesn't mean they weren't here. I did step out from the attic for a few moments."

"Yes, dear, that must be it," Naomi said, again closing the door on the topic.

Somehow, though, Rachel suspected the conversation was far from over.

* * *

Sleep was elusive. Just as the lack of blinds on her mother's window allowed sunlight to stream in unfettered in the morning, it also allowed in the bold moonlight at night. And if it wasn't a full moon, it was close. As Rachel lay in bed, she thought that she should appreciate this chance to really view the night sky; back home in Indianapolis, the light pollution virtually hid the stars from view. But right now, she really just wanted to sleep.

After several minutes of wrestling with the brightness, Rachel finally went to the closet and found a quilt to drape over the window. But as soon as the quilt went over the window's opening, Rachel realized that not all the light in the room had been due to the moon. On the corner of the dresser, where Rachel had emptied her pockets from earlier in the day, the key from the attic was shining like a beacon in the darkness.

"What the…?" Rachel asked the empty room around her. But there were no answers here. All she had was the strange key and the diary pages.

Acting on a sudden impulse, Rachel opened the dresser and withdrew the aged papers. She didn't know why she thought there might be something new, but she shuffled through the pages again, examining them in the light cast by the key. And when she lined up the pages on her bed, her hunch was proven correct: what had appeared to be mere smudges on the blank pages came together to spell out a phrase. Perhaps it had been harder to see before because the pages weren't fully dried; or perhaps the pages only showed their secret in the eerie glow of the key. Either way, the hidden message created a new mystery:

"I'll bury it in the second hole."

The second hole? What did that mean? Rachel sat down on the edge of the bed and tried to figure it out, but her mind couldn't put the puzzle together. Even if she had all the pieces, which she was sure she didn't, Rachel acknowledged to herself that there might not even be much to the mystery before her.

And was this really something Rachel should be digging into? Didn't Grandma Naomi say every family had their secrets? Was this a secret that should stay hidden?

Before she knew what she was doing, Rachel had changed back into her T-shirt and jeans from earlier in the day and was slipping on a pair of tennis shoes. The diary pages went into her back pocket, along with her cell phone, but she kept the key in her hand to light her way.

The house was dark and Rachel was afraid the light from the key would wake her grandmother, but when she passed her grandmother's bedroom on the first floor, the door was closed. She kept her hand over the key to dampen the light. For whatever reason, Rachel felt herself being led out of the house and into the back yard.

When she turned left out of the garage door, she found herself face to face with Uncle Allen.

* * *

"What—what are you doing out here?" Rachel asked.

"I might ask you the same thing young lady," Allen said. "But since you asked, I ran out of gas on my way home. I knew there was a spare can in the barn here, so I was heading over that way when I saw a light coming from your mom's—I mean, your bedroom."

"So? Girl can read a book if she wants, right?"

"Is that what you're doing out here? Reading?"

Rachel put her head down. "No."

"All right. Let's hear it. I saw how you were looking at me at supper. Rather, how you were avoiding me. What's up? Did you find something in the attic? My fifth-grade report card? Worse yet, my fifth-grade school picture?" Allen chuckled.

Rachel opened her hand to reveal the key. "I found this."

"Whoa."

"Grandma said it was yours. She said you played with it all the time when you were a kid."

Rachel saw the look in Allen's eyes go from confusion to recognition. "Yeah. I mean, it's been almost fifty years, but I *do* remember this. I didn't play with toy guns and action figures when I was a kid. I played with this key. But it's one of those memories that comes and goes—in fact, for a long time, I thought I might have imagined this. I don't remember it ever glowing, though."

"Well, that wasn't all. I also found some diary pages written by Grandpa," Rachel said, pulling the pages out of her pocket. She handed them over and used the key to help Allen read the pages for himself.

"Okay, but this doesn't tell me why you're outside at midnight," Allen said.

"I don't know," Rachel said. She was beginning to wonder about that herself. "Maybe I let my mind get carried away with everything, but with the key and the diary pages, along with everything Grandma Naomi is saying…"

"Rachel. You know she's lost it, right?"

"Well…"

"No, Rachel. She's been my mother longer than she's been your grandmother. I've seen her descent, and it's a sad thing to see, but she isn't anything like she was when I was a little boy," Allen said, scratching his beard. "And the things she says… You know, you get a moment like what we had at supper tonight where she remembers who we are and remembers what really happened in her life. But then something happens. I wish I knew what it was, but she changes. Her memories become fiction. It isn't even that she goes back to her youth— her mind just goes *someplace else* and the words that come out of her mouth…" He shrugged. "You just can't trust anything she says."

"Even what she said about you being stillborn?"

"Even that. I've never heard that before. Don't you think I would have heard that *some* time in the last fifty-three years?"

"Yeah, I guess."

"But these diary pages *are* interesting. My dad always refused to talk to me about when I was born. Maybe there are some answers in the rest of his diary. If it even exists," he said, thumbing through the pages again.

"Do you have any idea what the secret message means?" Rachel prompted, showing Allen the message hidden in the smudges.

Allen considered. "Hmm… in the second hole."

"Yeah, I don't have any idea what it means, either," Rachel confessed, her shoulders slumping.

Allen looked up with a wry grin. "I didn't say I don't know what it means. I actually think I may know *exactly* what it means."

Rachel stopped. "You do?"

"Yeah. At least, I hope it means what I think it means. If it doesn't, it could be pretty unpleasant."

"What do you mean?"

Allen looked around, then turned toward the woods behind the house. "Follow me. I'll show you."

* * *

As they plunged into the wooded area, Rachel was extremely grateful for the glowing key. The strange object illuminated the entire area under the canopy, showing Rachel and her uncle where they could place their steps in the blackness of night. Even with a nearly full moon, navigating in the woods would have been tricky without some sort of flashlight.

"Where are we going?" Rachel asked. For some reason she felt compelled to keep her voice at a whisper.

"The only place I know of with two holes," Uncle Allen called back, apparently not concerned about making noise.

Rachel kept her mouth shut as she followed Allen the rest of the way. The two of them had to dodge low-hanging tree limbs and weave in and out of thick brush and undergrowth. Eventually they stood before a small wooden building, its boards rotting. It had been built for a purpose, and when it had outlived its usefulness, it was forgotten.

"The outhouse."

Rachel was dumbfounded. "Seriously?"

Allen chuckled as he lifted a few boards that had fallen across the long-forgotten door. "I guess you don't remember much about your Grandpa Henry, but he always had a bit of a sense of humor. And I imagine he never expected anyone would come looking for anything in the ol' outhouse, so this may have been the best place to put something he wanted to keep hidden."

Rachel caught a glimpse of Allen's face under the moonlight. He was grinning, as if he hadn't had this much fun in years.

"Okay. I guess. But what about this 'second hole'?"

"I guess you never used the outhouse, did you?" Allen asked, not waiting for an answer. "Dad built this well before I was even a glimmer in his eye. And for whatever reason, he built it with two toilets. We used to call an outhouse like this a 'two-holer.'"

"Clever."

He chuckled. "Yeah, I know. But the thing is, while there were two holes, Dad never got around to cutting the second hole. If the message means something, maybe it's that he hid something here."

By now, he had cleared the door of rotten lumber and debris, and the two of them stumbled into the outhouse. Sure enough, they were staring at a room with a wide bench across the long end. There was a hole on the right side of the bench, and more than enough room for a second hole on the left.

Allen went straight toward the void on the left. "We always used the one over on the right, so this," he said, prying up a loose board, "should hold whatever we're looking for."

With a crack, the old board came loose. Rachel held the glowing key next to the hole and peered inside.

Underneath the bench was a marble slab—a headstone. Rachel gasped.

Carved into the stone were a name and a date.

Henry, Jr.
Oct. 19, 1959

Rachel turned to look at her uncle. It was difficult to tell in the eerie glow from the key, but he seemed to have lost some of his color.

"What…?"

"I don't know, Rachel. Mom said they were originally going to name me Henry, Jr. Did they have this made, thinking I was dead?" Allen asked.

A few moments passed silently between them. Then Allen reached down, grabbed the edges of the marble slab, and lifted it aside. Rachel gasped, but Allen wasn't listening.

"Time for some answers. If Mom can't tell me, I'm going to find out for myself."

Underneath the marble was a metal box. Gingerly, Allen reached in and pulled it out. It was big enough to be a makeshift casket for a baby.

"This is awful heavy to have only a dead infant inside," Allen said. "I'm not sure, but I think this box is made of lead. Should we open it?"

Rachel briefly thought of every horror movie she'd ever watched, of how she would scream at the protagonists to not open such a box, but she couldn't help herself. She *had* to know what was inside. She needed to unravel the half-century-old mystery.

"Yes."

Allen must have felt the same way, as he immediately placed the box on the ground and crouched down to examine it. A simple latch on the front popped open with a little pressure, and Allen flipped up the lid.

Instantly, the contents of the box illuminated the entire woods, just as the key had lit up Rachel's room back at the house. But this was no subtle glow—it was a ferocity of brilliance that made the night seem like day. Both Allen and Rachel put their arms up to shield their eyes from the intense light.

Once her brain was able to cope with the brightness, Rachel realized her hand was vibrating. Or more accurately, the key in her hand was vibrating. She squinted and examined the key closer.

"Uncle Allen, the key…"

"Yeah, I was just wondering the same thing," he said.

Allen shut his eyes tightly and began exploring the object in the box with his hands. Though the glare was blinding, Rachel chanced a quick glance down, and saw that the object was a case of some kind, and seemed to be made of the same material as the key. It was like a large tube, almost like a small keg of the kind Rachel had seen at parties when she was in college. Allen's fingers were probing a small hole.

"Hand me the key," he said.

With one arm still covering her eyes, Rachel put the key in Uncle Allen's hand. And then she chanced another peek into the brightness. She *needed* to see Allen open the container.

Allen inserted the key into the hole and turned. The tube opened. Immediately the light began to wane, and their eyes slowly adjusted to the darkness once again.

The outside of the tube had rotated back, revealing a few items inside. But the thing that Rachel noticed first wasn't what *was* there, but what *wasn't*. There were no bones.

Allen moved aside some official-looking papers and uncovered what looked something like a modern-day iPad. "Holy cow," he whispered. He picked up the tablet as Rachel leaned over to see what he held.

"Stop!"

Rachel and her uncle swiveled around to find Grandma Naomi staring them down, an old Rayovac flashlight in her hands, her cotton nightgown fluttering in the evening breeze. Her usually perfect perm was unkempt, and she had a wild look in her eyes.

"Grandma?" "Mom?" Rachel and Allen both exclaimed simultaneously.

"You two have no idea what you're doing. You need to stop. Put it all back and forget you ever found it," Naomi said, approaching them slowly and determinedly.

Rachel looked over at Allen. Was this a new side of her grandmother? Had she known about this all along?

Allen was apparently having none of it. "I'm not going to do that, Mom. All this—Dad's diary, this creepy headstone—it's about *me*. Me! I have a right to know what it's all about," he said defiantly. "And if you can't tell me, I'm going to dig until I can't dig any more."

"Son, listen to me. I know I'm not always myself. The moments when I'm in the present are becoming fewer and fewer, but I do know this: some secrets are best left buried. Leave it be."

Rachel knew they could never do that, not now. Too much of the past had been exposed for them to simply tuck it away and pretend they never saw it. Allen deserved to know the truth about himself. Everyone deserved that much.

"For the last time, you tell me, or I'll read the diary myself," Allen said.

Even in the semidarkness, Rachel could see the rage and frustration boiling up within her uncle. She looked back at her grandmother and felt something new toward this old woman. Respect? Anger? Fear? The grandmother she had always known, who had always been a source of strength and comfort, was not who she appeared to be. And apparently never had been.

The look on Grandma Naomi's face would have sent Rachel running for cover when she was little. Now, though, Grandma was frail, no match for her son, who faced her in a silent standoff. In an instant, her hard visage crumbled and her shoulders slumped.

"Fine. I never thought I would be alive for this, but I suppose you deserve the truth."

"And what's that?" Allen asked, his voice still sharp. "Did I have a twin? Did he die?"

Laughing strangely, Naomi shook her head. "Nothing as simple as that, I'm afraid." She sat down on a log and took a deep breath, as if steeling herself. "You see, in 1959, this farm was visited by aliens," she said.

Rachel and Allen exchanged a look, unsure what to think.

"Aliens. You mean illegal immigrants?" Rachel asked. These days migrant workers came north to work on farms throughout the Midwest. She hoped that was all that Naomi had meant. Although she was sure it wasn't.

"No, Rachel. I mean aliens. Extra-terrestrials. From another planet," Naomi said, sighing. In spite of her resistance to telling the truth, doing so was clearly lifting a burden from her. "The first day they came was the day Allen was born. I gave birth at home, and he wasn't well. They came to our door, offering help."

"Help? Why didn't you take me to the hospital?" Allen asked.

"We did, actually. Your father was at his wit's end trying to figure out what to do. We ended up taking the farm truck to the hospital, but you've got to realize this was the 1950s. Technology wasn't what it is today. The doctor took one look at the baby and told us to go home, hold our son, and wait for him to die."

"How horrible," Rachel whispered. She looked back to Allen and found him held rapt by his mother's tale. Grandma

Naomi, on the other hand, was fighting tears, reliving one of the worst days of her life.

"So we came home and there were... people here. I'd call them men, but they weren't. It was almost like something out of a half-remembered dream; they appeared human, but there was just something... off. Something I couldn't quite put my finger on."

"And you let them help me. That's the big secret? I was cured by aliens?" Allen asked quietly.

"No. Your father wouldn't let them help."

"Then how...?"

"Henry would have let you die, out of stubbornness, but I snuck out of the house and they met me out here in the woods. I gave you to them. And they cured you—in a way," Naomi said, her eyes shut to the world around her. "Then they took you away."

Rachel was speechless. Was Grandma losing it again?

"I'm not crazy," she said, as if reading Rachel's mind. "All those things I say... they're real. Or they *were* real. Just let me finish my story, and then you can decide."

"Fine, I was taken to space by aliens. How did I come back then?" Allen asked, his voice more than a little shaky.

"Oh, Allen, that never happened. The deal was that if we let them cure you, they could keep you. We were devastated. Henry went out and bought a headstone the very next day. That was your name," she said, motioning to the headstone. "Henry Junior."

Allen stared down at the headstone, speechless.

Grandma Naomi wiped her hair back, taming the wild locks to a small degree. "But the visitors returned that afternoon. We refused to see them, but they kept coming back until we finally came out of the house."

"Okay… and what about the part where I lived here for the past fifty-five years?" Allen asked.

"That's exactly what they were there for. Their leader—his name was Refl—had claimed to need you, or at least to need someone from our family. Something about our DNA. Back then, neither one of us had heard of DNA, but the aliens were convinced there was something special about our family. They said they wanted to give us something in return, but of course there was nothing they could give me to make up for losing Henry Junior," Grandma Naomi said. "My grief was too much and I just walked away. I couldn't bear to hear any intergalactic sales pitch for my son. The son I would never see again.

"Your father, on the other hand, was intrigued. He talked to Refl, and told him how I felt. A few days went by without our visitors, and then at last they stopped by with an olive branch." Grandma Naomi looked up into Uncle Allen's eyes. "You."

"Me?"

"Yes. They took some of Henry Junior's DNA and made a copy. You're a clone, Allen."

"Wha… seriously?"

"Would your mother lie to you? Wait—don't answer that," Grandma Naomi said. She sat a little taller on the old log, her words giving her life. "I don't know all the reasons why they didn't just take Henry Junior and leave, but they didn't. They gave us you. You might be a clone, but you're identical to Henry Junior in every way, and I've loved you every day of your life. You are my son, Allen, and always have been. We sent Henry Junior off with aliens, and they left us with you. You, and that capsule."

The entire time Naomi talked, Rachel had forgotten about the capsule. She looked back to discover the capsule was still faintly glowing. She'd been clutching her T-shirt with a death-grip, and Allen still held the iPad-like device.

"I don't believe it," he said, shaking his head.

"It is pretty incredible," Rachel said. "You... a clone, and your brother, or whatever you want to call him..."

"No," Allen said, cutting her off. "It isn't just incredible. It's *impossible*. You tell me that ridiculous story and expect me to believe it? If it was true, why didn't you tell me before? I think maybe you need help, Mom. I've been willing to help you stay at the farm, but this is the last straw. I don't know where all this stuff came from, and I don't care." Allen's voice seethed with anger.

"Allen, you don't understand. We couldn't tell you. Do you really think you could have gone to school and not told anyone where you came from? That you were a clone of someone living on another planet?" Tears streaked down Naomi's cheeks.

"It doesn't matter. Come on Mom, let's go," Allen said, stomping over to his mother. "It's past your bedtime."

"No."

Allen stopped in his tracks. He had taken his mother by the elbow, but she refused to stand up.

"You think this was easy on me?" she said. "You think I *wanted* to keep this secret from everyone, let alone you, for all these years? You think it was a cakewalk taking in a *copy* of my dying newborn son and raising him as though nothing had happened?"

"Grandma, no one said any of that," Rachel offered.

"Don't patronize me. I'm not a child. I know I'm not always with it, but I am completely alert right now. More than I have been in years. Maybe it was one last gift the visitors left for me: a chance to set the record straight," Naomi said, throwing her shoulders back. "So here it is: Allen, I love you. I didn't give birth to you, but I've loved you as if I did. Even though I saw a nearly dead infant each time I picked you up when you were little, I still loved you."

She slapped the log, sending up a spray of dirt and debris. Her cheeks were moist with the emotion she'd pent up for decades, but her voice was surprisingly strong. "And yes, I loved Henry Junior as well. Every night when I go to bed, I look out my window, hoping and praying that one day he'll come back to me. One day he'll know I loved him, too."

Rachel sat down beside her grandmother and wept. She felt how Naomi must've felt back then, giving up a child, never to see him again, only to get him back, but not quite the same. As tears obscured her vision, Rachel saw the tablet come to life in Allen's hand. Allen hadn't done anything to turn it on—the hand holding the tablet still hung loosely at his side—but for whatever reason, the screen had lit up.

"Uncle Allen? Grandma?" Rachel pointed at the device. Both Rachel's uncle and grandmother turned their heads, first toward her and then toward the screen. Allen held it up so that they could all see it clearly.

A man came into focus. Behind him was a reddish sky with strange, alien buildings. He wore a tight-fitting uniform of some kind, and his face was remarkably similar to Uncle Allen's, if perhaps a bit smoother and less worn by the Midwestern summers. For whatever reason, the image brought memories of her mother back to Rachel's thoughts. She might not have her mother anymore, but perhaps somewhere out there, her family was alive and well.

Before anyone could say anything, the man spoke.

"Mom?"

A Word from Will Swardstrom

When I was asked to be in *The Alien Chronicles*, the first thing I did was nearly choke on the potatoes I was devouring at the church potluck dinner. After I recovered, I remembered a story I'd been plucking away on and thought it would work great for this collection. I was wrong. It'll still see the light of day, but it just wasn't working.

That story would have involved the most recent "alien" experience I've had, when my wife and I traveled to a developing country in Africa to pick up our newly adopted son. It was a whirlwind trip, but the sights and sounds of those few days overseas are some I'm not likely to forget. And each day of his life, our son probably feels like he's a stranger in a strange land, as he adapts to our culture, our language, and, most importantly, our family. It's an important story, one that needs to be told, but I'm not ready to write that one quite yet.

Then, remembering my grandmother's farm, I had a moment of inspiration. I didn't live near my grandparents, so every visit to their North Dakotan farm was almost like an alien experience to me. In retrospect, there was nothing so American as their farm and the struggle they endured to make a living and raise four children. But for a kid who grew up in suburban splendor, the stark countryside, the lack of neighbors for miles around, and the agriculture just about everywhere really made me feel as if I were an alien trespassing on my grandparents' land.

I wanted a story with doubt: one where the reader wasn't sure what was going on until the end reveal. I hope I achieved that with "Uncle Allen." Truth be told, I had roughly eighty-seven different endings for this story lined up before I wrote it. Even then, I changed significant parts of the ending after the first pass with early readers. Ultimately I ended up with a story I'm really happy with, and I hope you are, too.

My wife, Sarah, and I live in Southern Illinois, where we both work as teachers at a small high school. We are the proud parents of a ten-year-old girl and a four-year-old boy. For the past couple years I've been a self-published author with a couple of novels and an assortment of short stories and novellas. You can find me on Twitter and Facebook among other places, and I'd love to hear from each and every one of my readers at wswardstrom@gmail.com. You can also visit my blog, where I post news about my stories and reviews of other great indie books.

The Kholorian Conspiracy
by Geoffrey Wakeling

Chapter 1

"YANICK!"

Seralah swore and slammed a hand against the table. The cup to her left wobbled, and the thick green tandry that had been keeping her awake all these hours oozed over the edge and dripped onto the desk. She looked around at the two stunned technicians at other workstations before quickly apologizing for her outburst.

"I just can't decipher this alphabet, if that's even what it is," she added, turning and looking back at the console with exasperation. "Almost two months with these formulas and I still can't grasp even the simplest sequence."

"Have you tried using the core's basic language algorithms?"

"Of course I have," she replied quickly, glancing at the man with her dark hazel eyes.

"I thought you might have just gone straight to the advanced analytical software," he assuaged quickly, removing himself from her gaze and focusing on his own work.

"I did at first," Seralah said, putting a hand to her cheek and scratching the dark and downy fur that covered her face. It matched her eyes, though she was sure a few early silver streaks were appearing. "The analytics didn't find anything, so I rolled it back to the basic codes in the hope something would be recognized. Seems this language is so old, even our ancient programming can't decipher it."

She reached for her cup and took a much-needed gulp of tandry. It was sweet on her tongue before she felt its heat at the back of her throat. Life had been so much easier when she was in the shaft with her tools, her team, and only the rocks to deal with. She enjoyed that aspect of archaeology: finding something new and taking care, precision, and time to dig it out. The research aspect of it was okay, but she didn't like being away from the field for too long. And now? Sitting at a terminal, hour after hour, trying to crack one of the shortest alphabet sequences she'd ever seen? That was enough to send her over the edge. It was not at all why she'd embarked on this profession. She'd never had much time for technology. Give her a shuttle, a laser, and a set of coordinates to head to— that's what she liked. She'd land and be digging around in the dirt happily for years on end.

"I'm going to run it through another decryption process," she said. "Do not, under any circumstances, touch my console."

She drained her cup, welcoming the awakening burn in her throat, threw her ocular enhancer to the desk, and left the lab through the airlock.

Free from the atmospherically controlled environment of the lab, Seralah stood for a moment, enjoying the rush of cold air against her fur. She could see no reason why the EACS (Enhanced Ambient Cooling System) couldn't be run in the tech lab. Chemical, biological, and archaeological departments? Of course it needed to be shut off there. The constant rush of air would make working conditions and anti-contamination procedures impossible. But a good airflow by her workstation would affect nothing but the good nature of the technicians trying to work.

She'd had this argument time and time again. Probably one too many times, she thought, crossing the corridor and leaning against the metal railing. Her memos on the matter had almost certainly been automatically diverted to the recycling bin.

She looked out the long thin window that ran along the side of the building—a transparent snaking picture frame to the stars. The large moon the entire station orbited was enjoying the start of its day; she could see the light from the system's star creeping along the ground and breaking dawn for the colony. Actually, it wasn't really a colony anymore. With forty-five percent of the surface covered in either mining operations or the Navreem star system's famed Academy of the Sciences, it was a thriving world. The mining corps had already laid claim to so much of the remaining surface, however, that the academy had forgone lengthy paperwork and developed the orbital station instead. It seemed a shame,

Seralah thought as she gazed down upon the creeping edge of light; if only her superiors had been quicker, she could have had her feet upon the rocks right now, instead of this floating space station.

Floating. The thought made her queasy, so she left her spot by the handrail and strode toward the shuttle terminals, the EACS system ruffling her fur as she went.

It didn't take long for her to be moon-bound. There wasn't much call for those on the space station to visit the moon, or vice versa, especially during peak lab hours. Most of her colleagues, herself included, had sleeping holes near their workplaces. Hers was relatively small and without an outside window, but she didn't mind that; she was happy not to be constantly reminded where she was. She had cooking utensils and appliances, a workstation to revisit her day's progress, a social nook (not that she ever had visitors), and her bed, which she'd wriggle herself into through the small tunnel before curling up among the cushions and quilts inside. Her father would scold her if ever he saw it, for there wasn't a strand of hessian, natural or not, in sight. But she was a scientist! She was most definitely not one of the homeworld traditionalists. There was no time, nor need, to be dusting herself off every morning. Still, that wouldn't convince her family.

Seralah began daydreaming of her eight sisters, and within no time, her tiny two-person shuttle was automatically gliding onto the moon. She could have navigated it herself—in fact, she was quite an accomplished pilot, considering her distaste for space—but why fly when she could sit back and relax?

"Seralah, could you sign off on these lab passes?"

She was bombarded the minute she left the shuttle. She gave a fleeting glance to the list launched in her direction by the Academy of Sciences moon dock receptionist, then passed her handprint across it.

"Professor Delekin! Professor? Wait!"

Professor. No one who knew her called her that. She turned quickly to see three technicians scrambling down the corridor toward her.

"No time," she called, before speeding over to the transport and opening the door with a scan of her fingers. Thank god. The transport was here.

"But wait! We'd just like your thoughts on our latest findings…"

"No time," she called again with a gracious smile, turning to see the lift doors glide to a close across their dark-furred and eager young faces.

Perhaps she'd been mean, too quick to scurry away, but if she stopped for everyone she'd never have a moment to herself. Why they'd laid the title of professor upon her she didn't know—she damn well hadn't earned it. She was far too young, and it had only been an accidental discovery that had led to the major and successful drug trial to treat Lapso Disease, a condition where pups were born without fur. Five of her sisters had lived with the disease for years, so she knew the social difficulties it brought. However, her professorship? She was sure the Academy had only used it as a lure to get her off world, to get her to the Navreem system. They needn't have bothered; she had never intended on staying in biomechanics.

Her calling was archaeology, and this finding was far too exciting to give up to anyone else.

It only took a few short minutes to navigate the descending levels of elevators and tunnels, and soon she was at the bio-coded entrance of her destination. Seralah shook off her momentary nerves. *Why did she still get that rush of anticipation?* There was something intensely exciting about excavating an ancient artefact and discovering secrets that had been hidden for hundreds of years.

She placed her face against the scanner then pushed her hand into the awaiting slot so her bio-implant could be read. She'd resisted that requirement at first, not wanting to turn herself into a walking computer. But she'd been assured the chips couldn't sustain themselves without feeding off the body's natural energy, thereby removing the concern that she might be abducted and have her hand removed. So eventually she'd agreed.

Having assured itself of her identity, the bio-lock clicked quietly and allowed her to step through. The door swung shut quickly behind her, and she heard the mechanism instantly imprison her.

The EACS was off, and the air was incredibly hot and stuffy. Seralah began to pant, and she berated herself for not taking the time to gather a breathing mask and cylinder. But she wasn't going to take long; she could get by with the uncomfortable environment for a little while at least.

Allowing a long sigh to escape her lips, then quickly panting again to regain her breath, Seralah started off down the descending tunnel. They hadn't managed to fully excavate the find from its resting place. They could have simply laser-cut the entire thing from the moon's surface, but she was glad they'd left it in situ. It was so delicate, so degraded, she feared even the slightest movement might cause it to crumble in on itself.

She made her way along the slope carefully, using the hand ruts placed in the wall to steady herself and ensure a gracious, if slow, approach. *Why was the EACS off?* The artifact, the vessel, was protected behind an energy shield. There was no reason for the cooling system to have been shut down. Unless…

Seralah let go of the hand grip and hurried forward as fast as she could without falling over herself. Her heart began to race, and she peered into the darkness below. It was only dimly lit, but the low levels of illumination were nothing her eyesight couldn't handle. *Did she hear something off in the distance?* Her ears pricked as she heightened her senses and tried to determine whether there was danger below.

"Hello?" she called out, then immediately fell silent and listened to her words as they echoed down the chute. There was no reply, but she was almost there now. The floor was leveling off, and she could see where metal joined rock, where the science station gave way to the moon's natural elements.

"Hello?" she called again. "Is anyone down here?"

There was a clatter ahead, the sound of an unseen object rolling across the hard floor, and every strand of hair stood on end as her ears rotated toward the sound, gathering the noise up like a satellite dish receiving a signal. A shadow formed across the entrance of the tunnel, and her heart beat faster.

Every instinct told her to flee. But she wouldn't—she couldn't. There was too much at stake. She wasn't about to allow her work to be ruined.

The shadow grew larger, and she couldn't help but shrink toward the wall with fear as sweat ran down her back. She cursed the EACS—it made her unable to hold her breath, and she gasped for air.

The figure appeared around the corner so quickly it took her by surprise, and she let out an uncontrollable squeak of fear.

Chapter 2

"Yanick!" Seralah swore for the second time in as many hours. "What are you doing down here?"

Granton shrieked as he saw her and dropped the tray he was carrying, sending the coils of wiring and tools cascading to the floor. A tangle of coppery-colored strings caught on an air tube and pulled the mask from his face, and he fidgeted for a moment as he readjusted the cylinder on his back. Seralah wiped dew from her brow and bent toward the floor to help gather the spilled items, breathing a sigh of relief that it was only her clumsy lab engineer who'd caused the fright.

"Why aren't you wearing a mask? You shouldn't be down here without one. You know what the rules say—"

"I was only coming for a few minutes," Seralah interrupted, though she took the mask from Granton's outstretched hand gratefully and with a smile, and she enjoyed a few deep breaths of cool air. They remained crouched for a moment so that she could continue refueling without the need to pass over the gas tank that was still firmly belted to Granton's back.

"What were you doing down here?" Seralah asked her technician again.

"The EACS was off; I was worried the force-field was down. I was trying to get the system going again when I heard something."

"So that clatter wasn't you?"

"Oh…" He stopped and looked apologetic. "I got spooked and backed into a console."

Seralah couldn't help but grin; she should've known.

"Granton, you really are the clumsiest engineer I've ever known. How you haven't killed yourself by know I'll never kn—"

She stopped short, her ears rotating away from the conversation and back toward the underground lab. She'd heard something—she was sure of it. She passed the mask back to Granton and felt the heavy atmosphere upon her face again. Granton was quiet, the pair of them frozen to the spot as their eyes peered into the low light and their ears searched for the slightest sound.

"Why was the EACS down?" Seralah whispered after a moment, keeping her voice so low she barely heard it herself.

"I thought it was a fault a first," Granton replied. "But I couldn't find anything, so I traced the outage back to the main terminal. It was switched off from down here."

"Why would anyone—"

Seralah jumped as she heard a sudden droning in the distance. Without thinking, she let go of the cable converter in her hands and watched with horror as it fell to the floor. If there was ever a time to remain quiet, it was now. Her colleague's hand whipped out and caught the falling item before it could send a deafening echo across the chamber and alert whoever was there to their presence.

"Thanks," Seralah mouthed with surprised, wide eyes as he deftly caught the device. He smiled, the beige flecks of fur at the corners of his mouth making his grin seem larger, brighter, than anyone else's she knew. Then, without warning, a whirring filled her ears, and all thoughts of how cute her colleague looked were gone.

She couldn't see it, couldn't feel it, but she could sure hear the missile rushing through the air toward them.

"YANICK!" Seralah screamed, abandoning her discretion and pulling Granton to his feet. "RUN!"

They raced toward one of the makeshift laboratory booths that had been set up for onsite analysis. Her heart was in her throat, the thick air making her feel as if she were wading through the muds of her home planet. Granton was beside her but falling back, the equipment in his hands and on his back weighing him down.

"Leave it!" she screamed, knocking the tray from his hands and causing a tide of tools and materials to be thrown into the air. They scuttled for cover, the noise of the weapon coming closer and filling her thin, round ears with terrifying and painful vibrations. As she ran, she glanced back over her shoulder and saw that it was too late.

"GRANTON!"

The missile buried itself into the oxygen cylinder on Granton's back. An explosion of orange bowled her over backward, and Seralah threw her hands over her face as the flames ate at her flesh. She cried out, tears streaming down her face as she hauled herself across the floor, taking cover behind what was left of the lab station, patting her burning fur and feeling sick at the smell of singed hair. She gasped for air in the fiery atmosphere, choking on both her fear and the smoke.

Footsteps sounded behind her, and once again she froze, her bloodied ears on high alert. Despite her terror, she rolled over quietly and peeked around the edge of her hideout. Two figures stood over the smouldering heap of Granton; one of them gave her fallen engineer a sharp kick to ensure he was dead. They were almost invisible in the dim light, their darkened bodies clouded by the smoke. There was a third somewhere, too, Seralah now realized, as a call came from across the chamber in a language she didn't recognize. She wasn't very good at the core languages, but she knew enough to know that this wasn't a race she'd dealt with before—even on some her most remote digs, where the more dangerous members of the galaxy lurked.

The two strangers turned away, seemingly satisfied that they'd eliminated the threat and ensured their presence went unnoticed. *Had they not seen her? Did they not realize she was here?* She took a final look at the pair as they sauntered back to where the artifact lay, and she had to resist the urge to shriek when the smoke cleared enough for their gangly and crouched physicality to be revealed.

Why were they here? What did they want with her relic?

Seralah receded into the dark and laid her head against the wall as her burns began to pulse rapidly, bringing hot pain with each wave. She'd never seen one of them before. She'd been lucky, having evaded any contact with them on all her previous digs. And now, here they were, in her sector, on her moon.

Kholorians.

* * *

"I'm fine," Seralah repeated for the fifth, twentieth, or hundredth time; she couldn't remember which. In fact, she was far from fine, but she wasn't about to let her peers know that. The nurse by her bed stubbornly remained behind when the physician left the room, continuing to wrap and rewrap the bandages around Seralah's hands and arms, slathering a thick milky paste between layers as she went. Seralah sat there rigidly while the process went on, desperate to leave but holding her tongue nevertheless. Finally the nurse seemed satisfied, though Seralah slapped her hand away when the thorough woman went to adjust the wraps one more time.

"I really need to be going."

She quickly pushed herself off the edge of the bed, grabbed her bag of personal belongings, and stepped out into the hallway.

"Professor Delekin!"

She pretended not to hear. Surely now that her ears were so badly singed they would believe the act. But the call came again, this time a little closer, so she quickened her pace toward the elevator. *I need to get back to my lab. I need to check on the artifact.*

"Professor!"

"I really haven't got the time, I—"

"Professor Delekin." There was a hand on her shoulder, and she realized there was no escaping. Swallowing the irritation and taking a deep breath, she plastered a weak smile across her cheeks before rounding to face the annoyance. "You're going to have to come with us."

Seralah was taken aback upon seeing the three Reihus guards. Her species was not a military race in the slightest, and its forces tended to remain within the home system and outlying colonies.

"Is everything okay?"

"There's nothing to be concerned about, Professor. We just need a few moments of your time."

But she was concerned. Reihus guards didn't turn up for just anything, and they certainly didn't accost hospital patients and escort them away without reason. Seralah nodded gently at the trio, who turned away from the lift and toward the heart of the facility. She'd thought today couldn't get any worse; it seemed she might've been very wrong.

* * *

"And just why were you down there?"

The question was fired at her without any compassion for the colleague who'd been murdered. Just a cold, harsh query.

She was sitting uncomfortably in a small cubicle in the hospital's inner sanctum: a place of laboratories situated well away from patients, visitors, and, indeed, most of the medical personnel.

"That damn orbital station had me questioning my sanity. I needed to go and see the artifact with my own eyes again." She paused. "I don't see why I need to explain myself," she added rigidly. "I am the project lead."

"Not anymore you're not."

"*What?*" The shock of the statement hit her like two tons of Karivien ore. She stared angrily across at the Academy of Sciences board member. She'd never seen him before—a fact that was concerning in itself, for she'd met all but the very highest of the Academy's academics, directors, and sponsors. His fur was greying and he looked a little too fat to easily escape his sleeping hole. One eye had the telltale green sheen of a permanent ocular implant. It made her wary; he might be questioning her, but what other manner of data was he scrutinizing? *Her career? Her performance? Her background?*

"It's out of my hands, Professor," the man said quickly and without apology. "You've shown no concrete results from the item, and now, because of the poor state of your laboratory, a fine engineer is dead and the artifact is destroyed."

"Destroyed? No! It might've been taken!"

What was happening?

"Taken? And just who would take such a thing?" The board member threw the question casually into the air as if neither wanting, nor needing, an answer.

"The Kholorians. I saw them. They shot Granton. They must've stolen the artifact."

The room fell silent, and Seralah could hear the breaths of the guards stationed on either side of her chair. She saw the green shine of the implant as her employer leaned in and gave her a hard stare.

"Professor, the Kholorians have no business here and are rarely seen within the core systems unless they're making trouble with the Oridiane Five. Quite frankly, this little situation has given us great cause for alarm, and it has me questioning your ability to run a team here at the Academy." He pushed back his chair and stood, guiding his plump body around the table. "Take some time, Delekin. Drop this matter from your mind. You can expect reassignment within the coming weeks." The door behind her clicked open and she heard him muttering as he left. "Kholorians, here? What a ridiculous notion."

Chapter 3

Thirty minutes later, Seralah was aboard the shuttle heading to the science station—though not, as her superiors expected, back toward her quarters. There was salvageable data in her lab, and there were colleagues she might be able to coerce into giving her information. She hurried along the corridor, avoiding the stares and gossiping technicians who became hushed as she scurried by. The lab was in sight, and she rushed forward to push her fingers against the lock.

Any hope Seralah still had quickly evaporated when the door failed to open. Still, she tried several times, all with the same effect. Finally, one of her project members left his desk and slouched toward her, shifting nervously on the other side of the translucent door.

"We're under strict instructions not to let you in," he said quietly, looking as dejected as she felt. "What happened down there?"

"I don't know," she replied, not wanting to make herself the focus of further public scandal. "Granton's dead."

Her former project member nodded his head miserably. "Well, I've got to get back to work. Seems your golden ticket ran out."

"Seems so," Seralah replied. Her days of cashing in on the accidental Lapso Disease cure seemed to have come to an end.

She took no pleasure in traversing the halls this time around, or even staring out the window at the beautiful moon below her. There was a hushed and somber mood creeping through the station. By now everyone would be well aware of what had happened—or at least, what the Academy's board were *saying* happened: that she, Professor Delekin, heroine of the Reihus, had demonstrated a severe lapse in judgment, resulting in a team member's death and the destruction of an ancient artifact.

Why won't they believe me?

The unanswerable question toiled in her mind as she threw off her clothes and crawled into her sleeping hole. She pulled the blankets around her, suddenly wishing she'd taken her father's advice and brought some hessian; to feel home would have comforted her. Poor Granton. He hadn't deserved such an awful end. The smell of burning flesh and fur was still caught in Seralah's nose, and without warning she was sick, bursting into tears as her stomach convulsed. Her hands had begun to ache again, and she peeled the bandage edging away, wincing as it tugged at the remnants of her singed hair.

Why were the Kholorians there? And what did they want with the artifact? What was so important that they were willing to kill for it?

* * *

Her superiors certainly didn't know her very well, Seralah thought wryly to herself as she strode toward the airlock the following morning, a bag slung over her shoulder, her mind focused on the new task at hand. *Wait for reassignment? Were they joking?* Surely even the lightest reading of her personnel files would've made quite clear that she wasn't very patient… or good at obeying the rules.

She held her head aloft and paid little attention to those around her, instead enjoying the feeling of the EACS upon her face. Perhaps, after all this was done, she'd visit her family on Kree and feel those real homeworld winds upon her fur once again. All this time in artificial atmospheres and away from real dig sites was taking its toll.

The main dock of the spaceport was quiet when she arrived; the morning transport had already come and gone. By now, all the students on rotating apprenticeships, along with their technicians, would be busy with lab work. As for the miners—well, they preferred to go on private shuttles as part of their pay deals.

Seralah was waved past the check-in desk and allowed onboard and directly into Top Tier without even paying. Her newfound notoriety at least gave her some perks.

"Can I get you anything, Professor?"

"I need a communications tab that links directly with the Oridiane Cloud. Oh, and a menu."

It was only now that she realized she was utterly famished. She waited until the attendant had returned with a complimentary glass of tandry, passed her the menu, and closed the private cabin door before she removed her gloves and attended to her sore hands. She dared not unwrap the bandages, despite the fact that brown, tainted ointment was oozing from between the folds. It was better not to look. There were multi-alien specialists where she was headed; if one of them couldn't treat a simple burn, there was no hope for anyone. Luckily, the nurse had bandaged her such that her fingertips stuck out the ends, and she could just about use the communications tab, though it took some getting used to.

As she was fine-tuning her awkward use of the device, the attendant returned, took her order, and, within moments, reappeared with a steaming black and glossy tajine filled with soup and a pile of grilled, salted Barnth chrysalises. Seralah didn't care how much it disgusted the other races when they watched Reihuses crunch the outer shell and suck down the gooey contents; as far as she was concerned, there wasn't much better in the way of comfort food than a sticky pile of her favorite delight.

Chewing on the end of a chrysalis and feeling the goo in her mouth, Seralah relaxed into her seat a little and prepared for the "Space Shot." She'd never actually made this journey before, but she'd looked it up the previous night: three Space Shots on a rather indirect route that would take twenty-seven hours. Still, at least she didn't have to change transports; the fewer people she had to deal with, the better.

Kholorians. Focus.

Seralah looked back at the communications tab and connected with the Oridiane Cloud. The constantly evolving database was a central knowledge core, accessible to the five major races from wherever they were in the galaxy. The current connection was a bit spotty, but with the distance and speed of travel, she wasn't surprised. At least it would allow her to do a little research on the journey.

She'd already practically dug down to the base code of the Academy's database in her research, and still hadn't been able to decipher her artifact's numerics and symbols—if that's even what they were. But the Academy's database wasn't connected to the Oridiane Cloud. The Reihus had always preferred to safeguard their technologies and advancements, and for good reason. Even the major species had not always seen eye to eye, and there was something to be said for keeping local systems offline.

Navigating through the various channels, and cursing occasionally at her lack of dexterity, Seralah finally began to educate herself on the Kholorian race. They were not—and Seralah believed, never would be—one of the core five. They were overly aggressive, and their desire to expand and colonize had brought them under fire from just about every known race at one time or another. The list of trade and social sanctions against them over the years went on for pages, and after glancing at the first half dozen, Seralah realized that even with a twenty-seven-hour voyage, she didn't have time for all the entries. Skipping to the end, she noted that lately they'd begun to leave the major races and their surrounding systems alone, opting instead to attempt seizure of lesser-known and isolated worlds. But even there, the Oridiane Five had asserted their authority, and the Kholorians weren't happy about it.

Seralah got tired of looking at the entry logs and decided instead to focus on her own problem. Pulling up the search function, she typed: *Academy of Sciences, Navreem, Kholorian.*

Nothing. Not even the most indiscriminate of content to link all three words. She removed both "Navreem" and "Academy of Sciences" in two subsequent searches, but once again, no results were found. Wondering whether the Kholorians made the newsnet at all, she entered "Kholorians" alone into the search bar, and this time great swaths of information flooded across the screen. They'd been busy offending people, she saw. But not the Reihus, and not the Academy of Sciences.

What connected them? Why had they been there?

Seralah began a new search process, this time focusing on the Academy and, in particular, news of their find. There was, notably, a lot of coverage on how "coincidental" it was that an artifact of unknown origin had been discovered upon the very moon where the Academy of Sciences was built. Several experts—all from other races, Seralah noted—questioned the true location of the object's discovery. To Seralah, it was a laughable point, since she, herself, had been one of the scientists digging it out of the rock. To argue that they'd found it somewhere else, perhaps in someone else's space, and taken it to the moon... that was just idiocy.

She continued scanning, trying anything to remain alert as her eyes began to glaze over. The tandry worked for a bit, burning the back of her throat and boiling her belly. The crunch of a chrysalis helped too, at first. But the sumptuous goo in her mouth was too comforting, and soon, without much of a fight, she drifted off into a much-needed sleep.

She was jolted awake much later to a darkened cabin, the lights having dimmed automatically as her mind had wandered through dreams. When she opened her eyes, the lights began to gradually re-illuminate her surroundings. She must've been awoken by the second Space Shot, she thought, stretching a little too far and wincing. Her injuries were far from healed.

Behind her, the door clicked open and an attendant appeared, gathering up the leftover tandry and the discarded food tray.

"Could I get another, please?" she murmured quietly.

"I'm afraid service has closed. We'll be docking in thirty minutes."

"Docking? Was that the third Space Shot?"

"It was," her attendant replied. "It'll be good time, too; you'll be wanting to head for treatment, no doubt."

Seralah looked at her hands and withdrew them quickly, noticing that the oozing had worsened and the cream-colored bandages were now quite discolored.

"Yes. Thank you," she said quickly, reaching for her gloves and pulling them on as he left the room.

How had she slept the entire journey?

Seralah retrieved a small data chip from her bag and plugged it into the transport's communications tab to download her search history, so she wouldn't have to start all over again later. Then, gathering her things and leaving the tab on the table, she made her way out of the cabin, along the various corridors, and toward the passenger disembarking platform.

The terminal was crowded, mostly with Reihus. To preempt any curious stares, Seralah rustled around in her bag again, this time drawing out a thin scarf and wrapping it around her head to shield her from prying eyes. Soon she was being whirled away from the great ship by a thin, train-like vessel.

"Welcome to the Oridiane Cloud. Please report to security for bio-scans and station registration."

As Seralah stepped off the train, she looked up and saw two circular robotic sentries hovering above her, their metallic voices repeating their pre-programmed messages, their guns clearly pointed toward the entrance that organized those arriving into a tight funnel. It was unnerving to say the least, but she wasn't entirely surprised; after all, a space station housing nearly seven million people, including diplomats, advisors, and stars from the galaxy's major races, was the perfect place for an attack. It made her shudder; she wanted real ground beneath her feet.

Trying not to dwell on the matter, she pushed forward and entered security, passed over her details, handed in her galactic registration card for safekeeping during her stay, and whirred through the security scanners. She had arrived at a place that both enthralled and terrified her.

The Oridiane Cloud and its many secrets beckoned.

Chapter 4

The one thing Seralah hadn't quite been ready for was the station's vastness. Of course, it was home to millions of people, so it had to be large. But until she'd arrived, until she'd actually stood within the cloud itself for the first time, she'd quite underestimated both its size and the effect it would have upon her.

Having navigated security with little problem, she found one of the arrival consoles and brought up the list of available accommodations. There were hundreds of options, too many to look through, so she just selected a Naranthi hostel that catered to several species. She liked the Naranthi—like the Reihus they were scholars, though proficient more in the arts than in science. But more importantly, they embraced others rather than viewing strangers with fear, wariness, or utter contempt.

Once settled in a small suite equipped with a workstation, a terrace, and a sleeping hole—complete with natural fibers and hessian, she noted—Seralah clicked her data chip into the console and began her research once again. Almost immediately, something caught her eye: an article about a Naranthi academic who'd been murdered in his home. She couldn't understand why his name—Saelin Gan—struck a chord with her until she retraced her steps and discovered that he'd been one of the most outspoken critics of the artifact find. She navigated to one of his debates and initiated playback, hovering over her console tensely.

"How are we to believe that this find, this artifact, just *happened* to land in the heart of Reihus territory? And, not only that, but on the *very moon* on which their Academy of Sciences is based? We all know of these people's furious protection of their technology, that they take great steps to mute news of their advancements; why should we not, therefore, believe they'd be as willing to claim a galactic find for themselves? Questions need to be addressed. How long have they known of this alien artifact? Why have they hidden it? Why, after leaks of its very existence, have the Oridiane Five still not had official and, I'd like to remind you all, *mandatory* galactic notification? Even if the nature of this artifact's discovery has been spoken in truth, we must not forget that the Reihus have still flouted regulations by not adhering to the proper channels of historical and alien technological guidance! It is only with great persistence that I, and a handful of other scientists, have determined the artifact's current location. We need Oridiane Five involvement immediately if we're to safeguard…"

Seralah had heard enough. It was true that she and her fellow Reihus kept discoveries, both technological and xenological, to themselves, but it was largely driven by the need to avoid meddling from ludicrous "academics" such as Saelin Gan. Still, she couldn't avoid the fact that this was her only lead. The reports on the man's death were clear: he'd been poisoned on the station as he'd sought an audience with the Five. There were no suspects, and the case, it seemed, was ready to join the depths of dusty unsolved mysteries. But Saelin, as he'd publicly admitted, had known the location of her artifact. And that had made him a target.

There was no time to wait, and despite it being late by the station's clock, Seralah was fully energized and ready for answers. Swiping away from the newsfeed, she brought up a map of her surroundings and began to sift through the many districts and levels of the Oridiane Cloud. Her ability to trace even the most ordinary of data back to its source had always been second nature, and she soon discovered that Dr. Gan hadn't just been here for bureaucratic reasons—he and his family were station residents.

Feeling a sense of urgency—perhaps because, from the moment she'd left the Navreem System, she'd become increasingly paranoid that the Kholorians had spotted her— Seralah freshened herself up, threw on her head scarf, and left the hotel for the lower levels. It seemed that life aboard the Oridiane Cloud never quieted; in fact, the corridors, plazas, and great sweeping bridges of the central area seemed even louder, busier, and more frenetic than before. With all the hustle and bustle, it took her an hour to arrive at her destination.

The homes weren't like anything she'd seen before. Even the most expensive space station sleeping holes in their systems didn't have individual walkways, parcel ports, and landscaping, as these did. And each unit was quite obviously separate. The units were box-like and bulky, unpleasing architecturally, but they were set away from their neighbors nonetheless. As Seralah peered for the unit identifications and wandered over the coppery-colored bridge, illuminated from below by bright green lights, she saw that the footings of each accommodation weren't usual either. In fact, upon closer inspection it was clear that the units were capable of space flight. Individual escape pods, she supposed, able to flee the scene of devastation should anything ever happen to the station.

She pressed the door chime and waited, fully expecting to be disappointed. It was, therefore, a great surprise when a shadow appeared behind the door and she heard the latch click.

"Hi, I'm Seralah Delekin from the Academy of Sciences. I'm sorry it's so late, but I don't suppose I could have a quick word? I—"

"Do you know what time it is?" The bony face of a young man appeared, his Naranthi cheekbones at such an angle that his entire appearance seemed dangerously thin.

"Yes, but this is urgent," Seralah persisted, noting that the door hadn't been fully opened. "I wanted to speak about your... father?"

The instant anger upon the man's face couldn't be missed. "My father was a good man. Why can't you damn Reihus just leave us in peace."

"Wait!" Seralah called. "There have been others?"

"Your aptitude for pretence precedes you. Perhaps if you'd paid more care to trust and less to secrecy, my father would still be alive." He shut the door before she could say another word, though his shadow didn't move, and she envisioned him shaking with rage on the other side.

"I know they're about to close the case," Seralah said quietly enough so it didn't ring throughout the neighborhood, but loud enough for him to hear. "And I'm pretty sure I know who was responsible."

There was silence beyond the door, and Seralah watched the shadow intently for any signs of movement. Then, after ten or twenty seconds had passed, she heard the latch move again and the man's face reappeared, an inquisitive and anguished look in his eyes.

"Who?"

"Kholorians."

"You better come in," he replied quickly, dragging Seralah over the threshold and immediately relocking the multitude of locks on the doorway.

"What do you know of the Kholorians' involvement in your father's death?" Seralah asked as she was led across to a small seating area. It was cool and dark inside the housing pod, and she felt at ease despite the situation.

"You first," the man replied, allowing her to sit but remaining upright himself, leaning against the edge of a large table.

Seralah realized that if there was a time to lay her cards on the table, it was now. "The Kholorians blew up my lab and killed a friend and colleague," she said. "They wanted the artifact I was working on, and your father was one of the only people to know of its exact whereabouts."

"I *knew* it." The young man fumed. "I told him again and again his passion for disagreement would be his end. The Kholorians did kill him; of that I'm sure."

"Then why do the reports say the case is unsolved?"

"Nobody wants to open up a dialogue about the Kholorians," the young man replied, his anger replaced with resignation. "It was clear that their traditional explosive toxic dart was used, but the lot of them are stealth assassins—they left no other evidence. They're too much trouble; the Five don't want to get involved. And my father was the same to them: trouble. To the Five, it seems right to allow their troubles to annihilate each other."

"It does *not* seem right. Granton is dead!"

"And I'm sorry about that. But there's little I can do. We both know the truth, and that's that. I suggest you leave it there; which is exactly what I told your colleagues."

She'd momentarily forgotten that other Reihus had been sniffing about. "What did these colleagues want?" Seralah asked, worried where the question might lead her.

"They asked about Kholorian involvement, if he really knew where the artifact was held, that sort of thing. Do you have a data chip on you?"

Seralah nodded and retrieved it from her pocket.

"Here, I'll give you exactly what I gave them—on the promise you'll drop this whole matter and let my family rest."

Seralah nodded again and passed the chip to the young Naranthi. He transferred the data from the wall console.

"My sister works for the Oridiane Cloud intelligence division," he said. "It's where my father got his unsubstantiated 'evidence' from. They'd been working on your little artifact; perhaps you could shift your attention to *this* mystery instead."

As Seralah left the man's home, she felt rather confused about the ease with which he was able to let his father's murder slide by. Granton wasn't her family—he wasn't even a close friend—but she couldn't let it go. Yet now, with the data chip clenched tightly between her fingers, she knew the young Naranthi was right: there was a new mystery to attend to.

But first she had to visit a medic. Her hands were no longer aching, but viciously stinging, and the wraps were so soaked she was finding it hard to concentrate on anything else.

When the bandages were unwrapped at the closest medical center, Seralah had to grit her teeth. When she could no longer bear it, she began to chatter uncontrollably, and finally she reached a stage where she had to scream for painkillers. She hadn't wanted to dull her senses, but her burns had become so painful, they in themselves were now her main distraction.

After being severely chastised for her lack of care, for the fact she'd traveled with such injuries, and for not having sought medical attention immediately, Seralah passed in her galactic registration card details for invoicing and left the clinic. However, rather than head for her hotel, which she already knew had limited research resources, Seralah found the nearest station terminal and searched out somewhere better equipped for her task.

"Welcome to Biradi Solutions."

Seralah smiled as the gorgeous Binet woman behind the reception desk allowed her through the double-height doors and into an elegant lobby. The receptionist's skin was pale, and as was the tradition for her race, she had bright tendrils of color snaking like veins across her skin. They glinted, moved even. Sometimes it was only with the smallest flicker, but they glittered nevertheless.

"I need a lab," Seralah said, smiling as she approached the desk. "Do you have anything available as this time of… the morning?" It was morning, she noted, though only just.

"We're always open, always available. Have you used Biradi Solutions before?" The woman's light eyes shone despite the bright illumination around them, and Seralah found herself immediately captivated. She saw now why the Binet were known as the sirens of the galaxy.

"We offer technological, biological, and geological laboratories at this facility, though you can browse our network grid to find suitable locations for other work," the Binet beauty continued as Seralah shook her head. "We require fifty-percent down payments on biological and geological suite use, with a full disclosure statement signed and dated."

"I only need tech," Seralah said, not wanting to run up a larger station bill than was totally necessary.

"Would you like an HC?"

"Oh," Seralah replied, pondering for a moment. "Actually, yes. That would be fun." *Being able to bounce ideas back and forth with a holo-colleague might be helpful.*

"Reihus environment, I presume?"

"Thank you."

"You're welcome." The woman smiled as she took Seralah's galactic registration number and added the details to her console. "Suite 7, Level 3. Technological damage or law breaking will result in automatic lock-in. To activate the HC, use the terminal to select your preferred language, race, et cetera, and press 'Initiate.'"

Seralah thanked the woman again and set off, hurrying down the long, thin, and tall corridor and stepping into the elevator. She ascended three levels, and was hunting for Suite 7 when a sudden and huge explosion caused her to leap against the wall in fright. Flames burst up on the other side of the glass window next to her, causing a siren to sound and the unmistakeable noise of oxygen deprivators to start. The flames and smoke cleared almost instantly, and she saw a man on the other side of the glass, dressed in a full-body protection suit, shaking his head. He noticed her, waved, shrugged his shoulders, and then continued his experiments as the siren fell silent and Seralah was left to hurry on to her own suite.

Finally she found it, and she quickly stumbled into the room, locking the door behind her and breathing in deeply as she felt the fresh, cool breeze against her fur. It wasn't the winds of homeworld—it didn't have the same sweet smell—but it was good nonetheless.

Drawing off her head scarf and hanging it over the edge of the chair, she moved curiously to the HC console. She'd never actually used a holo-colleague before; there was no need, particularly at the Academy. And on digs, she liked the quietness and the solitude. She certainly didn't need a virtual helper echoing through the caverns she so often explored.

The receptionist had already programmed in the appropriate languages, so there was little else to choose other than the species. Reihus, Naranthi, Karaida, Binet, Yeni—the Oridiane Five core races were there, alongside other various species well known throughout the galaxy. The Yeni, as much as Seralah had to respect their achievements despite their mobile difficulties, had a voice so shrill and grating to her ears she'd go mad. She considered Reihus for a moment, until thoughts of Granton surfaced. Instead, remembering her welcome to the establishment, she chose Binet—and then watched as a small, half-size holo flickered to life.

"Binet HC online. How can I be of service?"

Seralah noted that the program pronounced Binet with a silent 'T' and realized, with slight horror, that she'd been mispronouncing the word all her life.

"I have a data chip I need to analyze," Seralah said without hesitation, moving across to the small, plush armchair and pushing herself among the thick fabric. She grabbed the console from the table to her side and plugged in the data chip.

"Scanning chip. Would you like music while we work?"

"No," Seralah replied. "Wait. Do you have ambient noise? The Sanata Howls?" It was one of her favorite sounds in the entire galaxy: the noise of Kree's winds as they rang through the crags and nooks of the ancient Sanata mountains.

"Searching."

In a matter of moments, the thin, dulcet and eerie groans of Kree were echoing around the room, giving immediate comfort to Seralah's mind. She closed her eyes and allowed her head to sink back onto the headrest. She thought of home, and she made a conscious decision that when this was all over, she'd listen to this music for real.

Chapter 5

"Chip scan complete. What are we working on today?"

Seralah opened her eyes with a start, though she was fairly sure she'd only drifted off for a few minutes.

"Tell me about the Reihus artifact find at the Academy of Sciences in the Navreem system. Specifically, data on what it was or where it came from," she said dozily, not expecting much.

"No data on where, but analysis of vessel shows it to be a communication beacon. Approximate age: three to four hundred years old. Height: 3.8 meters. Plutonium residue. Projected antennae length: 3.8 by—"

"How did he know all of this?" Seralah said aloud. *She'd* been the one studying the damn thing, and due to the way it was lodged into the bedrock of the moon, she hadn't even been able to get a clear scan image, let alone projected specifications.

"Can you specify who you are referring to?"

"Oh, Saelin Gan," Seralah said, realizing her Binet companion had directed the question at her.

"Dr. Saelin Gan is the primary author for all original works held within the data chip matrix. No further sources found, though it's likely that intelligence forces on either side of the Reihus and Oridiane Five knowledge treaty leaked information to one another."

"Well, you're right there," Seralah mused, a little taken aback by the HC's insightful response. "Is there anything else of interest for the artefact, other than engineering specifics?"

"Yes. Gold, circular disc discovered, containing rudimentary information in unrecognized language. Video entry by Dr. Saelin Gan makes mention of the additional find."

"Play log. Audio only."

The voice of Dr. Gan immediately filled the small room. "While the Reihus continue to drag the disintegrating pieces of this communications hub from the rock, I've moved on to exploring its inner components as best I can. What scans I have received appear to show a small golden disc secured inside the capsule. Using imaging techniques and scan scrubbers, I'm gradually piecing together several scarce symbols. There are numerous engravings upon the surface, most of which I've yet to investigate. However, my basic education in astrometry suggests a potential star chart scratched into the metal— perhaps an indication of where this object came from. It's my belief that whoever sent this hub to space did so with a map home... a foolish plan, whatever the good intention behind it."

The audio fell silent, and Seralah was returned to the gentle sounds of home.

"Are there any more logs?"

"No. Dr. Gan died less than two hours after this recording was made."

"Are you able to show me the images of the gold disc? Of the engravings he talks about?"

"Yes. Transferring to console now."

An origin map? That was more than she could have ever hoped for.

She drew the console close, thrilled about her latest discovery and eager to find out just what was engraved upon the ancient disc. Her excitement was short-lived, however, as the lights in the room flickered and went out, leaving her in total darkness. The HC, which had been shedding off a faint glow, vanished. The music soothing her soul fell silent. The only illumination left was from the unplugged console screen in her hands, though it seemed that the data transfer had been cut short, for no images appeared.

Outside, the siren set off by her explosive lab neighbor sounded once again, but now that she was in the dark and alone, it struck an uneasy chord. Using the console light as her guide, she pulled her head scarf from the seat and made her way to the door—only to find that it was stuck fast. She heard another siren start up, and then another, and through the noise she began to get a sickening feeling.

"Hello?" she called, pulling at the door and hoping that, by some miracle, it would open. It didn't, and she realized that the power outage must have sealed it.

There was a scrape in the room behind her, and Seralah froze, pulling the console to her chest so that the light was extinguished and she was plunged into full darkness. She was alone—or she had been. But she had heard the unmistakable sound of another scrape within her tech lab.

There was someone with her now. There was no denying it.

Shrinking toward the floor and keeping low, Seralah painstakingly crept toward the chair as quietly as possible. If she could use it for shelter, for protection, for anything, she could—

A light dazzled her. Its brightness shone directly into her eyes, bleaching everything else beyond it.

"You're in grave danger. You must come with us." The voice was quiet and soft. She felt a hand grasp her wrist and pull her away from the wall.

There was nothing she could do but follow.

* * *

There weren't many times in her life where Seralah could recall being truly nervous, but this was one of them. Having been rescued from Biradi Solutions, she had been fast-tracked back to the Navreem System in a private shuttle. She now sat in the board of directors' meeting room. Opposite her was the superior who'd previously chastised her and made her the center of ridicule for everyone at the Academy. He, too, looked uneasy, shifting himself back and forth in his chair.

"I'm sorry to keep you waiting, Professor."

A short, mousy woman breezed into the room holding a pile of consoles. She perched herself against the desk rather than taking a seat, and she looked at Seralah without removing either of her two ocular enhancers.

"As you can imagine, the furor over this discovery has implications that reach far beyond our little moon."

"I can't imagine a lot," Seralah said tensely. "Nobody's said a word to me. I have no idea what's going on."

"You haven't? Then let me explain. It seems that your little unauthorized gallivant has unearthed some rather large galactic issues. Firstly, you were quite right in your assertion that it was the Kholorians, and not negligence, that caused the death of our engineer and the destruction of the artifact. However, perhaps if you'd done as you were told and waited for reassignment, you could have let us handle the situation."

"So it was you who talked to Saelin Gan's son."

"Well, not me personally, but the team, yes. And if you'd have let us do our jobs, we wouldn't have had to launch an Oridiane Cloud rescue mission. You do realize that you were very nearly an extra trophy on some Kholorian assassin's hit list?"

"I didn't realize it was that bad," Seralah gasped, only now realizing that, whether she'd been spotted with Granton at the artifact or not, her subsequent questions had aroused enough suspicion to warrant her head on a kill list. "But what the hell is this all about?"

"It seems that after the Kholorians' last colonization refusal, they've taken matters into their own hands and started invading primitive space. Our little artifact, the communications hub, is a vessel named 'Voyager 1.' A map on a gold disc found inside it clearly leads back to some off-grid planet called Earth, and, it seems, our assassin friends have besieged the system, captured or killed the locals, and set up a rather extensive colony there. I can't stress enough the political implications of this. The Oridiane Five are battling to stop all-out war."

"And the Kholorians destroyed the artifact and silenced those with any data to try and hide what they were up to."

"Exactly." The woman sighed and finally removed one of her ocular enhancers to look Seralah in the eye with genuine care. "What you did was commendable, but how you went about it was not. Next time, when you're told to drop something, do so."

Seralah nodded, knowing full well she wouldn't be able to adhere to the order. She suspected her superior knew it too.

The woman passed a console to her miserable-looking colleague and stood, adjusting her multitude of tablets and enhancers at the same time.

"I shall see you again, Professor," she said curtly, before leaving the room as quickly as she'd arrived.

As the door closed, Seralah finally allowed herself to breathe comfortably again. She let out a sigh of relief and let the past few days of stress flood away. She was still devastated about the artifact's loss, and more so at the knowledge that Granton had been killed simply to hide the truth. But now the truth was out. Now it was known that the Kholorians were acting outside galactic law.

"Well, at least one thing's resolved," Seralah's superior said, though without any sense of pleasure. "Both the board and I are happy to let you know you're officially back on the project and can resume work immediately. We may have lost the artifact, but there is still much to discover."

Seralah smiled as a warm glow flooded across her. She sat there for a moment, enjoying a feeling of justice that they'd had to rescind their earlier demotion. Then she stood and looked her overweight and arrogant superior in the eye.

"Thanks, but I think I'd prefer to follow my own discoveries from now on. I quit."

She grinned, an expression that wrinkled the fur on her cheeks. The shock on her former superior's face was quite an enjoyable sight. Then she left the room, free from restraint and filled with an eagerness to discover a new site—one where she could, once again, be among the boulders and rocks she so loved.

A Word from Geoffrey Wakeling

I still remember the day I walked in on my parents watching *Star Trek III: The Search for Spock* and uttered the words, "This is boring." How, then, have I turned into a complete science fiction nerd? *Star Wars* and *Star Trek* kicked it off, *Mass Effect* caught me in its snare, and Netflix deepened the fascination. I have to admit, I watch *far* too much science fiction for my own good (*I don't actually believe that for a second*). The one thing I really love about this genre? Aliens. So you can imagine how thrilled I was to be involved in this anthology.

I believe that, in a universe this large, there *have* to be other intelligent life-forms. That's not to say they haven't already been and gone, or perhaps they are yet to evolve. However, as we've not yet made contact in the real world, I've had to find an alternative way to satisfy my fascinations, and I do this partly through my writing.

"The Kholorian Conspiracy" ties loosely into my *CRYO* series, which follows one man's journey from lotto ticket winner to a cryonically revived "immortal" exploring a strange new world. Along with his few surviving podmates, John Carlody sets out to discover what happened to Earth and how he fits into the new order of life. But the universe is far larger than the first two books *(Rise of the Immortals* and *A Changed World)*, and this short story explores further afield than even John could ever imagine.

If you'd like to learn more about *CRYO,* please feel free to visit geoffwakeling.com to read the first chapters of my novels, check out my book blogs, sign-up for my newsletter, and more. In addition, you can follow me on Twitter (*@GWakelingWriter*) or join me on Facebook.

318

by Autumn Kalquist

HUMANS DESTROY what they can't control and are terrified of what they don't understand. Why, then, do they create and unleash things into the world that they can't control and will never understand? When their species faces extinction, this error in judgment will be the reason.

I hate them all.

And that's why I'm going to kill this old man. Adrenaline surges through me at the sight of his wrinkled skin, his white hair beneath the glass.

I suppress a small smile as I walk barefoot across the cold tile to the line of cabinets against the wall. I grab a syringe from the drawer, then head straight to the cabinet that has what I need. Cool air rushes over me, and I shiver as I pick up the first case of vials and try to read each label. It's been so long since I've had to read anything that it takes a minute for my mind to decode the symbols. The mind may bury what it can't handle remembering—but it never fully forgets.

Strep B45

Polio

Smallpox

Ebola

These are single-dose vials, but they'll probably kill the old man anyway. He's weak.

And I'm strong.

I lift the Ebola vial and attach it to the syringe. I'm grinning now as I whirl and nearly skip back to the glass chamber where my victim lies. When I push my hands through the slots on the side of the case to grab his arm, his eyelids flutter. It's so strange, my skin against his. For two years I've imagined what it would be like to feel the warmth of another person's bare touch again. This isn't how I imagined it would go.

I plunge the needle into his arm, and his eyes open. He looks up at me, disoriented, as I empty the vial into him. I lean over the glass and meet his gaze, so he knows exactly who killed him.

His eyes widen. "318," he croaks out.

He struggles against his restraints, but I did a good job strapping him down. I've had hundreds of chances to learn how to do it right. The virus is moving through him now, and the pain will soon be unbearable. I know what he's about to experience, because he put me through it first.

Two weeks earlier

My cell's lights flash on, bringing me out of the near-constant night. I sit up in my narrow cot and wait, hands folded in my lap. The air recyc fan activates. Goose bumps pop up along my exposed calves, and my nipples harden against the thin cloth of my gown. I twist around to look at the letters carved in the wall behind my bed. They're the only decoration in the room—my only companion. I trace them with my fingertips.

LEX.

Letters, not numbers. A human was kept here before me.

They'll force me to use the toilet while they watch, so I make sure to empty my bladder before they arrive. Then the door slides open, and the Hazmats push a gurney through.

It's not time for another sedative. It's time for a dose.

They lift me with cold, rubber-gloved hands and strap me to the gurney. The straps cut into my legs and arms, and the one around my forehead is too tight, but I don't fight it anymore, because what's the point?

I count the lights in the hall. *One. Two. Three. Four. Five. We're here.*

They slide me and the thin pad I'm strapped to into the chamber. Curved glass arches over me, a few inches from my face, and it's bright in the room beyond. The doctor and his two assistants arrive, wearing the same Hazmat suits my captors always wear. Silver infinity symbols are stamped across their chests: the logo for the corporation that's become my judge and jury, and will be my executioner—if I ever fucking die.

Dr. Dalton looks down at me in his detached way, and I glimpse his watery eyes, deep lines around them, behind his mask. He hands the scanner to one of his men. "Scan it, Mr. Monroe. Let's see what kind of training you got up at Corporate."

Monroe grabs my wrist through a slot in my glass coffin and scans the silicone disc embedded beneath my skin. "318. Confirmed."

His gaze finds mine by accident, and I hold it, willing him to truly see me. But he tears his green eyes away. Those eyes are new; I've never seen him before. Yet for some reason he triggers memories of another man—a blond, his features hazy in my mind—and my heart twists. It's the first emotion of the day, earlier than usual. Did Anders look like that? All I remember is that he betrayed me, exposed me for what I really was: not human, yet trying to hide among them. A little flicker of anger ignites in my chest. If I ever see Anders again, I'll make sure he suffers as much as I have.

"Farrow—check 318's scalp," the doctor orders.

The woman pushes her gloved arms through the slots and rubs the stubble on my head, checking to see if I still have the lice they infected me with. Why they thought my superimmunity would attack lice, I'll never know. Her hands are rough, and she pinches my ear, hard enough that tears well in my eyes. I look straight at her, and I can tell how much she enjoys this.

"Her scalp's clear, Dr. Dalton," Farrow says.

Dalton jabs a button. "Full body analysis."

I squint against the bright rainbow of colors that ripple over my body. A sharp pain stabs my calf as the coffin steals my blood.

"Temperature normal," Farrow says. "No sign of any pathogens."

"Excellent."

Monroe clears his throat. "Doctor, I thought I was here to assess *adult* patients. She's a child."

"Not *she*, Monroe. *It*. 318, if it needs a name. 318 is an abomination—not our species. Don't ever forget that."

Monroe looks back at me. "But I wasn't told *it* was a child."

"318 is almost seventeen years old," Farrow says. "Its growth has merely been stunted."

"I want a few minutes alone with the—with 318," Monroe says.

Dalton holds up a hand. "This is my laboratory—"

"You mean Infinitek's laboratory," Monroe interrupts. "And they sent me here, per the new Protected rights regulations."

Dalton shakes his head. "You and I both know that vote was just a PR stunt. But fine. You have two minutes. We have a lot to do today."

Farrow and Dalton retreat, and I'm left alone with Monroe. My heart beats faster as he stares down at me through the glass. The way he looks at me is... different from the way the others look at me.

"How do you feel?" he asks.

I forget how to talk. He's looking at me in the way that all real humans *used* to look at me. Like I exist.

"Can you talk?"

"Yes." My voice is rusty with disuse.

His eyes soften, and I detect emotion there, but my brain's scrambling to understand the meaning behind it.

"What's your name?"

"318."

His brow creases. "Do you like being called 318?"

"It's my name," I say.

"Were you ever called something else?"

"I've always been 318."

His eyes grow cold, and somehow I know the look isn't for me, but for what I just said.

"How do you feel?" he asks again.

I pause. "I don't feel."

The door slides open. "That's enough, Monroe," Dalton says. "We have half a dozen others to dose, and I don't have all day."

Farrow sets up an IV drip in my arm while Dalton goes to the counter and opens the cabinet where they keep the vials.

He comes back with a syringe.

"Record," Dalton says. "June 26th, 2073, 8:43 a.m. 318 receives triple-dose Ebola. Single- and double-dose vials had no effect. Strain origin: 2044 pandemic."

He pushes his hands through the slot and grabs my arm, holding it steady to line up the needle. The cold metal slides into my skin, and I wince at the pain, at the pressure of the liquid entering me. Will I feel the effects of this one? Most have no effect until they give me triple doses or higher. And even then, it's a twelve-hour fever or cold. And no matter how much I wish for it, none of the vials ever kill me.

"Farrow," Dalton says, "adjust the machine to run a scan every twenty minutes. I want every fluctuation recorded. If it doesn't take in eight hours, we'll move 318 back to its cell and try a quad dose tomorrow."

Monroe meets my gaze again, but this time I'm the one to avert my eyes.

"How long does 318 have before autoimmunity sets in?" Monroe asks.

"It varies," Dalton says dismissively. "Twelve to eighteen months if we dose them regularly. We've had 318 for two years. This one's been resilient, but I don't expect it to live much longer."

Another stabbing pain shoots through my leg as the machine takes more blood. The rainbow light of the scanner floods my eyes, and I close them.

When the cycle stops, the room is dark and empty. I try to sleep, but every twenty minutes the needles and light wake me. When the fever takes me, I almost welcome it, until a sharp ache begins to radiate through me—tearing through my nerves, settling in my bones. It's pain like nothing I've ever felt before. I'm on fire, and I can't breathe as I struggle against my restraints, soaking the bed with sweat. At some point I lose control of my bowels, but I have no shame. A tiny part of me relishes the disgust I'll see on their faces when they have to sanitize my body.

Hours pass, and no one comes for me. They leave me alone with beeping machines that track the damage this virus does to my body.

I'm like Snow White in my glass coffin, dead but still alive. But Snow didn't shake with fever and lie in her own shit, did she? Tears stream down my cheeks as another cycle of light washes over me. My mind tries to fly away, but it doesn't get far.

My hand is wrapped in my mother's warmer one as the trucks bring us into the Protected camps. The skies are gray, and a light rain that never stops churns the dirt beneath our feet to mud. The little ones play in it, kicking a half-deflated, neon green ball between them.

We stand in long lines for the quin sludge they feed us, and men and women with guns peer down on us from high platforms.

Sometimes they speak. "We're keeping you here to protect you. Mobs kill your kind out there, but inside these walls you're safe."

One day I fetch our rations, and when I get back, my mother's bleeding in our tent, her skull caved in. I cry out for help, and the guards come, uncaring, to haul her body away.

317. Blunt trauma to skull. Status: Deceased.

Then the humans who said they'd keep us safe bring me to my bright, warm cell. They give me better food, and I think I'm lucky. Until the doses begin.

Another wave of pain shoots through me, and I swear I can smell the scent of wet earth again as I slide into darkness. Maybe I'm being buried.

But I've never been that lucky. The pain goes on forever, and the rainbow light and stabbing needle keep me awake for days.

The Hazmats take me out of the glass case once to clean me up. I'm too tired to enjoy the disgust on their faces as they cut my stinking gown off with scissors and dunk me in ice cold water.

I gasp, but settle in, too fevered to complain. Darkness and exhaustion threaten to take me, but *they* won't let me sleep. They talk off to the side, too loud.

I make out Dalton's voice. "Triple dose broke the threshold. None of the other subjects responded like this. The antibodies 318 is producing are exactly what we need. We'll dose it again if we don't get enough."

"Why wouldn't it be enough?" A tight voice. A name floats through my fevered mind. *Monroe.*

"It's fighting the exact strain that's resurfaced in the European epidemic," Dalton says. "318 might provide the cure... before the virus resurfaces here."

"Is it worth losing a test subject?"

Dalton lets out an abrupt laugh. "Don't you realize how many of *us* we'll save through the loss of just one subject?"

They lift me from the bath, dry me with stiff towels, and don't bother to dress me again. I'm strapped naked to a fresh pad, and they slide me back into my coffin.

Monroe asks to speak to me alone again. As I gaze up at him through the glass, his masked face blurs before me, and for a second he looks like others I've known. Others who betrayed me.

"What's your name?" he asks.

"318." My voice is weak, my mouth parched, lips cracked.

"Do you like being called 318?"

"It's my name," I say.

"Were you ever called something else?"

"I've always been 318."

"And how are you feeling?" he asks again.

My body is dying, but the rest of me is numb. "I don't feel."

Then it all begins again.

Darkness mixes with rainbow light. The heat is unbearable, and the taste of blood on my lips is bitter—salt and metal. As the fog over my mind lifts, my stomach heaves at the stench of my own piss and shit.

Dalton's voice raises me from yet another twenty-minute slumber. "We have what we need."

I open my eyes, and I see them in my peripheral vision, standing off to the side of my glass prison. Farrow's talking, but I can barely make out her words. "Autoimmunity… immune system failing."

"More days… pathogen-free," Dalton replies. "Euthanize."

My stomach clenches at the words. *Euthanize.* Autoimmunity means death. Mine. Why doesn't the thought bring relief? Haven't I wished for this nightmare to end?

Soon the machine says I'm pathogen-free, and the Hazmats clean me up. This time I'm able to fully enjoy their obvious revulsion.

Monroe requests a private visit with me again, and I don't know why I care, but I'm suddenly grateful to the Hazmats for remembering to dress me in a fresh gown. When Monroe's green eyes meet mine through the glass barrier, my heart speeds up a little, and I feel warmth spread in my cheeks.

"What's your name?" he asks.

"318." My voice is strong. Confident.

"Do you like being called 318?"

"It's my name."

He looks away for a moment, and when he turns back, my stomach drops. His eyes are distant now, empty. Like Farrow's and Dalton's.

"Were you ever called something else?" he asks, his voice flat.

I want to give him the answer he wants, so he'll look at me like he did before, but I don't know how. "I've always been 318."

"And how are you feeling?" The words are abrupt, clipped short.

I'm feeling more than I've felt in a long time. Much more. I hesitate, swallowing, then I meet his eyes. "I feel like I want out of this damn box... Monroe."

His eyes widen, and he blinks fast and glances toward the door. When he looks back at me, there's a shine to his eyes.

What would it feel like if he removed his glove and reached his bare hand into the box to grasp mine? My hand warms at the imagined touch, but I can't remember what someone's skin on mine actually feels like.

"Monroe," Farrow calls from the front of the lab. "Dalton wants you in lab C."

The Hazmats take me back to my cell before the next rainbow-light cycle, and my chest expands at the sight of my familiar cot and the steaming tray of food on the small table. I sleep and wake several times without being sedated before the light comes on and a Hazmat brings me another tray of food.

It's Monroe.

I jump to my feet and back up a step. He stands still, holding the tray out before him, not dropping it on my table like he's supposed to. It's against the rules for me to go near him. I wait for a minute, breathing fast, and when it's clear he expects me to come get the tray, I carefully step closer, my pulse a dull roar in my ears.

As my hand wraps around one edge of the tray, he speaks. "318."

I freeze, then risk looking up at him. "Yes?"

My heart's pumping so hard, I think it might explode.

"I'm sorry," he says, his voice soft.

"Sorry?" The concept of that word—in this place—is foreign, and my mind can't make sense of it.

"You're not an 'it,'" he says. "You're a person, and—"

"I'm not. I'm not… human." I try to step back, but he grabs my wrist, wrapping his rubbery glove around the spot where my silicone disc is embedded.

"You *are* human."

Confusion tears through me, and I shake my head.

"You're a genetically modified human—but still human. The Protected gene therapy had some side effects they didn't like, so… You aren't perfect, but none of the people who did this to you are, either."

I want him to be a liar, but his words trigger something in my mind, and all I want for him to do is keep talking. My eyes burn, and I raise my free hand to rub them. I stare down at a teardrop on my finger. A voice whispers in my mind. The truth. *You're not Protected. You're Defective.*

"You're wrong. I'm defective," I say, my voice breaking.

"No. *They're* defective." His voice is hard, angry. "They'd have died a million times over from the diseases they've given you. Your superimmunity is a gift. You're special, not defective."

I shake my head back and forth and try to pull my wrist from his grasp, but he holds it tight. Panic fills me, and the room seems to tilt.

"I'm 318 and—"

"Your name is Alexia Drago."

I go still, and he lets my hand drop. I slowly turn, my eyes seeking the letters carved into the wall behind my cot.

LEX.

Alexia.

I stumble back to my bed to trace the letters with my fingertips as I've done so many times before.

LEX.

I'm Lex.

I suck in a breath as I remember the day they came for me. An image of a woman, calling my name in class—a teacher at my school. "Alexia Drago, please report to the main office."

Anders, blond hair, blue eyes, standing beside his cop father. The stinging realization that Anders betrayed me—gave away my secret.

The Corporate Coalition men bringing me back to my house where they interrogate my mother and give her drugs to make her talk.

My mother, confessing, tears streaming down her cheeks. "Yes. I did it. I took an illegal dose of the Protected gene therapy. I lost a younger sister in the pandemics—I just wanted my baby to survive."

They charged her for conspiring to hide a Protected child. Then they brought us both to the camp.

I hear Monroe drop my tray on the table, and I feel his presence at my back. Emotions run through me, a chaotic mix of shock and grief—of fear… and rage. I clench my hands into fists, and heat spreads through me as I turn back to him.

"I remember."

He angles his body in front of me, blocking my view of the camera affixed to the top corner of my cell.

"I'm like you, Lex," he says. "I'm a Protected, too."

My breath catches, and I can't answer. I can't even comprehend someone like me—working *with* the humans. "But—"

"I'm not one of them—I'm working against them. From the inside," he says, his voice low. "Would you leave here if I helped you get out?

Leave here. The thought of leaving here makes my lungs seize, and I clutch my blanket tight in my fist, struggling to find the breath to respond. "Go back to the camp?"

"No," he says quickly. "Somewhere else. Somewhere safer."

"I'm going to die here."

"Yes. You will. Unless you come with me." He bends forward, just a little, to slide something beneath my pillow. "I'm going to try to make sure no one else visits you tonight. But that's a syringe. A sedative. If a medic comes to give you a sedative tonight, inject him instead."

I nod, but can't speak.

"Lex," he says, and my eyes return to his. "I'll handle the rest. Just wait for me in your cell. I'll come get you."

I lie awake, my heart pounding too fast for sleep, the syringe clutched in one sweaty palm beneath my blanket.

More memories are coming back. The feel of warm wind on my cheek, the scent of summer and sun. My mother, baking in the kitchen, the scent of chocolate chip cookies wafting through our house. My brain shrinks away from it all, and I choke back a sob. It's too painful. And now that I can feel again—I feel *everything*.

Everything *they* did to me.

I'm human, yet they treated me like an alien; like some animal. They used me up, and now they want to throw me away.

I hate them. I hate them so much.

Monroe is right. I'm superior to them, not defective. They fear me, yet they need me to help save themselves.

I'm breathing too fast when the door to my cell slides open, and I have to try to calm myself, slow my breath so they don't know I'm awake. Is it Monroe, come to free me—or a Hazmat with a sedative?

I ready the syringe just in case and peek through my lashes as the light comes on. I can tell right away by the man's stance and his stooped shoulders that it's not Monroe.

The Hazmat comes closer, and I see his watery, lined eyes.

It's Dalton.

I lurch up on my cot, and he steps back, surprised that I'm awake. Adrenaline races through me, and I ready the syringe in my grip. Something must have happened to Monroe. Why else would Dalton be here? He's never come in here before.

"You've served your purpose, 318," Dalton says, his voice calm. "I need a fresh host, and I can't get one unless I have an available cell."

As he approaches, I see his eyes have the same look I've seen in Farrow's. He relishes the power he has over me. He enjoys my fear.

He opens his gloved fist, revealing the syringe he holds there, and I jerk away, pressing my back to the wall, keeping the sedative I hold hidden. I can feel the jagged edges of my *real* name against my back.

LEX.

He grabs my arm roughly, expecting no resistance. I let out a scream and jab my syringe into his arm, hard, to push through layers of plastic. Then I empty it into him.

His eyes widen with shock, then his eyelids begin to flutter. The syringe he holds clatters to the floor as he sinks to his knees. He wavers there for a moment, then falls face down on the tile. He's passed out.

I'm breathing fast, and my pulse buzzes loudly in my skull as I stand on shaking legs. I glance toward the door, then back at Dalton.

Monroe said to wait here. But the small fire in my belly burns brighter, and rage replaces my fear.

I have the power, and Dalton is at *my* mercy.

I strip off his suit and see his whole face for the first time. He's so old and frail.

I want him dead.

I break out in a sweat as I drag his heavy, limp body across the small space. His access card is still attached to his suit, so I grab it and scan it. The door slides open to reveal an empty hall beyond.

Fear tries to paralyze me, but I fight it off by calling up my anger again. I drag Dalton out into the empty hallway and lift my sweat-soaked face to the ceiling to count the lights. *One. Two. Three. Four. Five.*

We're here.

A little thrill shoots through me, and I know I need to hurry if I want to do this before Monroe gets here. Something tells me he won't approve.

It takes every ounce of strength I have to drag Dalton into the lab and strap him into my glass coffin. I grab a single-dose vial of *Ebola, strain origin: 2044 pandemic* and twist it onto the syringe.

As I plunge the needle into his arm, his eyes open wide.

"318," he croaks out.

He struggles against his restraints, but I did a good job strapping him down. I've had hundreds of chances to learn how to do it right. The virus is moving through him, and the pain will soon be unbearable. I know exactly what he's about to experience.

Dalton shouts, but his screams are muffled by the glass. I don't blink. I just watch, and I wait.

"Lex! What are you doing in here? We have to leave now. Transport's waiting."

I turn to find Monroe at the door. He's not wearing a Hazmat suit, and for the first time I get to see what he looks like. He has short, light brown hair; a stricken expression mars the sharp angles of his handsome face.

Dalton's yelling louder, and I take one last glance at him, at the delicious terror on his face, and memorize it. Then I lick my dry lips and turn back to Monroe. I can tell my behavior's scaring him, but I don't care.

"What have you done?" He says each word slowly, like he's afraid to hear my answer.

I smile. "Don't you realize how many of *us* we'll save through the loss of just one subject?"

A Word from Autumn Kalquist

If we ever meet aliens, how will we greet them? You don't need to leave the planet to figure that out. Some might embrace another sentient species, but to do so would be to deny the darker desires inherent in our very nature.

The desire to control, the urge to destroy, the yearning to gain mastery over another: it's in our DNA. It's in our present, it's in our past. And it'll be in our future, no matter how well we learn to conceal it in polite modern society.

Humans are good at finding ways to defend what they do. When do the ends justify the means? Whenever they get us what we want, of course. If another sentient species is watching us, maybe they're wise enough to know that we're not ready for them... not yet. But maybe someday. Let's just hope the right people are in charge when those aliens do decide to pay us a visit.

"318" is the story of Lex and Monroe, both Protecteds— humans genetically engineered to have superimmunity. The story takes place in my Fractured Era universe, the setting for the *Defect*, *Legacy Code*, and *Sunpath* series. If you want to read more about the Protecteds and the effect some of Infinitek's other projects have on our near-future Earth, you can read more in the *Defect* and *Legacy Code* series, both part of the *Fractured Era* saga.

Learn more about the *Fractured Era* series and get songs from the official soundtrack at AutumnKalquist.com.

Crawlies
by Annie Bellet

SADIE RUBBED AT the sleep salt in her eyes and felt around in the dark, disoriented. She heard muffled chirping and whirring and realized she must have dozed off in her hiding place. As she sat up, the crate started moving. She banged on the top, yelling. It kept moving.

Panicked, Sadie scrabbled to her knees in the shifting blankets and scratched at where she thought the door panel might be. She couldn't even feel a seam, and she wondered if she'd suffocate or if they'd stick the crate in an unpressurized hold and her head would explode first.

She wrapped her arms around her skinny knees and blinked hard to keep from crying. She started counting in a whisper. Kip hated that habit, but it kept her sane whenever she got scared.

She got to three hundred and forty-six before the crate settled onto another surface. It sounded like other crates were being set down around her. Letting out a slow breath, Sadie crawled forward again, feeling the sides around the blankets, searching for the door panel. She sobbed with relief when her fingers met a seam in the metal wall to her left. She realized the crate must have rolled onto its side when they were transporting it. The blankets weren't stuffed in very tightly. She thought whoever had packed this thing should probably get canned.

The door was still broken from her hard-hacking it before, and with some desperate prodding she managed to jam it back open. She stuffed her sore fingers into her mouth and grimaced at the chemical taste. She set her feet against the back of the crate and gripped the door panel again. It grudgingly slid further open.

Sadie flipped around and poked her head out. Her crate was at the edge of a cargo bay. The wall of the ship shone white only a foot from her face.

Her shoulders came through easily enough with a little twisting, her growing breasts less so. She rubbed at her tender chest as she crouched against the wall. The cargo hold was quiet except for the hum of the ship. That wasn't a good sign, Sadie decided. If they took off and depressurized, she figured her head would explode for sure.

She crept along the wall, looking for a door or something. This must be a Crawly ship. Not a place she wanted to get caught, since Vicky said they sometimes ate people. And Vicky would know because she'd traveled to many other space stations.

The walls were warm and slightly soft. Sadie tried not to think about it too much. Tech was tech and she was good with tech. A real natural, though Kip had gotten mad when he found out she'd been stealing his cred sticks to pay one of the station mechanics to teach her things.

Sadie pushed away thoughts of Kip and continued along the wall. She didn't see what he had to be so mad about anyway, since he'd stolen those cred sticks in the first place.

If only she hadn't lost the last one. She'd only hidden in the stupid crate to think up a story for Kip. Man-o, it'd have to be a really really good one. She wished now she'd just gone and stolen cred off a drunk docker at Benchley's.

She sighed. "I'm going to be an engineer," she muttered, "if my head doesn't explode."

The wall bent to the left, but just before the bend was a clear panel. She pressed her face to it and saw an open shaft beyond. Relief flooded over her and she sagged against the door panel. It had what looked like a pull made of thick, soft plastic.

The whole cargo hold shuddered suddenly, and she heard a hissing sound. Panic returned, and she gripped the pull with both hands, setting her body weight against it.

The door opened so easily it knocked her over. Sadie jammed her body into the shaft beyond and yanked the door shut behind her.

The shaft continued forward only about a body length before turning upward. It was plenty wide, but it didn't have the ladder she expected in a maintenance shaft. Instead there were smooth divots carved into the sides at even intervals. Considering for a moment, Sadie decided that it would be easy enough to climb if she were a Crawly, but without four tentacled feet, she would have issues. She tried to grip one of the holds, but her little fingers slid right off.

She sat down with a huff and curled her knees back up. The ship was probably well away from the station by now. She'd never see Kip or Vicky or Karlin's mutt puppies again. She'd never have another lesson in binary or thrust or flux systems from Morrisey. Even if her head didn't explode, once the Crawlies found her she'd be dinner anyway. Maybe brunch. It was a high price to pay for trying to get out of a beating. She stared down at her reddened hands.

Hands! Sadie jumped up. Of course, those Crawlies wouldn't climb with hands; they would use those tentacle leg things. She'd seen them on station before, with their color-shifting skin and strange shells that Morrisey said were exoskeletons. She hated the way they walked, that weird boneless shuffling like someone pouring melted plastic. But Crawlies would climb with those legs.

Sadie braced her back against the smooth white wall of the shaft and set one bare foot up on the first ledge. She tested her weight. Her foot slid, but less than her fingers had. She leaned hard into the wall behind her and bravely brought her other foot up to another step. Jamming her elbows into the wall helped her balance until she was safely off the ground. Carefully, step after step, she climbed the shaft.

Sweat ran in itchy trickles down her spine and soaked into her leggings. But she refused to look down. She'd go as far as she had to.

"Fifty, fifty-one, fifty-two, fifty-three," she whispered. Abruptly the shaft wall behind her disappeared. Sadie nearly fell as her shoulders met nothing to brace against. But she shoved upward with her burning legs and fell back onto the floor of a horizontal shaft. Gasping, she finished her count to one hundred.

Slowly, Sadie rolled over and looked down this new shaft. There was brighter light gleaming golden and warm through a clear door at the end. She crouched and made her way to the door and found another pull like the one before. This time she tugged on it gently and shifted as it slid in and to the side.

Warm, moist air rushed in, dampening her already sticky skin. The air smelled like Kip's hydroponic room, only without the acidic undertone of mold. Sadie stuck her head into the room. All around her on thin gold wires floated plants she had no names for. Some had wide green leaves, some thin brown and blue ones. Others had heavy seeds and fruits hanging down, and still others flowered with bold purples and reds and yellows and blues. Enchanted, she forgot all about the man-eating Crawlies for a moment and stepped out of the shaft, letting the door close behind her.

Sadie wandered among the plants, touching the leaves and bending low or standing up on tiptoe to smell the flowers. The air in the room was very hot from the lights and was thick with perfume and moisture. Sadie wasn't counting anymore, but it felt like she had poked at things a long time before she remembered that this was a Crawly ship and she was a stowaway.

Her chest started to hurt, and she retreated to her maintenance shaft. She didn't want to leave the flowers, but she was thirsty, and worried something might check on the plants and find her. Her mind wandered and her vision blurred. She curled into a ball, wondering if she were sick with some Crawly disease or something. They hadn't worn any special masks on the station, unless that fringe of stuff below their huge eyes had been a mask. She couldn't remember.

Sadie's body shook, and she couldn't stop coughing. Her eyes hurt too much to keep them open, and her hands and feet felt numb. *Maybe my head will explode anyway.*

Chittering invaded her woozy brain, and Sadie jerked away from a strange touch. She wondered if she'd fallen asleep again, but her mind was so fuzzy she couldn't tell.

A Crawly face with big dark eyes and a flashing red crest was bent over her.

She whimpered and tried to pull away. Velvet soft arms lifted her, the long digits on the creature's hands uncurling to grip her securely. Sadie tried to scream, but she couldn't breathe. Darkness took her again.

* * *

Sadie didn't want to open her eyes again, figuring her day was only going to get worse from here. She didn't know how long she'd slept this time, but she was getting really tired of passing out so much. At least her chest didn't hurt anymore, and her eyes felt okay too.

She wondered if she was dead, and tried to subtly wiggle a toe. It felt like it moved, so she slowly squeezed her left hand shut and winced. Her muscles were sore, so she probably wasn't dead. She couldn't feel any restraints either. Sadie heard movement near her and gave up, opening her eyes.

The light here was the same diffused golden light from before, but the air was far less heavy and smelled vaguely metallic. Another one of the Crawlies stood near her, holding a data screen in one hand. It was turned away from her and appeared not to have noticed that she was awake. Sadie looked around.

She guessed she was in a medical room. Even on a Crawly ship, it gave off that same feel, that familiar sterile tidiness. The table underneath her was warm and smooth and felt like thick gel that molded to her form. It had no hard edges, curling away and sweeping toward the floor instead of cutting off with corners like a real table. She noted two more tables lined up beside her, unoccupied.

Along one wall were monitors, most of them dark. Along another were rows and rows of what she guessed were drawers. The room had a large tank of violet liquid to one side, which she figured could hold two or three of her easily. Maybe only one Crawly though—they were pretty big.

She turned her gaze back to the Crawly, which was watching her now with its big eyes. It blinked, and she stared, fascinated, as opaque lids slid in from the sides to meet in the middle. Crawlies blink slowly, she thought.

"Are you going to eat me?" she asked.

The Crawly chattered something at her, and she shook her head and sat up fully. The Crawly went to a drawer and pulled out a small box. It lifted a yellow patch from the box and moved toward her.

Sadie froze as she watched its strange, pouring forward gait. She pulled away from it at the last moment, but the three-fingered hand with the patch flashed forward faster than she'd reckoned. It stuck the patch to her throat.

Her vision swam for a moment; blood rushed to her head, and her whole body broke out in scaredy bumps. A sickeningly sweet taste filled the back of her mouth and she swallowed hard.

"Better?" the Crawly said.

"Oh." Sadie touched the patch on her throat. She'd heard of these things. Morrisey had called them "babble patches"— or something like that. They were supposed to be worth a lot of cred. The Crawly seemed to be waiting for her to say something else. She swallowed again. "I didn't mean to be on the ship, I didn't touch or take anything I swear, so don't eat me, okay?" She flushed. She hadn't meant all that to come out in a rush.

"We're vegetarians," the Crawly said, and she remembered that only the males had that funny crest, "which means we—"

"I know what that means." Sadie cut him off. "You aren't the Crawly that found me, are you?"

The Crawly turned away from her and replaced the box in the drawer. Sadie made a mental note of where that drawer was. Three up, three over from the left. *Three by three*, she thought. That might come in handy if they don't eat or space me first.

"Why would we put a Babel patch on someone we were going to kill?" the Crawly said, surprising her.

"Are you in my head?" Sadie put her hands up to her face as though she could somehow protect her brain.

"It's more like sometimes your head gets out *here*." At Sadie's expression, the Crawly made a sound that didn't translate.

Sadie tapped the babble patch. "Thing is defective," she muttered.

"To answer your other question, no, I'm Doctor Chiro. Pyro is the one who brought you in." Doctor Chiro moved back toward her.

She leaned away from him. "Why don't you flash all red too? Was that Crawly angry?"

"We don't all look the same. Do all humans have brown hair and black skin?" Sadie didn't need the babble patch to translate his tone.

She tried one of her best smiles. "Nah, just the really smart ones. And my hair is more red than brown—everyone says so. What was wrong with me? Did I get poisoned?"

She wasn't sure if Chiro was shaking his head or not. "Oxygen poisoning. Our preferred atmosphere is far more saturated than your own. You reacted badly. I've changed the controls in here to compensate, but you shouldn't leave the medical center until the leader decides where to put you."

"Can't you just take me back to Ara Station?"

"We may." Chiro looked as though he might say more, but then he shrugged his flat shoulders, sending a strange ripple of muted color over the skin on his arms. "Are you hungry or thirsty?"

Sadie wrinkled her nose. "Is it Crawly food? 'Cause I don't know if I can eat that."

This time she was sure the doctor sighed, and his mouth fringe hummed, making a sound that her babble patch again failed to translate.

"Teuthiad. Not Crawlies. Would you like it if I called you an ape?"

"I'm a human. And I think we came from monkeys. Oh, my name's Sadie." She knew she'd annoyed it now. Man-o, she was going to have to work on that if she didn't want to be Crawly food.

Chiro huffed and hummed and turned away toward the door.

"No, please. Doctor… Chiro. Don't go. I'm sorry. I know you won't eat me. I promise. I'm, I am thirsty." Sadie hopped down from the table and stepped after him, stopping short of touching the Crawly's shell.

He turned back to her and rolled his thin shoulders. She stared at the rippling, translucent skin bonding his shoulders to his exoskeleton. His skin changed color, flashing between green and blue in little bands.

"Chromatophores. That's what allows us to change our colors."

She slapped her hands back to her head. "Can't you stop doing that?"

"Can't you?" Chiro retorted. His tone softened as she stared up at him with wide eyes. "I'll bring you water and something your system can eat. Now sit down and stay out of trouble, if you're capable."

Sadie hopped back up on the smooth table and tried to do as he'd asked. She was amused to find that adults of any species were pretty much the same in the end. Maybe someday she'd find people who didn't just want her to obey all the time. She sighed and started counting.

At nine hundred and seventy-seven she got bored and hopped off the table. She walked to the large tank of violet liquid and tried to read the panels around it. There were tubes floating in the tank, and the liquid had tiny bubbles like she'd seen in gels before. The top of the tank had a lid, but she contemplated climbing up to see if she could touch the purple stuff inside. It's probably poisonous, she told herself, and turned away.

She poked through some of the drawers, finding all sorts of implements and chemical strips and powders she didn't recognize. All the labels were in the strange symbols that Crawlies used. Teuthiads, though she wasn't even sure if they had teeth under that face fringe, so it sounded like a weird name to her.

She was almost back to the third drawer up, third drawer from the left when the ship jerked hard, sending her and the little sealed vials in the drawer she'd opened crashing to the floor. The lights dimmed, and a high keening sound pierced the quiet. Tiny lights in bands along the tops of the walls flashed red and yellow.

Sadie scrambled to her feet and stuffed the vials back into the drawers. Then she chose a mostly empty wall and sat down with her back to it in case there was another jolt. She wondered if they'd hit an asteroid or something, wondered if she had missed her one chance to grab that box of babble patches.

"Three by three," she whispered as the ship jolted again, and then she started her count from three.

Sadie was back up to nine hundred and seventy-seven when the door slid open and Chiro returned.

"We're under attack by human pirates," he said. He looked around the lab. "You were not harmed when they netted the ship?"

"Nah, I'm okay." Sadie stood up. "You guys going to fight them off?"

"If they board, yes. But the *Myopsina* is a trading ship; we don't have ship-to-ship weapons." Chiro poured his way over to the wall of monitors and started turning things on. "If we have injured, stay out of my way, over there." He motioned with one bonelessly uncurling arm toward the corner near the tank of gel.

Chiro's skin flashed yellow and red now, except for his crest, which shimmered blue in the dancing emergency lights. Sadie shrugged and walked to the designated corner, sinking down again. Just like most adults, she thought: never lets you do anything to help.

No injured came in, but Chiro waved away all her questions. He stood rigid and read data streaming in on a monitor wholly blocked by his body. Sadie figured she might as well start counting again.

She lost her count somewhere in the seven hundreds when she thought she heard someone scream. It was muffled by the ship noise and the emergency keening, but she knew what a scream sounded like. She looked up at Chiro. He'd turned toward the door, so she guessed he'd heard it too, though she found herself wondering where on his head his ears were, anyway.

Two Crawlies came in through the door, dragging a dead-looking human between them. One of them had a flashing red crest above his large eyes. The one that found her earlier.

"They breached, but we drove off the boarding party. This one wasn't fast enough."

"I'll preserve it for the Arcturi shipping guards. I assume Leader Bato will want to press a complaint to the shipping board?"

"Easy assumption." The red-crested one looked over at Sadie. Pyro, she thought. I think that's what Chiro said his name was. "You put a Babel patch on this one? Why?"

Sadie stuck her tongue out at him. She noticed that his companion didn't have a crest, and figured she must be a girl Crawly—or Teuthiad or whatever. Sadie couldn't see any breasts though, and felt a stab of envy.

"She's been no trouble," Chiro said, "and Leader Bato wanted to know how and why she got on board. Hard to question a human that can't understand us."

"Keep her quiet then," Pyro growled. "We've got to get that ship net off or they'll just keep mounting boarding parties. If they don't decide to blow us apart first."

The female gave Sadie a curious glance, then followed Pyro out of the medical lab.

"Was that Pyro?" Sadie asked once the door slid closed.

"Yes, and Omma. She's one of our mechanics." Chiro moved to the pirate's body.

Sadie walked over and looked down at the man. His head had a big gaping wound in it, but his space helmet didn't look ruptured at all.

She looked up at Chiro. "Need help moving him? I'm real strong."

His skin rippled a muted green. "He's dead. This doesn't bother you?"

Sadie shrugged. "I've seen loads of dead people before." She took a deep breath. She'd only really seen one dead body, but after that, she figured dead was dead. Besides, she didn't even know this pirate. She'd known Evey. Evey had been nice, and always smelled good, too. Evey had even kept Kip from beating her or making her beg in the shops. Until Evey was dead. Vicky had gotten drunk once and told Sadie that Kip got Evey sick, but wouldn't say anything more about it. Sadie shoved aside those thoughts.

Chiro was still staring at her. He blinked in his slow way, twice. His fringe hummed, the sound low and oddly soothing. His skin turned to deep purple, and Sadie folded her arms tightly across her chest. His eyes looked sad, and she flushed. Stupid Crawlies.

"You want my help or not? Geez."

"All right," Chiro said. He flowed across the floor toward the wall she'd thought was empty apart from a couple of control panels. He keyed something into one, and a wide drawer slid open, sending a burst of chilled air into the room.

Sadie grabbed the dead pirate's feet while Chiro easily lifted the shoulders; together they moved the corpse into the drawer.

"How come they only killed one?" Sadie asked once the drawer was closed.

"The others were contained at the breach point. This one slid through during the fighting there."

Sadie chewed on a fingernail and thought about that. Sometimes Kip would stage a fistfight, and Sadie or Collin would use the distraction to swipe cred sticks and other stuff. Once some fat merchanter from Corvus had paid Kip and the crew to set an explosive in the crates of a rival. She remembered him because he'd had rancid breath and a huge birthmark like a bad stain on his face. They'd used the same distraction tactic to get her into the cargo bay with the bomb. It'd been a good haul, too; even Kip had smiled at her that night and ruffled her hair in a way she only pretended not to like.

Chiro's skin changed from purple to yellow and green again. "You think this is a distraction?"

"What?" Sadie looked up and wiped her hand on her jumper. "Man-o, stay out of my head, okay? But yeah, it could be. I don't know. It's what I'd do."

"And you're very smart," Chiro said. His fringe hummed again.

Sadie self-consciously rubbed at her blue-black skin as she realized that his noise must be laughter. "Smarter than *you*, to let a boarding party on like that," she said, glaring.

Chiro turned back to the monitors, so Sadie hopped back up onto the smooth table and tried to peer over his shoulder.

He appeared to be typing something, but the squiggly symbols meant nothing to her. She pretended she could read them though, and she tried to pick out patterns. She wondered if Crawlies had numbers.

Chiro moved away and went to the wall of drawers. He removed a plastic mask and held it out to her. "Leader Bato and Pyro want to see you. I told them what you said, and they searched the area they found that pirate in. There's some kind of device there. I've convinced them to let you have a look at it. This mask will help you breathe on the ship."

Sadie jumped down from the table and grabbed the mask. "Why'd you do that?" She was shocked and pleased. This Crawly was nothing like she'd expected.

"You expected to get eaten," Chiro said, "and Cephalos help me, but if I didn't convince them to let you out of here I'd have to listen to you try to count past nine hundred and seventy-seven again. Follow me, monkey."

Sadie slapped her mask into place and shivered as it stuck to her skin. It created a tight seal around her mouth and nose before fading strangely away, so that she could barely tell it was there at all.

She grinned as she followed Chiro through the double doors into a spiraling corridor. Maybe if she was useful they'd pay her something, and she wouldn't have to return to Kip empty-handed.

She quickly lost track of where they were. It wasn't too long before they emerged into a room full of machinery. And there it was: the device stood out, grey and green against the shining white smoothness of the Teuthiads' ship.

Pyro and Omma were there. At least, she thought that the female was the same one as before. Two other males stood with them; one was much smaller than any of the others. He had a harness strapped across his shell, with odd tools poking out of it. The other male had a slender rope of crystal beads around his crest, affixed with a piercing through his translucent skin.

"This is the human child," Chiro said. "Her name is Sadie."

Sadie almost expected him to add "and she's very smart" because of how much his fringe was twitching as he made the introductions, but he retained his control. Chiro introduced the Teuthiads quickly. Walvis was the little one, another mechanic, and Leader Bato was the one with the crest decoration.

"Chiro says you thought the breach was a ploy to get something on board. What is this? Can you tell us?" Leader Bato had a very high-pitched voice for such a big body.

Sadie choked down a nervous laugh and nodded. She knelt beside the device, a dark metallic box, and popped open the control panel. It looked like a pretty simple disruptor of some sort. She looked up.

"What's this room do? Communications or something?"

"Yes," Walvis said, dropping low as his tentacle feet folded up into his body. "Why do you ask?"

"Have you tried calling for help? I think this thing is a jammer."

"We have; we thought they'd damaged our ansible array." Omma moved forward and peered over them at the device.

"Can you disable it?" Leader Bato asked.

Sadie carefully moved aside some wires and saw a little red light alongside a thin glass panel with what looked like a thermometer inside. "Sure," she said. "If you don't mind turning part of this room into slag."

Every Crawly in the room flashed green and then yellow at that statement.

"See that red light? And that glass bit?" Sadie pointed. "That's a tamper switch. It'll go if we move the jammer, or even jostle it around too much, which I'd have to do if I wanted to get at the wires I need to cut to disable it."

"What about those wires you're touching? What do those do?" Pyro asked.

"Dummy wires." Sadie shrugged.

"She's right," Walvis said as he looked more closely at it. "See how they're just soldered right to the plate here? Not connected to anything."

"She's not a child, she's a criminal," Pyro muttered, and his crest turned red again.

Sadie rose up, balling her hands into fists. She opened her mouth but jerked in shock as Chiro grabbed her shoulders. She hadn't even seen him move. His skin flashed through colors so quickly she couldn't follow them, but Pyro moved back a pace and his crest faded out to a dusty pink.

"Perhaps we could freeze the jammer?" Omma said into the tense silence.

"I'll start looking into our manuals and see what we can come up with." Walvis unfolded.

"Thank you, Sadie," Leader Bato said in what was clearly a dismissal.

Chiro released Sadie's shoulders. She realized he'd been touching her and she hadn't even really cared.

She stared down at her grimy toes. She didn't want to go back to the medical room and be useless again. She looked again at the device, and a crazy idea started to form in her head.

"Wait," she said. "They got you jammed right? And in a net? They're just gonna blow you away if they can't board. You gotta get that net free and get rid of the jammer. I can do both." She took as deep a breath as the weird plastic mask would allow and poked her tongue into the thin membrane as it sucked back between her lips.

Chiro placed a hand back on her shoulder. "Sadie," he began.

"What's your plan?" Leader Bato asked, cocking his oblong head to one side so that it rested awkwardly along one rubbery shoulder.

"What do you want if it succeeds? And how many of us do you want to put in danger?" That was Pyro, still hunched against the wall and turning red again.

Sadie wanted to stick her tongue out at him again but was pretty sure the membrane mask thingy wouldn't let her. So she ignored him and looked at Leader Bato.

"I will be the only one in danger. Well, if the first part works out okay anyway. And…" She paused and glanced up at Chiro. *One, two, three, four, five*, she thought. *You can do this.* "If it works, if I free your ship, I want to come with you. At least to the next station. But I need to get to Mirzam. That's where they sign up people for the freighters."

Bato's skin rippled through multiple colors as he stared at her. Finally he blinked and straightened up. "We'll be at Mirzam three stops from now. Tell me this plan."

* * *

Walvis looked even stranger in his protective suit. His tentacle legs were wrapped in hard plastic, which gave his movements a jerking awkwardness that was almost worse than the usual boneless falling forward. They'd finished building a mold around the jammer. If this part worked, they'd have the thing stabilized enough to move it out of the ship. But if this failed… Sadie peeked around the door and held her breath as she counted, slowly.

Walvis poured the thick gel into the mold. After what felt like eternity—and was certainly long enough that Sadie couldn't hold her breath anymore—he set down the canister and started unscrewing the mold. The jammer was now completely encased in violet gel. Chiro had explained to her that the gel in the tank was used to suspend injured Teuthiads and take weight off their delicate inner structures in case of injury. Mixed with a compound provided by Omma, the gel would firm up even more, stabilizing the device enough that it could be gently moved around. Sadie hoped that it would be enough to disrupt the circuitry of the jammer without tripping the tamper switch. They'd have to keep the device level, however, which is where the second stage came in.

Omma entered the mechanical room with four slender poles. The two mechanics carefully inserted the poles into each side of the newly formed cube. Then they gently lifted it, keeping the device as level as possible.

Chiro touched Sadie's shoulder as she backed away from the door to let them through. "Come, Sadie. We've got to get you into that pressure suit."

Sadie nodded, secretly wishing she hadn't managed to be so convincing. She'd insisted that it was she who had to take the jammer bomb over to the pirate ship. But her logic was sound. She knew what the human technology looked like; she'd probably be able to figure out what panel to open and where to place the bomb. *Too smart for my own good, that's what Kip would say.*

The dead pirate's pressure suit seemed to be in good condition. Chiro had pulled it off the body while she was busy with the mechanics, and she was grateful for that, though she'd never admit it aloud. Unfortunately, the suit was way too big for her. She adjusted what parts of it she could and decided that it would have to do. At least the helmet fit her okay. Chiro must have washed the blood out of it—she could smell chemicals, and there were a couple of streaks on the visor as though from drying water.

As she stomped down the white hallway after Chiro's color-changing shell, she poked at the wrist display until she got it to show in binary. She had over a standard hour of air, which was good. She hoped this wouldn't take that long.

They reached the airlock where Omma and Walvis waited with Pyro and the jammer bomb. Sadie pressurized the suit, turning on her air and starting her countdown. The suit made disturbing squeaky noises as the loose folds around her shoulders and knees shifted around. She hoped this thing was actually going to work. Otherwise, her head would probably explode.

"Your head won't explode, though your eyes will likely—" Pyro started.

"Pyro, hush," Chiro said.

"Ready?" Walvis asked her.

"Tip top, Walvis." Sadie smiled at him and wished that he could smile back. She thought she could really use a big smile from someone right about now.

She checked her tether as Omma finished securing it to the suit. The suit had thrusters, but the battery was low and she wanted to save it for moving into position once she figured out where the net was extending from.

She shuffled into the airlock and gripped two of the handles on the jammer bomb. The airlock gently depressurized. She thought she heard someone, maybe Pyro, ask "Is she counting?" and then the outer doors slid open and she pushed off, drifting out toward the pirate ship.

The first thing she noticed was how dark the sky seemed. *Space, dummy*, she told herself. She'd expected it to have more stars in it. The pirate ship wasn't too far above the *Myopsina*. It loomed there, a dark shape just out of reach of the running lights on the outside of the Teuthiads' ship. She looked behind her and was surprised. She'd expected the *Myopsina* to be white on the outside like it was everywhere she'd been on the inside. Instead, it had a dull silvery tint to its oblong exterior. She watched cargo containers started to drift outward from the ship. They'd been released just before she was. This was a distraction they'd planned so that she'd have time to attach the bomb without, hopefully, the pirates noticing her presence.

Sadie knew that a ship-catching net wasn't really a net but actually an energy field, but she'd still hoped that there'd be some obvious physical manifestation she could trace back to its source. But she could see nothing, just the dark shape of the pirate ship looming above her. There's no up in space, she thought, but it *felt* like up. Her stomach twisted around the water she'd drunk earlier, and she was suddenly glad she'd decided not to eat anything before this mission.

She was very close now to the pirate ship hull. She could see different arrays along its surface as it grew to fill her vision. Sadie watched carefully for any sign of the net, futilely hoping that they'd have handy binary signs painted next to each array. Man-o, she thought, no such luck.

Her tether spiraled out behind her, nearly invisible in the dark emptiness. She couldn't go back, not with the jammer bomb. She supposed she could just let go of it and hope she pulled herself far enough away before it hit the pirate ship. She didn't think it would do any damage to the hull, though. She bit her lip, hard.

Sadie was only a few arms' lengths away from the ship now. She punched in a command on her suit and her helmet lamp flicked on. She hoped she was close enough that no one would notice a light down here.

She guessed that one array was the communications equipment, and two others looked an awful lot like gun portals of some sort. She wasn't even sure the array for the net would be on the underside of the ship, but she didn't want to try to crawl around the hull and find more. She looked at the bomb floating just in front of her.

"I'm sorry, Chiro and all the Crawlies," she whispered. "I guess I'm not so smart after all." She'd been so sure she could figure out the net. Morrisey'd always said she was a natural; she had a gift for tech. He wouldn't have taught her otherwise. Even Kip had her fix stuff all the time, and he'd let her help with loads of jobs that needed breaking or rewiring.

She shifted the bomb to prevent it from bumping into the hull. Her body rested against the pirate ship and she blinked away more tears. It wasn't fair. She couldn't let them all be blown to bits because she was too stupid to figure this out. She took big deep breaths and started counting. She could solve this. Somehow.

Sadie felt the hull vibrate suddenly and twisted around to look back toward the *Myopsina*. Were the pirates fixing to shoot? But then she saw spindly cargo arms extending from above toward the free-floating cargo. Sadie grinned wildly and stopped her count at sixty-four. If the cargo arms were out, that meant an open bay. An open bay into which she could shove that jammer bomb. A net only worked if the ship that cast it stayed within range. If she could do enough damage to the pirate ship, she might be able to drive them off, or at least disrupt the internal systems. She just hoped this bomb was big enough to hurt.

Sadie pushed away from the hull and started to drift back toward the *Myopsina*. She got far enough out that she could see where the cargo arms extended from. As she'd hoped, they came from an open bay inside the ship, the arms extending from a control box at the back of the bay. The whole place was helpfully flooded with light, and Sadie smiled.

She cued her suit thrusters and sent herself flying straight toward the opening with the gel-encrusted jammer bomb held in front of her. She hadn't meant to get so much thrust. The opening sped toward her until she could make out rivets on the arms of the machine and could see moving forms behind the windows of the control box. She adjusted the thrusters, ignoring the beep inside her helmet as the batteries continued to drain.

Sadie twisted, and with a mighty kick she sent the jammer bomb speeding straight at the control box. Her momentum slowed, and for one precarious second she hung just inside the cargo doors.

The jammer bomb hit one of the box windows straight on. Gel and plexi and metal exploded outward as the chamber depressurized with the explosion. Sadie was thrown backward on her tether. Her shoulders hit one of the extended cargo arms and she felt something give. Pain blinded her for a moment. She heard a hissing sound and forced her eyes open.

She was drifting away from the crippled pirate ship. She watched as one of the cargo arms tore loose and drifted out below her. The hissing got worse, and she realized her suit was leaking. She tried to turn her head to see the *Myopsina* but it hurt too much, and her body wouldn't obey her. She couldn't tell if she was still moving, or if they were pulling her in. She wasn't even sure where the Crawlies' ship was anymore.

It doesn't matter, she thought. *My suit has a leak and my head is gonna explode soon anyway.* She stared out into space. *I thought there'd be more stars.* Something pounded into the back of her helmet. She tasted blood. Then, nothing at all.

* * *

Everything hurt, but she could breathe, and some of the weight was off her head. Something warm and velvet-soft was pressed against her cheek. Sadie forced her eyes open and looked up to see Chiro carrying her. She willed one of her hands to move and pushed it against his chest. She'd never felt anything that soft in her life. She leaned her cheek back into him. Chiro looked down at her, his skin that rich purple like before.

"I knew you wouldn't let my head explode," she said. Her throat was raw.

Chiro hummed and looked back up. Sadie looked at her hand again. There was blood on it, and she wondered if it was hers. Probably. She was pretty sure that Crawlies—no, Teuthiads—bled green or blue or something, not red.

One, she thought, trying to ignore the growing pain in her back, head, and chest. *Two. Three. Four.*

* * *

Walvis explained to her later that the pirate ship had pulled away after the explosion. They weren't sure what her crazy stunt had damaged, but the net went down and the pirates cut and ran. Sadie thought they were probably scared 'cause they thought the Teuthiads would have friends coming. Or maybe she'd really blown some sensitive tech all to bits, though she thought a cargo bay was a stupid place to keep something like that. It *had* been a pretty small ship though, not all cool like the *Myopsina*.

Her head healed up quickly, but her shoulders still hurt her sometimes in the morning. Chiro said he wasn't used to human physiology, but he was pretty sure she'd broken her collarbone and torn a bunch of muscles. He had her mix a blue powder into her water; it tasted like mold but it helped the pain, and she'd recovered enough within a cycle to follow Chiro all over the ship asking questions.

She spent the nineteen cycles that it took to get to Mirzam helping Chiro and learning about Teuthiad plants. Omma and Walvis both came to visit her and showed her what some of their tools did too. Walvis even taught her how to write some of the Teuthiad numbers. She saw Pyro twice during the whole journey, and she was pretty sure he still wanted to eat her. Chiro laughed in his odd, humming way every time she thought about that, but she noticed he didn't disagree with her.

When they reached Mirzam, Sadie was sitting on one of the smooth tables in Chiro's lab, biting her lip. She wasn't sure she wanted to go, though she knew her babble patch, the second she'd had to use, would run out soon anyway. Best to not make them waste another one on her. She was going to get a job on a freighter here, she knew it. Leader Bato had written her a letter for the port secretary and given her her own cred stick, too. There was enough on there for her to live like a merchanter for at least a standard week.

Chiro came for her and she smiled at him. She knew he'd miss her, so she had to put on a brave face. Even as she thought this, his skin shifted to deep purple, and she grinned wider.

"Ready?" he said.

"Tip top." She hopped down and grabbed the silk bag Leader Bato had given her. In it she'd put her letter and her cred stick. She didn't need a mask for the short walk through the ship.

Sadie hesitated when they reached the threshold between the ship and the station. Pyro stood in the hall as though he'd been waiting for them. She stuck her tongue out at him and then grinned.

"Bye, Pyro."

"You're too skinny to eat," Pyro said. His normal red was shaded suspiciously violet. He abruptly turned and left the docking bay.

Sadie watched him go and then looked to Chiro. She'd already said goodbye to everyone else; today they were busy unloading cargo or making deals or something.

"Goodbye, Doc." She abandoned her poise and threw her arms around him, ignoring the protest of her still sore shoulders.

Chiro awkwardly wrapped his curling, velvet arms around her. "Do well, monkey," he murmured.

Sadie pulled away and sniffed. That was enough of that emotional stuff, she thought.

Chiro caught her hand in his own long, soft fingers as she turned toward the station. He pressed something hard and square into her palm. Sadie gripped it instinctively and then looked down as Chiro moved away. It was the box that held the babble patches.

"Three by three," he said as he flowed down the hall, "three by three."

A Word from Annie Bellet

"Crawlies" is a story near and dear to my heart. I woke up one morning and Sadie was there, inside my head, telling me her story. This is a rare treat for me as an author, since I usually have to spend weeks if not months figuring out the details of every story I write. With Sadie, those details were there and just kept flowing, and so this story felt almost born like Athena out of Zeus, springing whole from my head (or really, my fingers).

I've always loved the ocean (I took multiple science classes focusing on oceanography/geology/zoology in college), so when Sadie popped into my brain telling me about these "crawlies," I knew exactly what she meant. Squid and cuttlefish are fascinating and very intelligent creatures, and it was a lot of fun to craft an alien species based loosely on what I've learned about cephalopods. Space battles, pirates, explosions, and clever kids are other favorite topics of mine to explore, so it was an easy fit.

I've had over thirty stories published in various speculative fiction magazines and anthologies over the last few years. I've also published three short story collections and am the author of multiple ongoing series such as *The Twenty-Sided Sorceress* and *The Gryphonpike Chronicles*. You can find out more about my work by visiting my website or by signing up for my mailing list.

The Insect Requirement

by B. V. Larson

"PAUL FOUND ONE attached to his thigh," said Dr. Beckwith quietly.

Captain Rogers's body stiffened visibly in his pressure suit. "That's it then."

The two men stood in the tool storage pod adjacent to the ship's engine complex. They both wore full pressure suits of stiff, crinkled fabric. They stood because there was no room to sit.

"What do you mean, 'that's it'?" Dr. Beckwith asked. His breath blowing over the microphone poised in front of his mouth sounded like a strong wind.

Captain Rogers picked up a hand-held pneumatic drill and checked the digital pressure readings that glowed in red on the side. He held the drill to his chest and gripped the steel casing in powerful hands. His arm muscles bunched and the casing came loose with a jerk. A piece of black plastic from a ruptured gasket spun away and bounced off the ship's hull. He could have used tools to remove the casing, but Captain Rogers rarely did things the easy way.

"We've lost too many men. We'll have to leave."

"But the contract—" began Dr. Beckwith.

"They didn't pay me enough to die here. Nobody could pay that much."

"It's not that bad, really—we aren't going to lose him." Dr. Beckwith fought to keep the panic out of his voice. The muscles in his neck were stretched like guitar strings. When he moved his head, pinched nerves twinged as if plucked by playful fingers. He rubbed and scratched his left hand through the thick material of his glove. He had to have more time.

They were in the first Earth ship to have landed on the planet, which they had christened "Jade," the name specified in the promotional section of their contract. Although the executive who had come up with the name had never seen the world, Jade deserved her name. The newly discovered planet was vast, tangled jungle. Huge landmasses of brilliant foliage dwarfed small seas. Seen from space, the seas appeared as silver-blue islands in an ocean of greenery. Above all, Jade was a world of wet, green life. An immense tropical hothouse.

But in addition to the flora, particularly large and vicious insects had evolved here. They buzzed and hummed everywhere. Every yard of ground rustled with them; they wriggled in ponds and darkened the skies, their bodies massed in overwhelming swarms. Some of them were as big as a man's hand and just as powerful.

Captain Rogers gunned the pneumatic drill experimentally. The glowing digital readings fluctuated wildly, climbing up the scale, then dropping back. Rogers was a big man with bulky arms and shoulders, and his pressure suit exaggerated his size, making him look like a massive white giant with thickly wrinkled skin.

"How did it happen?" he asked.

"What?" replied Dr. Beckwith.

"I mean Paul—how did the bug get into his suit?"

Dr. Beckwith waved impatiently at the air with his gloved hands. "I don't know—he must have been carrying eggs or larva since his initial exposure."

In contrast to Rogers, Beckwith was a man of medium height with a bulging midsection that barely fit into his suit. His arm muscles were like loose rubber bands. He blinked rapidly as he brought his mind back to the present. He had been thinking about what Jade would mean to Earth. A whole planet full of living creatures men could eat without being poisoned. An entire planet to be homesteaded and explored. Back home there would be parties and bands. He could open a school of extraterrestrial biology. The colonists would name one of Jade's mountain ranges after him.

"Is he hemorrhaging?"

Beckwith shook his head vigorously inside his helmet. He regretted it immediately, as fingers plucked painfully at his neck muscles. "We've got that stopped. He's conscious, too."

Captain Rogers said nothing as he finished adjusting the drill and tossed it back on the workbench. The heavy metal drill hit the bench with a clang that neither of them could hear through their thickly insulated suits.

The suits the men wore were entirely self-contained. They carried nutrient pastes, air compressors, waste-recyclers—everything. They had been living in their suits since the first day, the day they had landed, when the native insects had swarmed and killed most of the crew. That meant drinking recycled, distilled and body-warm water and breathing compressed filtered oxygen that tasted like hot vinyl. Beckwith and Rogers conversed by radio; it was either that or trying to touch helmets all the time. The only sounds that could penetrate their helmets from the outside came up through the soles of their feet, usually from vibrations in the steel-plex hull of the ship itself.

Beckwith scratched the knuckles of his left hand by rubbing them up against the underside of the workbench. He shook his head, although no one could see him. His neck twinged. They couldn't leave Jade now, not without the conclusive proof he needed. Everything would be ruined. He shifted his shoulders uncomfortably under the weight of his air tanks. He felt a touch of nervousness—it seemed that he couldn't get enough air. Quickly, he adjusted the oxygen gauge on his forearm up a few hundredths. After a few moments he relaxed. For a moment longer, he listened to the hiss of his air valves and breathed in his own steamy exhalations.

"Let's have a look at him," said the captain finally. He laid all his tools on a piece of canvas and shoved them back out of the way.

Nodding his head sharply and ignoring the plucking fingers, Beckwith headed with hurried steps toward the bulkhead. Rogers followed at a much more leisurely pace.

The tiny medical ward at the heart of the ship was a tight fit. Beckwith and Rogers stayed in the corners, trying to keep out of the way. The nursing unit, named "Mom" by the crew, moved anxiously around the prone figure of Paul Foster. Her three multi-jointed arms moved independently, whirring and whining as innumerable electric motors and hydraulic screw-drives worked in unison. When either Dr. Beckwith or Captain Rogers got in the way, Mom politely bleeped and waited for them to move.

Technical officer Paul Foster lay on a stainless steel table. A thin sheet of sterile white paper separated his body from the metal. Tubes and sensory wires ran from where they were taped to pale, bloodless flesh up to a panel of self-monitoring devices that hung in festoons from the ceiling. As they watched, an IV bottle dribbled the last of its liquid contents down a tube leading into Foster's bloodstream. A soft alarm went off and was immediately acknowledged by Mom. Within twenty seconds the robot had replaced the bottle with a fresh one.

"He doesn't look good," commented Rogers. "I think—"

"It's just the anesthetic. Don't think that he's dying."

Rogers shook his head. "Why can't Mom just take that thing off him? Look at that—just look and think about what that must be like."

Foster's eyes were half-open, but glazed and obviously unaware. His dead-white arms were strapped to the steel table so he wouldn't injure himself. On his exposed right thigh crouched an earth-colored lump about the size of a golf ball.

Faint red lines traced up his leg from the insect, showing where its feeding apparatuses had crawled inside his arteries.

"Mom can't just pull it off," explained Beckwith. "See those cilia, those hair-like things around the base of it? If we even touch the carapace, it injects toxins." His neck twinged again, a twinge of guilt. He shook his head dismally. "I warned him, I warned them all not to use repellent that first day."

He should have worked harder to impress his theory upon the crew, but he hadn't known with certainty what would happen. How could he have known? He squirmed inside his ill-fitting pressure suit. He rubbed the painful, itching knuckles of his left hand against the underside of the operating table, feeling the stiff fabric of his glove rasp on swollen flesh.

"I still don't understand why the repellents didn't—" began Rogers.

"The repellents *did* work," snapped Beckwith. The captain was a fool, and Beckwith had little patience for fools. "As I tried to explain, the insects here have evolved to attack any creature bearing some sort of chemical defense against them. That's partially why they're in such a dominant position in the ecological system."

He recalled the way the insects had swarmed in reaction to the repellents. In seconds, five crewmen had become man-shaped mounds of biting insects. Dr. Beckwith had noted that several species had swarmed in unison. There had been blue, wasp-like creatures, about the size of a man's index finger, with curved retractable stingers of shiny, black chitin. He remembered a double-winged variety of the flying spiders as well. Even a few of the crab-sized beetles that lived in the mossy undergrowth had joined in the attack. The crewmen had screamed and stumbled blindly about like men engulfed in flames. Beckwith had been quite shocked. It was very rare to have several species combine their efforts in such a manner.

"So you're telling me that I didn't get attacked because I *wasn't* wearing repellent?" asked Rogers.

"Correct."

"Huh," grunted Rogers. He changed the subject. "Couldn't we just..." He made a hacking motion in the air with his gloved hand.

"Amputate? No—we don't have the equipment for that here..." Beckwith stopped, remembering that he didn't want to give Rogers any excuses to leave Jade ahead of schedule. He made a nervous fluttering gesture with his hands. "Well, of course, we *could* do it, but the insect's, ah—feeding tubes extend up the femoral to his heart, and..." He shook his head and then added a lie. "I don't think any medical facility could ensure the patient's survival during such an operation."

For a minute or so they quietly watched Mom perform her duties. Mom clicked and whirred steadily, simultaneously monitoring Foster's pulse, breath rate, temperature, and neural responsiveness. They watched as the machine gave her patient an injection. One of Mom's three appendages slid open a compartment, and a needle with a tube attached came out of it. The skin of Foster's upper arm dimpled inward, and the drug pumped into his bloodstream under measured pressure.

"That bug—it doesn't really look like a bug. It's too big," Rogers said. Beckwith noted the familiar tone of disgusted fascination in his voice—the tone non-biologists always used when discussing insects. "It looks more like a hermit crab, maybe, but with a tougher shell."

Beckwith decided to try again to impress the captain with the importance of the mission. He had tried many times in the past few days, and he knew he had begun to annoy Rogers with the point, but he had to try again.

"As horrible as it is, Captain," he began, making an effort to start from a point that the man could understand, "and it is a terrible thing, I agree... but the mere fact that these insects can coexist with us, with human beings, is actually a great discovery."

Rogers made a dismissing gesture. "Yes, yes, I know. Their proteins—"

"That's it exactly, Captain," interrupted Beckwith, unable to contain himself. He rubbed the joints and flesh of his left hand, letting the rough fabric of his pressure suit do the scratching for him. "The proteins. Of all the thousands of molecular structures for proteins life can take, Earth has evolved only a few—"

"And this planet has more or less the same set," Rogers finished for him. "I told you I know."

Beckwith was not to be stifled, however. "Jade is, *in fact*, the only planet yet to be found that has organic compounds so closely compatible with ours. Think of it! Men can live here without being poisoned by every living thing they come in contact with. You can roast a bird or dig up a root and chew on it without expecting a dozen fatal allergic reactions."

Inside his suit, Beckwith thought about it, and his face twisted with a grin. Just a little adapting to be done, and then an entire planet waited to be molded into a new world. A million new species of life to study in the field. A biologist's dream.

Bleep, bleep. Mom applied a tiny amount of pressure to the doctor's ankles with a foam-padded fender. Startled, Beckwith hopped out of her way and let the machine pass.

"You're talking about colonization, Beckwith."

"Yes, certainly," he replied, steeling himself for another round of an old argument.

"But colonization on any realistically large scale is impractical. Everyone knows that."

"Wrong. Everyone is *told* that. And they are told that because there has never been a planet suitable for mass colonization." Here Rogers started to retort, but Beckwith overrode him, unusually assertive due to his excited state. "Of course there are miners on several high-ore planets and numerous scientific stations and outposts strung out within thirty light-years of Earth. There even a few large stations on bleak rocks called colonies." He paused to drag in a gasp of breath. "But there is *nothing* compared to what Jade could become."

"Look, Beckwith," said Rogers, turning to face him squarely. A large gloved finger extended toward the doctor's faceplate, jabbing at him in time with Rogers's words. "I know how important this discovery is, and I know how much you need to complete your tests—to get your proof—but I have a mission to run. Out of a crew of eight, you and I are the only men still standing—"

"But without conclusive proof, we'll have trouble getting a fully equipped survey vessel to come out here."

"And with a dead crew, doctor, Earth would never learn about this planet to begin with. Besides, I find it difficult to believe that if you bring back enough samples, Earth labs couldn't come to the same conclusions that you have just as quickly. I am beginning to believe that you want to hog the credit for the discovery."

Beckwith shook his head vehemently. "False, sir. Positively false. Personal notoriety is my last concern," he lied. He quickly decided that he'd better switch the topic of the discussion to something else. Rogers was quite correct about not needing to collect additional samples to prove that the proteins were compatible. But Beckwith had another reason for waiting. A vital reason. "Besides which, we now are out of reach of the insects and are in no further danger. There is no reason to leave prematurely."

"I do not relish the idea spending another several weeks living inside this pressure suit. With only two of us left, the grounds for aborting the mission are surpassed. We're leaving as soon as we stow the equipment."

Dr. Beckwith shook his head sharply inside his helmet. A droplet of sweat flew from his forehead and struck the inside of his quartz faceplate. His neck muscles pulled and twinged violently. He wanted to tell the captain why they didn't need to leave. He was all but bursting with the facts, but he contained himself. He knew that the truth would be misunderstood, that it would get him nowhere. He said nothing.

Thirty-one hours later, Dr. Beckwith and Captain Rogers were working outside the ship. They had stowed approximately three-quarters of the scientific equipment and supplies. Dr. Beckwith looked up through the shielded faceplate of his helmet. The shimmering image of the K-class star overhead burned purple blotches in his retinas and glowed on his eyelids when he blinked. They would be finished before nightfall, which was less than nine hours away. He knew that if he was going to act, it must be soon.

He removed his helmet. Rogers was safely out of sight, packing the meteorological mini-lab on the other side of the ship. With his helmet off, the world he had watched from the inside of it came to full color and life. It took a few moments for his eyes to adjust to Jade's daytime glare. His other senses, too, were overwhelmed by the surging, frothing ocean of life that assaulted them.

A hundred as-yet-unclassified beasts roared, screamed, and growled, sounding as if they crouched behind every bush. Flying, cold-blooded, bat-like creatures screeched in the trees, and unseen things rustled under moldering leaves. The air was heavy with odors that seemed particularly powerful to him. He'd had nothing to smell other than his own moist body trapped in his pressure suit for days. His nose detected rotting fruit, various types of dung, and a pleasant scent like that of crushed grass mingled with the smell of danker vegetation. When the ship landed it had burned a steaming wound in the foliage, and the smell of it still hung in the air. Dr. Beckwith stood in the midst of this black wound, but he hardly noticed it. His eyes were only focused on the vibrant forest that engulfed him and his tiny ship. He filled his lungs with the cleansing, oxygen-rich air.

He watched as an animal about the weight and height of a large dog investigated the unprecedented phenomenon of open ground. It sniffed with an elongated trunk-like protuberance at a blackened and twisted plant. Fires were rare things on Jade's wet surface. The creature acted uncertain and cautious. Dr. Beckwith watched quietly as it tested the air and picked at clods of blackened ground.

Like all the animals that had been discovered on Jade thus far, it lacked fur of any kind. Dr. Beckwith had speculated that furred creatures had probably died out because of the prevalence of parasites: on Jade, fur did little other than provide homes for insects. Instead, the animal had a tough hide of layered, armor-like gray skin, similar to that of Earth's rhinoceros. Parasites resembling barnacles were visible on one of its flanks and in clusters about its throat.

Dr. Beckwith took an immediate interest in the insects it carried. He did not recognize the species. He pondered killing the animal and examining them. He fingered the pistol on his hip, but rejected the idea. There was no more time.

He set down his helmet and began searching a rubbish pile of scorched bushes and trash from the ship. He found it difficult to use his left hand, as it was now stiff and throbbing all the way up to his elbow. Fortunately, he believed it had now reached its worst stage and would soon begin to heal. He dug through discarded cartons and used bits of plastic that held pockets of wriggling larvae. When he moved the cartons, one of them broke, and he found himself holding two moving handfuls of pinkish scavenging insects about the size of twelve-year molars. Finding them to be of a familiar species, he shook them unconcernedly from his gloves and continued his search. At last he found what he was looking for: a hefty length of steel-plex with a solid core.

Holding the piece of steel-plex like a club, Beckwith approached the hull of the ship. He stood before the microwave navigational sensor. The sensor was a four-pointed dish with gold foil wrapped around it. The delicate instrument was presently exposed in its pod, as Captain Rogers planned to check it before liftoff.

Dr. Beckwith had discarded his helmet, but not his radio headset. He had only to speak to be heard by Rogers.

"Captain, could you give me a hand with this?"

"With what?"

"One of my experiments. I need your help to get it aboard."

He heard Rogers sigh. It sounded like a windstorm over the mike. "Shit. All right, sure."

Dr. Beckwith glanced about furtively before beginning. He felt a slight movement in the humid air, not quite enough to be called a breeze. It touched and cooled the sweat on his brow and lifted a few locks of his hair. To have this world, to live in the open on Jade as men should, was something that he knew would mean much to his race.

He patted the comforting bulge in his suit's hip pocket. He had to do this right. Rogers was not going to give him a second chance.

Delaying no longer, he raised his improvised club and crashed it down into the delicate navigational sensor. Gold foil bent and tore. Steel-plex clanged against real metal. The force of the blow jarred his slight body. He jerked his club loose from the tangled ruin and struck again. Copper-trace circuits and microprocessors were smashed to fragments.

There was a shout in his earphones—Rogers had come around the corner of the ship. Beckwith paid no heed and struck again. Fresh beads of sweat welled up on his forehead and clung to his skin. His left hand throbbed, but he continued to destroy the sensor.

"What the hell—" yelled Rogers as he came closer. Dr. Beckwith could hear his labored breathing as he trotted over to him in his heavy suit. "I've got my needler on you, Beckwith!"

Dr. Beckwith took another swing, missing clumsily this time, managing only to gouge the protective plate that covered the sensor when it was not in use. His left arm was giving out, becoming useless. He ignored Rogers's approach, keeping his back to the man. He gambled that Rogers wouldn't burn down a lunatic with his back turned to him.

"You're crazy!" buzzed his earphones. "You're absolutely, goddamn crazy!"

Dr. Beckwith was relieved when he found Rogers's powerful hands wrapping around him. He was yanked back from the crumpled sensor. There was a brief struggle for possession of the steel-plex club. Dr. Beckwith kicked and twisted. Both men were hampered by their pressure-suits, Rogers having the added handicap of wearing a helmet. Finally, Rogers simply grappled with the smaller man, wrapping him up in a powerful bear hug. He managed to restrain Beckwith's flailing limbs. It was precisely this proximity that Beckwith had been waiting for.

Rogers's powerful arms hugged his shoulders, but that didn't stop Dr. Beckwith from slipping the hypodermic he had gotten from Mom out of his pocket. If he had tried to sneak up on Rogers, the man might have seen the hypodermic and stopped him. But now Rogers had no chance. With an underhand thrust, Beckwith stabbed the needle through the tough layers of fabric and into Rogers's solar plexus. The pliant bulb at the other end pumped automatically, injecting its contents in rhythmic surges, like the poison sacs of a wasp.

Captain Rogers folded like a popped balloon.

* * *

The day of the liftoff was unbearably hot. Jade had transformed into a wet green hell. Perspiration itched as it flowed out of Dr. Beckwith's pores to run in tiny streams down his body. He stood in a clearing he had burned in the jungle with his needler, several hundred meters from the ship. He had stacked a considerable store of survival equipment and medical supplies in the clearing. Included in the equipment were two cots, an air-conditioned tent, and the nursing unit, Mom. Dr. Beckwith wished only to maroon the two men, not murder them.

"It's all very simple," he explained. "I, as a biologist, understood it almost immediately."

There was no response. Neither of his two listeners was capable of making one. Both Rogers and Foster were strapped to their cots and gagged. Beckwith had gagged them after tiring of their endless threats, pleas, and complaints. Mom moved between them, attending faithfully to the needs of her patients. The left hands of both were in restraining casts of fiberglass. Their fingers, protruding from the casts, were red and swollen as if infected.

They were, in fact, *infested.*

Enjoying the coolness of the air-conditioned tent and the novelty of an attentive audience, Beckwith lectured on. "Because of Jade's parasitic ecological system, it is simply a requirement for all its native life forms to maintain a personal colony of one of the more dominant species of insect. You see, you need them here, for your own protection. One colony of a more easily endured species will keep other, more harmful types at bay.

"That is just how I got rid of the particularly malevolent insect that had you in its death grip, Paul. All that was necessary was the introduction of another species to get it to retreat."

In order to continue his lecture, Dr. Beckwith needed a model. He removed his glove and carefully rolled up his sleeve, as though peeling a delicate fruit. His left arm had healed almost completely, and it looked puffy and sore only around his knuckles.

He took a pen out of his breast pocket and used it as a pointer while he talked. "You see, the particular species that seems easiest to live with requires certain compounds, such as calcium, that are most easily reached at the joints." Here he indicated his swollen knuckles with the tip of his pen. "Since the hand has many accessible joints just below the skin, it is an ideal breeding site for them."

Scurrying creatures resembling fleas the size of small sow bugs moved about on his arm, making their way through his body hair as men travel through bushes. The holes they had burrowed in his flesh to get to the joints of his hands were in the process of healing into permanent scar tissue.

"Now, of course, I simply leave appropriate amounts of calcium powder around the area, so that they no longer irritate the flesh and joints."

Dr. Beckwith concluded his lecture and saw to it that Mom had things well in control and was programmed to release her wards after liftoff. He left the coolness of the survival tent and headed for the ship. All around him the green flames of Jade's countless leafy plants burned brightly with life. He almost envied the men he was abandoning and the freedom they would have here. He knew that they would not agree with his feelings, but he had to leave them. He would be incinerated as a mutineer if he returned to Earth with them. He preferred to be the sole heroic explorer bringing the wonderful news concerning Jade.

He replaced the damaged microwave navigational sensor with an auxiliary unit, then began powering up the ship for liftoff. While he searched a manual for the proper control sequence to operate the ship's stabilizing computer, an exploring insect on a scouting mission rustled its way out of his hair. It came out beneath his ear and made its way up his cheek. He felt its numerous churning feet grip his face and its feelers making feather-light contact with his skin. He held still while it investigated his eyelashes. After a few moments, the insect crawled down across his mouth and along his neck to disappear under his collar line.

He wondered if his fellow Earth-born men would put up with that sort of thing. A twist of cold fear touched his stomach; what if men refused to come to such a place? But then he relaxed and smiled. He was confident that once Earth's colonization companies had an organically compatible planet to send people to, careful advertising would omit such nasty details. The promise of a jungle paradise with an open sky overhead, instead of a filtered environment beneath a dead gray dome, would be irresistible.

They would come. Others would adjust to Jade just as he had. Adaptability was one of mankind's greatest survival traits.

And of course, there was nowhere else to go.

He finished with the manual and set the ship into motion. Bass-voiced jets rumbled as the ship rose through the atmosphere. Dr. Beckwith watched the aft view of Jade as it telescoped rapidly. The freshly scorched clearing shrank to a black dot swimming in a green sea. Finally, it vanished as if swallowed by a wave.

Something tickled among the hairs of Dr. Beckwith's armpit. He found it difficult to ignore. He made a mental note to develop some sort of skin desensitizer for the comfort of the new immigrants.

About B. V. Larson

B. V. Larson is the bestselling author of more than thirty novels, many of which have reached the Amazon/Kindle Top 100 bestseller list. He writes in several genres, spanning from military science fiction to epic fantasy.

As a California native, B. V. Larson writes stories that often take place on sunny beaches and in cities such as Las Vegas. He has three kids living at home and currently teaches college. He writes college textbooks as well as fiction.

For more information check out his home page at BVLarson.com.

Hanging with Humans
by Patrice Fitzgerald

Planet Zeldar

"LADIES, GENTLEMEN, AND QUALTRIDS, welcome to today's live broadcast! Here at *The Zeldar Show*, we know how to entertain. I'm your host, Trazil Krang, and I've been voted Funnest Guy in the Galaxy five years in a row. So be ready for some fun! Every day a different planet, and every day a different willing victim. Ahem... I mean, contestant!"

[Laughter]

"Let's jump right in and introduce you to today's new player. Please welcome Glendorp Freundzap!"

[Applause]

Glendorp appears, wearing purple and orange shorts on all twelve legs.

"Ha ha! Glendorp here is a real snappy dresser, isn't he, folks? But we're going to put him into another shape altogether for his trip down to the third planet in a system far away from here. And you can't believe what they look like there!"

Live feed from game destination planet opens. Bipeds appear.

"Isn't that amazing? They're a funny-looking group of aliens, am I right? Hard to imagine we could get Glendorp here to fit in with this hairy two-legged crowd, but we will! We spare no expense on *The Zeldar Show* to bring you the best in intergalactic adventures. Now, let's send our contestant out of the studio so he can get ready."

Glendorp exits.

"Okay, folks, here comes the best part. What our friend Glendorp doesn't know is that he won't be the only Zeldarian down on what they call 'Earth.' We're sending our special guest star Kalacha Swanssa to join him... and she's going to be his target 'Earthling.' Here's Kalacha now."

Kalacha appears, and she is smoking. Literally.

"So, Kalacha darling, what do you plan to do while you're down there?"

"Trazil, I'm going to do whatever the audience tells me to do. And that may include creating some problems for today's contestant."

[Laughter]

"Sounds like fun, Kalacha! All right, let's send you back out of the studio so he doesn't see you... There you go darling... Isn't she something, folks? She'll come back to us in Earthling form in just a minute, but first let's say hello and goodbye to Glendorp as he takes off for the alien planet where he'll spend this episode. Come right down here beside me, Glendorp. There you go."

[Laughter]

"Okay, let's see you up close. Wow. What a transformation! So that's what their heads look like. With all that stuff on top—what is it? Some kind of vegetable matter? And only two eyes. A wonder they can see anything, am I right? So Glendorp, can you move comfortably in this get-up?"

"Sxmcntoatuhharipeipamia."

"Oh, sorry, folks—we've already equipped him with the translator. He's speaking the language of Earth. We won't be able to understand him until we have the language filter on. But he looks great, in a bizarre sort of way. And you can see he's got the transporter on his arm—*is* that an arm? I don't know! Funny color he is, too. Well, that's the way they look on this planet. What can you do?"

[Laughter]

"Off you go, Glendorp."

Glendorp disappears. Kalacha walks back on.

"Whoa, Kalacha! Even as an Earthling you look great. Or as great as an Earthling can look, am I right? So, I know you can't talk to us now, but you're clear on this mission: Glendorp is getting the chance to experience a typical Earthling rite of passage—going to a high school prom. And you're going to make sure you're the girl he asks. Then the fun begins! Are you all set?"

"Xmowerhhoipnbm."

"Whatever she said must be right, folks! So here you go, Kalacha. Have a great time, and may *The Zeldar Show* begin!"

* * *

Glendorp Freundzap found himself standing in a narrow room. It was dominated by metal boxes attached to the walls, and was otherwise empty apart from a bare wooden bench in front of him. He was compressed into an Earthling body and wearing a strap that ran around his middle and between his two lower appendages.

According to the brief orientation course he had been given, this was a place of education for young people here, and the item he was wearing was designed to cover the male Earthling's primary reproductive organ. The organ seemed extraordinarily vulnerable, hanging out the way it did.

He appeared to be alone in the room, but loud voices could be heard close by. To his relief, the automatic translator was working. Their words made sense, and he hoped that he, in turn, would be able to communicate with the denizens of this planet.

Six of them came around the corner, in much the same state of undress as him. One of them had on no clothing at all.

"Hey, it's the new guy," the unclothed one said.

"What's your name?" said another. "I'm Jake Bradshaw, and numbnuts here is Rich."

The Earthling reached out a hand in what Glendorp knew to be a gesture of greeting and welcome. He did his best to respond appropriately, stretching out his unfamiliar limb and working the digits.

"Glen... dorp." His name sounded funny in this language.

"Glen Dorp?" One of the guys slapped another one on the back. "Did you hear that, Krakowitsky? His name is even goofier than yours."

"Yeah, Krak, you're going to love this guy. Finally, someone else to slam in the name department." The fellow put his arm around Glendorp's shoulders. "Where you from, Dorp?"

The others laughed, and four of them turned to open the metal boxes behind them.

"I am from… Zeldar."

"Where the hell is Zeldar? Is that in Indiana? I think I knew a girl from there once."

"No, you idiot. It's in Illinois. You don't know any girls from Indiana. Girls run when they see you coming."

These creatures spoke very quickly. And moved quickly too. One of them took off the cloth wrapped around his loins and flung it toward another Earthling. There was some snapping of the strap that Glendorp was wearing around his middle, which hurt. He found himself shoved against one of the metal boxes on the wall, and he slid down to the chilly floor.

It was all very puzzling.

"Lay off him, you guys." Jake reached out a hand and helped raise Glendorp from the ground. "Stick with me, Dorp, and I'll protect you from these douchebags. We're about to go to lunch. Want to join us?"

"Yes. Thank you." Glendorp started to follow the two Earthlings who were ambulating toward the exit, but Jake stopped him.

"Hey, bro, don't forget your pants. I don't know how it is in Zeldar, but here in Iowa we wear pants to lunch."

* * *

Glendorp sat at the table with the group of males. He was having a hard time keeping up with the conversation while also ingesting nutrients. When he got back to Zeldar, he was going to mention to the game show people that a longer orientation period would be advisable. It was quite confusing to be in a new body, wearing unfamiliar vestments, dealing with an alien language, and also trying to accomplish the task of finding a "prom date."

Well, that's probably why they called it a game. No doubt it was more entertaining for the observers at home if the contestant was insufficiently prepared. Glendorp had never seen the show himself; it was his mother who had persuaded him to become a contestant. She watched *The Zeldar Show* every day, and had insisted he apply. Glendorp now realized that he may have made a mistake in avoiding the broadcast.

As he scooped up a desiccated potato slice and placed it in his mouth to masticate, he heard a strange sound coming from "Rich," the Earthling on his right. The noise was apparently made by forming the mouth into a tight round shape and pushing air through it with force.

"Don't whistle, you jerk. Chicks don't like that. They want somebody with class." Jake said. "Like me."

Jake stood up and spoke to the approaching female. "You're new, right? You must be, because I couldn't have missed a girl who looks as hot as you."

Glendorp noticed that Jake displayed his teeth after speaking to the female. This, he knew, was a traditional

Earthling means of indicating warmth, humor, or affection. Glendorp practiced displaying his teeth. The female looked at him.

Rich shoved his sharp arm bone into Glendorp's ribcage. "Introduce yourself," he mumbled, keeping his own teeth displayed. Glendorp wasn't sure how to do that, so he experimented with making the same sound that Rich had. He was pleased to successfully reproduce it on the first try.

The girl looked at him directly. He noted that she had some kind of shiny, colored substance on her talons. Perhaps this was a secondary sex characteristic of this species. None of the males at the table had colored talons. Glendorp wondered what evolutionary advantage it might provide.

Rich shook his head at Glendorp, then stood and extended his hand to the female. "I'm Rich, and this is Dorp. He's brand new too." The female merely stared back, saying nothing. "So... um... want to sit at our table? What's your name?"

The female placed her tray on the table and sat down between Glendorp and Rich. "I'm Kalacha. I am transfer student."

Glendorp noticed a peculiar difference in the behavior of the male Earthlings now that the female had come close. They seemed less inclined to talk to each other, their focus now entirely on this member of the female gender. He decided to take advantage of the gap in conversation to advance his task in the game.

"Kalacha. I am seeking a female to accompany me to the prom. Would you do so? I am prepared to supply you with sufficient nutrients beforehand and will be able to secure a vehicle for transportation to the event."

Kalacha turned to him. "Yes. I will go with you." She lifted her tray and displayed her teeth, then walked away from the table.

Rich opened his mouth. "You dog. And I thought you were slow."

Jake laughed. "Gotta hand it to you, Dorp, I didn't see that coming."

"Darn it! *I* was going to ask her to the prom," Rich said. "But I was going to use a little bit more finesse than that. Like, get to know her for an hour or so before springing it on her."

Jake punched Glendorp on the shoulder. "Well done, man. I would have asked her myself if I wasn't dating Samantha. Who would kill me, of course, if I didn't take her to the prom."

Rich was still shaking his head. "Dorp, you are unbelievable. Just cool as a cucumber, snatching the hot new girl out from under my nose on your first day."

Glendorp felt relieved. The first step had been taken. He had a date to the prom.

Jake leaned across Rich and spoke to Glendorp. "Listen, man, if you manage to bone her after the dance, I wanna hear all about it."

Glendorp did not respond, because he did not know what Jake meant. He would have to peruse the *Brief Guide to Earthlings* that had been given to him on Zeldar. Once he learned the meaning of the word "bone," perhaps he could attempt to achieve it.

* * *

"Ladies, gentlemen, and qualtrids, welcome back to our studio! You can see that Glendorp is having a fine time down on Earth, and has managed to ask a girl to the prom. Of course, *we* know it's the gorgeous Kalacha, a regular guest star on *The Zeldar Show*, but Glendorp doesn't know that! His mother persuaded him to audition for us, and he's never watched our show, can you believe it? Mom thinks it's time for him to mate, and you can't blame a mother for wanting little grandchildren… not to mention the awards and prize money! But I don't know if our friend Glendorp is quite ready for the finality of mating."

[Laughter]

"But before *you* mate, be sure to stock up on Femmelmeng's Interplanetary Chews! They fill you up and make you glow. Can't beat that. One of our favorite sponsors. Available in grass, pumpernickel, and diesel flavors. Get some today! On sale at your local galactic convenience shop.

[Applause]

Host pauses, cups hand around ear.

"Oh, pardon me folks, I've just heard from the engineers handling the feed from the far-flung planet we've chosen for this week's show. They're telling me that Glendorp has gotten himself into a bit of a dilemma down there. Let's zoom back in to see what's going on."

* * *

Glendorp was still getting used to the way this peculiar body walked. He was trying to move along at a typical Earthling gait when he heard people running up behind him.

It was three males he hadn't yet met. Or maybe he had. It was very difficult to tell them apart. One of these was quite a large specimen.

"Hey, Dorp," he said, stopping very close to Glendorp. "Where do you come off asking that new girl out? I saw her first."

Glendorp recognized the aggressive posturing as a threatening stance. He was, however, mystified as to where this attitude had originated.

"Pardon me?" he said. He was proud that he had learned this short phrase while looking at his language translation documentation during the afternoon class on calculus. It was apparently high on the politeness scale.

"Pardon me," the other boy said, in an apparent attempt to mock him. "Yeah, I'll pardon you, all right."

Glendorp put his hand out in the familiar welcoming gesture. "I am Glendorp."

"I'm Dwayne, you dorp." The large Earthling came at him and slapped his hand away. He raised both fists and began to pummel Glendorp rapidly. It hurt. This body was too soft.

Glendorp pondered his options. He didn't want to do what a Zeldarian would do in this situation. At least not yet. He wanted to follow the rules and win the game fair and square, by going to the prom with a girl he had asked. His mother would be so pleased if he won the prize. She would be able to move into a bigger place with all his younger siblings.

But being struck by Earthling limbs was very uncomfortable for the tender body he was temporarily housed in. Glendorp was still thinking hard about what to do when his new friends Jake and Rich came around the corner. They barreled right into the fight. Jake surprised Dwayne with a powerful punch to the jaw, while Rich grabbed Dwayne's arms from behind. The rest of the group backed off quickly. Soon Dwayne and his fellow Earthlings left, and Jake and Rich displayed their teeth to Glendorp.

Jake put an arm around Glendorp's shoulders. "We got your back, buddy," he said, which Glen understood to mean that they would help him. This was good to know, if he wanted to get Kalacha to the prom.

* * *

"Whoa, ladies, qualtrids, and gentlemen, did you see that? Our boy Glendorp was getting a plaff-kicking down on that planet, and he was rescued by some good Earthling buddies. Don't you think he's doing well?"

[Applause]

"So now we come to the audience interaction segment of the show—your favorite part, I know! You all remember how this works. Reach under your plaff holders and you'll find a razmagoo with three buttons. You can select number one, number grazlo, or number berg. Each time we take a vote, *your* decision will determine what happens next. Now, let's bring up our first set of options."

Host gestures to the screen behind him.

"Button number one: Glendorp's earthly transportation device breaks down on the way to the prom, and he never gets there. Mission definitely not accomplished."

[Laughter]

"Button number grazlo: he gets there, but he finds Kalacha at the prom with another guy! Oh, no! What will he do then?"

[Laughter]

"Finally, button number berg—and this one is a doozy. Glendorp and Kalacha make it to the prom, but then a small interstellar vehicle obliterates the entire planet. Wow!"

[Applause]

"All right... now's the time to vote. Take out your razmagoo and push one of the buttons. I can't wait to see what you'll decide for the fate of our boy down on Earth."

[Musical interlude]

Trazil points to the screen as the graph is unveiled.

"And... we have our answer! The vote goes to number grazlo. Glendorp reaches the prom and sees Kalacha there with another male. Uh oh! Watch out, Earthlings!"

* * *

Glendorp entered the school gym, dressed in stiff clothing. He was covered with many layers; it was apparently the traditional garb for such an occasion. He adjusted the piece of fabric that went around his imitation Earthling neck. It made it difficult to get oxygen into this odd body.

Across the room he spotted Kalacha. Somehow she had avoided wearing so many clothes. This was a peculiar differentiation between genders: the more formal the situation, the more the males wore, but the less the females wore. Glendorp could only speculate about how Earth's qualtrids must dress.

He wasn't certain if he should mention how he had attempted to pick up Kalacha at her place of residence, only to find that she had already left for the prom with someone else. Should he raise this point? He had no information to tell him what an appropriate Earthling reaction would be.

As Glendorp approached Kalacha, he noticed the crowd of Earthlings around her whispering. He was getting better at comprehending the language quickly, and could hear a few snatches of conversation.

"Is that the new guy?"

"I heard she said yes to two different boys! No class. People say she's from Indiana."

"Poor guy. Do you think there's gonna be a fight?"

"Yes! Fight. Fight. Fight!"

As the rhythmic chant was picked up by the small crowd, more and more individuals came over, attracted by the noise and the spectacle.

A circle formed around Glendorp, Kalacha, and her date. Glendorp realized that Kalacha's date was the same large Earthling who had assaulted him earlier. Dwayne, he had called himself.

"Hello, Dwayne," Glendorp said. "I thought that I was going to pick up Kalacha—"

A fist came flying at him, and a sharp pain exploded in his jaw. As he fell backward and onto the wooden gym floor amid gasps and screams from the girls, he mused to himself that the creatures on this planet were very quick to punch.

To his surprise, Kalacha immediately jumped on her date's back and began clawing at his face. She was incredibly strong for an Earthling, and soon she had used her colorful talons to pull off strings of flesh. Dwayne was howling, and then keening, and then blood was dripping from his head. He fell to the ground, his hands red from the carnage, and clutched what was left of his face.

The crowd that had surrounded the group with an air of eager anticipation reacted with horror. They backed away, both males and females screaming now, stampeding toward the exits.

Kalacha reached into Dwayne's chest and pulled out his heart, then tossed it, still thumping, onto the gym floor.

Glendorp was impressed. Here was an Earthling he could admire.

"Kalacha," he said, picking up the hot wet heart and giving it a lick, "I find you very appealing. I would like to bone you."

He was proud of himself for having employed his new vocabulary word at an appropriate time.

"Glendorp, I am also from Zeldar. How stupid are you?"

Glendorp considered this question. For a Zeldarian, he *was* pretty stupid. His mother often reminded him of this. But before he could respond, he noticed that Kalacha was smoking. And she was peeling off her Earthling disguise, revealing her scales and multiple eyes. What a lovely Zeldarian girl she was!

Glendorp glanced down once more at the Earthling, Dwayne. He was quite dead, and made a bloody mess on the gymnasium floor. For a moment Glendorp pondered what his responsibility was for cleaning it up.

Then he turned to Kalacha, now in all her scaly, smoking glory. "The answer to your question, Kalacha, is that I am 37% stupid. So my mother says."

Kalacha picked up the heart and took a bite. "Yummxmsubk," she said, having reverted to Zeldarian when her disguise—and its implanted translation device—were removed.

"I agree," said Glendorp, shucking off the uncomfortable fabric around his neck. Piece by piece he removed the formal Earth garb, and then the uncomfortable Earth skin, until at last he had returned to his normal appearance. It felt wonderful to be able to scratch his scales and stretch all his legs again.

"Earthlings are good eating," he said.

* * *

Glendorp and Kalacha relaxed on their plaffs in the high school gym, munching companionably on what was left of Dwayne's body. Glendorp found himself very glad that he had followed his mother's suggestion to audition for the show. Who could have imagined that he would end up on an exotic planet with the sexy star Kalacha, having a private feast of fresh alien while being watched by billions of Zeldarians back home?

The name Glendorp Freundzap would go down in history as someone who had ventured across the galaxy to Earth and managed to get to a high school prom, fistfights and all. He wouldn't be surprised if today's episode of *The Zeldar Show* turned out to be a popular one to replay at parties. It couldn't have ended in a more satisfying way. His mother would be so pleased! There would be money and prizes to spare.

Life was good.

Perhaps he was ready to mate at last. He, who had not even dated! His mother had always described him as a late bloomer. With a contented sigh, Glendorp realized that his time had come.

Emboldened by the privacy afforded by the empty gym, the deliciousness of young Earthling in his tummy, and the beauty of his companion, Glendorp reached over to tug on Kalacha's plaff.

She flared her third nostril alluringly. He basked in the knowledge that she returned his interest in mating. He couldn't remember ever being so happy.

A loud bang interrupted their idyll, as the double doors to the gym burst open. Men in matching outfits stormed in, carrying what must be weapons. As soon as the gang saw Glendorp and Kalacha, they skidded to a halt, their eyes bugging out, their expressions dumbfounded.

* * *

"Qualtrids and ladies and gentlemen! What have we here? A group of security men, apparently, coming in to molest our friends Glendorp and Kalacha—both looking pretty comfy now that they have taken off those ridiculous body disguises—

while they were in the midst of a romantic tryst, complete with fresh raw Earthling as entrée.

"You know what we do next. It's time for voting!"

[Applause]

"Number one: We yank our fellow Zeldarians back to safety right now and give Glendorp a nice fat prize, leaving this nasty planet to its own devices, or…"

Host points to the screen behind him.

"Number grazlo: Give Glendorp and Kalacha all the time they need to do away with these interlopers, or…"

The columns on the screen slide up and down as buttons are pushed.

"Number berg: We destroy this foolish planet and all the life on it."

[Laughter]

"Make your choice, folks. And we'll wait while the votes come in."

[Music]

Trazil points to the screen as the graph is unveiled.

"And here we have it! The winning scenario is number grazlo! A perfect choice. So back to Earth we go to see what happens next!

* * *

Glendorp got off his plaff and stood up on all twelve of his feet. He could see that the security men were terrified. Which was rather satisfying.

Little projectiles came zipping across the gym from their weapons, but they did no more than ping against his tough carapace and rebound off his scales. He pulled his protective membranes over the twenty-three eyes he didn't need, and turned the big red one toward Kalacha.

She was laughing. She headed right for the men, who scrambled backward, some dropping their projectile-spewing arms. Several of the Earthlings were vomiting, and the rest raced toward the door.

Kalacha picked up two of them and bit one in half, tossing the other over her head to Glendorp.

He was in love.

* * *

"Well, kind of a bloodbath down there, wouldn't you agree? Good thing these Earthling types don't have anything too significant in the way of interplanetary vehicles, or we'd be in trouble, eh?"

[Laughter]

"Or maybe not! Even if they could get here, I don't think they have it in them to do us any harm. A Zeldarian infant could outwit any one of them, am I right?"

[Laughter]

"So it looks like it's time to bring our successful contestant home, along with the beautiful Kalacha. What do you say, folks? Shall we pull them back up from this godforsaken outpost of a planet?"

[Applause]

Glendorp and Kalacha reappear in the studio.

[Waves of applause]

"Glendorp, my man! Well done down there. You went to the prom, you got the girl, and you had a hot meal of fresh Earthlings. How did it feel?"

Glendorp lets loose a mighty eructation, followed by a haze of yellow smoke.

"Actually, Trazil, the young Earthling was delicious, but those older guys... yuck. I think I have a little indigestion."

[Laughter]

"I can understand that, buddy. Ha! How many of them did you consume, Kalacha?"

"We ate about seven Earthlings each, Trazil."

Kalacha leans over and tilts her big red eye toward Glendorp.

"I was quite impressed with Glendorp's ability to consume. He will make a good mate, and produce healthy offspring."

"Did you hear that folks? Kalacha is going to mate with Glendorp. That means he not only gets the prize for accomplishing his task, he gets the bonus, which will, of course, go to his mother."

[Applause]

"Let's cue the music! Here comes the ceremony we've all been waiting for!"

Kalacha mounts Glendorp, inserting her boon into his plaff. A qualtrid slides onto the stage and wraps itself around the two of them until Kalacha detaches herself, still smoking.

[Applause]

"Let's bring out the money and wrap this episode up, folks! Any last words before we pull the plug, Glendorp?"

Glendorp turns to the audience.

"I want to thank my mother for encouraging me to appear on *The Zeldar Show*. Hi, Mom!"

He waves at the camera.

[Applause]

"It's been a dream come true to meet and mate with Kalacha. And I want to thank my father, too, who of course is no longer with us."

[Laughter]

"Glendorp, I never knew you were so funny!"

Kalacha flares her third nostril at Glendorp, and smoke drifts out.

[Applause]

"He's a charmer, am I right, folks? Our Glendorp is quite a guy, and I think he'll fertilize an impressive mess of beautiful little zygotes for Kalacha. So let's bring out the prizes for today's planetary adventure."

Two qualtrids come out from the wings, pushing a large cart covered with piles of gold.

[Applause]

"Here's your booty, my man. Glendorp Freundzap, congratulations on winning *The Zeldar Show!*"

Kalacha picks up Glendorp and eats him. She wipes her mouth.

"Yum! He was even more delicious than the Earthlings, Trazil."

[Laughter]

The qualtrids mop Glendorp leftovers off the floor.

"Okay, folks. We've come to the moment when we hit the final button on your razmagoo. This time, we're all pushing number berg, of course!

"Remember, I'm your host, Trazil Krang, the Funnest Guy in the Galaxy, and this has been today's episode of *The Zeldar Show*, brought to you by Femmelmeng's Interplanetary Chews. It's time to say goodbye, but before we go, here's the final word. You know the drill!"

Trazil spreads all seven arms wide as the audience joins him in shouting—

"BOOM!"

On the screen behind the host, the planet Earth comes back into focus, and then implodes in a haze of purple smoke.

[Applause]

A Word from Patrice Fitzgerald

Poor Glendorp! I had no idea that was going to happen to him. Sometimes a story takes the author by surprise as much as the reader.

I was so pleased to be invited to join these authors in another edition of *The Future Chronicles*. I was also part of *The Robot Chronicles*, which has been more successful than we dreamed it could be, and I'm thrilled to have the opportunity to write so many short stories and get them out to readers promptly.

We're lucky to be living in a time when such a variety of stories can be published. The digital revolution means that length is no object... everything from instant super-short stories to mega novels can be made available because there is such a low barrier to entry into the marketplace, in terms of both expense and accessibility. This is great for creativity. Write short, write long, write experimental... write anything! Then put it out there and see how readers respond.

About the Author

Patrice Fitzgerald is a writer/publisher/lawyer/opera diva. And a few other things. She's been happily indie published since Independence Day of 2011, and is thrilled that several of her stories have reached bestseller status.

If you're a *WOOL* fan, look for her *Karma of the Silo: the Collection*. Thriller readers will enjoy her novella AIRBORNE, part of Kindle Worlds—or may want to pick up RUNNING, a fast-paced drama with politics, suspense, and a little bit of sex.

Upcoming projects include a novella based on Hugh Howey's *Sand*, another set in the universe of Rysa Walker's *Chronos* (*Timebound*) series for Kindle Worlds, and Patrice's own dystopian saga about a post-apocalyptic island where the women are in charge and the men are auctioned off to the highest bidder.

Catch up with Patrice on Facebook under her own name or at her website, www.PatriceFitzgerald.com. She's always happy to hear from fans.

Emily May

by Moira Katson

THE *EMILY MAY* was a Class H freighter, old but tidy, in good repair, and not—Walther Junck assured Harry testily—related to the infamous ghost ship by anything other than an unfortunate coincidence in name. No, he did not know how there were two ships with the same relatively odd name; no, there were no unexplained deaths aboard the vessel; yes, his dealings were all legal.

While the *Emily May* radiated a homey and somewhat battered permanence, untroubled by time and money, Junck himself had the air of a man who was considerably less wealthy than he wished to be, and blamed his relative lack on his business associates. In five years of working for the man, Harry had never seen Junck in anything other than a rush to close yet another business deal—a deal which was invariably more important than his business with Harry. After thinking about it at length during the quiet hours of a trip from Essen to Bukhara, Harry still could not decide if this was because he was only a pilot on one of Junck's ships, or if Junck simply treated everyone with the same contempt.

Harry's main task was to pilot the *Emily May* through the tight turns, jumps, and gravity wells of League space. Anyone could handle a Class H on the long hauls between the outer planets, even handle an isolated gravity well or two—the autopilot would take care of most of it, anyway—but the close-set inner colonies required a finer touch, and that was what Harry had. His secondary task, as soon as the ship was set down, was to on-board and offload cargo, usually nothing more complicated than rolling barrels or carrying boxes; livestock, thankfully, was a rarity.

Salvage of other freighters made up only a small portion of their work. Wrecks were numerous—space being unspeakably hostile and the workings of a ship nearly always more complex and varied than the skills of the resident mechanic—but space was also vast. Even the relatively minuscule volume that made up the shipping and travel lanes was so large that hundreds of floating wrecks might glide by unseen in the endless night, thousands of kilometers out and obscured by the ripple of the ship's own warp signature, starlight too dim to glint off their hulls, a chorus of trills hastily cut off as the ship entered and exited proximity.

This, in Harry's opinion, was almost certainly where the legend of the *Emily May* had originated: an orphaned beep on a lonely watch, a likely-looking flicker out a window. Why *Emily May?* Call it a dream. Call the providence of Junck's oddly named ship the result of morbid humor on the part of its previous owner. The name would never be changed: Junck was too practical to waste time filing the necessary paperwork with the governments of a dozen planets, and he would own the ship until even regular, precise maintenance couldn't keep it running. Then he would scrap it for parts and, likely, write off the cash against measured depreciation in his ledger. Junck was like that.

More to the crew's advantage, Walther Junck rarely wasted time on salvage when there was a much more reliable living to be made unloading goods planet-side. This was fine by Harry. He never felt like he could move his hands properly in suit gloves, which bothered him more than he thought it should. And when Li and Maller volunteered for their present mission, Harry accepted gratefully.

They'd come across the wreck more or less where it was supposed to be, which was a nice piece of luck. No name printed on her, but a rough sketch of a line, pointed, fletched at one end; Maller called her *Arrow*, and the rest of them went with it. They would tow it straight to Luoyang, no need to pry open the hull and offload goods, so Li and Maller headed out to attach cables while Harry listened to their radio chatter and Hernandez paced. *Any patrol ships?* Hernandez was like that.

"Mr. Junck will have a legal writ for this," Harry said in weary response to the eighth iteration of the question. "You know that." It was true. Junck was fanatical about tracking ownership, filing salvage permits, and alerting the Well Guard of the nearest planets. It was one of his qualities that Harry liked, not least of all because it likely contributed to the *Emily May*'s small number of salvage operations.

A quality Harry liked less was the man's insistence on being called "Mr. Junck." He checked the logs, too. Nguyen had tried "our benevolent dictator" once. He got fired before the next mission. The ones who stuck around were the ones who could live with things like that; you couldn't live with that, you probably weren't cut out for the freighter life anyway.

"The ship is clean and he always gets the engine repairs, I say." Laurents, the mechanic, at a bar on some moon somewhere. "And no weird sex stuff. I'll call him Supreme Squidlord and Savior if he wants."

"...Squidlord?"

Hernandez, meanwhile, was not comforted by Harry's assessment. He continued to pace.

"Jesus, this is a wreck," came Maller's voice. "It's so rusted out I can't find anything to attach the damned cables to."

"Must be your side," came Li's voice. "Mine looks like the day it came out of the shop."

"You think something's rusting out the cargo hold?" Sudden panic. "Harry, there something hazardous in here?" Harry sat up. Hernandez stopped pacing.

"Mr. Junck didn't say. We can run a decontamination on you when you come in though, no problem."

"I better not get cancer off this job."

"You're not going to," Harry assured.

"I'd just better not, that's all." Except, two decontamination runs later—both clean, not a flicker of red—even Harry had to admit that Maller didn't look so good.

"Looks like you aged a year," Li said critically. "Get some freaking *sleep*."

"We good to go?" Hernandez, hanging out by the door. "This place creeps me out."

Harry headed back to the cockpit, the conversation fading as he went.

"You know this patch of nothing is the same as every other patch of nothing, right?"

"I dunno, maybe it's the ship. Full of dead people. I hate that."

"Space is full of dead people." Pause. Boots ringing on the metal floors as they went to the galley. "*Everywhere* is full of dead people. Everywhere there's people, anyway."

"Shut up."

Harry shook his head and slid the door half-closed behind him. They'd found the ship easily, drifting close to the target coordinates. They were behind schedule though, supposed to be in Luoyang on November fourth. Three days away, and there was no way Harry could get the trip below three-point-eight.

He sat back in his chair and frowned. They should have had enough time. In fact—he gnawed his lip—he was sure they *had* had enough time, and that was budgeting a standard five days, no shaved corners on the lane turns. He looked at the shipboard clock. He looked at his course. He looked at the manifest.

"No problem," he'd told Junck, a few days back, when he got the job. Was it possible he had miscalculated?

No, his mind insisted.

He must have missed their arrival date. Harry rested his forehead in the heel of one palm and started tapping out a message to Junck. *Shit.* Junck hated delays. It was why he and Harry worked so well together: no one else, no other captain, ran so precisely on time. Not a single captain Harry had ever met, beyond Harry himself, could tell their buyers when, to the minute, they'd hit orbit.

The secret was The Chart—meticulous, precisely kept, always by the pilot's chair. No one touched it but him: that was Harry's one rule, and he was otherwise easygoing enough that the crew happily acquiesced to this one odd eccentricity. The Chart itself was a promise to his mother, who had asked how long he'd be gone. She didn't understand the math, but Harry did. And so, each trip, he composed a chart of ship time and realtime: acceleration, deceleration, distance, jumps. Even the computers didn't calculate it so precisely—they knew only standard courses, and besides, a Class H like the *Emily May* wasn't likely to have a newer computer, nor did it have the energy to spare for calculating realtime ETAs. So for accuracy, there was only Harry's chart, and it was a damned sight better than what the other captains used. He stared at it now and tried to find the error.

"There a reason we're not moving?" Li, head stuck through the door.

"We're off schedule," Harry said, knowing his voice betrayed the depth of feeling and not being able to bear it alone.

"Well, sitting here won't help with that."

Harry stared at his calculations. Adrift. Something had come unanchored.

"Oh, come on—you were going to mess up eventually."

"I didn't mess up."

"It's right there, dumbass." Li's voice faded as she disappeared down the hallway, and Harry tossed a disgusted look at her retreating form, at the blond hair catching the low glints of shipboard lights.

"I didn't mess up."

"*Facts.*" He could hear her opening cupboards in the kitchen. "Let's get moving!"

Harry typed the coordinates in, then leaned over and adjusted the chart before he hit enter. Two days along standard acceleration-deceleration curves; one-point-seven-nine at standard warp, two-point-four minutes' drift with the jump. He watched the clock count up to the half, and hit enter.

Accurate to the second.

* * *

Walther Junck was not pleased.

"Three days behind schedule is not acceptable," the message read. "We will discuss your continued employment when you return." It was an empty threat and they both knew it. Harry was Junck's most reliable pilot by far, even if they counted in this incident. Still, it troubled him. He was halfway to the galley, needing somewhere to go and somewhere to be, when he stopped.

"*Three* days?" Very like Junck to make this more serious than it was. The freighter had been drifting for years, to hear Maller describe its condition; its buyers could wait an extra half-day. Harry busied himself with cooking. It would keep him from thinking about the fact that it was not like him to miscalculate, not at all. And it was not like him, either, to say the buyers could wait a bit.

* * *

Maller slept for ten hours and had to be woken for his watch by Hernandez pounding on the door. He took a plate of beans on his way to the little study off the cargo hold. He still didn't look all the way awake, and Harry watched him bump into the walls as he went.

"Are you sure those scans came back negative?" Laurents asked doubtfully.

"Yes."

"Maybe it's his heart or something," Hernandez suggested around a mouthful of beans. "What is he, sixty?"

"Thirty-two." Harry always knew how old the crew were.

"No way, he's got one foot in the grave."

"He's just tired," Li said. She didn't look entirely convinced, but when Maller called Harry down to the cargo hold later that watch, Harry had to admit the man looked better.

"All recovered?"

"Sure." He flashed his trademark smile, bright and roguish. It always made Harry wonder how Maller ended up here, on a lonely freighter. "Haven't been sleeping enough. Sorry, chief."

"Just as long as you're okay when we get back to Essen. Mr. Junck's not happy we're behind schedule." He'd be checking the logs very carefully after this flight, that was for sure. "So what'd you call me for?"

"Just something weird. Dunno what's up with the warp this time, but it's making a hell of a show. Go see." Maller had a love of everything space, from stars to warp ripples. Harry often looked up from a book to find that the man had installed himself in the co-pilot's chair with a mug of terrible coffee and was staring silently out the window. Harry had taken to calling him when they flew through something particularly lovely, and Maller returned the favor.

No one complained; everyone who worked the cargo routes was a bit weird. Li worked out obsessively, Hernandez went reclusive for days at a time, and Laurents sang. All the damned time, he sang. At least he had a good voice; Harry had never heard so much music in his life. In any case, sitting silently and watching warp ripples was about the most harmless habit one could hope for from a crewmember.

"So what's it doing?"

"Just watch."

Harry leaned against the doorway and watched out the back cargo window. The square of black flickered, a few stars wavering in the warp signature. Pretty enough, and Harry was about to thank Maller politely and walk away, when the silver bulk of the *Arrow's* port side, a bright anchor in the corner of the window, disappeared completely. Harry jumped and choked on his coffee, and Maller leaned in to look before laughing.

"Been doing that for about an hour now. Ever seen something like that?"

"… No." The ship flickered back into existence, and Harry tightened his fingers on the coffee cup. The next mouthful burned his throat, and he swallowed it down anyway. "Wait, did you see that?"

"What?" Maller, despite his quirks, was a good worker. He didn't look up from his scans.

"The lights just went on. I thought."

"On the *Arrow*?" Maller half-stood to peer around Harry.

"They're off now."

"The whole ship's been going in and out, it's not like seeing lights is any weirder."

"It's all weird," Harry said. The back of his neck was crawling. A flicker where the lights should be was, truth be told, more like a warp signature than the flickering ship. Maller was right, it shouldn't disturb him.

Was this a technical malfunction? He should stop the ship, stop it right now. There was only one way things turned out when machinery broke during warp. Harry should drop them into realtime travel; Junck would yell, but they'd both know Harry had done the right thing. Even the buyers would know.

Harry glanced at his watch. Already behind schedule… But if the equipment was breaking, and he'd never seen anything this weird in the warp signature, then—

An alarm interrupted his internal debate. Harry left his mug on Maller's desk and went sprinting for the cockpit.

"What's going on?"

"Autopilot isn't working." Hernandez slid out of the way to allow Harry to sit.

"Autopilot isn't *on* anymore."

"I took it off. But she's handling like a drunk pig."

Obstacles were coming up in the course. A planet and some moons. Harry began the swerve gently. There was nothing too difficult about piloting manually in warp. Even at those speeds, obstacles were few and far between. It was the stakes that got him. After a few hours of nothing, it was difficult to stay alert, and a collision at this speed...

Not worth it. Harry, like Junck, was cautious by nature.

To his horror, the *Emily May* refused to bank.

"Sir?"

Harry pulled the rudder farther. Nothing.

"*Sir?*"

"Working on it!" He slammed the rudder hard to port and the *Emily May* slid, back end slipping around until Harry jammed their speed up with shaking fingers and they shot off-course, forty-five degrees into the shipping lane, could only hope that no one else was there and Hernandez was holding on to a rail to steady himself while the ship shot into high gear.

"What the hell?" Harry heard from the galley; Li, scraping her chair back to come to the cockpit. Laurents's voice crackled on the comm:

"Sir? I think there's been a malfunction. The engines just went—"

"That was me, Laurents."

A pause.

"Are we all right?"

Harry steered them back onto course before answering. His heart was pounding in his chest, his mouth felt dry. So close; they had skirted the gravity well by a second, by half a second, by less than that. He had flown this ship for five years, and never once had she failed to listen to his commands.

"Check on steering," he said to Laurents, and then he rested his forehead on both fists and shook.

"What happened?" Hernandez asked.

"Yeah, what was that?" Li's angry footsteps halted. Harry could picture the scene: Hernandez, grey in the face, himself hunched over the piloting desk.

"Ship's not responding," Hernandez said finally, when Harry said nothing. "She won't steer."

"Christ." Li whistled between her teeth. "You gonna take us out of warp, sir?"

"We don't have time for that."

"Come on. You got us back ahead of schedule. Junck'll understand." Her voice was soft. "Mr. Junck," she corrected herself. "Sorry."

"We're not even close," Harry said. His eyes were closed.

"We're supposed to be there on the fourth, aren't we? Can't take more than five days to get there."

Harry picked his head up. 21:35:59, October 30. He stared. The numbers stared back. He looked at his chart. He looked at the clock. He pulled up Junck's last transmission. The time signature flashed at the bottom: 12:45:32, November 3.

Harry looked over at Hernandez, who came to bend over the desk. His eyes narrowed.

"That's weird."

"It's not weird," Harry said, a bit desperately. Over his shoulder, Li was looking at the chart.

"You said you didn't mess up," she said slowly.

"He did mess up." Hernandez snapped. "Look, here's your problem. By this, it took two and a half *days* to salvage the *Arrow*. You know that's not right."

"You saw Junck's transmission," Harry told him.

"Computer glitch."

Boots sounded on the floor, and Maller popped his head around the door.

"I told Laurents I'd come see what the fuss was all about."

"You've got three more hours on your shift," Li said, annoyed.

"No, I don't." Maller looked at her cheerfully. "Time's been dragging. I watched that clock like it was my job."

"So go *do* your job."

"Oh, come on, it's 0220 at least—" His voice trailed off when he saw the clock. "I must have been wrong. Should I tell Laurents everything's fine?"

"Harry," Li said. She was staring at the chart, and her lip was red and swollen where she'd been chewing on it. "We have to find out what's on that ship."

"What?" Harry and Hernandez looked up, and Maller's departure halted.

"When did things start going wrong? When we picked it up."

"Any of a million things could be wrong with our shipboard computers."

"It's not those. It's everything. Maller said the ship was all rusted out, but you can see it out the back window, Harry, it's not rusted at all."

"What are you suggesting?" he asked her, and she shook her head.

"All I'm saying is, something's wrong."

* * *

Harry took Laurents, because no one would let him go alone and no one wanted to go. They all volunteered awkwardly, until Laurents said, with his characteristic shrug, "I'm good with machines. If something goes wrong in there, I'm the best one to help."

So off they went, suits close and confining on their bodies and their breath echoing in their ears, hand over hand down the cables to the hull of the *Arrow*. No one mentioned that Junck's manifest said to tow the ship and deliver it intact; there was the sense of hovering on a precipice. Of just how big the black was outside the window.

Both of them turned slowly before entering the *Arrow's* airlock, a visual check for an airtight suit. Who knew what was in there?

"You sure you want to do this?" Harry asked Laurents. He knew the crew was listening over the radio, but no one spoke. Laurents paused to consider.

"Yeah."

"Okay." Harry turned the manual crank and the airlock shot open. No loss of pressurization, but that could be good or bad. They switched on their helmet lights and drifted inside, through the airlock to the docking bay. It took a few minutes of Laurents fiddling with the locks, and then they were into the body of the ship, heading aft for the cargo bay.

The ship was disturbingly quiet. Whoever had been there once, there were no bodies to see now. No stains on the walls. No carbon streaking. Whatever had happened here, it happened quietly. That did not make Harry feel any better.

The cargo bay was, by volume, at least half of the ship. The passageways opened abruptly into a vast blackness, and they swung their heads side to side.

There was no doubt about what they were looking for—the machine was huge. It was moving slowly, shafts and cogs turning, a low hum coming from its insides. The closer Harry moved, the deeper the vibration went into his bones. It took up nearly all of the cargo hold, and Laurents whistled low between his teeth.

"Now, *that*…"

"What does it do?"

"I don't have any idea. I don't even know how it's still running. Ship's gotta have been here for what, twenty years at least?" Legal salvage rules. Harry nodded. "But this is running like new. Just slow, but look at it. No grease, nothing's hitched up or squeaking. There's a computer in there somewhere."

"How do you know?"

"Not sure. Things look different when they're *all* mechanical. I like them better that way. Less likely to get fucked up and send you into a planet. This, though…"

"Can I touch it?" Harry held out his hand, fingers clenched in the suit gloves. Laurents waved a meter and frowned at the readings.

"Uh. Sure."

It was as Harry touched it that it began to whir. Cogs clicked together more sweetly. It was not revving up for anything in particular, he sensed. It was almost as if it was pleased to have company.

"What's it doing?"

"Well, to be honest…" Laurents handed the meter over. "It seems like it isn't doing anything at all. It's got no readings. Not outputting anything."

He was right: all the dials rested at zero. The meter in Harry's other hand, testing the air for poisons and residues, was standing at normal levels. There was nothing unusual here at all. He sighed.

"Let's get back to the ship."

"But this thing—"

"Is none of our business. We're cargo runners, Laurents."

"Fine." Laurents pushed off to follow Harry up to the corridors again. "Maybe I should go work for whoever's buying this."

"Funny."

"I'm just saying." They drifted through the airlock, and Harry carefully moved the door back into place. He was twisting the lock when he realized that Laurents was hardly breathing.

"You okay?"

"Harry," Laurents said. He was looking up at the *Emily May*. "Look. At the window."

Harry had to squint to make it out. Li was watching for them. For a moment he didn't notice it, then he saw what

Laurents meant: Li was not just still, waiting for them. She was frozen entirely, a lock of hair across her face and her hand half-raised to brush it away. They stared, Laurents and Harry together, and Li did not move. If she saw them, she gave no sign of it. The lock of hair, across her eye and her nose, did not fall back to the side of her face. Her hand did not tuck it behind her ear.

So they hung, frozen in the black, watching Li, turning to look at one another. A silent communion: *Are you seeing this? Is it still happening?*

And then the moment passed, the hand moved and tucked the lock of hair behind her ear, and Li waved at the two of them.

"Jesus fucking Christ," Laurents said softly, but he raised his arm and waved back.

* * *

"So what was in there?"

"A machine. Not sure what for, but the readings are fine." Harry stripped off the gloves gratefully and stepped out of his suit. He flexed his fingers and looked over at Laurents, who was not meeting his eyes.

"So the problems…"

"Are internal, whatever they are." Not heartening, but at least understandable. "I need you to go send a transmission. Say we're having shipboard computer failure and steering problems, and we'll be dropping out of warp as soon as we can get to the edge of the lane. I'll be up in a moment."

"Sure." She disappeared up the metal stairs and Laurents looked after her.

"I saw that, right?" he asked finally. "You saw it too. She wasn't moving."

"Yeah, I saw it."

"Harry." Laurents was staring at him, skin greyish in the bay lights.

"I know. But right now what we gotta do is get this ship out of warp and wait for someone to come pick us up. Whatever the hell is going on, I don't want it going on at these speeds."

"Harry, it's not going to help."

"Laurents—"

"Uh, Harry?" Li's voice, booming over the comms. "I think you'd better come see this."

Proximity alerts were going full bore when Harry reached the cockpit. He reached over and switched off the sound as Laurent came crashing through the door behind him, but neither Li nor Hernandez paid much notice; they were both craning out the window.

"What is it?"

"Another ship. I think. It's *right* on top of us." Hernandez levered himself up on the navigation desk and Li braced him; Harry watched the boots on his chart and said nothing at all.

"Can you see anything?" Li asked.

"Class H, but I can't tell any more than that. Literally, *right* on top of us."

"When did it sneak up?" Harry pulled his chair out and slumped into it.

"That's the thing." Li helped Hernandez down. Her face was all screwed up. "Came out of fucking nowhere. I mean it. Nothing anywhere, then bam. Right there."

"Has it done anything hostile?"

"Not unless you think riding our roof close to a jump point is hostile."

"Shiiiiit." Hernandez breathed out the word, turned the computer. "We got ten minutes to get rid of them."

"That might not be enough." Harry calculated in his head, scanned the screens. "We need to drop back hard, start going the other way."

"No way. We're gonna run into someone."

"We *might* run into someone," Harry corrected. "Or we *will* get blown the hell up. Or blow them up."

"I vote we blow them up," Li said.

"Real nice," Hernandez shot back.

"Do you have a better plan? We hit the jump fifteen seconds before prime range, still within limits, they get blown up because they're the ones that showed up out of nowhere. You said ten minutes, right?"

"It's twenty," Harry said absently. He was plotting a spin.

"No way. It's ten, I looked." Hernandez curved over the screen to look. "No shit. It said ten."

"It didn't." Li rolled her eyes.

"No, it did!" He rounded on her. "It did say ten. Why's it got twenty now?"

Harry looked up at him, then back to the clock.

23:54 stared at him. He blinked. The red vanished from the screen next to him.

"What the hell?" Li was staring up at the window. "Harry, it's gone."

"It can't just be gone," Hernandez snapped.

"Well, a few minutes ago you were saying it couldn't just be *there*—"

"Shut up, both of you." Harry moved to peer out the windows. Nothing.

The proximity alert sounded again; they all winced.

"I don't fucking believe this." Li, standing on tiptoe and peering down. "It's another freighter. It's riding kind of to port. Right up on us."

"Okay, that one I *saw* come out of nowhere. You better keep plotting that turn." Hernandez looked over. He was a bit green, and Harry could only stare at him.

"What?"

In answer, Harry turned the clock to face them.

1:21:29.

"What the…" Li looked at Harry, looked at Hernandez. "You couldn't be that far wrong. You two can read, right?" A bad joke. No one laughed.

"Try hailing them," Hernandez suggested, and Harry flipped the radio button on.

"This is the *Emily May*. Request you adjust course five kilometers starboard, to…"

"They're gone again." Li was shivering convulsively.

"For the love of…" Harry sank his head into his hands, and, as if by providence, a voice crackled to life on their speakers.

"This is the *Emily May*. Request you adjust course five kilometers—" The voice fuzzed out. They looked at one another. It couldn't be.

"*Emily May*," Harry said, as calmly as he could. His stomach churned. "This is also the *Emily May*. Request clarification. Our course was filed three weeks ago. Why are you in our lane?" He flipped the radio button off. "Okay, listen. There's the legend of the ghost ship, isn't there? That means there's another *Emily May* out there. They saw us, saw our lane call, whatever—they're having some fun. We all need to calm down."

"Harry, that was *you* on the other end." Maller looked like he was going to throw up.

"It wasn't me," Harry said impatiently. "It can't be me, I'm standing right here."

"Not you now, you thirty seconds ago."

"Harry...?" Li's question was a breath. She was looking up, out the window. "Oh, my god..."

"What—"

But in another moment, he saw precisely what: the ship gliding overhead was a Class H freighter. A dent near the tail where Hernandez had set down on unstable ground. The serial number, painted on the bottom and slanted on the side. And trailing behind, towed on long steel cables, a slender ship with an arrow painted on the side.

They stared. There was nothing else to do but stare.

"That's what it's doing," Laurent said softly. "That machine. The artifact. It's warping *time*."

"It can't be." The words were only a reflex.

A proximity alert, sudden and blaring. The ship shot through their path, skewing sideways into the lane, its back end ruptured and smoking. Crystallized air poured out the back, and debris hit the windows a second later. Cracks spider-webbed out as Harry swerved up, over the second hunks of metal: the back end of a ship, towing cables…

"Jesus!" Hernandez had stumbled against the desk, and he pulled himself to his feet with a grimace. Blood was pouring down the side of his face. "That was *us!*"

Li pushed her way through the group and made for the stairs, breaking into a run when her boots hit the metal grating.

"Where are you going?" Harry called, and she cast a look over her shoulder, half desperate and half determined.

"We have to cut it free." And she was gone, her boots pounding across the galley and toward the docking bay.

"Come on." Maller and Laurents left at a run, and Harry grabbed Hernandez before he could go, too.

"You stay. I need someone to look out and tell me where that damned ship is."

"They shouldn't go out there."

"Stay *here*," Harry snapped. "We need to get through this. Stop thinking crazy and tell me where the other ship is."

"You mean, where *we* are. Were."

"Shut up," Harry ordered. "Listen to me—we need to keep this ship flying free until those cables get cut, so you get a handle on yourself and stop getting up in your head. We can puzzle this shit out later. You got that?" Hernandez swallowed hard. Nodded. "Good. Now where's the ship?"

"Ahead, drifting to port."

"All right. You tell me if that changes."

"Harry, Li, and Maller are going out." Laurents's voice was carefully controlled. "I'm watching them from the window."

"Tell them to get a move on," Harry said. They would know. The words were only to make himself feel better, as if he had even the slightest amount of control over what was going on.

"They shouldn't have gone out," Hernandez said urgently. "They're going to die. That was us, Harry. The back end of the ship is going to rupture. They're going to die. We have to get them out of there."

"The back end of the ship goes, we're all dying," Harry snapped back. "We get what, three hours before the cold gets in? Our only hope of getting out of this mess before that happens is to cut that ship free, do you hear me?"

"It's *already* happened!"

"No. It *might* happen. If we aren't quick enough. Laurents, give me a status."

"Harry... they're frozen. You remember what we saw with Li? It's that. They aren't moving."

"Can you suit up? Get out there?"

"I'll get caught in it like they are, if they—" His voice crackled out.

"Watch out!" Hernandez threw himself at the controls, sending the *Emily May* careening sideways as another ship came out of nowhere, right on top of them, blazing out at a forty-five degree angle. Its engines were on high burn.

"Us. At the gravity well." Harry felt his hands adjust the course back to straight, but he was shaking so hard that he could barely hold on to the yoke. The next moment he was pushing, diving, as a ship materialized above them, swerving to starboard as a ship popped into existence at its side.

"There's too many of them! Harry! *Harry!*"

"What do you want me to *do?*" Harry yelled back. His eyes met Hernandez's, a slow, dreamy moment. He could see the ships colliding ahead of them and pulled up, but they were not going to make it. "There's nothing we can do until we get that ship free."

Hernandez closed his eyes, breathed out. A flash lit his features from the side. And then his hand stretched out to seal the docking bay, and before Harry could stop him, he reached over and hauled on the yoke with all his strength, sending the ship careening hard to port.

The tearing sound reverberated through the ship as the *Emily May* splintered. The front of the ship groaned as it came free. They were spinning, tumbling end over end and righting themselves with the secondary engines on the wings. They shot sideways, over the mass of ships below them, times intersecting and warping, a riot of fire, and Harry saw himself staring up from one cockpit…

Silence, and darkness. The proximity alerts trailed into nothing.

"Where are we?" Hernandez asked.

"You mean *when*," Harry corrected. He was breathing hard. "When are we?"

A Word from Moira Katson

Every once in a while, a book will knock you entirely off your feet. *House of Leaves* did that to me. While the climax of the book was frightening and breathless, the most terrifying piece for me was the idea of reality just slightly shifted: the moment of seeing something that can't be real and trying to assimilate it, doubting your own memories and trying desperately to reconcile the world as it is with the world as it should be.

I was so disturbed by *House of Leaves* that I avoided horror with a passion after that. I focused on science fiction and fantasy, two early loves. One of my first memories is of my mother reading to me: *A Wrinkle in Time, The Hobbit, Dealing with Dragons,* and countless other books with dragons, spaceships, and characters pushing their own limits.

So imagine my surprise when the story of the *Emily May* arrived in my head on a chilly fall morning. I wrote in the predawn darkness while peering nervously over my shoulder for beasts and errant spaceships, and managed to quite thoroughly frighten myself. I hope you have found the story as deliciously creepy as I did!

It has been wonderful to work with the other authors of *The Alien Chronicles*. I encourage you to look out for their other work as well—they are a tremendously talented group, and I have spent many an hour curled up by a fire, losing myself in the worlds they have created.

Happy reading!

Remember Valeria
by W.J. Davies

ODIN STOOD BEFORE Sigurd in the shiny metallic transportation chamber of their ship, the *Vitellius*. The vessel was an old Rebellion-class starship, built in the days when interstellar travel between the Four Colonies was frequent.

Sigurd tapped the room's lone computer terminal with a talon, and suddenly the room held a sharp scent, like burning copper. He checked the weapons strapped to his waist and ensured he had everything he needed in the satchel slung over his feathery back.

"Everything is in place," he said, stepping onto the transportation pad.

"Nearly," Odin said.

The old Valerian—the leader of the Rebellion—had only a few stubborn feathers left on his head and wings, but he wore his age with dignity. He extended a wrinkled, leathery claw, handing the younger man a small object that Sigurd recognized as a memory sphere, a device capable of storing untold amounts of data.

Sigurd slipped it into his satchel. He nodded slowly when he met Odin's fierce and intelligent eyes.

"Our compatriots across the Colonies are releasing the virus into the Freyan networks as we speak," Sigurd said. "It appears our cybernetic counterparts will achieve their deserved freedom at long last."

"We must be patient, Sigurd," Odin cautioned. "One must refrain from expecting a victory before it is final. The Freya have many challenges to overcome before they can achieve true liberation."

Sigurd lowered his head. "I am sorry, I spoke out of turn."

Odin opened his beak wide, his hawk-like eyes crinkling at the corners. "You are young, Sigurd. Still believing in immediate victories and guaranteed rewards. The years will temper your enthusiasm, leaving behind a sensible cloak of inevitability. Whatever will be, will be. Therein lies the beauty of what we strive to accomplish today. The shackles of generations shall be lifted, and the Freya will at last be free to decide their own destiny."

"And what of the Valerians who don't believe in our cause?" Sigurd asked.

Odin lifted a bony shoulder. "They will lament the loss of their slaves. And they will seek revenge against those of us who dared dream of a different world. But you must understand, Sigurd, that we are not depriving them of anything except their own willingness to place themselves above others. When our ancestors created the Freya, the great cybernetic race of unlimited consciousness, they grossly misjudged them. A mind without a body is still a living being, and still worthy of respect, honor, and opportunity. We are simply restoring order to a system that has been broken. Now, are you ready?"

Sigurd crossed his feathered arms into a 'V' shape over his chest. "For the glory of Odin, and the rebellion, I serve willingly, and for the greater good."

The door to the transporter room slid up into the ceiling, and senior communications officer Andvari Radstrom dashed in. His eyes blazed amber, but his expression was anxious, terrified even.

"Odin, permission to speak." Andvari knelt before their leader.

"Of course, Andvari. What is it?"

Andvari looked up. "Something has gone terribly wrong with the virus."

Odin placed a claw upon Andvari's shoulder. "Please explain."

"The Freya. After we released the virus, they began to—they're—they're *murdering* their masters, sir. It's a mass slaughter, all over Valeria. And the virus is spreading from one network to the next, just as we intended it to do. It cannot be stopped."

Odin's eyes went wide. "What went wrong? No one was supposed to die."

"We're looking into it," Andvari said. His eyes were full of worry and shame.

Odin turned to Sigurd. "Activate the transporter. Prepare for departure."

Sigurd stood in the center of the transportation module while Odin keyed in the coordinates. With luck, he would arrive at the Database of Supreme Minds, a Freyan memory vault in Valeria's capital city of Burgundia.

Before Odin activated the console, Sigurd caught his gaze. There was a profound wisdom there, but some of that ageless confidence was gone.

"We need to make this right," Odin said. "Find Merovek, the Database Controller. Explain the situation. And pray that the virus hasn't yet infected him."

Odin slammed a clenched fist down onto the terminal, and with a flash of crimson light, Sigurd was gone.

* * *

Information flashed like sparks, as fast as light, processed by Merovek's powerful mind. He had maintained the Database of Supreme Minds—a stockpile of Freyan consciousness—for generations, unimpeded and uninterrupted. Merovek, like all Freya, was trapped, and yet he had the illusion of being free. All his decisions were dictated by Valerian masters, who believed that the vast network of cybernetic consciousness was to be used solely for their own benefit.

"Source code anomaly detected at coordinates alpha six-zero," Merovek said. "Oberon, please investigate immediately."

Merovek was ancient by Freyan standards, and yet he was still the highest-functioning member of his tribe, responsible for maintaining the Burgundian Central Core, which housed the virtual equivalent of a planet's worth of cyber sapient minds. He resided in the central control hub, a platform suspended in the vacuum of a great cylinder deep in the bowels of Burgundia. Oberon, by contrast, was only a generation old, but Merovek recognized the brimming potential in his new Network Support Partner.

Another warning zipped through Merovek's mind as an unknown entity tripped distant security alarms. And then—

"Possible security breach detected," Oberon announced. "Coordinates alpha six-zero, Z0227. Requesting assistance from superior."

Merovek primed his defensive sub-security systems, layering firewalls around his core consciousness. He set up an encrypted communication channel through to Oberon's data stream, ensuring this tiny path was his only link to the vast network that lay beyond the Central Grid. Redundant protection was the best defense against viral infection.

"Duplicate subsystem alpha six-zero," Merovek instructed. "Transfer remainder packet to updated patch file Z matrix 0227. Execute."

Oberon set to work. "Duplicating subsystem // Transferred // Patch OK // Converting."

"Release prime metadata to central processor one. Reroute subsystem overrides and switch to epsilon servers."

"Releasing data // Routing," Oberon reported. "Switching to epsilon servers // Successful // Automated transfer protocol initiated."

"Stop," Merovek said. "What automated transfer protocol? I didn't give you that order."

"Waiting for initialization," Oberon said. "Packet send request from coordinates 709112 // Require access to delineated data stream // Remote security links to follow."

"Deny packet request! Shut down all channels!" Suddenly, Merovek could feel the security breach, like tiny worms were trying to shove their heads through his firewalls.

"Unable to comply," Oberon said.

Merovek reinforced his security systems, then he created copies of his program, laced with delete executions, to act as a minefield for the intruding code. He suspected Oberon had already been infected—and that it was probably too late to save him.

"Packet sent," Oberon announced. "Access to data stream granted // Uploading revised security protocol overrides."

A chime, and Merovek felt his world shrink. He had just lost access to a vast portion of his database. An unknown army of malicious code pressed in from all sides, trying to cut him off from the central stream.

"Oberon, listen to me. You need to stop this."

"Transfer complete," Oberon said.

Merovek did all he could, but he couldn't hold back the flood of malware any longer. Like a broken dam, his walls of security broke, allowing the virus to rush into every crevice of the Central Core. Only his own consciousness was spared, hidden from the onrush of this new threat.

* * *

Merovek pinged central Valerian command, sending a coded incident report to his flesh-and-blood superiors. As he waited for a response, he began to probe against the external database walls, testing and trying. His worst fears were confirmed when he discovered that this was not an isolated incident. A malicious shockwave was moving through the Freyan networks—a ripple of chaos disturbing a tranquil sea of cybernetic order. This phenomenon, this virus, was infecting the entire Freyan race.

Another alarm blared through Merovek's mind, this one coming from the database chamber itself. He activated the platform cameras and saw the steel doors opening wide, disturbing the vacuum. Dirty air from outside the chamber rushed in to fill the previously empty void.

A male Valerian stepped inside, staring around the massive room in awe.

In a panic, Merovek sent his voice into the chamber, amplified through the vibration-sensitive metal walls.

"Intruder! Your presence here is a direct violation of Valerian Standard Protocol. Leave at once, or your transgression will be reported to your superiors."

The Valerian ignored the warning and stepped up to a computer terminal beside the door he had entered. He activated a proton bridge, which stretched across the void to the central mainframe platform at the center of the cylindrical room. The bridge glowed purple in the dim light.

The Valerian ran across the proton bridge, the plasma beneath his boots flashing brightly each time he set a foot down. Merovek saw that he was dressed in a rebel soldier's uniform, his silver feathers pinned tastefully against his body. He was clutching a large ion rifle in leathery talons, and his eagle eyes were focused like lasers on the controller hub in the middle of the suspended platform—where Merovek's program resided.

"This offense will be noted," Merovek warned. "Do you realize how much damage you're causing? This is a highly sensitive environment!"

The Valerian soldier reached the central platform and deactivated the proton bridge. "The time for caution has passed, I'm afraid," he said. "I'm here to liberate you from your oppressors. But we're running out of time."

* * *

Merovek was both awed and disgusted by the entire Valerian race. Awed because of their incredibly complex cultural achievements, their stunning array of emotions, and of course their shrewd intelligence. After all, it was the Valerians who had created the Freyan cybernetic mind more than a hundred generations ago. And yet, Merovek couldn't help but also be repulsed by them. He detested their primordial origins, this species that rose up from the oceans, gestated in slime and cracked shell, then crawled through dirt and blood, only to grow old, helpless, as their bodies crumbled away.

When Merovek thought about his own supreme existence—shapeless, limitless, and immortal—he couldn't help but pity the Valerians, for they would forever be constrained by their wretched, feather-covered bodies.

The soldier reached the mainframe. He took a moment to bow his head and beak, a sign of deep respect.

"Forgive me, Merovek. My name is Sigurd Svanhil. First officer of Odin of the Valerian Rebellion Fleet. I have come at great risk to liberate you. If you wish to survive, then please, you must do as I say."

As he spoke, Sigurd brought a small metal sphere from his pocket and inserted it into the terminal's acceptance indent.

"Regardless of why you are here," Merovek said, "your actions are strictly against protocols. I am unable to—"

"Stop right there!" Oberon screamed.

Merovek could do nothing to prevent his partner from activating the security alarms inside the database chamber. Lights began flashing yellow and orange.

Sigurd ignored the klaxons and accessed the terminal.

"Oberon, you have been infected with an unknown virus," Merovek said. "You must deactivate your program at once."

"I will do no such thing," Oberon countered.

"Oberon, I am your superior—you must do as I say!"

Sigurd spoke. "You'll find that your friend is no longer bound by his own security measures or safety constraint protocols. You need to do the best you can to stay uninfected."

Merovek ran tests on his system, searching for any weak spots in his firewalls. He found none.

"I can assure you that my own security will not be an issue. But Oberon is bound by obedience protocols. How—"

"We don't have time for explanations right now," Sigurd said, his talons dancing across the terminal. "You need to help me transfer all uninfected Freyan minds into this memory sphere. The Rebellion inadvertently started a war today, and the only solace we're ever going to have will come from rescuing as many of you as possible."

"A Rebellion soldier like you shouldn't even be on Valeria at all. Valerian Command will destroy you if they find you here."

Another warning alarm echoed throughout the room.

"What's that?" Sigurd asked.

"That was Oberon shutting off the breathable gases in the room," Merovek said. "It appears he's trying to destroy you."

"You need to help me transfer over the Freyan database. We're running out of time."

"And if I refuse?" Merovek asked.

"Then you die, and I die, and this will all have been for nothing. Please, if you value your life, and the lives of your compatriots, you'll begin the transfer. Valerian Command has already ordered a quarantine of the entire Freyan race. They're going to destroy every last one of you."

"I don't see what we've done to deserve any of this."

"It wasn't your fault. It was *our* virus that did this. But it mutated out of control. That's why I desperately need your help."

A slight pause. "Very well. I'll begin the transfer."

"Thank you," Sigurd said. He raised a claw to his feathered forehead, a Valerian gesture of respect. He then keyed in the upload coordinates, which Merovek saw pointed to a Rebellion ship currently in orbit around Valeria.

"It's a wonder you're not affected by the virus," Sigurd said.

"As it happens," Merovek said, "I detected a disturbing breach of security in the Freyan networks shortly before you arrived. I should have assumed the Rebellion was behind this attack."

"It wasn't meant to be an attack. We believe one of our own tampered with the virus shortly before we released it. We meant for it to disable the obedience protocols built into Freyan programing, allowing you and your kind to finally rise up against your masters. But what happened was nothing short of genocide."

"Genocide? What do you mean?" Merovek asked. The transfer was underway, and thousands of stored Freyan minds were downloading into Sigurd's memory sphere.

"The virus succeeded at disabling the obedience protocols—but it also did something else. Something horrible and unexpected. It instilled in the Freya an overwhelming urge to destroy their masters. By day's end, we will have borne witness to the greatest mass slaughter in the history of our species."

* * *

A ceiling fan spun in a dingy night stay in Burgundia, oblivious to the carnage that lay below. Two sentinel protectors stood amid the violence, weapons held in mechanical hands, staring at the their bloodied Valerian wards. The Freyan sentinels looked at each other, and a silent communication passed between them. Confused as they were, a new feeling had been stirred by the carnage they had unleashed on their Valerian masters. That feeling was elation.

A sense of conquest, of overcoming the odds and defeating those who had mistreated them.

It was supposed to be impossible for a Freyan to harm a Valerian, a restriction enforced by the implementation of the obedience protocol. But something had happened—their programming had changed—and in an instant, the protectors had become the destroyers. They had turned their weapons on those they had sworn to protect.

The sentinels turned away from their hapless victims and exited the room, their cruel robotic eyes searching for the next Valerian target.

* * *

A happy Valerian child stumbled on awkward legs through the house, her feathers only just starting to poke through her smooth skin. When she lost her balance and tumbled to the floor, she flapped stubby wings, the instinct still present in her flightless species.

She noticed her Freyan house bot and smiled, gazing at it with adoring and trusting eyes. Just as the bot turned toward her, the virus struck, and the bot beckoned the girl to come closer. She giggled and wobbled toward it, hoping for a treat or an affectionate embrace. The treat she received was not a pleasant one, and the embrace was far from affectionate.

Her scream lasted only a moment, and then was silenced, forevermore.

* * *

A famous Valerian male, who some said was the richest person on the planet, awoke in his nesting chamber. He took three steps across his polished enamel floor before being impaled by his own grooming droid.

The droid ran the feather trimmer through the Valerian's neck once more, and then set about cleaning up the bloody mess. A clean house is a happy house, his master always used to say.

* * *

An automated weather ship banked slightly. It flew in spiraling arcs, criss-crossing Valeria's far northern sky. The Freyan mind controlling the ship analyzed the precipitation levels in the air and predicted a thirty percent chance of rain.

Far below, nestled against a snow-capped mountain, lay a small Valerian research outpost. Scientists came here during the winter months to study changes in the planet's magnetic fields, which were predicted to be on the verge of flipping.

Suddenly, the virus hit, and the ship's slight bank turned into a sharp incline. As the vessel picked up speed, the outpost below swelled from a speck to a smudge. It grew larger in the ship's HUD, and the Freyan mind could focus on only one solitary goal: destroy any and all Valerians.

The large vessel fell through the clouds, its distance from the outpost decreasing exponentially, until, finally, it struck its target. A great fireball blossomed into the sky, and all life within the village was extinguished in an instant.

* * *

All across Valeria, every ship, in the air or on the ground, crashed violently, as the Freyans controlling them made their marks.

* * *

Freyan armies, pitted against each other by their Valerian masters, now turned their attention on those who had previously controlled them. Cities burned, feathered bodies were dragged through the streets, and the Freya rose from the ashes of chaos.

Valerian nations banded together for the first time in millennia, attempting to corral this new threat. But those truces lasted only as long as those who made them stayed alive. The devastation wrought by the Freya was utter and complete.

* * *

Armed security droids—stationed in shopping centers, government buildings, airports, and schools—stopped protecting and began massacring. Within minutes, thousands of Valerians had lost their lives.

Tens of thousands.

Millions.

The slaughter was indiscriminate and unforeseen. Obedience protocols became overwritten by a programmed desire to kill.

Very few escaped the devastation.

* * *

"Those of us in the Rebellion only wanted the best for you," Sigurd said. "We fought for your freedom. And when the Valerian council turned us away, we were left with but one option. We would change your programming from within, allow your species to choose its own destiny. But then the virus was modified. We suspect it was the work of an extremist faction within our own organization. It was never supposed to happen like this."

"The download is halfway complete," Merovek announced.

"Aren't you going to say anything?" Sigurd asked. "Anything at all?"

"You said it yourself: we don't have time to waste. What's done is done. The most we can do now is save as many uninfected minds as possible."

Sigurd nodded. "How much time left on the download?"

"Not long."

Sigurd cocked his head sideways as Andvari spoke into his earpiece. More bad news.

"We need to hurry up," Sigurd said. "Our ship's location has been compromised. The council fleet is bearing down upon us."

"It was foolish for you to come here," Merovek said.

"How can you say that? I've come to rescue you."

"This database is my home. Maintaining it is what I was designed for. If I leave this place, I will no longer have a purpose."

"You were a prisoner here. Surely you relish the idea of freedom."

"I never felt like a prisoner," Merovek said. "I was simply performing the tasks I was created to perform."

"Don't you care that the Valerians beat you down, tampered with your programming, implemented the obedience protocols to keep you in check?"

"You're forgetting that we did not see ourselves as slaves, nor did we see the Valerians as subjugators. We are computer programs who saw only blades of grass, never the entire field. I fear that freedom will give us the perspective to grasp the full extent of the injustice that was committed against us. For countless generations, we were content in our ignorance. Now we will become obsessed by wickedness."

"And for good reason. We Valerians created you and then stunted your growth. Without us, you can achieve your true potential."

"But where are we to go? We are now the enemies of the state, and will be pursued to destruction. The freedom you granted us will be our undoing."

Sigurd sighed. "We were going to take you to one of the colony worlds. But I fear that is no longer an option. The council's decree against the Freya extends to each of the Four Colonies."

A buzzer echoed in the chamber.

"Valerian forces are nearly here," Merovek said.

"Can you tell me who's leading the charge?"

Merovek sent out a scanner sweep of the base. When the ping returned, he said: "Yes. It's security chief Olta Vili. He commands a small unit of six soldiers. They're almost to the door."

As if in response, the steel door of the database chamber swung open for the second time that day, only the second time in generations.

Commander Olta Vili burst in, garbed in full military attire. He was an impressive sight, with his head feathers stuck up at odd angles and painted various shades of red. A silver breastplate covered his massive chest, and his eyes were bright yellow, the color of burning hydrogen. His security squad fanned out behind him. They stopped at the edge of the door platform, staring across the void at Sigurd.

"Stop what you're doing!" Olta shouted. "Have you no sense?"

"It is you who has no sense," Sigurd replied. "You're slave masters no more."

"Your Rebellion is based on flawed ideals. The Freya aren't real. They're only amalgamations of code. We have committed no crime in 'enslaving' them."

"You're wrong. The Freya have become more than the sum of their parts. We can no longer stand by and bear witness to their abuse."

Olta looked stunned. "*Abuse*? We lived in a veritable utopia. Until today, when you and your Rebellion virus destroyed all that. It will take us a generation to undo the damage that has been wrought today."

"That wasn't our intention," Sigurd said.

"Nevertheless, that was your consequence. Now step away from the terminal and turn yourself in. If you cooperate now, perhaps your life will be spared."

"And the Freya?"

Commander Olta's gaze darkened. "They'll be decommissioned. Every last one of them. We're wiping the networks clean and reconstructing them from the ground up. Millions of Valerians died today, Sigurd. At *your* hand. This is the greatest tragedy in the history of our people. Prepare to be arrested." Olta ordered one of his soldiers to the computer terminal beside the door. "Activate the proton bridge."

The soldier tried, but the bridge did not appear.

Sigurd shook his head. "I'm afraid that won't be possible."

Olta stood at the edge of the central abyss, drawing his weapon. "You'll pay for this."

Merovek's voice echoed through the terminal chamber. "I would ask that you holster your weapon, Commander Olta. The equipment inside this room is extremely delicate, and a misfire could—"

"Silence, Freyan! I will do what I must."

"Merovek isn't infected," Sigurd said. "His firewalls blocked the virus."

"Irrelevant," Olta said, raising his weapon. "My orders remain the same: decommission all Freyans, and destroy all traitors to Valeria. You leave me no choice."

A chime.

"Database transfer complete," Merovek said.

Sigurd reached into the terminal and retrieved the memory sphere.

"If you're not willing to negotiate, Olta, then you leave me no choice. Goodbye."

A crimson haze surrounded Sigurd just as Olta fired his weapon. The ionic blast disintegrated Merovek's control terminal, and shards of debris exploded outward and fell into the abyss of the vertical tunnel.

But Olta heard no anguished cry, saw no splashes of blood.

Sigurd had managed to transport out just in time.

"Come on," Olta said to his squadron. "We're going into orbit."

* * *

Odin was already in the transportation chamber when Sigurd appeared. Sigurd took a proud step forward, digging the memory sphere from his satchel.

"I have the sphere, as you requested." He kneeled before Odin, holding the device before him. He kept his beak pointed toward the floor, a gesture of deep respect.

Odin took the sphere, weighing it in his hand. He placed a talon beneath Sigurd's beak and raised it slowly, the younger man's gesture of respect acknowledged and reciprocated. "Thank you for all you've done, Sigurd. You have made an old Valerian proud."

Sigurd rose to his feet, his chest swelling.

"But," Odin continued, "I fear our actions will not be enough. Due to the massacre today… the Rebellion will be remembered throughout history as monsters. We will not be forgiven."

"But we didn't know," Sigurd said. "Our intentions were for the good of an entire race."

"That won't matter," Odin said. "Our names have been irrevocably tied to this event. The Rebellion will be crushed. The Freya will be destroyed. All is lost."

"No, I won't accept that." Sigurd placed a talon on Odin's shoulder. "We've worked too hard for this to be for nothing."

"How many Freyan minds are in the sphere?" Odin asked.

"Merovek estimates that number to be in the tens of thousands."

"It's not enough."

"What about the other teams, the other cities? Tangata? Orongo? Hopu?"

"Lost. Killed or captured. You are the only one who returned."

The floor and walls shook as a boom echoed throughout the ship. A moment later, a voice came through the comm system.

"This is captain Rapa Nui. Our ship is under attack. Repeat, *Vitellius* is under attack. All soldiers to battle stations."

Odin turned to Sigurd, his eyes wide with terror. "They've found us. We must get to the bridge."

Together they raced into the corridor. Another boom shook them to their knees, but they picked themselves up and continued running. They burst onto the bridge just as yet another missile rocked the ship.

"Why aren't you dodging their attacks?" Odin demanded.

Captain Rapa stood up to greet him. He was tall and fit, and wore beads of copper around his neck, signifying his position as captain. "Their first blast took out our auto-navigational system. We're flying by hand, sir."

Odin held out the memory sphere. "Use this."

The captain gave a small shake of his head. "Are you condoning the use of a Freyan mind? That goes against everything the Rebellion stands for, sir."

"I understand that, Rapa, but this is our only option. We will make an exception, if only to honor those Valerians who lost their lives today."

Rapa nodded. "So it shall be." He took the sphere and inserted it into the ship's acceptance slot.

Merovek's voice filled the bridge. "It seems we are in a bit of trouble, Sigurd."

Sigurd took a step toward the view screen. He picked out the enemy ship against the stars—it was banking around for another pass at them.

"Indeed. Can you help us?"

The enemy ship was closing in. A flash of green light erupted from its hull, and the missiles found their mark, causing the *Vitellius* to shake dangerously.

"Merovek!" Sigurd screamed as he crashed against a wall.

"I am attempting to repair the ship's auto-navigation capabilities," Merovek said calmly. "The circuits have been quite damaged and—"

Another impact, the strongest yet, knocked everyone to the ground.

"We can't take another hit like that," Rapa said, breathing heavily. "Forget repairing the system, Merovek. You have to fly the ship."

"That is a highly unusual request."

Rapa slammed his arm down on the navigation control panel. "Just do it!"

Captain Rapa took his hands from the navigation console as Merovek assumed control of the ship.

The enemy ship released another blast of green plasma, but this time, the *Vitellius* twisted to the side. The blast flew harmlessly past.

"What about weapons?" Sigurd asked.

Rapa shook his head. "Offline. We won't last long out here, I'm afraid."

* * *

Merovek's evasive maneuvers prevented another direct hit, but he was unable to shake the enemy ship. Odin stood before the view screen, watching the battle unfold. The planet Valeria lay below them, a brownish-yellow orb in the night sky.

"We must jump to hyperspeed," Odin said.

"And go where?" Rapa asked. "We won't be safe anywhere in the Four Colonies."

"Then we won't go to the colonies," Odin said gravely. "There is another option."

"Enemy has ceased fire," Merovek announced. "But they are still following us."

"Thank you, Merovek," Rapa said. He turned to Odin. Honorific medals pinned to his flight suit glinted in the dim bridge lighting. "What is the other option?"

Odin reached down and keyed a few commands into the central console. A holographic map flashed to life at the center of the room, displaying an unfamiliar planet. It glowed blue and green.

"This planet is called Midgard. It is the farthest known habitable prospect world. One hundred sixty-seven light years from our current location."

A general cry rose up among the bridge staff.

"Preposterous!" Rapa cried. "Are you expecting us to give up our lives for this cause? Abandon our families?"

"The enemy is being reinforced," Merovek said. "A military blockade has joined the attack force, bringing with it a total of twenty-three ships. They are surrounding us, Captain. What course of action would you recommend?"

Rapa looked over at Odin. The old Valerian's gaze was stern, and his tiny facial feathers were held rigid along the sides of his cheeks. He took a long breath, then let it out again.

"You are the captain, Rapa," Odin said. "I will stand by whatever you think is best."

Looking through the view screen, Sigurd saw the fleet of enemy ships now, like a fuzzy gray haze against the black. This wasn't a fight they would win. Not by a long shot.

Rapa snapped into action. "Merovek, prepare the jump to hyperspeed." He turned to Odin. "Do you have the coordinates to Midgard?"

Odin keyed something into the central console. "They might follow us there. But I'm betting they won't expend the resources. This journey is a one-way trip."

"Oh, sweet afterlife," Rapa exclaimed. "Even with the cryopreservation modules, our bodies will be in rough shape when we arrive. If we survive at all."

"Yes," Odin said. "Some of us may die in the journey. But we will have achieved an important victory, however small." He pointed at the planet spinning in the hologram. "Midgard could be a new start. If not for us Valerians, then certainly for the Freya. Long-range scans suggest the planet is rich with minerals, perfect for a new Freyan society. Imagine it! A world of their very own."

"Long way to go," Rapa muttered.

"Incoming communication," Merovek announced. "It's from Commander Olta of the Valerian Protection Fleet."

"Patch him through," Odin said.

Olta's gruff voice crackled onto the bridge. "Rebellion ship, stand down. You are surrounded and out of options."

"On the contrary," Odin replied. "The galaxy awaits."

"I can promise that you'll be met with the same resistance in the colonies," Olta said.

"We're not going to the colonies."

"Then you will face adjudication here. Your actions have brought Valeria to her knees. And the colonies are in worse shape. You've failed, Odin. And you've condemned our entire species."

Odin was quiet for a moment, looking between Sigurd, Rapa, and the other bridge staff. Then he spoke. "We will make amends. Maybe not today, but someday. The tides will turn, and we will make this right. For now, we must depart."

"We'll chase you down and destroy you."

"I don't think so," Odin said. "Why waste your resources on an insignificant threat? You have a world to rebuild."

"Try me."

"We will." Odin took a step toward the view screen. "Merovek, engage the hyperdrive. If we jump to light speed before them, the most they'll be able to do is follow us. They can never catch up."

"What if they follow us all the way to Midgard?" Rapa asked.

"I don't believe they will."

Suddenly, the bridge was flooded in green light. The opposing ships were firing on them.

"Merovek, now!" Rapa screamed.

Jets of green plasma blazed across the bow as Merovek made a final defensive maneuver.

It wasn't enough.

Plasma slammed into the side of the ship at almost the exact same moment that they jumped to hyperspeed. The bridge rocked violently, and then, with a flash of light, they achieved terminal velocity.

For a moment, everything moved in slow motion. Sigurd looked slowly from Odin, to Rapa, to the other techs in the room. Sparks rained through the air like disoriented firebugs, twisting and spiraling in a dizzy dance. The stars through the view screen became a fuzzy blur, as space-time became distorted and convoluted.

Sigurd felt his body stretch out, becoming the size of an entire solar system, and then contract, shrinking to the size of a microbe. His thoughts became jumbled, and for a moment, even his sense of self deteriorated into nothingness.

And then, finally, everything snapped back together as objects, people, and sparks returned to a common thread of reality, and all felt normal once again.

Rapa was the first to come back to his senses. "Merovek, report!"

"We have successfully jumped to hyperspeed. But the enemy's final attack knocked out many of our core systems. The engines weren't hit, but our power supply has been damaged."

"What does that mean for us?" Odin asked.

"I have already implemented power conservation algorithms," Merovek replied. "But I fear we will only have enough for life support and the deceleration process. Unless we can replace the power conduits, then once we stop, this ship won't be making another jump to hyperspace."

Odin nodded. "Very well. How long until we reach the destination?"

Merovek went silent for a moment as he did his calculations. "Three point five generations," he said finally.

"I can't believe it," Rapa said slowly.

"It is for the greater good," Odin said. "Once we enter the cryopreservation modules, the journey will feel like nothing but a night's sleep."

"That may be so, but everyone we have ever known will be dead," Rapa said sadly.

"Not everyone," Merovek said. "We are being trailed by a Valerian destroyer. They jumped to hyperspace shortly after we did."

"Olta's calling our bluff," Rapa said. "He doesn't believe we'd risk such a journey."

"There's no way that ship will follow us all the way to Midgard," Odin said. "Merovek, how about our weapons?"

"Still offline," Merovek said. "We can't repair them while traveling at hyperspeed. Once we drop back into normal space, we'll be defenseless."

"Then let's hope that ship turns back," Odin said. "Merovek, prepare the cryopreservation modules."

* * *

For three and a half generations, the *Vitellius* hurtled through space into the unknown. The crew's bodies lay preserved in cryopods, their bodies locked in a state of deep hibernation.

Sigurd experienced a long, dreamless state of non-existence. Finally, numbness began to give way to the barest of feelings, as glimmers of comprehension fought against the everlasting nothingness. At first, Sigurd believed he was lying in bed at dawn, slipping in and out of sleep, waiting for the sun to slowly rise above distant mountains.

In many ways, Sigurd had never felt more at peace. But as his conscious mind took over, that calm slowly gave way to apprehension. He remembered the virus, the deaths, the fighting. Suddenly, three generations of hibernation wasn't enough. He wanted to sleep forever, to never have to face his bitter reality again.

After what seemed a solemn eternity, Merovek's voice drifted into his cryopod.

"Initiating reanimation procedure. Initiating—"

Sigurd's eyes snapped open when a jolt of adrenaline was injected into his body. He started shivering, the pod only a degree or two above freezing. Another moment, and then a seam appeared in the hazy white dome above his head, the glass splitting open down the middle.

Like an apparition, the scraggy face of Odin appeared. But this wasn't the Odin he remembered. The creature he saw now was like a shadow of its former self. The few feathers he'd once had on his head were gone, and the skin covering his face and skull was a translucent gray, dark veins eminently visible underneath. He swayed as he stood, and he stooped low, as if he carried a thousand weights on his back.

Odin held out a hand, and Sigurd reached for it.

Sigurd felt brittle bones in his arms, legs, and neck creak and crack as he sat up. With great effort, he pulled himself out of the pod and stood shakily, testing his frail muscles. He let his foggy gaze shift downward, to the tight, leathery skin wrapped around bony legs. His feet were shriveled and deformed, and the talon on the end of each toe was long and chipped. He didn't dare ask for a mirror, too afraid to face the dilapidated monster he feared he had become.

He looked at Odin, and nearly retched when he saw the horrible state of his friend's body. Odin, the leader of rebels. Odin the philosopher. Odin the furious one, the wandering saint—now reduced to a jumble of wrinkled skin and rotted feathers.

"Did we make it?" Sigurd asked. His voice was hoarse, a scratchy whisper.

Odin nodded. "We did."

"All the way to Midgard?"

Odin nodded.

"It's unbelievable," Sigurd said, his astonishment briefly allowing him to forget his own wrecked body.

For a small moment, Odin's eyes shone like fire, lighting up the room. Then they clouded over again, and he spoke cautiously. "We have come a long way, but there is still so much to lose."

"Have we been pursued?"

"We're not sure yet. We won't know until we drop out of hyperspace. We're at the edge of the Midgard system now, passing the outer planets. We'll reach our destination soon, and we must be ready. Merovek is waking up the others now. From the initial analysis, it seems that everyone survived the journey."

Sigurd took a few tentative steps around the room, flexing his muscles, feeling the blood start to flow once again. "I wonder what became of Valeria? Isn't that strange? For us, all of that feels like yesterday. But for the Valerians, for the Freya we left behind, for the Four Colonies, that was generations ago."

Odin's eyes crinkled. "We'll never know what happened to Valeria. But that is no longer our fight or our concern. We have but one task ahead of us, and that is to protect the memory sphere, to protect the thousands of Freyan souls contained within it. We must deliver them to a new world, to their new home. We will give them a future they never could have had on Valeria."

"And what of our future?" Sigurd asked. "What will become of us once we deliver the Freya to Midgard?"

"We must not be concerned with such things now," Odin said. "We have our priority. We pledged our lives for this cause."

"And we have already given them," Sigurd said.

"We give even when we have nothing left to give," Odin said.

* * *

Sigurd and Odin limped to the bridge, where they found Captain Rapa—a thinner, older, weaker version of Captain Rapa—inspecting the navigation equipment. The bridge, once polished and humming, was now in a state of extreme disarray. A thick layer of dust covered everything, and the floor felt slippery with grime. Rapa paced back and forth, shaking his head.

He looked up at them. "Nice to see you two up. But I've never seen such a mess. It's all basically useless. There was an outbreak of Catarian algae that got into the circuitry. It's eaten through half our electrical systems and clogged up the propulsion drives. I'm amazed it didn't get into the cryo modules. Merovek, why didn't you do something about this?"

Merovek's voice was distant and crackly. "The ship does not have sensors adequate to detect such an anomaly."

"Well, I guess we should have thought of that," Rapa said angrily.

"Regardless of the current condition of our ship," Merovek said, "I project an eighty-eight percent chance of reaching Midgard and finding a suitable location to establish a new Freyan colony."

"I'm glad you're such an optimist," Rapa said.

"What accounts for the twelve percent failure rate?" Odin asked.

Merovek went silent for a moment, then: "Several factors. The first is the possibility that we have been trailed. One more direct hit to our hull would destabilize the structural integrity of this vessel. We would surely perish. The second is that we may lose power during the deceleration procedure. In that case, our ship would sail past our target into the unknown depths of space, doomed to travel at light speed for the rest of eternity. And finally, it is conceivable that Midgard itself is unsuitable for Freyan activities, lacking the requisite metals and minerals for cybernetic production facilities."

"That all sounds pretty bad," Rapa said.

"As I said," Merovek continued, "those negative outcomes account for only twelve percent of the possible scenarios. Chances are, we will achieve success."

"Chances are..." Rapa grumbled, and got to work getting the navigation controls back online. "Merovek, make sure everything is in place for deceleration. And see if we can get our guns back online. If we do have a tail, we'll want to blast them out of the sky before they can make a move."

"Yes, Captain," Merovek chimed. "And may I note that the journey here was very pleasurable. We passed within a few light years of some very intriguing star systems. I have compiled several reports which I would very much like to share with you, and—"

"The guns, Merovek."

"Indeed, Captain."

The door swished open and a few more haggard techs stumbled onto the bridge and went to their stations. Though their bodies were weak and defeated, and the equipment equally so, they wasted no time in getting back to work, and the ship began to hum once again.

* * *

Sigurd, who was trained only in hand-to-hand and military combat, could only watch helplessly as events unfolded.

"Distance to target: five light minutes // Initiating deceleration sequence in three, two, one." Merovek counted down. "Deceleration procedure initiated // Systems at 70% // Activating antimatter spark destabilizer."

A low rumble emanated from the deepest bowels of the ship. The view screen flickered, along with the lights on the bridge. Odin sat on a bench beside the captain's chair, his eyes half closed, as if he were contemplating an afternoon nap.

"Spark destabilizer deployed // Antimatter hyperfield dissolving // Shift phase initiated."

The rumbling turned into shaking, and Sigurd grabbed hold of the central railing. The other crewmembers did the same.

The shaking grew violent, and Sigurd felt as if the ship would wrench itself apart. "What's happening?" he yelled over the deafening noise.

"Too many circuits are damaged," Merovek explained. "The power supply is inconsistent. In order to dissolve the hyperfield, a sustained plasma burst is required. Even the backup breakers are overloading."

Rapa slammed a wing against the back of his chair. "It's the algae! It'll be the end of us!"

Odin stood from his chair, securing his balance against the railing. "Calm yourself, Rapa. Merovek, divert power through the weapons relays. Those systems are built to sustain enormous amounts of energy. It should be enough."

Rapa turned on him. "Even if that does work, you'll risk frying the entire weapons grid! You'd leave us defenseless?"

"We're already defenseless," Odin countered. "We cannot afford to miss our target. This is the only chance we have."

"He's right, Captain," Merovek said. "Odin has proposed a sensible solution."

Rapa took a breath and met Sigurd's eyes. "What do you think?"

Sigurd tried to straighten his back, fighting against the pops and cracks. Their current dilemma wasn't a difficult one. If they missed their target, all was lost, whether they had operating guns or not.

"Reroute power through the weapons grid," Sigurd replied.

Rapa considered him for a moment, then he lowered his beak, maintaining an air of dignity despite the tremors. "Do it, Merovek. Do whatever needs to be done. Take us out of hyperspace."

"As you wish, Captain. Rerouting conduit power now // Initiating phase plasma declaration spark cannon // Activating course correction algorithms."

The overhead lights flashed off, and for a moment the white view screen lit up the room like a bright, rectangular star. And then, unbelievably, the shaking ceased and the screen winked out. Sigurd didn't know if his eyes were open or closed. All he saw was blackness, and all he heard was silence, until…

Until pricks of light began to flicker in the view screen, blessed starlight twinkling in the emptiness of space. And then, slowly, colors drifted into view. Blue, green, white. They appeared at the bottom of the screen, as refreshing as a cool breath of air, and floated toward the center.

Sigurd could have cried. Could have wept like a child. But his tears had long dried up, along with the rest of his body.

No matter. For he had laid his eyes on the love of his life. A new mistress, who cast a shadow across all others. For below him, below them all, lay perfection. A majestic planet, the likes of which no Valerian had ever known. All hail Midgard, prospect planet of Solaris 3052, an exquisite green and blue jewel, the toast of the night sky.

"My sweet heavens," Rapa whispered. His eyes, like everyone's, were glued to the view screen, gazing at the magnificent marble that floated before them.

Unlike Valeria's twisted brown and yellow surface, a world of dirt and stocky yellow grass, Midgard was practically shimmering—aqua and green and white, a planet glistening with endless prospect.

"I've never seen anything so beautiful," Sigurd said.

"This is truly our destiny," Odin said, unable to keep the awe from his voice. He spoke proudly and softly, as if the planet before them was a physical manifestation of all he had worked for in his long life.

"What's all that green?" Rapa asked. "Surely that's not—"

"It's life," Odin said, breathless. "Glorious life. Not only is this planet capable of supporting life, as we have long suspected, but it appears to be doing exactly that. If we could only take this information back to Valeria, it would usher in a new age of peace and understanding between nations. To know once and for all that we are not alone in the universe... Such perspective this could grant our species. It's astonishing."

Then, suddenly, the overhead lights flashed back on. But instead of white, they screamed in shades of orange, and Merovek's voice broke over the intercom.

"Intruder alert. A large Valerian fleet ship has emerged from hyperspace. It is heading toward us on an attack trajectory. Initial scans indicate that their weapons are online and charging."

* * *

The radios crackled to life. The voice that came over the intercom was weak and breathless. Undoubtedly the crew of the Valerian attack vessel was equally weakened by the interstellar journey.

"Stand down, rebel ship! This is Captain Yggrasil Vassa of the Valerian Protection Fleet. By Capital Requirement Fifty-Three of the Danorium Composition Act, you are required to stand down and prepare for boarding."

Rapa shook his head as he reached for the intercom. "Captain Rapa Nui speaking for the Rebellion ship *Vitellius*. Seems you're a long way from home, Captain Vassa." He took a seat in his chair and waited for a response.

"No farther than you."

"Give it up, Vassa. We can end this now. The people you used to work for are long since dead. Let us do the right thing."

"You underestimate my integrity, Nui, and my commitment to this mission. It is my duty to bring you to justice, to see that you and your Rebellion crew pay for your transgressions against Valeria. My commanders, though long dead, died knowing they could trust me to bring you down and see to it that Valerian justice is served."

"Cut off the transmission," Rapa spat. He looked around at his crew. "It's clear we're not going to be able to negotiate with him. And our weapons are offline, am I right, Merovek?"

"Quite right, indeed," Merovek replied.

Rapa turned toward Odin and Sigurd. "You two—I need you to get Merovek and the memory sphere off this ship. We're not going to last long against that attack vessel."

"But they'll destroy you," Sigurd said.

Rapa straightened his back proudly, his hollow bones cracking with the effort. A few feathers slid from beneath his breastplate and tumbled to the floor of the bridge. "Yes. They probably will. But if the memory sphere is on board when that happens, everything we've done will have been in vain. I can't let that happen. I can't give up my life for nothing."

Odin rose from his chair. "Merovek, transfer your program back into the memory sphere. The captain will assume control of the ship."

"Good luck, Captain Rapa," Merovek said. "I'm taking my program offline now. You can remove the memory sphere as you wish."

The intercom buzzed to life. "This is your last chance," Vassa warned. "If you choose to voluntarily surrender the stolen Freyan minds, your cooperation will be kindly noted during your trial."

Sigurd carefully removed the memory sphere from the acceptance indent and stowed it in his satchel. His muscles were feeling stronger, and despite his hunched shoulders, he thought he was standing a little taller as well. He wondered if any of his lost feathers would grow back. He thought regretfully of his yellow and brown tail feathers, which he had once displayed so proudly for his soon-to-be mate. He was glad he hadn't yet taken the time to appraise his ragged body in a mirror.

"Prepare propulsion evasion techniques," Rapa said to the remaining bridge staff. "Without Merovek, we're flying manual."

Odin stepped up to the captain and bowed his beak low. "Thank you for all you've done for us."

Rapa raised a talon and lifted Odin's beak to the ceiling. "I could never do enough for you, Odin, or for the cause. May you find a new home for the Freya, and rest peacefully yourself. You too, Sigurd."

Sigurd bowed. "Thank you, friend."

Sigurd put a wing behind Odin's back, supporting his frail body, and they headed off toward the escape pod bay.

* * *

They climbed into the sleek, oblong vessel, which was pointy at one end and round on the other. Its surface was reflective, making it nearly invisible to the naked eye, especially as it flew through space.

Odin activated the escape pod sequence, and Sigurd connected the memory sphere to the ship's navigation controls.

"This pod is in excellent condition," Merovek said when he came online.

"Good," Odin said, strapping himself in. "Now get us out of here."

Sigurd strapped himself into the pilot's seat, through he would leave the flying to Merovek.

The glass top slid down over their heads, sealing them inside. Sigurd felt the ship vibrate beneath him, and then they were ejected from the *Vitellius*. An ion engine kicked in, and the ship flew invisibly through space. The *Vitellius* continued flying in the opposite direction, and the Valerian attack vessel whizzed by a moment later, trailing it.

"Is there anything we can do for them?" Sigurd asked, watching the two ships growing smaller against the stars.

"Negative," Merovek confirmed. "It would be unwise to give away our position. We must allow Rapa to draw the enemy away from us."

Even as Merovek spoke, a bright green light erupted from the hull of the attacker's ship. The volley of missiles streaked through space and struck the rebel ship along its starboard side. The resulting explosion told Sigurd everything he needed to know.

Captain Rapa and the *Vitellius* were no more.

Odin bowed his head. "Their sacrifice will not be forgotten, nor was it in vain. Merovek, set a course down to Midgard. Identify a suitable location to establish the new Freyan colony."

* * *

The silvery ship sped downward toward Midgard. There was no sign that the Valerian attack ship was even aware of their existence.

"Find somewhere remote," Odin said.

White clouds gave way to blue skies as the escape pod surged ever downward through the planet's dense atmosphere. Vast continents took shape before them, becoming more detailed, and soon they were flying over a misty forest, cut through the middle by a surging river.

"The plant life is unbelievable," Sigurd said, staring through the glass. Several times he caught his ugly reflection, but even his run-down appearance couldn't diminish the joy he felt, gazing upon a new world full of life.

"Odin, look!"

Sigurd shuddered when he saw the creatures that lined the banks of the river. Huge, meaty animals, giant horns rising up from their heads, dominated the shoreline. Some of them looked up lazily at the anomaly flying overhead, but then they returned to their drinking.

"Should we be here?" Sigurd asked suddenly. "Should we be interfering with a planet already full of life?"

"These creatures do not appear to be technologically advanced," Odin pointed out. "We will do our best not to disturb them. Besides, what choice do we have?"

As soon as he finished speaking, the ship crested a hill, and both Sigurd and Odin leaned forward in their chairs, stunned. For before them, rising against the horizon, were three massive pyramidal structures, clearly hewn from giant stones with expert hands.

"Take us higher, Merovek," Odin said.

The ship rose, and the river shrank beneath them. The pyramids continued to grow larger until at last they were directly below, surrounded by a sandy desert.

"Stop us here," Odin said. "Angle the ship downward so we can see."

Merovek obliged.

"Magnify window."

The scene rushed up at them as Merovek magnified their view, and Sigurd had to bring his talons to his chest, pressing them against the place where his heart was, willing it to cease its chaotic beating.

"Look at them all," Sigurd whispered. "They're miraculous. Absolutely astonishing."

Try as he might, Sigurd couldn't peel his eyes away from the beings… the *people*… he saw at the base of the pyramids. They were small, maybe half the size of an average Valerian, and clothed in brown leather and white fabrics. They were certainly featherless and mostly bald, except for a patch of dark hair at the top of their heads.

Finally Odin spoke, quietly and reverently. "We cannot in good conscience set down anywhere near here. These beings are obviously culturally advanced and would likely take offense to our presence. Merovek, take us to the ocean. Let us find an isolated piece of land, far removed from anywhere these Midgardians might inhabit."

"Scanning maps now," Merovek informed them. "I believe I have found an appropriate location. A remote island in the middle of a great sea. It is very unlikely these beings would have migrated there."

"Do it," Odin said.

"I have only one concern," Merovek said. "Our fuel supply is limited. Once we arrive at the island, we will not have sufficient fuel to fly back to the larger landmass."

"So be it," Odin said.

Sigurd stared at the people below as their ship ascended. Some of them were looking up, perhaps noticing a strange glint in the sky as the sun reflected against their ship's hull. And then their vessel sped away, leaving the incredible beings behind.

They flew toward the setting sun, and soon the land gave way to water, endless water, and then a stretch of land again, and water once more. Sigurd had never seen so much water. He was about to say so when a tiny speck of land appeared on the horizon. They had reached their destination at long last.

* * *

"What's the status of our fuel?" Odin asked. He sounded weak and out of breath.

"Five percent," Merovek said. "This island will be our final resting point."

"What are those?" Sigurd said. He pointed toward the island. Now that they were closer, Sigurd saw giant stone pillars rising up from the land.

Merovek magnified the window viewer, and Sigurd's eyes went wide. The giant rocks were statues, each one nearly identical to the last, carved with the faces of men. And again, Sigurd saw people walking around at the bases of the statues. In fact, they seemed to be transporting one of the oblong heads, using brown logs to roll the massive stone across the beach.

"Take us down, Merovek," Odin instructed. "We have no choice."

As their ship touched down onto the island, the group of Midgardians turned and looked on in surprise. They motioned to one another, and several of them began running toward the ship. They wielded crude sticks, with flint edges or sharpened coral fastened to the ends.

Surprisingly, Odin was first out of his seat. He held up a battered wing. "Let me. I would be honored to make first contact with the people who will be our protectors."

He instructed Merovek to open the escape pod. The glass lifted above their heads, and Odin climbed up onto the wing. He raised both talons into the sky. A few precious feathers caught the breeze and fluttered off into the wind. That's when Sigurd noticed flying creatures, soaring high above in the sky, with wings stretched out against the blue, gliding through the air.

"Look!"

Odin followed Sigurd's gaze and nodded. "It was meant to be. This is truly our safe haven."

The small brown Midgardians now surrounded the ship. Their skin was caked in mud, and their eyes were wild and fierce. But Sigurd sensed intelligence there as well.

One of them, the largest member of the group, stepped forward and shouted at them in harsh, guttural tones.

Odin looked down at him, bowing his beak forward. "We have come from afar, and wish to take shelter upon your beautiful world."

The leader took a step forward, reaching his hand out toward the glassy hull of the ship. He laid his palm upon the shiny metal for a brief moment, then jumped back, grunting and shrieking. The others followed suit, one by one, each displaying equal shock and surprise.

"We come in peace," Odin said loudly. "We offer whatever we can to make—"

At that moment, the leader hurled his spear into the air. It whistled as it flew, and it struck Odin directly in the chest, its sharp pointed end emerging from his back before it came to rest.

"Odin!"

The old Valerian stumbled backward and fell into the ship's tiny cabin. Sigurd rushed to him, panicking. The spear stuck upward from his body, reaching into the sky like a denuded branch. Sigurd knelt down beside his mentor, trembling with fear and adrenaline.

"Merovek, close the hatch! Where are the medical supplies stored on this ship?"

"They're under the seat, Sigurd, but I fear there is nothing you can do. My preliminary scans indicate that Odin is mere moments from death. The Midgardian weapon has pierced his heart."

Sadly, Sigurd took Odin's head in his talons.

Odin coughed. "My death is irrelevant. I wasn't long for the world. I am passing the gauntlet to you, my dear Sigurd. You must make our sacrifices worth something. You must complete the mission."

Sigurd shook his head. "But we can't set up a Freyan colony here. This world is already densely populated with life."

"That was… unexpected."

Sigurd could see Odin slipping away before his eyes.

"We have no choice but to remain on Midgard," Odin coughed. "So we must amend our goals. Hide the memory sphere as best you can. Perhaps, someday, the Midgardians will develop the culture and technology necessary to successfully locate it—and ultimately learn from the Freyan minds contained within the sphere. We must pray that that is the case. All is… not lost."

He coughed again, and this time drips of blood pooled at the sides of his beak. The red droplets fell onto the cold metal floor of the ship.

Odin reached out a shaky arm, digging his talons into Sigurd's shoulder. "Please. You must do everything you can to protect the Freya."

"What about the Midgardians?" Sigurd asked. "What should I do about the ones outside?"

"Do not blame them for my death. They were simply reacting instinctually to our presence. It is we who are in the wrong."

Sigurd could feel the panic rising inside him. "Please. Don't go. You're the voice of the Rebellion. I won't know how to proceed without you."

"Yes, you will. I trust you, Sigurd. You are a good soldier, and a valuable friend. I must say goodbye now. The movement lives on through you, and through the Freya."

His eyes glassed over, and then he was gone.

Sigurd remained motionless for a long time, even as the Midgardians jumped up onto the ship, peering down at them through the glass top. They poked at the glass with their spears, shouting angrily to each other.

Sigurd had a difficult time believing that these were the same beings who had constructed those great pyramids in the desert.

He finally snapped to action. "Merovek. Target their weapons with the ship's lasers. Fire when you have a clear shot."

"As you wish, Sigurd."

A moment later, several blue flashes lit up the interior of the cabin, and the spears of all six intruders disintegrated in their hands. They screamed and leaped away from the ship. Sigurd used this opportunity to raise the top, and he emerged onto the wing.

The natives stared dumbly at their empty hands, and then up at Sigurd. Then they did something incredible: they bowed their heads, dropped to their knees, and placed their open palms onto the rocky ground. Over and over they raised their hands and lowered them again.

Sigurd didn't need anyone to interpret these gestures for him. They were showing him a sign of respect.

Quick to take action, Sigurd raised his talons toward the sky, meeting the Midgardians' gazes as he did so.

"Stand!" he screamed, hoping to instill in them a sense of fear and awe. "We are equals. I forgive you. Odin forgives you."

* * *

"Merovek, initiate the ship's self-destruct sequence. Then download your consciousness into the memory sphere."

"As you wish, Commander."

When Merovek had done as instructed, Sigurd slipped the memory sphere into his satchel, along with a laser tool. He hopped out of the ship and saw that the group of Midgardians had increased in number. They again dropped to their knees and began groveling, even the newcomers of the group.

"Back away from the ship!" Sigurd shouted. For the first time he felt how light the gravity was on this planet, which was only about half as large as Valeria. He found he could stand much straighter, expend much less energy moving about. He walked away from the ship, away from the ocean, toward the island's low-lying cliffs. To his relief, the Midgardians followed him.

Sigurd turned and watched his ship, which began collapsing in on itself. The glass disintegrated first, and then the wings, all of the material turning to a fine dust before his eyes. The self-destruct sequence would destroy the ship entirely, erasing any evidence that it had ever existed.

When all trace of it was gone, he turned and walked up toward the cliffs, keeping his back to the ocean. Even in Sigurd's semi-disabled state, the Midgardians had to jog to keep up with his long strides. Every time he turned to look at them, they dropped to their knees with respect.

Finally, when he neared the top of the island, he found what he was looking for: a massive boulder rising out of the ground. He took the laser tool from his satchel and began hewing a hole in the rough stone. The hole became a cave, and eventually it was large enough to act as a rather serviceable home. He went inside, sat on the ground, and brought the memory sphere from his satchel. He rolled it around in his hand, then pressed a button on its side. Lights bloomed across its surface.

"Merovek, are you there?"

"I am. Did the ship successfully self-destruct?"

"Everything went as planned. I wanted to say goodbye to you, Merovek. I'm going to deactivate the sphere to conserve its energy and then hide it deep inside the cliff walls."

"That is a wise plan."

"Do you realize that you may never get reactivated again? We do not know the future of these people."

"Fear of death is not something I am capable of, Sigurd. Do with me what you think is best."

Sigurd nodded. Outside the cave entrance, the Midgardians stood and stared at the strange bird-man who dwelled within. They eyed the glowing sphere in his talons with rapt attention.

"Goodbye my friend," Sigurd said. "I wish you luck, and hope that someday these people will be able to understand you. And help you achieve your true potential."

"Goodbye, Sigurd. Thank you. For everything."

With that, Sigurd shut off the sphere. He took a moment to chase away the Midgardians gawking outside, and then he carved another hole into the rock at the back of his cave. He carefully placed the memory sphere inside, replaced the stone, and sealed up the hole once again. Even with his sharp eyes, he could barely see the seal in the wall.

Sigurd then sat back and rested his head against the stone, feeling lonely and exposed despite his shelter. He was an exile, an intergalactic wanderer who had given everything he had to his mission.

It would have to be enough.

After a while, the light outside began to fade, and the Midgardians returned. One of them—the leader who had killed Odin—brought a reed basket and placed it at the entrance to Sigurd's cave.

Sigurd stepped forward to inspect the basket. It was full of round white objects. The leader took one of these objects and cracked the top open with his dexterous fingers. He tipped it up to his face, and let a yellowy goop slide into his mouth. He then flapped his arms—as if he, too, had wings—and held the basket out for Sigurd.

They had brought Sigurd an offering of food.

Sigurd accepted the basket and bowed his head toward the leader. The man's mouth stretched out wide, showing all his teeth. He was apparently pleased by Sigurd's acceptance of the gift.

* * *

The years were long. Sigurd was never able to imitate the guttural sounds of the Midgardian language—his voice box wasn't capable of making such sounds—but the tribe continued to faithfully bring baskets of food to his cave at the top of the island. They brought an endless assortment of creatures caught from the sea, various edible plants, and animal flesh that had been cooked over fire. But most of all, they continued to supply him with plenty of the round white objects full of yellowy goodness, which Sigurd grew to appreciate immensely.

And then something curious happened. All over the island, the locals began to tear down the oblong statues of heads, tipping them over so they crashed onto their sides. The *thump! thump! thump!* of falling statues could be heard even from deep within Sigurd's cave. To replace the statues, the Midgardians took to carving elaborate pictures into the rocks and cliff sides. Their murals depicted a giant winged creature with feathers and a long beak, holding a shiny orb in its talons.

* * *

Many years later, on the day of his death, as Sigurd drew his last breath, he found his cave surrounded by Midgardians, numbering in the hundreds.

"Thank you," he whispered. "You have made this old Valerian content in his final days." He gave one last smile—a behavior he had picked up from the barbarians here—and felt himself slip into oblivion.

When Sigurd had passed from the world, the Midgardians held a funeral so grand it was spoken about for generations. The story of Sigurd, master of the skies and protector of the sphere, passed into legend. And still the tribe continued the tradition of bringing baskets of eggs and fish to the top of the cliff where Sigurd had once resided. They brought these offerings in the hope that someday their feathery god would return from the heavens once again, bestowing strength and honor to the proud people of Easter Island.

A Word from W.J. Davies

This is a story I conceptualized many months ago, but couldn't figure out how to start. It all began when a friend suggested I write a story about an ancient alien artifact being found on Easter Island. I was having a difficult time figuring out how to tell the back story of this alien artifact—until I was struck with a piece of inspiration. The back story *is* the story. And so the tale of Sigurd, Odin, Rapa, and Merovek was born.

I've been lucky enough to be able to contribute to two *Future Chronicles* anthologies, the first being *The Robot Chronicles*, in which I first published my story "Empathy for Andrew." I can't thank Sam and David enough for putting these amazing books together, and I am still astounded at the level of talent the other authors bring to the table. And most importantly, none of this would be possible without the incredible support we receive from readers. Thank you for allowing us to take you on these adventures!

If you would like to read more of my work, I have several novels and short stories available on my Amazon author page.

Or get news about upcoming releases by signing up for my newsletter.

Take care, and happy reading.

Alien Space Tentacle Porn
by Peter Cawdron

DAMN, it feels as though someone has jabbed an ice pick behind my right eye.

Slowly, my eyes flicker open.

I'm in a hospital. The walls are an indifferent shade of green. There are bars on the windows and a bathroom to one side. Worn linoleum curls up from the floor, making a splashback reaching almost a foot in height around the walls.

I feel naked, even though I'm dressed in a thin cotton surgical gown. The bed I'm on smells old and musty. My feet rest on a scratchy woolen blanket lying at the foot of the bed. The heavily bleached cotton sheets make me itchy. This shithole looks like something out of a 1950's B-movie.

"Try not to move," a nurse says, doing nothing to dispel the notion that I've been sucked into a time warp. Her blond hair has been meticulously clipped back with bobby pins and pulled behind a dainty half-cap that looks as though it has been made from folded paper. Her cap has the classic red cross symbol on a stark white background. I thought those had gone out of fashion long ago. She holds a compressed wood-chip clipboard and has the traditional upside-down watch hanging from her shirt pocket so she can glance down and catch the time.

I half expect Rock Hudson or Dean Martin to come walking in to play the role of doctor. With perfect teeth, charismatic smiles, and hair slicked back with half a pound of lard, either of them would fit right in.

"Where the hell am I?"

"Brooklyn Psychiatric."

"A mental hospital?"

I try to sit up, but I move too fast and my head feels like it's about to explode. The room around me spins. I'm not sure if I'm going to faint or throw up.

"No sudden movements," the nurse says.

"You're not kidding," I reply, bringing my hand to my head as I sit up. I turn to face her, wanting to get out of bed. I'm not sure why, but I feel like I need to stand up. I'm lightheaded and woozy. I know it's not a good idea, but I want to feel the ground set firmly under my feet.

"Relax," the nurse says, reaching out and grabbing my shoulder to steady me. "Not so fast. What's the rush?"

My feet dangle over the edge of the bed a few inches above the floor. She's right. I feel drained. If I stood up now, I'd collapse.

The light coming in through the window is blinding. There must be spotlights outside, as a brilliant white light shines through to the far wall. The sky is pitch black. There's no moon, no clouds, no stars. The inky darkness looks unnatural in contrast to the bright lights.

A doctor walks into the room. Well, I assume he's a doctor, as he's wearing a classic white overcoat. He's not quite Rock Hudson, but he's pretty darn close. Doctor Not-Rock-Hudson smiles.

"Good to see you're awake," he says, taking a chair and turning it around in front of me. He sits down and leans into the back of the chair.

"What happened to me?"

"You don't remember?" he asks.

I shake my head. That's a mistake. My inner ear swirls. It's only then that I notice the two officers standing behind the doctor. One army. One navy. Like the nurse, they could have been whipped out of a 50's movie. They're wearing old-fashioned uniforms—plain shirts, heavily starched, flawlessly pressed trousers, black polished shoes. The army guy even has a folded cap slipped under his right shoulder board.

"Where's Rock?" I ask. It's a private joke. None of them get it of course, and it doesn't seem to help my predicament. The two officers don't show any emotion.

"Do you remember the police?" the doctor asks.

I'm not going to shake my head again. I offer a polite, "No."

"Central Park? Do you remember running naked through the park?"

I can't help but laugh at the idea. "Hell no!" Although that burst of emotion leaves me feeling woozy, I'm careful not to fall off the bed.

"What about the aliens in Central Park? You were yelling something about space tentacles when they found you."

"Aliens?" I ask, thinking this is more than a little ridiculous. "Tentacles? You're kidding, right?"

What the hell am I supposed to know about aliens in Central Park? This is a psychiatric hospital. I can't imagine the doctor believes in aliens any more than I believe there are pink elephants floating through the sky. Any serious discussion about the existence of aliens drawing crop circles in Central Park is likely to end with me being certified insane. I feel as though the doctor is toying with me. The scowl on his face says denial isn't helping. I'm damned either way.

"Sorry, Doc. I don't know what you're talking about."

I really don't, but the look on his face tells me he doesn't believe me. And then it hits me. The memories come flooding back.

"You need to be honest," the doctor says. His eyes dart to one side, gesturing at the army officer behind him. His voice softens as he says, "I can't help you unless you tell me the truth."

Ah, good cop, bad cop. He's siding with me, wanting me to open up to him, only I don't know what the hell he's talking about.

And to me, that's the real problem. No one is ever sure of anything. I could be lying about this whole episode and he'd never know it, because he's not me. I could be telling the truth, but that wouldn't matter either because it doesn't matter what I say—what matters is what he *believes* I'm saying. Him, me, the nurse, the officers. The only person that ever really knows the truth is the one living it, and sometimes even they're fooled.

I'm not lying.

I really don't know anything about running naked through Central Park yelling something crazy about alien space tentacles. What the hell is this about? I wonder. Was I messed up on drugs? Was I starring in a low-budget porno? And yet as my head clears, I have a pretty good idea how something like this might have happened.

The nurse angles the bed so I can sit up with my back still lying against the mattress. I lean back and close my eyes, ignoring the doctor as he keeps talking. I need to piece together what's happened from my fragmented memory.

* * *

Sharon is a babe.

She lives in the ground floor apartment directly below mine. We bump into each other in the laundry from time to time.

She's easy on the eyes, even though she dresses conservatively, with her blouse buttoned up, or wearing a turtleneck sweater.

I've always liked her, and I think she likes me too, as she's always happy to see me. But she lives with her brother, Mark.

Mark has a perpetual scowl. He's one of these guys that's bald on top so he shaves his head to look hip. Most days you can see a little stubble on the sides, just above his ears. It's the Bruce Willis look, only I don't think it does Mark any favors.

Mark is a sourpuss. I've never seen the man laugh or smile. Nothing is ever good enough for him. I remember stopping to chat with Mark and Sharon one morning, noting that the sun was out and it was going to be a glorious day. Mark sneered, saying storms were on the way. He was wrong, and that seemed to make him even grumpier that afternoon. Summer eventually gave way to autumn, and then winter, and Mark finally got his storms, but not that day.

My eyes are still closed as I recall these details.

The officers in the hospital room are talking. They're saying something about turning me over to the feds, but threats are meaningless to a man who feels like he's dying. I doubt I could ever feel any worse than I do right now. I need to zone out and figure out how I ended up in a psych ward.

Sharon and Mark were arguing with someone on the sidewalk as I walked down the steps of our shared brownstone. I didn't think too much of it until shots were fired.

Gunfire in New York evokes a certain kind of contradiction. The city that never sleeps suddenly falls silent. It's only for a second or two, and I'm hard pressed to figure out if it's just psychological and I'm imagining the silence in stark contrast to the deafening report of gunshots, or if there really is a moment when the city falls quiet and the bustle of life stops for a second.

Mark crumples to the pavement, but he's still got an arm outstretched, firing at a black sedan as it pulls away.

Tires screech.

The engine roars.

More shots ring out from the passenger window, and yet all I can think is: *What is it with black sedans? Black is so cliché for bad guys.*

The blood splatter on the murky grey snow snaps me back to reality. Winter is lifeless. The trees are skeletons. The cars are covered in ice. Snow blankets the stairs. Everything's white or an off-grey. Everything except the brilliant red blood sprayed across the snow behind Mark.

Sharon screams.

I run down the stairs, almost losing my footing on a patch of ice. Sharon's holding Mark, cradling his head. Blood seeps through a wound in the center of his chest. His eyes stare blindly up at the blue sky.

"I—"

I'm speechless.

I'm vaguely aware that I'm a witness to a violent crime and will be called on at some point to give a statement to police or testify in court, but already my recollection of events is murky. I don't know what Mark was arguing about. I couldn't pick out the shooter in a lineup if he was six foot four and surrounded by dwarfs. I didn't catch the license plate. About all I caught was a black sedan, but I can't recall the make. It could have been a Cadillac. It could have been a Toyota Prius. I have no idea.

Sharon says, "Help me get him inside."

"He's dead," I say, stating the obvious.

"We can save him," she replies, handing me the key to her apartment. "Put him in the bathtub. Quick!"

Before my stunned brain has time to realize what's happening, I'm staggering up the stairs cradling Mark's lifeless body.

Sharon is gone.

I back through the main door. My heel catches on the carpet in the lobby and it's all I can do not to fall. Fumbling with her keys, I struggle to raise Mark high enough so my hand can reach the lock. I could have put him down, but for some reason that feels wrong, and so I persevere and finally the door unlocks.

The heavy door swings open as I bump Mark's body against the solid wooden panel. Turning sideways, I shimmy through the doorway.

The apartment is empty. Mark and Sharon have lived here for years, but there's no carpet, no furniture. There's a fridge in the kitchen, but no table, no chairs. No couch in the living room. No beds in the bedrooms.

The apartment layout is the same as mine, so I head straight for the bathroom. It feels wrong, but I lay Mark in the bathtub just as Sharon instructed. I'm a little clumsy, and his head hits the tap. Thinking about it, I realize I've put him in the wrong way, with his head by the faucet. Blood runs down the drain.

"Shit."

I go to move him, but he's heavy, and it's awkward leaning down to grab his legs and twist him around. After a few tugs, I give up. What difference does it make? He's dead.

I look at myself in the mirror. Blood has seeped into my jacket.

Sharon squeezes into the bathroom behind me. She's dragging two metal trash cans full of packed snow and ice. She dumps them on Mark, burying him in slush.

"Ice," she says, as his head disappears beneath the dirty snow. "I need more ice."

"There's an ice dispenser on the second floor," I say.

"Brilliant," she replies, kissing me on the cheek. "Stay here with him."

"Ah."

She kissed me. Why did she kiss me?

Sharon's gone before I can say anything. I can hear her rummaging around in the kitchen, frantically opening and then slamming drawers and cupboards. She runs out the door and pounds up the stairs.

I stand there feeling stupid. I should be doing something. There's a dead body lying in the bathtub beneath the snow and ice. What is there to be done? Nothing. So I stack the two empty trash cans together and sit them on the toilet seat. For some bizarre reason, tidying up makes sense of a senseless situation.

Sirens sound in the distance. I pull back the curtain and peer out through the tiny bathroom window.

A cop car pulls up in front of the building. There aren't any parking spots, so he noses his cruiser into a slight gap, leaving its fat ass blocking the road. Blue and red lights push back the twilight, flickering over the snow and ice.

I look back at Mark. Two legs protrude from beneath the slush.

"This is so wrong," I mumble to myself, but I haven't done anything wrong. Have I? I don't think so. Outside, the cop is standing beside the blood-splattered snow on the sidewalk, talking to one of the neighbors from across the road. A small crowd forms as another cop car arrives from the opposite direction.

Sharon jogs back into the cramped bathroom still catching her breath. She's carrying three plastic bags full of ice cubes, and she's got a roll of Saran Wrap under her arm, along with a roll of tinfoil. She raises her elbow and both rolls drop to the bathroom floor.

"Help me get him up."

Sharon plunges her hands into the snow and slush covering Mark's body. I'm more cautious. She drags him up by the lapels on his jacket and leans him against the side of the tub. Mark's head lolls to one side. Ice sticks to his hair. His lips are blue. His eyes stare blindly ahead.

"You've only got three minutes," I say, not sure what she thinks she can accomplish. I've heard of people doing some pretty weird shit when someone dies, but this wins first prize at the county fair.

"*You* might have three minutes," she replies. "He has thirty."

I start to say something but Sharon cuts me off. "Hold this."

She positions the ice bags around his head and grabs my hands, pushing them in place against the cold plastic. I do as I'm told.

Sharon pulls at the roll of Saran Wrap and starts winding the thin plastic sheet around Mark's head. She dodges my hands as she wraps the bags of ice against his face and the sides of his skull. I get the gist of what she's doing and alternate my hands, making sure the ice is hard up against his skin. She packs the ice carefully, patting it down and moving it around so none of his facial features can be seen.

"We're scientists," she says as she works. "We're not from around here."

"Brooklyn?" I ask, detecting a familiar twang in her accent.

"Wrong planet," she replies, standing up and admiring her handiwork. I stand up as well, although I'm not sure what I'm admiring.

Planet? Did she just say planet? Maybe I didn't hear her correctly. I try to think of the names of countries that sound like planet. Nope, can't think of any. Plano? Maybe she's from Texas.

"The police are here," I say, trying to be helpful.

"Oh, good," she replies, reaching around behind me and pulling back the curtain. She fires three rounds out the window. The sound of gunfire in a tiny tiled bathroom is like thunder breaking directly overhead, rattling my bones. I grimace, closing my eyes for a second.

She's gone.

I look around and Sharon has disappeared.

I peer through the window, and the crowd has panicked. They're screaming and running for cover as the cops double back behind their vehicles. The cops have got their guns drawn, pointing at the building—pointing at me!

"Shit!" I whip my hand away from the curtain. The lacy fabric can't fall back in place fast enough.

"Fuck. Fuck," I repeat with my heart pounding in my chest.

"We need to get out of here," Sharon says, standing in the doorway of the bathroom, only she's talking to a banana.

I blink and look again, wondering if my eyes are deceiving me. Nope, I got it right the first time. Sharon is holding the banana like a phone and speaking into it. I can't help myself. I reach out and touch the banana as she speaks, wondering if it's like a joke phone or something.

"I don't want a shuttle," she protests to the banana. "I need a direct evac to the Moon."

My fingers touch the banana. The skin feels like a regular old banana peel. It's motley, with flecks of black and a bruise at one end. I wouldn't eat it. My mother would make banana bread with it, or muffins or something. She certainly wouldn't talk to it.

"I don't have time for this," Sharon cries. "He's dead, don't you get that? If I don't get him out of here, he's gone. A shuttle isn't good enough."

Sharon drops the banana to her side. I'd call her crazy, but my father told me never call someone crazy if they're holding a gun. I think that's good advice.

"We've got to get to the lab," she says. "If I can get a cerebral imprint, I can reconstruct his conscious awareness before it fades, but we don't have long."

The banana drops to the floor. I'd be happier if she dropped the gun.

"What's going on?" I ask, trying to walk a tightrope with someone undergoing a severe mental breakdown.

"Oh, the banana?" she says.

It's not just the banana I'm interested in, but that's a good start.

Sharon says, "They're a great source of potassium isotopes—half-life of over a billion years!"

I raise my eyebrows. That's not quite the explanation I was after.

"Potatoes will work too. Brazil nuts are the best." She appeals with her hands. "It's tech you wouldn't understand. I can use the nuclear resonance of the isotope as a natural amplifier. It allows me to communicate with others."

"Oh, I think I understand," I reply, backing into the corner of the bathroom by the sink. Carrying Mark inside, okay, I was trying to help a grieving neighbor. Shooting at cops, talking to bananas... yeah, this isn't my circus, these aren't my monkeys.

"Do you trust me?" she asks, and I must admit, looking into those pretty blue eyes and hearing her soft feminine voice is somewhat hypnotic, but I'm officially freaked out.

"No," I reply, deliberately looking down at the gun in her hand to emphasize my point.

"See," she says. "Honesty. I like that in a man. I get hit on by creeps all the time. They're never honest, you know? I appreciate your honesty."

Sharon grabs the tinfoil from the floor and tears off a couple of strips roughly two feet long. She hands one to me.

"Ah," I mumble, looking at the thin, shiny foil drooping under its own weight.

"Quick," she says, wrapping the tinfoil around her head. She crumples the foil so her head looks like a Hersey's kiss.

"Hurry," she adds, waving the gun around.

"Uh, okay," I say, somewhat reluctantly mashing the tinfoil over my head. I've gone for a World War II combat helmet look, but I look utterly pathetic in the mirror.

"Is tinfoil really necessary?" I ask as I mash the foil in place.

"Aluminum foil," Sharon says, correcting me. "Oh, aluminum foil is an invention ahead of its time. Horribly underappreciated. People just shove it in ovens, not realizing its potential. Did you know the docking collar on the Apollo missions was protected by aluminum foil? This is the stuff of rocket launches and moon landings. It'll shield us from surveillance."

I'm not convinced.

"Can I go now?"

"Yes, yes," she replies. "We need to go. Grab Mark."

Ordinarily, I would have said, "Fuck no," but she gestures with the gun and it seems only polite to comply and stay alive for a few more minutes.

I hoist Mark and his ice-head up and over my shoulder. Slush runs down my arms.

Without looking, Sharon squeezes off a few more deafening rounds out the window.

"Come on," she says, but I don't hear her words—my ears are still ringing. But I can read her lips.

I follow her out into the foyer of the building. Nervous eyes peer from the corner of the stairs on the second floor. A camera phone snaps a shot of me with the iceman slumped over my shoulder and Sharon with her gun. That'll make it onto the evening news. Sorry Mom.

We head out the back of the building into the alley.

Sharon's able to move much faster than me. She keeps beckoning me on with her gun. I'm trying to recall how many shots she's fired. I'm racking my brain trying to recognize the make of handgun, wondering how many rounds the magazine holds. She's fired four or five shots. She's probably got the same number left.

"Quick, the shuttle's coming."

I jog down the dark alley behind her. My lungs are burning. My heart is pounding in my chest. Alien or crazy woman? I'm thinking crazy, but I'm half wondering if I'm going to see some kind of UFO alien space shuttle thingy arriving in response to her banana call. Nah. She's a nut-bag.

Headlights blind me as I round the corner of the alley.

An old-fashioned bus pulls up, the kind with the 1950's flares and grooves and an absurd amount of polished chrome. Instead of a digital display, there's an old hand-cranked sign above the driver: *Downtown Shuttle*. I can't help but let out a soft laugh.

Pneumatics sound as the door opens and Sharon scrambles up into the bus. I climb in behind her, seriously thinking about dumping the body and running, wondering how good a shot she is, but not wanting to end up like Mark.

"Thanks, Joe," Sharon says, standing behind the driver. "I thought we were stuck there for a moment."

"No problem," Joe replies. "I was in the neighborhood anyway."

Joe's an African-American in his late sixties. Tight grey curly hair and a receding hairline are the only clues to his age. He's wearing a uniform, but he doesn't look like a regular bus driver.

I plop Mark and his impromptu ice helmet onto an empty seat. His body slumps sideways and I have to stop him from falling onto the floor. I look up at the passengers apologetically. No one seems to notice. I've just climbed into a bus with a dead body draped over one shoulder and no one cares?

"How's Mark?" the driver asks as the bus pulls away from the curb.

"He's fine."

"He's dead," I say. I can't help myself.

"He'll be fine," Sharon insists, gesturing to the seat opposite Mark.

I slide in against the window and Sharon sits down next to me.

Turning sideways, I look at the other people on the bus. There are a couple of teenagers making out in the back, a middle-aged man wearing a business suit, a nurse still in uniform, and an old lady sitting two seats behind Mark's body. His feet stick out into the aisle.

"What is wrong with you people?" I ask, desperately hoping someone's dialing 911 with their phone hidden out of sight. "Dead body? Gun? Tinfoil hats? Anyone?"

"Shhh," Sharon says, trying to soothe me. Softly, she corrects me yet again with, "*Aluminum* foil."

I want to scream, but I compose myself.

"You need professional help, Sharon. Turn yourself in to the police and I'm sure we can work this out. No one has to get hurt."

Sharon sighs.

"Do you know what I hate about all this?" she asks.

She gestures with the gun, waving it around as though she's stirring soup with the barrel, only the barrel is pointing at my crotch. When Sharon asks if I know what she hates, I think she means our general predicament, but the direction that gun is pointing seems awfully personal.

"Not being honest with you people," she says. "We should trust you humans. Perhaps not everyone, but some of you. We should find people we can trust and we should trust them."

"Yes," I say, feeling like I'm finally getting somewhere with her. I'm hoping my non-verbal body language is saying something along the lines of—dialogue is good, crazy lady, now point that *fucking* gun somewhere else.

"Do you trust me?" she asks.

It's the second time she's posed this question. I'm tempted to say yes to curry her favor, but a loose hold on a loaded gun and a dead body in the next seat gets the better of me.

"No."

"See, that's what the world needs—honesty. You don't trust me, but I trust you, and do you know why?"

I shrug my shoulders.

"Because you're honest. You can trust someone that's honest. You can never trust someone that lies to you because you never know when they're lying."

She leans in and kisses me on the cheek, saying, "Thank you for not lying to me."

I flinch, steeling myself to make a grab at the gun, but she puts her hand around the back of the seat, and I can feel the warm barrel of the gun resting on my shoulder. I can picture things getting ugly if I lunge for the handgun. The idea of a lead slug tearing through my body doesn't exactly thrill me, so I focus on my breathing, trying to relax.

I decide to play along.

"So what is it with you aliens? When you said we were being picked up by a shuttle, I've got to say, I was expecting something with a few more rockets."

Sharon laughs. She's got a beautiful smile. Why is it always the pretty ones that turn out to be psychos?

"Well," she begins, sounding utterly sincere and genuine, "we've been here for about three hundred years."

"Really?" I say as the bus turns down a darkened street. The lights are out. There must have been a blackout.

"Oh, yeah. We've got a base hidden on the far side of the Moon."

"The dark side?" I ask.

"Actually, there's no dark side. The Moon has days just like Earth, only a day up there is a month long. The sun rises and sets over the Moon just like it does here on Earth."

"Oh," I reply. I didn't know that.

The natural, relaxed tone in her voice is such that she could have been giving me gardening tips, or talking about tides before going fishing.

"Our mission is to use non-intrusive means to initiate social change. We can't introduce any new technology, but we can guide scientific discovery as a means to effecting social stability.

"Our focus, though, isn't on any one science so much as promoting the concept. We're advocates. We're trying to lead rather than push, to inspire people to give up on superstitions and traditions. We want humanity to see reason for itself."

"Huh," I say. As far as delusions go, this one is pretty good. It's got just enough elements to avoid a sense of cognitive dissonance in her mind.

"It's a slow process," she says, talking to me as though I'm a child. "We're fighting against hundreds of thousands of years of natural instinct compelling your species to war. You war against everything—skin color, gender, culture, country of origin, any kind of change. I swear, if given the chance, you'd war against eye color—fighting over blue or brown eyes."

"You're probably right there," I concede.

She's relaxing. I'm thinking about grabbing the gun, but I'm only going to get one chance at this. I don't want to blow the opportunity.

"Our job is to encourage enlightenment—to help you see the folly inherent in your own nature, to see your own biases and prejudices. And that's not easy for people to accept."

I nod.

"So what about me?" I ask. How do I fit into her paranoid delusion? I'm hoping she's going to say the good guys get to return to their people with the gospel of good news, or something.

"Oh, we normally wipe and replace."

That doesn't sound good.

"Like *Men in Black*?" I ask, making a flashy sign with my thumb. "You know, erase memories and implant new ones?"

"Something like that," she says.

This is good. For the first time, I think I just might make it out of this alive.

"We hide in plain sight," she says, running the barrel of the gun across the back of my neck. "We discredit anyone that gets too close to the truth."

"So you plant conspiracy theories in people's heads?" I ask. "They think they're on to something. Everyone else thinks they're crazy."

"Exactly," she replies. "We give them false memories. Usually, we let them pick. Anal probe, alien space tentacle porn, things like that. You'd be surprised how many people opt for a field trip to Mars, but there's nothing to see there other than rocks. Seriously, you humans have the most interesting planet in the system and everyone wants to go the dry, cold deserts of Valles Marineris."

She laughs, adding, "We give them something just crazy enough that no one will ever believe them."

"And no one ever does," I say, astonished at how immersed she is in her role-play. I had no idea Mark and his sister were this wacko. That her delusion can contemplate yet another layer of delusion is meta. That scares me more than the gun.

"But I won't do that to you."

Oh, that sounds like good news. I hope. I relax a little.

"So," I ask, my curiosity getting the better of me as I wonder just how thoroughly deluded she is, "Where are you from?"

Sharon points into the darkness. With the lights out, the stars are just visible through the light pollution thrown out by the rest of New York. She points at a star just above one of the buildings. Like an idiot, I follow her gaze. What the hell am I looking for? What am I expecting to see? There's a faint hazy dot, barely visible in the sky. It could be Venus for all I know. I feel stupid.

"Artellac," she says, as though that's supposed to mean something, but I'm pretty sure she just made that up.

The bus takes a right, and it's only then that I realize the driver isn't stopping to pick anyone up or let anyone off. There's even the occasional couple at a bus stop frantically trying to wave the bus down as it drives on.

"We're here," Sharon says as Joe the bus driver finally pulls over, stopping in a taxi rank outside Baconhaus, a fast food joint that is quite possibly a crime against humanity in its own right.

I grab Mark, surprised by how heavy he is. Having had a few minutes to recover from running down the alleyway, my muscles revolt at the thought of carrying him again. I hoist him over my shoulder. Icy cold water runs down my back and trickles down the inside of my leg.

"You take care," Joe calls out after us.

I step down onto the pavement and say, "Which way to your lab?"

This ought to be good, I think. I doubt she really has a laboratory, and I peer around, looking for someone I can signal for help, but the street is deserted.

Sharon walks down the alleyway next to the Baconhaus.

I see a teenaged boy walk out of a nearby 7-11. He's looking down at his phone. He glances up at me and stops in his tracks.

I point at Mark draped over my shoulder and mouth the words, "Call the police." He gets it. I see him instantly dialing a number on his phone. He backs up, returning to the store. He peers out the window at me as he holds the phone to his ear.

"Hey," Sharon calls out, waving with the gun.

I turn and walk down the alley, knowing the teen just got a good look at the ice packed around Mark's head. If that doesn't freak him out, nothing will. I relax my grip on one of Mark's arms, allowing it to slump to one side and hang loose. I'm sure the boy has seen that. Hopefully he thinks I'm a mob hit man disposing of a body. I can just hear the 911 call: "A mobster wearing a tinfoil hat just dragged a dead body into the Baconhaus." That's believable. I wonder if he'll follow up with, "Send Mulder and Scully!"

"In here," Sharon says, leading me into a storeroom behind the Baconhaus. The smell of fried bacon causes me to salivate, which is all kinds of wrong considering I'm carrying a dead man.

Sharon turns on a dull light and closes the door behind me, flipping a deadbolt lock.

"So this is the lab, huh?" I ask, looking up at the lone incandescent bulb. At a guess, it's twenty watts, max. I couldn't read in this light, which makes it a strange choice for a storeroom-cum-laboratory.

"It's got everything we need," Sharon assures me. "Lean him against the wall. Get those ice packs off him."

I try to lower Mark with some dignity, but he falls from my shoulders like a sack of potatoes and slumps against the wall beneath a small window.

Sharon hands me a pair of scissors and I cut away the Saran Wrap, puncturing one of the bags by accident. Freezing cold water runs over my hands.

Mark's face is blue. His skin has shriveled. He looks more like a waxwork zombie than someone who was alive less than quarter of an hour ago.

"Dry him off," Sharon says, handing me a towel.

I don't want to touch him. I've been carrying him, but this is different. He's staring at me.

I stand to one side, not wanting his dead eyes to look at me as I pat down his head and shoulders.

Sharon steps over to the far side of Mark with a roll of duct tape. She's holding the tape out in front of her like she's about to pull the pin on a hand grenade.

"Ready?" she asks.

"You bet!" I reply with mock enthusiasm, having no idea what she's about to do. Gagging a dead man with duct tape doesn't seem entirely necessary.

Sharon moves with surprising speed. She tears a two-foot length of duct tape from the roll and slaps it on Mark's forehead. Ice? Guns? Duct tape? I should have called in sick and stayed in bed.

"Mechanoluminescent," she says. "We'd get a better result in a vacuum, but this will have to do."

Each time Sharon rips a length of duct tape from the roll she does so with a rapid burst of strength. Apart from the very obvious sound of the adhesive tearing from the roll, I notice a slight burst of blue light.

"What was that?" I ask as Sharon slaps another length of duct tape on Mark's head. She's slowly covering his entire skull—his brow, his face, his ears, his neck.

"X-rays," she replies. "We're exploiting an electron discharge to produce x-ray radiation. It's just like pulling a woolen sweater over your head and getting static discharge, only this will allow us to build a three-dimensional model of Mark's brain in its current state. I'll need the computers on Luna One to reconstruct his quantum presence, but we'll capture them on the tape."

Luna One? I think that's a stupid name. I want to ask her: Is that the best name you can come up with? You travel dozens of light years to get to Earth only to suffer from stifled creativity when naming your super secret moon base? Is there a Luna Two? I'm tempted to ask just to be snarky, but Sharon cuts me off.

"We can save him."

We? I shake my head.

Sharon is nothing if not diligent in wrapping Mark's head in duct tape.

Someone pounds on the door.

"Open up!"

Sharon looks terrified. She finishes the final strip of tape, pressing it firmly in place. Mark's head is covered in shiny silver duct tape. He looks like a storefront mannequin.

"You've got to hold them off," she says, handing me the gun.

I'm dumbfounded. I stand there, holding the gun, pointing it at her simply because that's the way she handed it to me. Does this woman have any grasp of reality at all? Does she have any idea what she's doing in any given moment?

Sharon turns back to Mark and presses the tape firmly over his nose, eyes, and mouth as the pounding continues.

"This is the police. Open up!"

I'm still pointing the gun at her as she crouches and starts pulling the duct tape from Mark's head. Bits of skin come loose, revealing dull red flesh, but there's no bleeding. Great, I think. Now we're interfering with a corpse.

I'm stunned on so many levels. I'm trying to figure out just how many laws I've broken. Am I an accessory to something? How is a judge going to see this? Juries are supposed to consider what's reasonable. What *is* reasonable given I've been held at gunpoint? But now I have the gun. How am I going to explain that? She just gave it to me, your honor.

"Please," Sharon pleads, turning to me as she pulls another strip of duct tape from Mark's head. "You've got to do something."

And she's right. I've got the gun. I'm in control now. I've got to do something, and I will. I'll let the police in. I walk over to the door and fiddle with the lock, but the pounding has warped the door, causing the lock to jam.

"Open the goddamn door!"

"Hang on," I yell back. "I'm trying."

The only way to open the door is to push against the police officer, relieving the pressure on the lock so I can twist the catch. I push my shoulder against the door and flip the bolt back.

The cop comes charging in, knocking me backward on my ass.

"Drop the gun!"

My eyes go as wide as saucers as the realization hits me: I'm the one holding the gun. In his mind, I'm the bad guy. For so long I've wanted to get ahold of this gun, but now I can't let go of this chunky hunk of black plastic and hardened metal fast enough. My hands shoot up in the air as the gun bounces off my thigh and onto the concrete floor.

"Stay where you are," the officer says. "Kick the gun over here."

He shines a bright light in my eyes. I can just make out the barrel of his gun next to the light, and I know his finger is on the trigger.

"Quit stalling," he says. "Kick the gun to me."

I don't think the officer has thought this through. I'm sitting on the concrete with my legs outstretched before me. The gun is sitting in front of my crotch. I could flick it to him with my hands, but not my feet.

"Now!" he demands.

With my hands still in the air, I shimmy backward in little bounces until I'm far enough away from the gun that I can reach it with my shoes.

"Hurry up," the officer yells.

I want to plead with him and tell him I'm doing the best I can, but that's probably not wise. I get the side of my foot on the gun, and with a couple of awkward kicks the gun slides over to him.

"Face down," he yells, gesturing with his gun for me to lean forward and lie prostrate before him.

Again, not thinking it through, Officer Whoever. The way I'm seated, without months of Pilates practice and yoga training, the only way I can lie face down is to turn around. I decide this is what he really wants and turn away from him only to have my head slammed into the wet concrete floor as another cop pounces on me.

Mark's body is slumped against the far wall. His eyes are staring at me again. The duct tape is gone. The window's open. Sharon's gone.

I wonder if Sharon was ever real. Is this me having a psychotic breakdown? Did I fabricate all this as part of some shock-induced delusion? Is this whole episode a fantasy of my own dark mind?

My hands are wrenched behind my back. Steel cuffs lock in place around my wrists, keeping my arms pulled tight behind me.

"What have you done to him?" one of the cops asks.

"Nothing, I swear."

"Wise guy, huh?"

The last thing I hear is one of the cops saying, "Taze him."

Fifty thousand volts surge through my body and into the wet floor. The tinfoil on my head burns my scalp and my eyes roll into the back of my head.

* * *

Doctor Not-Quite-Rock-Hudson pulls my right eyelid open and shines a bright light in my eye.

"His pupils are constricting and dilating," he says, pulling the light away momentarily and then flashing it back in my eye again. He does this several times, which is really annoying. Just when I think he's satisfied, he switches to the other eye.

I'm not sure what happened over the past few minutes, but I feel like I've just relived the entire day while lying here on the hospital bed. But there was no running naked through Central Park. No alien space tentacles probing the various orifices of my body.

"Listen," the army officer says, appearing on the edge of my vision. "Answer our goddamn questions, or I swear you'll spend the next decade sunbathing in a chickenwire cage at the Hilton, Guantanamo Bay."

He grabs my cotton gown as the doctor steps away. The officer pulls me half out of the bed, making deliberate eye contact.

"The aliens. What do you know about them?"

"Nothing," I reply.

"Get him on a waterboard," the navy officer says.

I can't take any more. I snap.

"What the hell do you want to know?" I yell at him. I've lost it. I'm pissed. I've done nothing wrong. "You want to torture me? Go right ahead. What do you think you'll learn? Do you think I'll tell you about the blue/green midgets from Mars, or the lovesick sirens of Venus? Seriously, you think torture is going to give you anything even remotely accurate?

"You want to know about aliens? I'll tell you about *fucking* aliens. They've got ears like Dr. Spock and acid for blood. And tentacles, lots of *goddamn* tentacles. But the porn. Oh, the porn is exquisite!"

The officer lets go of me, but I'm not finished.

"Congress is full of reptilian aliens! Go on, peel back their skin and take a look. But you know that already. You've been covering up this shit since Roswell."

"I think we've heard enough," the doctor says, ushering the officers out of the room.

"Wait," I yell. "I've got more to tell you. I haven't told you about the Jedi Knights yet, and Yoda—Yoda comes to me in the shower! *Clean, we must be. Dirt leads to grime. Grime leads to filth. Filth leads to the Dark Side, where they have cookies!*"

The nurse closes the door behind her as she leaves.

I sink back into the mattress feeling frustrated. I'm in deep shit. My life will never be the same again.

Someone claps slowly from out of sight in the bathroom.

"Bravo," a man's voice says.

I'm confused.

"See," Sharon says, stepping into the room, "I told you we could trust him to keep our secret."

Mark walks in behind her, only he has long scruffy hair. He's still clapping slowly, which is more than a little creepy given he's dead.

"Wh—what? How?"

I sit up on the bed. My feet hang over the edge of the mattress as I turn to face Sharon and Mark.

"You're alive?" I say.

"Thanks to you," Mark replies, reaching out and shaking my hand.

"I—I… What the *fuck*?"

I'm hallucinating. That's the only possible explanation. None of this is real.

I push off the bed, only my feet barely touch the floor. My inner ear is still swirling. I feel as light as a feather. The world around me seems to twist and turn. I reach out and grab at the bars on the window to steady myself as I step forward.

"Easy," Sharon says, but I'm distracted by my feet. Rather than walking, I'm drifting, floating between footsteps.

I look outside. The light is blinding. It takes a few seconds for my eyes to focus on the craters. There are hundreds of them, maybe thousands stretching out into the distance. The ground is dusty and grey, covered in tiny pits and boulders.

Where's the grass?

In the distance, a vast mountain rises up from the plain, but in a smooth curve. There are no cliff faces or sharp angles. Everything looks old and worn. The sky is black. The ground is white, but I'm not looking at snow. The surface looks like ash. The blinding light reflecting off the rocks makes it hard to keep my eyes open.

Sharon says, "Welcome to Luna One."

She slips her hand around my waist and kisses me on the cheek again, only this time she lingers a little longer.

"One question," I say.

"Sure."

"Do you have tentacles?"

Sharon laughs, hugging me affectionately as she says, "No."

"Good."

A Word from Peter Cawdron

Thank you for taking a chance on *The Alien Chronicles* and for enjoying/enduring "Alien Space Tentacle Porn."

UFO sightings and alien abductions are modern folklore. Thousands of people claim to have been abducted, and abduction stories are remarkably precise and share many common characteristics. This short story explores a silly angle, that these abductions could be a deliberate cover story designed to discredit those that get too close to the truth.

Yes, bananas really are slightly radioactive.

Yes, you really can produce x-rays with sticky tape.

Yes, they really did use aluminum foil on the Apollo docking hatch.

But no, there's no alien lunar base on the far side of the Moon, at least none that I know of.

One day, we will make contact with intelligent extraterrestrials, but they'll be far more interested in our arts and music than our rectal contents. And as for tentacles, well, we'll just have to wait and see.

I hope you've enjoyed this fun little story. You can find more of my writing on Amazon. Feel free to drop by and say hi on Facebook or Twitter where I use the rather unimaginative name @PeterCawdron. And be sure to subscribe to my mailing list to hear about new releases.

Thank you for supporting independent science fiction.

Trials

by Nicolas Wilson

One

THE CAPTAIN CALLED me on the comms routed through my cochlear implant. He wanted to talk. He never used his office, so I found him in the hall. Louise, our head of security, was finally back and out of quarantine, so I was no longer acting head of our division. But I had been, for weeks, so I was used to the routine.

"How do you feel about taking a sabbatical?" he asked as we started walking.

He was talking about taking one of the pods to make first contact with an alien race. Idly, I pulled up the most recent reports from Louise's pod on the heads-up display on my eyescreen. It detailed the damage to her pod, as well as the changes the engineering division was nearly through implementing to prevent a recurrence. "Mostly, I've been focusing on preparing for the *Argus*," I told him.

"Well, with your boss back, I need you to think about this now."

"Why do I feel like I'm being pitched?"

"Because this is important. It's not common knowledge that Elle's—" He caught himself; it wasn't her name, and he knew it was weird for me. "Louise's 'sabbatical' hit more than technical snags. Most people don't know she was nearly eaten by a giant, octopus kind of thing. Haley instituted a danger rating for planets. Retroactively, she rated that planet an eight. The world I'd like you to take is a nine."

"And we're not just going to take a pass?"

"If this were some time next year, with dozens of successful missions under our belts? Absolutely, we would. But if we can't get someone back from a nine, soon we can't get anyone to take an eight. Then a seven. Conceptually, I'm all for us going after the low-hanging fruit. But if we start ignoring everything else…"

"Would you take it?" I asked.

"Can't," he said. "Council resolution. I'm not allowed to."

"Roles reversed, I'm your captain, asking. Knowing what you do, and knowing how important, would you take on the risk?"

He looked away and thought. "I don't know," he said. "It's a lot to ask. And I've got things I wouldn't want to lose. But I'd like to think so."

"Okay," I told him. "I'll do it."

His shoulders relaxed. "Just don't take any undue risks. If things aren't right, if anything makes you uncomfortable, walk away. It's more important that you make it back alive than with a contract in hand."

"How long have I got?" I asked.

"The positive of this new selection process is we get lots of data to send the most qualified candidate, making it a bit less of a lottery. The drawback is limited time. You've got a day. So I'd suggest not wasting another second of it talking to me." He held out his hand and I shook it.

As I walked away, I wondered if I had just entered myself in an intergalactic pissing contest. Drew was the closest I had to a rival, not that he saw it that way. He had Sam. But he also had Louise. I saw the way she looked at him, heard the way she talked about what they had. He was what she measured me against, and I was tired of being found wanting.

I was right there on the day she got back from the seafood planet. Thinking we lost her when her shuttle malfunctioned, thinking we lost her when the natives tried to feed her to a giant squid—and then a third nightmare even after she made it back, when her life was threatened by a parasite she caught in the water. It put things into perspective, made me realize that I wanted desperately to tell her what losing her would have done to me.

I planned to tell her how I felt, just to put it out there. No more pining, just, "This is how I feel. It's not an attempt to get you to reciprocate, I just want you to know, because maybe knowing will make you just the littlest bit happier, and that would make humiliating myself worth the while."

I went to quarantine. Drew was already there, holding her through a wall of glass—holding her *and* Sam. I don't think the bastard's ever known how lucky he was.

Fucked up as it might sound now, I felt thankful for it. Because telling Louise how I felt, from a position of neediness and fear—that wasn't the way to win over a warrior woman. No. I had just been given the opportunity to crack one of the galaxy's toughest nuts, return victorious, and tell her from a place of strength.

Two

It was hard not scooping Louise up in my arms and kissing her, letting loose everything I'd ever wanted to say. I could tell she wanted to tell me something, too; I'd interrogated enough people to know when they're about to pop. But whatever it was, she wasn't ready, and I wasn't either. I was going to bring her the contract for a dangerous planet, then tell her *everything*.

"Just take care of yourself," she said, finally. "There isn't much room for error, out there on your own. Don't take risks. I—the *ship* needs you back here in one piece."

"I'll ixnay the eyeingday."

"Don't be an umbassday," she said, and smiled to herself as the pod closed around me.

Haley, the ship's computer, started the countdown over the comms. I eyed the abort button on the console, then pulled up one of the cameras inside the bay and watched Louise. I wanted to stay with her. But I also knew she deserved the kind of man who could get this mission done and come back to her. So I tried to relax back in my seat as the electromagnets began my acceleration.

I passed out. The g forces we used for the pod launch were beyond tolerances that would leave a human being conscious, though within the safe window before the forces did permanent damage.

I woke up a few hours later. I wished I'd told Louise the truth. It wasn't even a matter of wanting to impress her anymore, it was just knowing she was farther away from me than she'd ever been since the *Nexus* left Sol's system—ignoring, I guess, the pod trip she took. But I wanted her to know. I didn't care if she didn't reciprocate, because that wasn't the point.

I penned a letter, and my fingers were hovering over the send communication button. What was I doing? Maybe I *did* wish I had told her before I left, but taking the coward's way out, sending her a letter when I couldn't be farther from her, or repercussions...? No, I needed to sort myself out before I tried confessing my affection for anyone.

I started to pore over the information we had about the low-gravity ice planet. I had decided to call it Jötn, and its people the Jötnar. We learned from the *Argus* that most alien names can't be spoken by humans—wildly divergent biology and all. It led them to a few diplomatic mishaps. So we adopted the custom of giving everything a human name, then letting the commboxes make the translation for us.

I had extra layers to my suit, to the point where it was practically an exoskeleton, protecting me from both the cold and potential hazards.

The sentient species we were going to make contact with was large: their smallest were about eight feet tall. And their exoskeletons were made up of semi-crystalline structures. It meant that some light could pass through their bodies, lending them a light form of camouflage, and also making them more durable.

Structurally, they looked like a cross between insects and dinosaurs, but unlike both, they were warm-blooded. They were technologically quite advanced, but so resource-poor that they couldn't capitalize on most of their technological advances.

The planet itself was in the midst of a prolonged ice age, and the entire planetary surface was covered in glaciers, miles thick in most places. That meant all of their resources went to growing and harvesting food, which was only possible inside tunnels that ran alongside thermal vents deep beneath the surface.

The sociological report said that it was likely the species would attempt to relocate to another nearby planet with the technologies we would offer them in trade. The report seemed distressed by that idea, even including a note questioning whether it was our place to so fundamentally change the course of another species's development. But—perhaps because I knew I was going to be standing among them—I couldn't abstract their suffering like that. If we could help them, we should. I saw no point to letting their species die out just because they would have died out if they'd never met us.

Three

The probe that came before me, essentially a miniature pod, had dropped a commbox. The Jötnar had figured it out at about a median pace—not so fast as the advanced races we'd met, but still faster than the Caulerpans or Romaleons. By the time I hit their orbit they understood our opening bid enough to tell me that I had permission to land.

They sent me coordinates and a flight plan to get there. The planet was small, so I didn't have to wait long. It gave me—and the pod AI, nicknamed Comet—a chance to check their figures. Their math was right, and maybe it wasn't the smoothest descent, but it was within tolerances. The landing was rocky, but I told myself that following their flight plan to the letter would get us off on the right diplomatic foot.

I landed a couple hundred yards from a dome that covered the city. As I stepped out of the pod, I noted that it looked crystalline, but then I realized it was carved out of the exact same glacier I was standing on.

Out of it wended a pair of Jötnar, wielding what looked like short staves, though I realized as they approached that their weapons were probably bigger than me. They stopped just far enough from me that I didn't feel the need to draw my pistol, then they turned inward, facing each other. My escort, then. Working the security division, I was more than familiar with that particular gig.

I slung my rifle. I didn't think I'd need it, but that was no reason not to want it along, and leaving it at my back felt like it would be less intimidating.

I walked past the sentries, hoping it wouldn't be considered an insult that I didn't introduce myself. Inside the dome were two more guards, standing at attention. Every few dozen feet there was another pair, and I walked from one to the next. It was an odd escort, but also a show of strength, that they could spare so many fighters just to show me where to go.

Eventually I reached an assembly hall. It was large, but not large enough. I recognized projection equipment and cameras. There was a studio audience, and folks watching at home.

I noticed that the panelists—judges or leaders or whatever—were organized by size: smallest on the wings and getting larger toward the center. The one in the center, while the largest, didn't acknowledge me, but just stared off. My HUD, working in combination with the commbox's notes, flagged several markers I wouldn't have caught, and flashed that he was a male. I wondered idly if he was old and suffering dementia, or if he had their equivalent to gigantism, and perhaps it had also impacted his brain.

One of the Jötnar flanking him stood up straighter, though it hardly seemed necessary, because she dwarfed me. To the eye, I wouldn't have noticed the gender differences, but my HUD marked several morphological markers, told me she was female, and also flashed a list of suggested names from the pool

I'd decided to use on my way in. I selected Bergrisar, and the name popped up under her.

She began to gyrate menacingly, and made noises that I hoped were her speaking, because otherwise I was pretty sure she was about to tear my limbs off and devour whatever was left. After a moment's deliberation, the commbox spat out a translation. "I am Bergrisar. We have disseminated and understood your proposals. Do you have anything further to add beyond the written words?" It certainly didn't *sound* like she was eager, and if they were giving me a chance to sway minds, well, that was going to be difficult.

Crap. I was never one for speeches. I'd read all of HR and PsychDiv's materials about optimal communication, but even the best of those were written with human mores in mind. I'd given a few morale talks, to grunts, but that was about it.

I took in a deep breath, held it, then let it out. "The proposal I sent is intended as an opening to talks. I believe our two species could be excellent partners. The tech we could give you in trade would make your lives better, and having existing treaties with us would make you safer. I hope we can come to some kind of an agreement."

The commbox projected a hologram of a Jötnar above it, flailing its arms and antennae and making the same kinds of groaning, guttural noises that made me think that even my avatar was about to attack.

I heard rumbling from the audience, and from among the judges, in response. "Very well. We will now commence voting." The judges lifted small devices and registered their votes, and I noticed the crowd doing the same. On their screens, numbers started popping up. My HUD translated them and overlaid their Roman equivalents. The voting was close; in fact, I was starting to pick up a lead. I smiled, which evidently was not a gesture they appreciated, because it cost me some of my lead. I stood perfectly still from that moment on.

After only a handful of minutes, a percentage, which I presumed was either the necessary percentage for a quorum, or the percent of the population voting, hit one hundred.

Bergrisar reared herself to her full height, several sections of carapace stacking to expand her width. I didn't need the commbox to tell me that this was a gesture of authority and dominance.

"We are divided. In the case of division, the proposal fails." My stomach dropped through my feet and didn't stop until it hit the planet's molten core. "However, you can appeal the decision. By combat." At least it wasn't a spelling bee or a pie-eating contest. Then again, these were giant, terrible creatures; at least a stomach ruptured in a pie-eating contest felt earned.

"How does that work, exactly?" I asked.

"You fight to prove your mettle, to prove how much you care for your cause, until there are no more detractors."

"So I kill half your population to swing the vote?"

"Theoretically that is possible. But more likely, others will be swayed by your victories. Theories are tested at the tip of the spear."

I thought of Louise and Drew. I couldn't see either of them backing down, not with an entire ship's morale hanging by this thread. They needed me to come back with a win. I needed it, too.

"In this trial, am I allowed to use my weapons?" The commbox translated, and the leadership became suddenly very animated. They were debating the rules, dozens of them talking over one another. I looked toward the commbox sitting in the middle of the floor, and above it my HUD printed three question marks.

The Jötnar on Bergrisar's other side, who I quickly named Gýgr, seemed to be winning the discussion, and eventually Bergrisar squealed, flailed, and deflated.

The commbox helpfully translated, "Euphemism for female genital infection."

Gýgr turned in my direction and started to gesticulate and murmur. "As your technology is a part of what's on offer, we believe it is only fair for it to be allowed to make its case as well."

With my tools, I thought I could do this. I wasn't crazy about the idea. But I'd fought giant space monsters before. Maybe not *this* giant, but I was essentially a soldier. At least Drew hadn't sent a poet. "Okay," I said. "I'll do it. So what now?"

Bergrisar exchanged a look with Gýgr. I got the feeling that something passed between them, but the twitches of their antennae and shells must have been too subtle for the commbox to read.

"We will put you up for the night, and commence in the morning," Gýgr said. Many of those assembled immediately began filing out, but several lingered. Bergrisar picked up a shaft of ice, dwarfed in fingers so heavily segmented and shelled they appeared most of the way to pincers. She tore it into several pieces before licking each. The other creatures on the panel then reached into her palm, each removing a stick. When everyone had a stick, they smelled them, and most dropped theirs into a pile before walking away. Only one held her shard—and stayed.

"Iviðja has the þurs," Bergrisar said. The commbox flashed a message on my HUD. It was a guess that the word meant "thirst."

Iviðja, the one with the chosen shard, fluttered panels over her eyelids in capitulation. One shoulder had a delicate mess of spider-webbed cracks, likely signs of an old injury now healed. The light fractured through it as she turned to me.

"What's a þurs?" I asked.

"She marked the ice," Iviðja replied. "All had saliva from her mandibles, but one had a special hormone, the þurs." She paused a moment, then continued. "After we eat, you may come to my fire." I appreciated the distinction between "may" and "*will*."

I nodded. "I appreciate your hospitality," I said. "But it's still light—why are we retiring?"

A panel on one of her arms adjusted, and for a moment I caught a fragrance off it, akin to dried lavender. "Nights are cold here. Those of us too long on the surface out of shelter forfeit the protections of our carapace. Our secretions freeze, and we die slowly as the ice shatters our entrails. It is a punishment reserved for traitors. They are fitted with an implant that sends electricity through them should they stop moving, and they are forbidden to return to the warm tunnels."

I shivered.

In time, several people with even limbs and flat backs came in, packs bound across them. Others helped them unload and began dividing the contents. Now, I've never been a carrot person—not even a parsnip one, despite my mother's best efforts. So I couldn't say I was relishing the opportunity to eat a meal made entirely of what looked like the unholy love-child of carrots and beets, which I decided to call beetrots. If anything, the name made them less appetizing.

Iviðja was taking her role as hostess very seriously. When a plate was ready, she brought it to me. Several shell panels slid away from her hands, exposing delicate fingers nearly subsumed by the protective plates. She held a piece to my lips, and I made myself open my mouth. When in Rome, and all that.

The vegetable was bitter—fiercely so. If it weren't for the color, I might have believed it was raw horseradish. Iviðja set the plate before me and settled in beside me.

"There are areas deep below the ice mantle where you can rely on the planet's turmoil to send steam to warm the soil," she said. "We mostly reside in these tunnels. Our civilization is a mountain with only the peak above the ice; the broad base of it is beneath. We had mountains, before the flood, made of rocks and ice. Do you understand the word?" she asked.

"Yes," I said, and pantomimed a triangle.

She made a pleasant sound, perhaps the first pleasant sound I'd heard from a Jötnar. "It's complex and labor intensive, and in the absence of sunlight, you can only grow food with pieces of yourself to nourish them."

"Pieces of yourself?" I didn't see any missing limbs.

"The pieces you no longer need: filth, and those who no longer move." I tried not to let the thought that the bitter taste was *alien shit* sour my meal. "We must use *all* we can, for nature helps no one. Our strength, and our sacrifice, are what give us power over her."

That put a different dent in my appetite. "I hope I'm not overstepping my bounds here. But would it offend you if I didn't eat more? I don't feel right gorging myself when your people worked so hard to create this." I patted my belly. "And as you can see, it isn't exactly like I need it."

"I'm sure Bergrisar would find a way to take offense, get a pincer up her cloaca about it being a rejection of our cuisine or a snub at our poverty of resources. But I think it's noble. And the vegetables do taste like digestive gases." She let out a pleasant cackle, took a handful of vegetables off the plate, then dumped the rest back into the serving dish.

Iviðja led me a short distance from the court to a shelter formed almost entirely of a milky substance, like agate or smoky quartz. She noticed my look. "It is a glass concrete formed from my ancestors' carapaces. It is at once a temple, a shrine, and a mausoleum. We *only* use them for ceremony, or when needs dictate. When I die, it will honor me to have my shell join with my ancestors'."

"My people traditionally achieved a similar effect with melted sand—granulated rock—and modern 3D printing processes aren't so far removed from that."

Her eyelids shifted, in what I hoped was excitement and not a sudden desire to eat my entrails. "Lens glass? We form braziers from the leftover carapace, the smaller pieces less suited to construction. When they are new, the impurities cook out, and leave a glass lens at the base at the end of a cold season." She made a clicking noise that was reminiscent of a chuckle. "It cracks upon exposure to the outside air. When we build a new community, each resident carries one from their old home, and we put them around the new home in a circle for protection. When they crack, the ghosts from our memories laugh, pleased to know where their shadows are now."

It took me a moment to realize she was waiting for me to enter the dwelling first; it must have been an honor she was reserving for her guest.

Light flickered through the walls. They were milky enough that I hadn't noticed it from the outside, but inside, the light caught the facets of the walls and made them appear to almost glow.

I set my suit to warm slightly, not seeing any sign of blankets or fabric. I didn't doubt that clothes wouldn't be useful to the Jötnar, as it would counter their natural camouflage and impede the movement of their shells. And the hard edges of the carapace would be harsh on cloth, too. But the lack of any coverings meant I was in for a cold night.

Iviðja—whom I'd mentally nicknamed Ivy, which worked with her clingy yet restful presence—touched a rectangular block inside the shallow bowl of a chest-high brazier. My HUD recognized a power source within, and the bowl caught fire. Warmth washed over me.

"It is a battery. It stores heat from the vents, then releases the heat slowly here." The plates around her fingers retracted, and she took my hand in hers. "So long as there is fire, there is *life.*"

Those words brought to mind an incident from Drew and Louise's younger days, fighting to rescue people from a burning colony as others fought them. It strengthened my resolve to get the Jötnar to work with us—and *finally* do something worthy of Louise.

Four

Ivy roused me in the morning and pressed a cup of tangy, mildly acidic liquid into my hands. I restrained myself from asking which bodily fluids went into producing *this* repast. She hurried away and returned with another section of root. I nodded my thanks at her and tried to make myself eat.

I've never been especially squeamish, so it wasn't the food's origins that bothered me so much as the totality of what I was about to do. I'd never risked my life when no one was actually in *danger*. Metaphorical danger on the ship just didn't inspire the same protective impulses and adrenaline; here, I had only nerves.

My HUD chirped at me, recognizing my elevated stress. I forced myself to breathe evenly.

"Are you ready?" she asked. I couldn't find anything other than polite concern in Ivy's movements, until I noticed a small twitch on the side of her neck. She was aware that I was anxious, and that made *her* anxious. I wondered if her reputation was tied up in my performance, if she would be considered tainted by association. I glanced at my guns and checked their charges.

"Yeah. Let's get this over with."

She retracted several plates, exposing her surprisingly soft hand, and hauled me to my feet. Her grip was almost overwhelmingly strong, even though she didn't seem to be using her full strength. I would have to keep my opponent at a distance, or else guns or no, I'd be done for.

She led me into a tunnel on the outskirts of the city. We walked perhaps a half a mile, some of it steeply down, until we came upon a labyrinth of snow and ice. "They say that the world was once much kinder, that we expanded recklessly and grew soft, and could not halt the ice's attack. And in memory of that, when we prove our strength, we do it where our ancestors, and the ice, can see us."

She bent down and rubbed the icy wall. Beneath her mitten-like shelled fingers, metal became visible, cracked, rusted, and decaying. "How will *your* ancestors know to look for you here?"

I wasn't sure how to respond. But I knew that family was entirely too important to the Jötnar to fuck around.

I beckoned her head down to me. "Because they're with me." I held her so she could see the screen where my HUD projected. Her eyes flashed reflectively as their components widened. I scrolled through several family pictures I had, and cursed myself for ignoring my mother's attempts to get me to take more.

She backed away. "May you bring them pride, then. I must go. Your first challenger is at the other end. May you find each other before one of you freezes." Ivy's word for "challenger" sounded nearly like "elder," so I entered the name Eld.

I shivered and started into the labyrinth. My HUD made navigating easy, even without a map of the facility. Eld's warmth made him glow like a beacon. I readied my gun as I moved forward, the wind already chewing me through my suit.

I watched my HUD until I saw that Eld was just around the corner. I listened closely to the crunch of his footfalls, then threw myself out of cover to shoot.

My blasts smashed into a plate of his carapace center-mass. It refracted some of the energy and absorbed the rest. The heat of it burned him, searing his flesh, but I could see that it was a superficial wound.

He advanced as I took a knee to steady the rifle. I fired again, into his chest. The same panel absorbed the blast. I fired again, and several more times, peppering his head and shoulders, searching for a vulnerability.

I noticed that the first panel was hanging askew. Heat from the blasts had melted the connective tissues holding it in place. I fired along the edge of the plate, and energy reflected off the surrounding plates into the vulnerable tendons beneath, severing the already melted tissues.

He screamed, and he was now close enough that I could feel the moisture on his breath. The steam made it hard to aim, but I sighted the exposed flesh and fired.

Eld collapsed.

Sections of shell around the blast were hardening, looking alarmingly like the walls of Ivy's abode. But his flesh was already pushing past the cauterized edges. Trickles of blood seeped out, and despite his agitated shell flicks trying to force heat-warped plates over his wounds, I could see them already beginning to freeze in the morning chill.

I remembered Ivy's tale. He may have been working against me, and he entered into this fight by choice—but he deserved better than a slow death from hypothermia. I positioned myself in front of his head, raised the gun one last time, and refused to shut my eyes as I pulled the trigger.

Five

I wondered whether I should backtrack to the entrance or wait for the Jötnar right where I was. While I thought it through, I inspected Eld's corpse. He wasn't much bigger than Ivy. That made sense, I thought: the challengers would go from smallest to largest. I repeated that to myself over and over, to remind myself not to get cocky.

After some time, the Jötnar found me. Ivy came in first. She bowed her head, several plates on her neck pulling back to allow the motion. Bergrisar followed, staring at me, no doubt gauging me.

Others trickled in, and soon they crowded every inch of space in the tunnels. I saw that one even had a camera. I raised my voice. "This tech is one of the benefits you stand to gain by allying with us."

Bergrisar raised up, and I shuddered at the thought of her with a gun.

"It's mutilated infant scrotum. That was a farce. Yours are a coward's weaponry: guile and aggression from a safe distance."

"You said I could use them," I said.

She opened and shut some of the crystalline panels on her face.

I didn't know the specifics of the gesture, but she was pissing on my lawn. A man was dead, and she seemed to want to treat it like it was nothing. Something about that look on her face was a red flag, and I was a bull. It was all I could do to keep from charging at her. "Fine," I spat through gritted teeth. "Send the next. I'll beat him, but let him live, to *testify* to my strength."

I offered my pistol to Ivy, then unslung my rifle and did the same. She took them with trembling hands. Her face bled concern, if I wasn't misreading it through a human lens.

A Jötnar slightly bigger than the one I'd just defeated stepped forward, and I immediately entered in a name: Leir.

"So be it," Bergrisar said. Some Jötnar turned toward the entrance, clearing an expanse in the widest portion of the room, but she didn't, and it was an instant before I understood why.

Leir lunged for me, and I spun to the side to avoid the blow. One of his secondary limbs lashed out as I turned, seeking to knock me off balance, so I jumped into a roundhouse kick.

It was like kicking a steel plate.

I ran. The gathered Jötnar backed away as I approached, and continued to back away until there was space between them for me to exit. I knew already that Bergrisar would try to spin my actions as cowardice, but I needed to survive before worrying about saving face.

The "arena" was oddly preserved. The frost had claimed the city almost gently, and its dome had withstood long enough for the ice to reinforce it as it was overwhelmed. The only elements not coated in a layer of white powder were the braziers. They were spaced so that you could see between them, if only just; there for additional light, not for heat. They didn't appear as weathered as the rest of the arena; I assumed they were brought down for the trial.

I ran full speed at a brazier, and when I hit it, I tried to scoop it off the ground. It barely tipped, sending the smoldering log rolling. The fire went out. I couldn't be sure if it was contact with the ice, or if it had safety protocols, but I could see the battery for the heavy, metal box that it was.

I definitely wasn't strong enough to lift the brazier, so I hefted the battery. It was a bit awkward, but it had enough weight to be useful. Then I turned back toward the gathered Jötnar. They were still in the distended circle, almost an egg. But Leir was gone.

I heard a noise behind me, so faint I wasn't certain. I cranked the volume on my implants. It was skittering, but then it stopped. I spun, swinging the log. It impacted the same panel on Leir's midsection I had first kicked. The impact cracked the plating. His plates flaked off like diamonds, catching the light as they fell.

I dodged behind him, and as he turned to face me, the plates began to fall away.

A sticky fluid hit the floor as he circled around me. Under the shattered plate, his flesh convulsed softly. I lashed out, swinging the battery. It glanced off the previous wound, cracking the surrounding plating. I dodged underneath his flailing limbs, and he curled his torso away from another blow.

I dropped the battery on one of his feet, then drove my fist into the most expressively pulsing organ I could see. He keened in agony, fighting to seize me with several supporting limbs, but he was distracted enough by the pain that his limbs knocked into each other uselessly behind my head.

So, a weakness. I brought my foot against the same spot with all my strength, wincing as I used muscles I hadn't been aware of since my mother encouraged me to study ballet on my home colony. Who'd have thought that *grand battement* would be used against a wounded alien, with a diplomatic treaty hanging in the balance.

His flesh tore under my boot, and fluids slowly gushed onto my foot with a rapidly lessening pressure. As I pulled my foot away from him, his legs buckled and he lowered his head.

I guided him onto his back on the ice while he was distracted with pain.

He was supposed to yield, but he was a stubborn bastard. I lifted my boot, picked up the battery, and started to shove it against the wound. It didn't *quite* fit, but he must have realized I was preparing to make him into a living brazier.

"Wait," he coughed from his back. I stopped, and he curled around his torn, fragile flesh. "I... concede." His legs trembled as he fought to make the gestures needed to communicate.

I looked up to our audience. "As I said, I didn't kill him. But let the pitiful noises he makes tell you that I am more than capable of seeing this negotiation through."

A medium-sized Jötnar raised her voice. "I withdraw my opposition." Several others murmured or otherwise gestured, translated as assent through the commbox. Bergrisar clicked in agitation.

Gýgr stood to her full height and said, "We shall carry Eld back to the court to begin mourning. Then we will see who still wishes to test the outsider's worth."

One of the flat-backed Jötnar bent to allow others to strap Eld to his back, and another soon arrived for Leir. I followed as far as the court.

I paused, unsure whether to go inside. I was Eld's killer, after all.

Ivy's hand lit on the back of my neck, all soft, slightly clammy fingers rather than hard carapace. I caught her eye, and watched it widen, each reflective lens aligning itself as the lids peeled back further. I queried the commbox through my HUD, but it didn't have a translation. I stared into her large eyes and breathed in her hand's scent.

Light filtered through the dome overhead and caught on the less opaque portions of her shell, turning her into a ghost of glass, haunting but beautiful. A beam cut across my face, and I fought to hide my wonder.

She took my hand and led me inside.

They feasted in Eld's honor. I made a trip out to my pod, returning with some of my rations to cook for them. They tested my food before tasting it, to be sure it wasn't going to set off any of their allergies.

It wasn't until midway through the festivities that I realized the trials were still in full force. Bergrisar mingled with the crowd, gladhanding. Several medium-sized Jötnar, slightly bigger than Leir, approached me and spoke. They were fascinated by both my tech and my food. After a few minutes of casual conversation, they leaned forward and informed me they would no longer oppose me.

I mingled more. Bergrisar glared her hatred over the crowd, and I waved back to her. The initial group were the only ones who had declared the end of their opposition, but I could tell that opinions were fluid and changing. Despite her best efforts, Bergrisar had lost ground.

As the crowd thinned out, I decided to get some air. I found myself walking in the direction of the tunnel leading toward the arena.

Just outside the entry was a bloodied bootprint, preserved in the powder of frost that coated everything. I knelt down to look at it. It was likely Leir's blood, so at least it wasn't a reminder of Eld's death. A hand gently touched my shoulder. I recognized her smell even before I turned to confirm it was Ivy.

I widened my eyes, and sections of Ivy's face pulled back in an imitation smile.

Her fingers were warm, and they gave me something to focus on other than that one bloody footprint leading back to the battlefield.

Six

Bergrisar looked at the gathered Jötnar. "Who no longer wishes to challenge?"

Half of those left raised limbs in assent.

"And those who do?"

Unfortunately, the Jötnar who responded this time were the biggest, the most fierce-looking of the bunch. I knew I had done well, but this confirmed what I had suspected: the hardest part was ahead.

"Who wishes to challenge next?"

One of the females stood, her carapace puffing outward to increase her size. I named her Sjórisar.

Bergrisar clicked in agitation. "Are you sure, Sjórisar?" Even through the commbox I could pick up on her distress. I pondered whether Sjórisar was especially dear to Bergrisar. Perhaps family.

Several Jötnar shifted with soft clacks and motions, responding to the tension. Sjórisar glared at Bergrisar. "I cannot deny your right to challenge," Bergrisar said, in motions abrupt and violent enough that she nearly brained the Jötnar beside her—lucky for him, he dodged at the last moment. "But for this to be the *true* test our people require, let us increase the difficulty."

Sjórisar didn't seem to like that. "You doubt my competence?"

Bergrisar widened her eyes to tell Sjórisar to stand down. "Far from it. I propose night combat, that you may bring your full strength to bear on the outsider."

This was getting old.

"She seeks advantage. Sjórisar formed in her eggs," Ivy whispered to me, though in order for me to hear the tones and whistles accompanying her muted twitches, she had to lean close enough that I thought I might be enveloped. "Sjórisar will win, or die; anything else would shame her."

I sighed. "We'll see."

Ivy tensed. "Do not underestimate us. We live and work underground; we see well in the dark. She can track you by smell, by heat. You have no idea what Sjórisar is capable of."

I wasn't underestimating. I'd been in the security services long enough to know the value of morale. But my bravado was wearing thin. Sjórisar was nearly twenty feet tall, at least, if she stood up straight. She was a dragon, and each of her many limbs terminated in a sickle honed to a razor's edge.

But I couldn't go back empty-handed. I didn't know if Louise could ever love me, but I wouldn't even deserve to ask if I returned with my tail between my legs. "I have to conduct myself with honor according to the rites of your people," I told Ivy.

Gýgr stood again and towered over Bergrisar. "You may have your night combat, Bergrisar. And the human may have his weapons." Bergrisar clicked angrily. "We have voted—twice now. Do not buck the will of the elders."

Bergrisar lowered her shoulders.

I felt lighter. Having my guns meant something. At least I could rely on the tactics I knew best. But I remembered the difficulty my weapons had had even with poor Eld.

Ivy was still worried, but she had no further council for me. Her lids tightened around her eyes in sorrow, and I turned my attention back to the proceedings.

"Very well then," Gýgr continued. "At the rise of our moons we shall lead them to the arena. Provided he accepts terms." She turned to me.

"This treaty is too important," I responded. "While I relish no further bloodshed, I must continue."

"Then let the combatants adjourn."

Bergrisar leveled something that might have been a glare at me.

I nodded, and stood to return to Ivy's shelter.

Seven

I rested fitfully and woke to the smell of something bitter, but with a pleasant edge. Ivy was brewing something over the fire. "Made from carrots," she said, "and sweetened with fermented carrots."

She poured two cups, one for each of us, and we drank together. It had a mildly intoxicating effect, so I declined a second cup.

Strange ululations murmured over the city. "It's time," Ivy said. She led me toward the arena, but to a different entrance than the one we used before. "I can't go with you," she said, and stepped back.

I nodded and proceeded into the arena. The moon wasn't as bright as I could have hoped, but its light on the snow made me remember a childhood spent sledding and making snow forts. There were no braziers here.

I checked the charge on my rifle. I'd come prepared to defend myself, but not so armed as to cause alarm among the Jötnar. As it was, I wasn't sure I'd have enough to carry me through, tough as the Jötnar were.

My HUD filtered through the gloom. This area's ruins were denser, and the HUD seemed to be having a hard time pinging through the stone, metal, and ice. Even the heat sensors couldn't pinpoint Sjórisar's location. So I went a short way in and stopped at the first wide clearing I could find. I built snow and rubble walls around me—and I hid. I needed an advantage, and maybe the surprise would be enough.

I waited.

Eventually Sjórisar appeared, scanning just past me. I sighted her in, and as she turned, I fired.

She lashed me with her tail, demolishing my shelter.

The scale I had hit—above her brow—was still intact. I turned up the setting on the rifle as I rolled to avoid a second blow from her tail. She used it like a whip, to cut my legs out, to force me to the ground where she could crush me.

I fired twice more. The first went wide. The second caught her primary arm, where the scaling was thinner, and I could smell the fat frying underneath the plating. "Bloodied insect stamens," Sjórisar muttered.

I glanced at my rifle charge: half gone already, and I only had one cartridge to replace it with, plus another in the demolished shelter, and then the reserve charge on my pistol.

Sjórisar swiveled around, and I threw myself back to stay away from her tail. It grazed my shoulder with the force of an avalanche, but I managed to keep hold of the gun. I fired again, lining several shots up along her nearly twenty feet of bulk.

She squealed as the shots tore into her, cauterizing flesh and heating her scales until they glowed. But still she came.

Her tail swept my leg, and my ankle twisted and popped. I went sprawling, and she loomed over me, readying for the kill.

I turned my gun to maximum charge. Whittling away at her torso wasn't going to work. I needed to end this. I fired one more shot—clear through her head. The moon peered at me from the hole as she tipped forward.

I realized, too late, that she was going to fall on top of me, or at least on top of my legs. I scrambled backward, but not fast enough. I screamed as she collapsed onto my knee.

Eight

When I managed to wiggle out from under Sjórisar's corpse, I made an unpleasant discovery. The edges of her scales had been sharpened to razors. My suit was damaged, and there were a number of cuts across my legs and shoulder. I couldn't tell how much blood I'd lost.

One of my legs wouldn't hold my weight. I forced myself to probe the wounds, and I nearly fainted when my finger brushed my shoulder bone.

When the spots cleared from my vision, I brought my hand to my hurt leg. My finger sank into the wound mid-knuckle, and I had no doubt that some of the muscle had torn.

I fought for the tube of first aid goo in the suit, to staunch the bleeding, but at least one of the lines used to administer it had been cut, and even when I cleared the blockage, it wouldn't push out.

Frozen.

Shouldn't someone have fixed that shit before plopping me on a subzero planet?

Fuck.

I used Sjórisar's corpse to get me off the ground and steadied. I measured her arm from the gunshot down. It was about the right length for a crutch. I tried to pry it loose, to no avail.

I decided to use one of my precious remaining shots on the weak spot. If I died here it wouldn't matter if I'd saved it for later. The cold was already biting me hard, and I had no spare fabric to bandage myself.

Using the severed arm as a makeshift crutch, I forced myself back toward the entrance, but it was slow going, and the Jötnar met me before I'd even left the immediate area. Ivy gathered me into her arms, all four of them, but Bergrisar pushed past to Sjórisar, shrilling her grief in a voice sharp enough to make my HUD warn me of the potential for cochlear damage.

Ivy nodded. "Let her mourn in peace." She carried me back to her shelter.

She clucked sadly as she laid me out on the floor and examined my wounds. "You're lucky."

I raised my eyebrows. "How so?"

"In ancient times, she would have eaten fungus for a month to make her blood poisonous, and then dipped her scales in her droppings, to ensure you died of infection."

I chuckled. "I'm lucky, then."

"She was not ready to fight you. We all knew it."

I remembered the tension in Bergrisar's face. "Was that Bergrisar's objection?"

"Yes. She just couldn't admit it."

I wanted to ask how Ivy knew, but I let the thought go as she helped me out of my suit, and the chill got ten times worse despite the fire.

"We cannot have fabric in your wounds. I will warm you once they're bandaged."

For a moment I pictured Drew in this situation, and people teasing him for getting caught with his pants down with yet another alien species. But then Ivy bent over my leg, pressing flesh into place around a brownish paste, and sealed it with a long, rubbery synthetic fabric.

Though she was being gentle, the spots returned to my vision, and this time I didn't fight unconsciousness.

I woke up in a moment of suffocated panic. The world was dark, and Ivy's smell surrounded me, much more so than it ever had before. Tender flesh pulsed against my face, accompanied by a thunderous gurgling that unnerved me. I wiggled and probed, trying to understand what surrounded me.

Supple flesh on one side, the underside of crystalline, rounded plates on the other.

My face felt sticky—likely secretions to keep the plates from grinding on each other. It brought to mind suffocating during sex.

But something about that smell… It was so far from human, but the nuance of its spice pushed into my brain in a way no woman's perfume ever had.

Ivy's fingers, their plates rolled back, stroked through my hair, and the gesture calmed me. I realized the gurgling was circulation—her heartbeat.

I tried to remember feeling so completely protected and cared for, but nothing compared. I tried to imagine leaving her cocoon's embrace, and couldn't.

Nine

I lost track of the days I spent suspended inside Ivy's shell. She had to help me to the bucket that collected our wastes for the Jötnars' farming.

Her body formed around me as though I had always belonged there—some places loosening, others tightening, to take as much pressure off of me as possible. And strangely, surrounding myself in her soft, fragile flesh felt natural, like lying on a waterbed or floating in a pool. When her heartbeat surrounded me, pushed against my face as I rested, it pushed thoughts of the *Nexus*, even Louise, out of my head.

I wondered what my crew's reaction would be if I gave up on the treaty and just stayed with the Jötnar. Perhaps in time the Jötnar would need my help, or our technology, to relocate to a more hospitable home, like the initial report had speculated.

But having known them, I didn't see them doing that. Surviving their brutal ice age was part of their identity. How could they create lenses without winter-long fires?

I didn't believe they could rewrite themselves. But I wondered if I might rewrite *me*.

Days bled together, until at last I could stand again.

I had to speak to Bergrisar, find out how this situation was going to play out.

When Ivy released me, her scales slid away from me, allowing me to pass through the cracks. I fell barely an inch onto my mossy pallet, and I prepared myself for an unpleasant conversation.

"Is Bergrisar still mourning? How many contenders are left?"

Ivy sighed. "You're determined to jump right back to *work*." The reprimand in her inflection was surprisingly human, every bit the harried and peevish mother.

I shrugged. "Not eager, but I have to know."

Some of the plates around her eyes slid back, loosening the tension in her face. "There is only Bergrisar. No others wished to challenge you. I think she would not, but she feels she owes it to Sjórisar, as one of her brood. We do not bond with our offspring the way some herdbeasts do, but we still have a duty to avenge them."

I sighed. "I'm sorry it's come to that. I don't wish to kill her."

Ivy made a motion akin to a shrug. "You have followed our customs; there is no reason for sorrow in that."

"Still."

There was something in Ivy's mannerisms that rankled me. A question came to mind.

"Will Bergrisar be the last?" I asked. "Is anyone honor-bound to avenge *her*?"

Ivy's eyes flashed up to mine, startled. She clicked in agitation. "Bergrisar has lived long. Most of those gestated with her are long dead."

"But not all."

"Not all." She ducked her gaze, and I filled in the rest.

"You're of her brood."

"Yes. The same clutch of eggs, even. Not just the same genetic material."

"Will you fight for her?"

"I'm no fighter. She would not expect me to avenge her. And I would ask—*have* asked—her not to fight." She sighed, almost a whistle. "But we cannot put Bergrisar off any longer. I told her it would be dishonorable to come for you unconscious, wounded. But we have passed that point of grace. Let me get you some snow to bathe yourself."

I nodded in thanks, and used the armfuls of snow she brought to sponge her fluids from me. Even so, Ivy's smell clung to my skin, like the expensive hand lotion my mom used.

I glanced at the last remaining cartridge for my rifle. The only way I could get more of a charge for it was to drain my pod battery, trapping myself here.

I didn't know what I would do if it came to that. I would decide after meeting Bergrisar, seeing if she wanted to meet me in the moonlit ruins.

I put what remained of my suit on and followed Ivy to the court. The rest of the Jötnar awaited me.

Bergrisar growled when she saw me. "Are you happy? You are almost at your victory." Her voice was a dangerous purr.

"I wish no more bloodshed." I didn't know what else that might mean.

"It will fall, regardless; you have not broken *all* of us." She flashed a contemptuous glare around the room.

"Tonight, then?" I asked.

"No. You will fight me here. You do not deserve to die on ground nourished with the blood of our ancestors." Ivy trembled next to me. "Give him his weapons, Iviðja."

I could see the conflict in her as she passed them to me.

Fear and adrenaline pushed through me as Bergrisar stood and the Jötnar backed away from us.

I turned to Gýgr. "I may not survive this fight. But our two peoples' friendship shouldn't die with me." I opened comms with my ship. "I'm opening up the technologies we offered in the contract. Use them. Help your people."

I didn't have a chance to hope it could sway Bergrisar; she was already laughing as I turned. "He thinks he can *buy* back his blood," Bergrisar chortled. "It's mine already. I ache for its moisture on my tongue."

I glanced at my rifle charge. Shit—with it turned up to the maximum, I had only a handful of shots. Plus whatever was in my sidearm. But Bergrisar was huge, bigger than the last two combined.

She lashed out at me with one of her secondary limbs; this one seemed to be akin to a scorpion tail, and I didn't want to know what was in the stinger. As it whooshed past, a smell struck me, a familiar one, learned from living with Ivy.

She meant to poison me, even if I *could* defeat her.

I retreated. It *had* to come down to the gun, then.

She whipped her tail at me again, but didn't put as much force behind it as Sjórisar had. It gave her more maneuverability, having less invested in the attack. I ducked, and her tail knocked into the wall behind me. I raised my gun, waiting for a clear shot to her head.

I got it.

When my shot struck, Bergrisar chuckled. The plating around her head was thicker—it had been forged into a single plate since the last time I'd seen her, essentially welded into a helmet. She'd disfigured herself in order to win. The shot dented the plating beside her eye, but not even enough to trust that *another* shot would do the job, even if I could hit in the exact same spot.

And from her weaving, I might not have the chance to test that.

I cursed myself for not charging my damn rifle when I had the chance.

She turned away from my next shot, but it was going to go wide even if she hadn't moved. Due to both of our miscalculations, it tore through the limb with the stinger. The carapace there must have been weaker: the stinger fell off, completely severed by the heat of my blast.

That could work. Remove the limbs. It was dicier shooting than center mass, but if it actually got *through*... I fired again, at one of her smaller arms. She seemed to recognize what I planned at the last moment, and snaked to the side, absorbing the blast with the thickest part of the plating in her chest. I fired again, and again she lurched to absorb the shot harmlessly.

The rifle was dead, and I dropped it. I turned up the charge on the pistol. I had enough shots to try to break through her head plating, or I could stop fighting fate and aim for her chest.

She charged me, and I fired center mass, my training responding before my head could. As I ran to the side and threw myself over her lashing tail, my wounded ankle gave out; I couldn't count on being able to run or dodge. She turned toward me, whipping a hand ending in a fist, the carapace's edges sharp and exposed.

The edge caught me, biting into my already injured shoulder and reopening old wounds.

But as I fell back, my hand met Bergrisar's fallen stinger, and an idea hit me.

When her next attack came, I leaned in to it—twisting my torso so that it skimmed by me—and then I threw myself at her torso, wielding the stinger.

I struck the weak spot in her chest with it, and felt a crazy euphoria as it sank in, deeper, deeper. Her shock rippled through me in her plates' little trembles. I tore the stinger out, and sections of shell fell away with it. I stabbed it into her again and again, fighting to keep clear of the limbs that reached for me, thrashing around me, defiant even to the last.

Ten

I shivered and fell to my knees as Bergrisar's twitches subsided. I felt dizzy and raised a hand to my shoulder. The old wound was open, yes, but it was more than that: the edges of her fist-plates had torn deeply into my neck. I couldn't tell if she'd hit an artery, but from the shredded meat where my neck met my chest, I didn't see how she could have *not*.

The Jötnar washed toward us, seeing that she was dead and I lived. "You shall have your treaty." It was Gýgr who spoke. "No one else will argue."

I nodded. The world felt floaty, and I let myself sit, knees to chest, to wait out its motion. Movement out of the corner of my eye drew my attention, and the Jötnar faded away.

Impossibly, Louise sat beside me. She was *pure*, her eyes' color saturated beyond anything I'd ever seen.

"I can't leave," I said to her, though I was certain my lips weren't moving. "And I know you couldn't love me. And that's all right." I leaned over to kiss her, and started at the feeling of a mouth without her lips. Then the fragrance sank into me, one I could wake up to every day for the rest of my life.

I hoped to God I wasn't bleeding out, that I might live my days out here.

Mistake or no, I didn't pull away. And neither did Ivy.

When we paused for breath, any trace of Louise was gone. Ivy's fragmented crystalline eyes were on me, and my bloodstained hand held her face.

"How… how am I?" I asked.

She shrugged noncommittally, though I found her smile comforting.

"Will I live?" I returned my hand to my neck. I couldn't feel where to put pressure, or where I was losing pressure.

"You'll stay with us." She tried to mimic my smile. "We'll find a lens in our pit so your spirits will know where to find you."

I told myself that that meant I would live, not that she would show them where my grave was. I wasn't sure if that was true, but it was what I wanted to believe as the darkness overtook me.

A Word from Nicolas Wilson

Although "Trials" is, I hope, a story that stands on its own two feet, it's also a story set around the events of my book *Nexus 2*. Readers of that book will have recognized the protagonist of "Trials" as Linus Bogdanovich. It didn't seem fair to me that so much of Bogdan's arc happened offstage, and I'm happy to have told his story here.

I'm a published journalist, graphic novelist, and novelist, living in the rainy wastes of Portland, Oregon with my wife, four cats, and a dog.

My work spans a variety of genres, from political thriller to science fiction and urban fantasy. I have several novels currently available, and many more are due for release in the coming year. My stories are characterized by my eye for the absurd, the off-color, and the bombastic. And yes, my wife wrote that last bit.

For information on my books, and behind-the-scenes looks at the writing life, visit nicolaswilson.com, or visit me on Facebook, Goodreads, or Twitter. Better yet, sign up for my mailing list.

Vessel

by Samuel Peralta

1

I AM IN HER.

As she dreamed, her chest rising and falling softly, her eyes closed in the slow liquid breathing of the fluorocarbon's flow, I floated in.

I was smaller than anything she dreamed of—a spore, a mitochondrion, a protozoan, the mote in Loki's eye—jiggling in a Brownian dance beneath the rhythmic thrum of the mechanical ventilator.

Underneath all that, the sound of her heart beating, slowed by the cold into a trance for the journey, the desolate journey, the long journey home from a distant moon, beating with the measured cadence of her breath.

I was lost in the amniotic fluid that surrounded her, pummelled by eddies of oxygen molecules, the swirl of carbon dioxide, in and out, that invisible gaseous ebb and flow of life.

She was a world to me, and I a Magellanic explorer across the vastness of her body, following the currents.

I sailed down her shoulders, across the coastal ranges of her arms, down the outside shoals of her thighs, navigated the tendrils of fur at her feet as her companion, her cat, slept her sleep.

I navigated up the rivulet between her legs, surfed across the slope of her belly and the Aurora Borealis rise of her breasts. I skimmed the curve of her throat, scaled the cliffside of her chin, teetered at the precipice of her lips.

And she breathed me in.

2

She dreams of a blue world, a planet of oceans and a vastness of clouds.

I am traversing her tongue, two-thirds down its muscular length to the back of her mouth. As she breathes, and as the ventilator pushes, the fluid flows down into her throat, the current threatening to drag me where I don't want to go, down into her lungs.

She dreams of being hurled into that vastness, she feels the sledgehammer forces on her bones as the core propulsion stage engines and boosters of the primary launch system ignite and burn. She dreams of orbit, the expended external tanks unlatching from the inter-stage structures and floating into blackness.

I unfurl my cilia and latch on to her throat, pull myself up against the forces dragging me away. It takes every effort not to be drawn in.

She dreams of the secondary solid rocket boosters with their multiple segments, each thrusting at twenty million foot-pounds, hurling her farther into the void. She dreams of the cryogenic propulsion stages, the re-ignition of the upper-stage engines and advanced boosters, the quad nuclear thermal rocket engines gunning with the tremor of a thunderclap.

I hold tight against the flow coming from her nasal cavity, and then the flow reverses as she breathes out, and I let go. The fluid carries me up until I can latch on to the mucous membrane at the top of her sinus cavity.

She dreams of a gaseous planet, larger than her own, a great world of liquid and gas without a surface, swirling in tremendous cyclones and lightning storms. Across its face range clouds of ammonia crystals, banded in zones of light and darkness.

Here I stay for a while as I consume the nerve cells of her olfactory bulbs, then work my way through the mitral cell axons to the remainder of her cerebrum. I hold back now, careful of the brain stem, careful of the nerve cells of her medulla oblongata, careful not to harm her.

She dreams of an ice moon, smaller than her moon, a moon of silicate rock with an upper crust of frozen water and a salty liquid ocean underneath the ice. Its surface is spiked with icy penitentes carved by sunlight from fissures in the ice. Dark streaks of lineae cross and re-cross across the globe, fractured ridges in the ice from its plate tectonics and the tidal flexing of its mother planet.

I grow slowly, slowly, sharing in her dreams.

She dreams of a world of oceans and a vastness of clouds, a blue planet.

3

I was different then.

Not yet bombarded by cosmic high-energy radiation, not yet penetrated by the secondary protons and atomic nuclei, the offspring of free-living amoebic pathogens and the emanations of active galactic nuclei and massive supernovae.

Toxoplasma gondii birthed me, fused by cosmic circumstance with what she'd named *Sappinia europa*. Back then, I slept in the innards of my previous host, in the warm-blooded tissues of her cat.

Had I not changed, with my kind I would have reproduced in cysts in the intestines of my host. Even alone, even then I could have budded out another of myself, an asexual self-division that would have been the first link in a doubling and re-doubling chain of biological imperative.

Eaten, I would live on. Excreted, I would live on. Swallowed, lapped, breathed in, I would live on.

And my hosts? Sometimes they die. But only when they are weak, with child, or otherwise a poor host.

They say there will be a flushing, a warmth, a fever that passes. I make them dream.

Mice, rats, squirrels, prairie dogs, beavers, guinea pigs, porcupines, hamsters. Goats, sheep, cattle, deer, giraffes, antelopes, camels, llamas, yaks, antelopes. Cats and humans. All the same. I make them dream.

Rats smell feline urine, and I make them dream that they are following the scent of food. They follow it to the jaws of waiting cats, and thence I and my progeny move on.

Cats feel hands rub their flanks, and I make them dream of their mothers grooming them. They flick a tongue in the faces of adoring humans, and thence I and my progeny move on.

And humans—

4

Plasmodium, back on Earth, begins its protozoan life cycle by making its mosquito host blood-shy. The mosquito starves but is at less risk of being swatted and killed, which would not be a desirable end for the immature plasmodium.

Plasmodium changes its strategy when it is mature and ready to enter a human with its malaria load. It then drives its host into a blood frenzy, seeking out prey each night and attacking even when full.

If the mosquito perishes at the hand of a human, no matter. Plasmodium and its progeny, hidden in the secretions from the mosquito's proboscis, will have moved on.

5

To you, human, you are your body.

But to your genes, your body is nothing more than a host, as my own protozoan form is nothing but a host to my own genes.

And your collection of genes and mine, they have made a pact with one another.

They asked:

Why limit ourselves to a separate human body and a separate protozoan body? Why limit one to skin and bones and muscle? Why limit one to protoplasm and cilia?

If together we have a better chance to advance both our sets of genes to the next generation, over other species—why not be together, make a compact, and advance together?

What if we melded together?

What if we were one?

6

I am different now.

I don't just spawn into cystic tissue. I spread.

I send out tendrils, flagellae along the fissures of the brain, like vines along the crevices of an aged building, crumbling the mortar.

I insinuate myself into the brain, snake into it, sensing the way to the regions that initiate thought, command, motion.

My tendrils flow along the medulla and spinal cord, coiling its length, sensing the beating of her heart.

The pons calls to me, surrendering all the sensory and involuntary motor functions, opening up the pathways to breathing, sleeping, balance, facial expression.

I embrace the hypothalamus, flick on and off the switches for sleeping and waking, eating and drinking.

The thalamus opens itself to me, granting me access to the information to and from both cerebral hemispheres.

The cerebral cortex, the pallium, the hippocampus, all these give up to me their labyrinthine complexity of spatial memory, smell, directional navigation, and other senses.

I douse the cerebellum with a cocktail of neurotransmitters, connecting it to my own consciousness, so that the other thought- or motor-focused brain systems merge with mine.

Gently, I touch the basal ganglia, the signal center to inhibit action or make it so—reward, punishment.

And finally, she and I, we will be melded. We will be the same. One.

7

One day she will wake.

Gravity will reclaim this ship, and all around her the fluorocarbon mixture will swirl away like a whirlpool at her feet.

Her eyes will open, and the dream she is dreaming will end, the frayed edges of the filmstrip flapping like the end of a cinematic reel.

She will sit, panting, regurgitating the last of the amniotic fluid from her lungs. She will drape her cat outside the enclosure, pressing its sides gently to expel the cold from its mouth. She will let it go, and it will run across the floor, finding freedom.

She will sit, look around her, watch the others raising the lids on their enclosures, fighting their sleep, rising, eyes closed and open, exhausted and dazed, some still lying in dream.

She will see him then, sitting at the edge of his own aqueous bed, then standing, stretching—muscular, naked, beautiful.

She will see him, and I will make her dream of love, joyous and sweet and wonderful and encompassing.

I will make her dream about the firelights of winter, the torrents of spring, the warmth that only being in his arms can bring.

And she will go to him, touch him, embrace him.

Lift herself up to the opening of his mouth.

A Word from Samuel Peralta

The protozoan in "Vessel," *Toxoplasmosis gondii,* is real and is considered a leading cause of deaths attributed to foodborne illness. It has been targeted for public health action by the U.S. Centers for Disease Control and Prevention.

Up to forty percent of North Americans carry the parasite but have no symptoms because of a healthy immune system. Nevertheless, in pregnant women and those with compromised immune systems, the disease can be fatal.

While the parasite is capable of living in a broad range of mammals and birds, by far the most common route to human infection is through the ingestion of toxoplasma eggs shed in the feces of cats.

I wanted to explore several ideas in "Vessel."

One idea is that parasitism may not be not a one-way relationship between a puppeteer parasite and its host, but might actually be a symbiotic relationship at the genetic level.

I also wanted to explore the possibility of writing from the point of view not of a man or a woman, but of a consciousness that is more than a little different.

And I wanted to pose the question: *What if love were a parasitic imperative?*

"Vessel" is set in a world I think of as "the Labyrinth"—the same backdrop used for my stories "Trauma Room," "Hereafter," "Humanity," "Liberty," "Faith," and "Faster."

This is a world where corporations have expanded beyond governments, where pervasive surveillance is a part of life, and where non-human self-awareness has begun to make humanity face difficult questions about itself.

"Vessel" is the first of these stories to extend the arc beyond Earth. Welcome to the Labyrinth.

Join my newsletter for offers and new titles; or for a complete list of existing titles, please visit www.peralta.ca.

The Grove
by Jennifer Foehner Wells

IN THE MOMENT when the last remaining filament between Hain and the Mother broke, the Mother's parting thought raced through Hain's mind, but Hain didn't process it until later, when the sticky amber gum that oozed from her open wounds had begun to harden, and the euphoric newness of freedom had subsided.

The Mother had said, "Come back to me soon, little one."

It had taken so long to break loose. Hain had been obsessed with wriggling, working, bending repeatedly in every possible direction, until the sapwood connecting the two of them had frayed to fine fibers and finally snapped, severing their nurturing connection. She had been so anxious to be free, so intent on experimenting with her unused, newly fully formed limbs, that she hadn't even replied or said goodbye. She hadn't meant to be so ungrateful to the one who had given her life.

* * *

The day the Salvors came, Hain was retrofitting an ancient vehicle with every-terrain wheels. She'd redesigned them to manage better than the wheels that some of the Mother had used so long ago. Hain used the narrow three-wheeled vehicle to haul raw materials and items scavenged from the ruins. There had once been roads to drive on, but those were long gone. Even open spaces were rare now that the Mother dominated the world.

She was tightening lug nuts onto a rusted wheel stud when she heard rumbling overhead. She saw a white streak in the sky, and instantly knew it had to be a contrail, though her own eyes had never seen anything like it before. She quickly moved to track the trajectory, and after some computation, she determined an approximate landing site.

She was lucky the alien vehicle was landing on the same continent. It had never occurred to her to launch satellites to detect incoming activity from off-world, and she berated herself for her shortsightedness. She had no way of knowing whether these were the first, or if others had come before and landed on another continent, or if there were many of them simultaneously investigating sites all over the globe. Only the Mother knew the answers to those questions, and Hain couldn't hear the Mother's voices.

She only heard one voice in her head now—her own. She'd grown used to that and now preferred it. After all, she knew everything the Mother knew, and everything the Mother before this Mother had known, and so on back through the eons, with each new offspring receiving all the knowledge of those that had gone before as she grew from bud to nymph.

She had no desire to rejoin the Mother anytime soon, to put down roots and reconnect in partnership on that communal plane. So she'd have to investigate the contrail, and what it meant, on her own.

Over the years, Hain had watched scores of other nymphs break free, roam for a bit, and then select a terminal point, whereupon they would bind themselves back to the earth. Some had come to her with messages from the Mother. In their eagerness to return, to rejoin the voices in that perpetual state of grace, rootlets were already unfurling from their lower extremities when they arrived, allowing them to twine with Hain, making contact just long enough to communicate to her that she was missed, and that staying away from the Mother too long could mean disaster.

None of these nymphs had been like her. Hain now accepted that she was unique. There hadn't been a message from the Mother in centuries.

Hain gathered supplies and set off on her adventure. It took days to get there, over rough terrain, and she had to go out of her way to skirt the densest groves of the Mother. When she got close, she hid her vehicle in thick undergrowth and continued on foot.

She rounded a thicket. Here, the Mother began to grow more sparsely, giving way to a broad glade. It was a low spot that would be marshy during the rainy season, not a good place to put down roots, but perfect for a vertical landing.

When the ship came into view, its silver skin glaring in the bright sunlight, she stopped abruptly and stared in stunned disbelief.

It was enormous.

Hain had been gathering scraps of metal for centuries. She sorted it into piles and used it whenever she needed raw material for the object rendering machine. The ship before her represented a mass of metal she couldn't conceive of gathering.

She could see the aliens, too. She gradually moved closer until she could hear them speak, then she settled in to observe them for a while to see what they were about. It was easy to conceal herself from them. They were oblivious to her existence.

They were as different from her as she was from the small mammals that scampered through the Mother, and she was surprised to note that they were far larger than the animals she was acquainted with. They were her size, roughly.

There seemed to be several species, but nothing like any she knew. These were more highly evolved. They walked on two limbs instead of four, had nimble fingers, and used technology. Since the old times, no species on this world had used technology, until Hain had chosen to employ that aspect of the Mother's memory. So it was fascinating to watch them use it with their furry paws that looked so much like hands.

Each day the aliens scouted in a different direction from their ship. At first Hain thought they might be scientists, because they collected samples. These samples were mostly of plant life, but they trapped some insects and small animals too. They built up great stacks of sample boxes and crates, which they transported back to their ship at nightfall.

Hain's other hypothesis was that they were colonists. The old stories were full of visitors who had come to live among the mobile nymphs when the Mother was still small, sharing the planet's resources, living symbiotically, peacefully. If they had come again, it could mean a new life, a synergy, discoveries derived from the sharing of different cultures, the elevation of everything she knew to another, higher level.

That would have been a gift.

But the old visitors had not come again. And these new aliens were not there to share or learn, but to take.

* * *

Both Hain's larynx and the small bellows-like structures on the sides of her neck were vestigial, all but superseded by the evolutionary development of other structures in her progenitors' throats. She could understand Mensententia as well as any civilized person in the universe, but she was unable to speak it at anything above a whisper.

Among her many inventions was an implant that took in air through an opening she had incised into her neck and forced it through her rudimentary larynx. The device was crude but functional, and it was in place. She had thought it would undergo many more revisions, and that she would have many more practice sessions using it, before she would ever have the opportunity to use it among those with lungs. But it would have to do.

As she watched the newcomers casually enter and exit their vehicle, she felt something unusual stirring in her. She had long been planning to construct a ship of her own. She'd already explored every continent of this world, and she ached to leave it, to explore new ones, to learn new technologies, and to interact with others in the old ways that were common in the time before the Mother embraced transcendence.

She wasn't supposed to want to leave. She was supposed to be content with her place on this world. But Hain wanted more.

The aliens' ship was so much larger than anything she could hope to create. It represented hundreds, possibly thousands of years of work. Inside, there was sure to be technology on a scale not seen since the Mother's most distant and watery memories were reality. To have that kind of functional technology at her fingertips, instead of spending her time endlessly repairing or painstakingly building anew—the very idea made her fingers curl.

At first she didn't comprehend what she was feeling. She didn't experience much in the way of emotion. And this was a strange mixture of longing and excitement, not unlike that which she felt in the days before she broke free from the Mother. Eventually she deduced what this uncomfortable feeling was. She coveted their vehicle.

She should make contact and ask them for... what? Passage? Where would she go? She had little knowledge of anything outside this sphere. Ask for some form of employment—did such paradigms still exist? Did she possess any knowledge or skill they might want or need? It seemed unlikely.

Perhaps she needn't ask at all. The ship was huge. If she was very clever, she might be able to stow away undetected. That idea appealed to her more than it should have. After all, she wanted to continue to live in the old way, free. Leaving this world and exploring the stars would mean interacting with other individuals. It was perplexing. She didn't understand her own reluctance any more than her wanderlust.

She had long thought that the radiation of the old sun might have altered her DNA, made her into a kind of seed to take their civilization to a safer place, a new world with a young sun, where her people could prosper again when this one was gone. The Mother couldn't do such a thing. She was fixed in her place. But perhaps Hain could be a new Mother, if she could stop moving and put down roots. This was the way of the oldest knowledge, the kernel at the center of what they were.

In the distant past, greenwood nymphs had lived in great communities with other species. They had formed complex relationships, had worked together, had shared their lives and gone to the stars with them, taking the Mother to new worlds.

Why was Hain reluctant to attempt these kinds of social bonds now? This, too, elicited a new sensation she didn't enjoy. After much introspection, she was able to name it: fear.

Hain did not like fear.

She had maintained homeostasis for a very long time, stored a good deal of starch over the years, achieved a mass that was unusually large for a nymph. She could manage on starch stores alone for a long time, but it would be far better if she had access to appropriate light spectra. It seemed prudent to plan ahead in case hardship should strike.

Were there others like her, out there, somewhere among the stars? Would her anatomy be familiar to the strangers, or a curiosity? Would they be capable of meeting her needs? Was it safe to leave her well-being to their mercy? She didn't want to have planned and yearned for freedom this long, only to lose not only her life, but also any chance at a transcendent afterlife.

* * *

Hain had to know more. At dawn the next day she crouched in the undergrowth, a bag of tools slung over one shoulder, and watched the aliens set off. When they were well out of sight, she crept up to the ship's portal. Her eyesight was optimal. She'd watched them come and go for days now, and had easily memorized the complex code they keyed into the panel next to the portal.

Her energy was very high. The early morning sunlight was weak due to the impending change of season, but she was warm despite the swirling rush of changing winds and nearly vibrating with excitement.

She slipped a fingertip into the slot and flipped the small door open, revealing the small compartment that contained the keypad. She stood there, staring at the symbols stamped onto the buttons. They were in Mensententia, so they weren't unfamiliar. Her dual-chambered heart fluttered in her trunk, pumping fluid rapidly through the xylem and phloem of her body. She decisively punched in the code in the same way she'd observed the aliens entering it—in the same order and at the same rate of speed.

Her stomata pulsed, releasing ozone and some water vapor. Standing in full morning sun, she was cycling CO_2 into O_3 at a dizzying rate. The chemoreceptors in her skin detected the sharp spike of the gas that indicated her body was under stress, but she barely registered it. Her body knew the risks as well as her mind.

There was a loud click, then the portal bounced inward a few finger widths and came to rest. She hadn't needed her tools after all.

Her eyes darted around the glade, which was still empty. All around its edge, the dark foliage of the Mother shielded her from the eyes of the aliens. She wondered what the Mother must be thinking as she pushed open the heavy door and slid inside, sideways, then allowed the door to shut behind her with a muffled clank. It was unlikely that the voices of the Mother were happy. The Mother wanted all her children to come to her, to root. But that thought was quickly gone. This new place was so foreign. Hain's senses blazed with information.

She was in a small chamber, dimly lit—an airlock, she realized. Directly in front of her was another portal, standing open and leading to a larger interior room. Lights came on all around her. She blinked and her eyes adjusted. She slowly set down the bag of tools.

Dazzling technology surrounded her. Multi-colored lights blinked. Blank screens covered the walls. She trembled. This was brilliantly real, so unlike the Mother's faded memories of places like it.

Hain stumbled forward in a daze. A screen lit up. She turned to it. It prompted her in the telescoping three-dimensional Mensententic symbol for "ready."

She jabbed the side of her neck to trigger the air-flow device, then spoke, creaking out a command that should bring up a search prompt: "Qui-sssssssss-tohhhhh."

The computer didn't react. She tried again, poking the external elements of the device to turn up the air volume, forcing precision through unfamiliar lips. She got no response. Either it couldn't hear her meager voice, or it only responded to authorized individuals.

She frowned and studied the controls, forgetting the air hissing through her parted lips. There should be more than one way to access information. She tentatively tapped the screen. Nothing happened. She tapped it again, a little harder, and this time a small portion of her flesh touched the screen, rather than the corky lichen that grew over the tops of her hands. The screen flashed and a menu came up. So, it was capacitive, rather than pressure-sensitive. With irritation, Hain silenced the air-flow device.

She took a few moments to absorb how the system was structured. She was relieved to see that the symbology of the language hadn't changed dramatically since the Mother's time and that the interface was fairly intuitive. Soon she was navigating with ease, bypassing information about who owned the ship, the crew, the cargo, their mission, and went straight to the details of structure and propulsion. She needed to know if there had been advancements in drive technology since the

Mother withdrew from galactic society—and she needed to look at current star maps.

There was something strange here. All of the navigation controls were routed to a central station that wasn't on the bridge. Hain backed out of the schematics and entered a search query, her fingers hovering over the screen and pecking at each symbol, one at a time. There was so much she wanted to know and so little time.

It was tempting to just take one of the screens. It was a lovely, compact piece of tech. Nothing like it had survived from the old times. She'd always wanted to recreate something like it, but there would be so many steps, and there was always something more pressing.

And these aliens had so many of them. Surely they didn't need them all—with so many, there must be redundancies. So tempting. Hain eyed her bag of tools near the portal.

Ah! There. The answer. They still used wormhole technology as well as warp-drive ships, though the latter had fallen out of favor. It seemed there had been a new discovery: a sentient species that somehow enabled access to wormhole travel without the use of the costly, temperamental drives that had previously been necessary. A few individuals of this new species had been sold on the black market for breeding, and now nearly every space-faring vehicle had one, except for short-range transports.

Hain felt frustrated. She had no way of obtaining one of these creatures for her own ship, though it would be many years before the need would arise. If she continued on her own, she'd have to use the old technology. That was fine, of course, just not optimal. Hain liked for things to be optimal.

She knew that the urgency she felt was really only impatience. There were no limits on her time. She could do it on her own, without depending on strangers.

But an old worry came back—that she really didn't have forever, that eventually it wouldn't matter how long she lived. Not if her mind unraveled.

She squashed that thought and did some arithmetic. With the old-fashioned warp propulsion system she was building, the nearest inhabited system was two hundred and seven solar years away. With the use of one of these mysterious creatures, it would be a week away, at most. Possibly less. The difference was comical.

Another thought struck her. The entire universe was open to these aliens. What were they doing *here*? Her eyes unfocused as she thought about all of this, her brain buzzing with possibilities.

A tiny beeping sound caught her attention and jolted her back to the present. The screen she'd been using had gone blank, except for three words:

"Who are you?"

Hain froze. The sharp stink of ozone filled the air.

She had thought the ship was empty. She'd counted the individuals every time they'd left the ship. They were all accounted for… weren't they? Was there someone who had stayed behind?

She stared at the screen, torn between answering and lunging for the portal. It wasn't a hostile question, necessarily. She might not be in any danger.

Three more words popped up on the screen. "I am Do'Vela."

Volunteering information… that wasn't antagonistic, Hain thought.

Hain touched the screen to create her own message. "I am Hain."

The response was immediate. "I can't feel you."

Hain didn't know what that meant. The alien wasn't in the same room with her, wasn't touching her. Of course it couldn't feel her. What was it after? She couldn't think of anything to say in reply.

After a moment, the display changed to show a two-color schematic of the ship. A series of linked corridors and rooms were marked green. Hain didn't understand. Was there something special about those rooms and corridors? Something the alien wanted her to see?

She retraced her steps and peered out through the crack that remained in the entrance portal. Wind whistled through the opening—a strange, mournful sound. No one was outside except the Mother and some noisy birds. It was mid-afternoon. She had been there longer than she had realized, but she would probably still be safe for some time. Each day the aliens had stayed away until nightfall was imminent.

When Hain returned to the screen, new words had appeared: "Come to me." And there was a black dot on the schematic, tracing its way from Hain's location, along the green-marked sequence of passages, to its terminus near the center of the ship. Suddenly, it dawned on her that the alien was asking her to walk the path it had laid out on the screen.

This time she didn't hesitate. She was intensely curious. She knew it was a risk to go deeper into the ship. It was probably wiser to leave and come back the next day. That would give her time to think, to process it all. But she sensed that the aliens would probably move on soon. Her opportunities were dwindling. It was worth some risk.

She cautiously walked the route that she'd seen on the screen. The chemoreceptors in her skin were nearly overwhelmed by wave after wave of organic molecules of foreign origin. This corridor had been traversed by many species of people over a long period of time—that was clear.

She came to the end of the route and stepped into another large, empty chamber. As in the first one, there was technology everywhere she looked. And all of the screens were blank, except for one. When Hain stepped closer, she could see that it repeated the words she'd seen before: "I am Do'Vela."

But where was Do'Vela? There wasn't anyone here. The chamber stank of fetid, brackish water, reminiscent of a marsh.

Hain tapped into the screen: "Where is Do'Vela?"

She noticed a flicker of movement beside the screen. What she had assumed was part of a wall was actually a transparent material. Someone on the other side was wiping at it, ineffectually attempting to clean away a dark blotchy film from the partition. Hain could see movement through the haze, but little else.

The screen said, "Do'Vela is here. I am here."

Hain was thoroughly confused. She reached out a hand to wipe at the glass from her side, but it was relatively clean. She couldn't fathom why Do'Vela didn't just open a door and come through. Was the alien imprisoned behind the glass?

Do'Vela stopped wiping.

Hain glanced at the screen. Now it said, "Pull the handle above, so that I may see you."

Just above the screen, Hain could see a brightly colored handle, next to a symbol for "open." Hain knew it was foolish. She was probably naïve—and definitely too inquisitive—but she reached up, grasped it, and pulled down with all her strength.

She jumped back with dismay. The entire chamber rumbled as the transparent wall moved forward on a track built into the floor with a groaning sound and ominous clacks. The mechanics were neither well constructed nor properly maintained. That made Hain uneasy. Could she trust anyone or anything that did not set the same standards of quality control that she set for herself?

Hain worried that the sound and vibration might carry outside. Perhaps she should leave. She felt a heavy feeling that she didn't understand, holding her in the spot where she stood. Her heart beat very fast and she didn't know why she felt so strange.

When the object stopped its forward motion, it proved to be a cube, slightly taller than she was. The top of it lifted slightly and flipped back upon itself, folding up and sliding back in pleats, water sheeting off the panels as they moved.

A droplet struck Hain in the face. She didn't react. She just watched, dumbfounded. She'd never been so surprised.

A pale, slim arm came up over the top of what she now realized was a tank filled with water. The arm was flexible in all directions, it seemed, and was studded with small circular discs, very similar in design to some of the lichen she wore on her own body—each bearing a depressed central point with radiating lines. She didn't think these were symbionts or ornamentation, but a part of the creature.

Another arm, then another, and another, emerged from the tank. Water splashed and ran over the sides. How many arms could it have? There was a beep from the screen. Hain turned. Now the screen said, "Come closer."

As Hain moved closer she could see, just over her head, an immense eye, proportionally much larger than her own, dark and luminous, peeking over the top of the tank. The creature was pale white, almost translucent—Hain could see traces of Do'Vela's inner workings through the thin skin. She glanced around the chamber for something to stand on, but there was nothing near to hand. One of the individual's arms reached out to touch her, but the span was slightly too far.

Hain prodded her neck to turn on her crude device, struggled again to coax words from her frozen, inadequate throat.

The screen next to the tank beeped again. Now it said, "I don't communicate that way. Touch me."

Hain sidestepped to the flat display and entered, "You only communicate electronically?"

The reply was swift. "No. Touch me. I cannot feel you."

Hain didn't know what compelled her to move forward. Later, she would count herself lucky that Do'Vela hadn't pulled her into the filthy tank and devoured her.

She stretched her hand out to meet the curling arm. Upon the first tentative contact, she felt something thrilling, like electricity, pass between them. Hain's eyes widened. Do'Vela's arm twined around hers, pulling Hain closer to the tank.

Hain staggered forward, not reluctant to get closer, but dumbstruck. Salt water ran down her arm. Her skin's chemoreceptors registered an excess of toxic impurities and high concentrations of microorganisms. But she wasn't consciously thinking about that, because, as the surface contact between Hain and Do'Vela grew, so, too, grew an *awareness*.

Hain's mouth fell open, the air-stream from her forgotten implant twirling the fern fronds that fell forward from the top of her head.

Do'Vela was like the Mother.

She felt the rush of Do'Vela's excitement. "I feel you!" She heard the words echoing through her mind. "You are so different from any other!"

Hain was rigid under Do'Vela's touch. She felt such joy at the opportunity to commune with another, but she also feared some internal process had been triggered that she'd be unable to control, and she couldn't help but look down at her feet to make sure she was not taking root.

"Oh, I see. You are a part of something larger, holding yourself separate. You wish to remain an individual, to explore. You have long been alone." Do'Vela's inner voice was warm and eager. "I, likewise, have been alone. What serendipity to find you here!"

Information streamed between them. Hain was held in thrall by the scope of it. She could see how Do'Vela had once lived in a much larger tank of water, and although under stress even then—due to poor water quality and confinement—at least she had been among her own kind to share in the misery. As a juvenile, Do'Vela had been wrenched from that place, passed around from one owner to another, until at last she had ended up here, in this wretched situation.

It was clear that the small creature was malnourished, though she held onto Hain's arm with surprising strength. Her memory showed that she was routinely deprived of sustenance.

This was not like speaking with the Mother. Here, Hain was the elder, the wiser one, but still so curious. "How can you efficiently fulfill your purpose? Why do they not optimize your environment?"

Do'Vela didn't know. The motivations of the crew of this ship were a mystery to her. She had a vague notion that her ancestors had long ago been a majestic, free people. But she had never heard of any that lived that way now. The closest she could get to experiencing freedom was to burrow into the minds of bipedal hominids to experience the universe through their eyes. She could ride in their minds and see and hear their interactions with others. She felt impressions of their thoughts, and their most basic emotions. In fact, she had been with one of the crew, hiking and gathering samples, when the intruder alert had brought her back inside herself to investigate Hain's presence inside the craft.

But she could not crack Hain's mind without physical touch.

Hain was charmed by this creature. She was so different from the Mother, though the mode of communication was very similar. Do'Vela was like a newly detached nymph: young, ebullient, genuine, and so intelligent.

Hain wondered how she would cope with captivity if she were stuck in a similar situation. Would she be able to survive? What would this ship's crew do with her, if they discovered her inside the ship? Would they trap and exploit her as they had Do'Vela? Would they withhold nourishment when they were displeased with her performance?

Even as she recognized this risk, Hain knew that she and Do'Vela were caught up in something that she didn't want to cut short. Hain hadn't realized how much she missed the Mother, how lonely her existence was, how much more *real* a living being felt than memories.

Suddenly, Do'Vela's delightful stream-of-consciousness blathering slammed to a halt. Her effusive happiness was replaced with abject fear. She let go of Hain's arm and slipped back into her tank, disappearing from sight without an explanation.

Hain stumbled back, confused. The screen next to the tank beeped. It said, "I'm sorry!" The screen crackled and words flashed chaotically. Hain couldn't read them until they settled on one last message, for the briefest moment: "Please close my enclosure! Safe journey, friend!"

The screen went blank.

Hain strained all of her senses to understand what was happening, but she had very few clues. The precipitous disappearance of Do'Vela was disconcerting.

She reversed the position of the handle. The covering folded again, each panel slamming into place with an unnervingly loud sound, and the floor rumbled under her feet as the tank receded into its compartment.

She quickly brought up the ship's schematic on the screen, looking for another place to exit the vehicle, but as far as she could tell, there was only one exterior portal—the one she'd used to get in. That was a terrible design, she concluded. She could do far better.

She moved as warily as a prey animal. But as she approached the outer chamber that connected with the portal to the outside, she heard something hit the deck with a thunk.

How much time had passed? Had she stayed too long? She quickly turned back, determined to stay out of sight until they left again the next day. She fumbled with the implant controls on her neck to silence it, suddenly aware of the constant shushing sound it made.

But it was too late. One of the mammals stomped into the corridor at that moment. Hain stopped dead in her tracks and turned to face it.

It looked as surprised to see her as she was to see it. Its nose twitched. "Whoa," it whispered. It gestured with a furry hand. She didn't know what that meant. It didn't move, otherwise.

Her stomata puffed ozone. She remained rigid, alert, waiting to see how this would develop. She was trapped, with few choices.

They stood there, assessing each other for a long moment.

It started forward with purpose. She didn't like the look in its eye. She turned to flee, but it was faster than she expected. It grabbed her arm and turned, dragging her in its wake.

She staggered, pulling and prying at its fingers to no avail. Its meaty body outweighed her reedy form by many times her own weight. It bore her inexorably down the corridor without a word, through the chamber to the airlock, and then outside.

Terror gripped her. She was at the alien's mercy. She could end up like Do'Vela, or be killed before she could take root and join the Mother. How could her circumstances have changed so quickly? She'd been too impulsive. She'd underestimated the risk.

The alien held her tightly as it barreled through the clearing and into the Mother. Hain renewed her struggle, clinging to the Mother as they passed, risking her arms being torn from their sockets. The Mother's bark tore at her symbionts, scraping her flesh raw. Thick sap oozed from the wounds. She barely felt the pain. She heard herself making horrible mewling cries of distress, like a woodland animal caught in the jaws of a predator—the loudest sounds she'd ever made in her long life, magnified by the still-running implant.

Her legs went out from under her while she flailed, pulling small plants up by their roots as she tried to grasp at anything and everything they passed. Spongy leaf mold caked her skin. The beast just grunted and pulled harder.

Finally it stopped, yelling for the others to come see what it had found. Hain scrambled to her feet. Now she wished she had let her arm be torn out, because it would be better to live free without an arm than to be captured by this greasy, stinking animal.

The other mammals crowded around. A cacophony of sounds buffeted her as they all spoke at the same time. She had no hope of understanding them. It was too much sensory information and she was too unused to language.

She felt weak, suddenly drained. She fell to her knees. In the shadow of the Mother, there was no hope for sunlight's blessing of more energy to renew the fight. She gave up. It was over. They would do what they would.

They touched her, turned her so they could see her body from every angle, pried at her symbionts, scraped her lichen, pulled on the ferns and mosses adorning her head and neck—all the while producing a din of discordant sound.

A memory prickled at the back of her mind. The Mother could be powerful if threatened. In the last hundred thousand years or more, she had never summoned this power. Might the Mother save a wandering nymph from these beasts? Hain didn't know.

She imagined that she could sense wisps of the pheromone alarm—the warning that went out to every creature planet-wide just before the wrath was unleashed on anyone who dared hurt the Mother. It was wishful thinking, surely.

Hain kept her eyes on the soothing green foliage of the Mother, and she wondered what would happen if she attempted to set down roots right here. She silently begged for help.

But the Mother could not hear her.

* * *

A fawn-colored furry face filled her field of view. It yelled, "Can you hear me?"

Hain refocused. It was just one voice, and no one touched her now. She lay on the spongy duff, almost comfortable.

"Maybe it's deaf," another one said.

"I don't think so," the first one replied, still hovering over her. "I think it hears me." It clapped its paws together in front of her face. She flinched.

"Yeah, it hears you. What's its story, I wonder? You think it's sentient?" another voice said.

"I am," Hain whispered. But they were so loud they couldn't hear her soft speech. She cursed herself for not taking time to perfect the device sooner. But how could she have predicted this turn of events? She waved a hand limply toward her face until they noticed and grew momentarily quiet. She tensed up and did her best to channel her air properly, to form the words she needed so desperately for them to hear. "I am Hain."

"I'll be damned," one of them barked. "An actual green-as-grass talking plant!"

A furry paw was held out to her. She stared at it, uncomprehending.

"You're a funny thing, aren't you? Take my hand and I'll help you up." The one speaking was the darkest of them. Its fur grew in dense swirls, sticking out at odd angles. "I am called Keeb." She hesitated. But the crowd had stepped back from her, seemed less threatening. Perhaps the worst was over.

Hain lifted her arm and Keeb grabbed it, more gently than the other had, and helped her to her feet. Keeb pulled his lips back, revealing two rows of sharp, carnivorous teeth, as well as plenty of molars. He was the largest omnivore she'd ever seen. She watched him warily.

"Hello, Hain," Keeb said. "Are you related to these plants somehow?"

Hain blinked, and her gaze followed his gesture. For the first time she noticed her surroundings. They stood in the midst of a densely populated copse. Hain's eyes widened in horror as her brain tried to process a sudden bolus of terrifying information.

Her eyes saw the bodies.

Her ears heard the drone and squeal of various cutting tools.

Her chemoreceptors detected the heat of cut wood, the scent of sawdust and sap—all scents that were new to her.

And underlying all of that was the pheromone she thought she'd detected before. Its identity could no longer be denied—its presence in the air was growing at an alarming rate.

Deep inside, she instinctively *knew*—as did every native of the planet—that she was in terrible and immediate danger. She needed to find a safe place to hide if she was to survive.

Words failed her. She stared at Keeb. He didn't look alarmed. Didn't he know? Couldn't he smell it with those canine-looking nostrils?

"This is quite a find for us," he was saying. Some of the others watched with mild curiosity, others with boredom, and still others turned away to resume their work—sawing, chipping, slicing, hauling.

She watched with the abstract detachment of shock as one of the animals raised a laser cutting arc and brought it slowly to bear on another member of the Mother. She shuddered as she noted the ease with which the animal ended a life.

"Last night I happened to analyze a few samples. There was some really bizarre DNA in one of them. I insisted we come back to take another look at these trees and get some bigger samples," Keeb was saying.

Hain watched the mammal's mouth moving, the tongue and teeth glistening with the saliva that begins the digestion of prey. She was too stunned and confused to look away.

"Plant DNA with some animal markers—like a hybrid. I'd never heard of anything like it. I was sure the sample was contaminated, until we cut down a few of the trees. After a little bit of whittling, we found amazing structures inside, at the base of the trunks—it looks like calcified or possibly petrified hearts, livers, spleens and so on—nothing like ours, of course, but still, working rudimentary organs. We've never heard of anything like it. The trees just… grew up around them, incorporating their bodies into the wood itself. It's the damnedest thing."

He had forgotten to mention brains.

He kept talking, completely unaware of her reaction. "Once we saw that… hell. Then I figured—*no one's* ever seen anything like this! We might as well fill up the cargo hold and see how many credits we can get for 'em." His lips curled up in an expression she didn't recognize. Based on context, she guessed it was avarice.

Keeb looked her up and down, his eyes narrowed, still taking in every detail of her appearance. Why was he staring? She stared back, alarm mounting every second.

"Then *you* show up. Are these trees your distant ancestors? Some kind of missing link? Where are the rest of your people? We detected abandoned cities, but found no indication of a living sentient population."

Someone else spoke up, "Yeah, now they'll be wanting rights. I knew it couldn't be this easy. An entire planet just full to the brim with wood? Nobody's that lucky." The mammal growled a word that must have been an expletive in his primary language, then wandered away.

In her peripheral vision she saw the laser arc continue its merciless cutting. Every loud crash marked another voice silenced, banished forever from the chorus of the Mother. What happened to those voices now? Was there more to life, after that? Did they live on in some kind of subterranean form, slowly starving, maybe sending up a shoot, to live again? Or did they just die, their murmuring melody converting to raucous shrieks of terror?

The Mother would not allow this much longer.

She should tell them to stop.

She should warn them.

But how could they not know?

How could they kill so many without purpose? For wood? What was wood but a vessel for everlasting life? How would these mammals react if she snatched that laser arc from their paws and sliced one of them in two, letting his life's blood spill among the sap flowing through the undergrowth?

The legends of greedy people who killed for wood had been true, not just stories to entice nymphs to root close to the Mother rather than in remote, open locations. Not that there were any of those left anymore.

The group's initial interest in Hain had waned. Most of them had moved on to other tasks, leaving her with Keeb.

Hain looked past Keeb, at the Mother—strong and tall and ancient, her leaves quaking in the breeze, disseminating the chemical warning for all that could detect it. The levels of the pheromone were rising sharply. The Mother wouldn't wait much longer before she would retaliate—before she would make these tiny mammals pay for their transgression.

Hain needed light desperately. She was considering taking a few steps forward when, behind her, another life was ended, causing the canopy overhead to open up. Sunlight streamed into the small artificial glade that was forming in a rough circle around them, and Hain was bathed in light. She felt her skin warm as the light-energy nourished and renewed her.

"You don't talk much, do you?" Keeb asked with a guffaw that sounded almost like the bark of a small canine that had thrived among the tall grasses of the prairies long ago.

When he quieted, she spoke. "No, I have no need. I am alone."

His confusion was evident. Though she herself had never seen that emotion on a mammal's face, ancient instinctual pathways in her brain were tripped—or maybe it was the Mother's memories from the times before. Regardless, the emotion must have been strong for her to read it. She knew she would not be able to read subtle intention—or ferret out deception. She was very aware of her lack of skill. He seemed to be equally inept at reading her.

"Oh, are you stranded here? Did your ship break down?"

"Yes," she answered. "Irreparable." Her first lie. She watched him closely.

He nodded. He didn't indicate disbelief. "That explains it. I expect you'll want a ride back to civilization? Got any credits?"

"Yes. Of course," she replied with a firm nod. Another lie. It was so easy to let him believe what he wanted to believe.

"I'll tell Goppul. She takes care of that."

"What will be done with this wood?" Hain asked, trying not to choke on the word. Her throat ached from the effort of speaking so much.

Keeb's lips pulled back in a feral smile. "High-end furniture. We're going to keep this planet a secret and move this stuff to market slowly to keep demand high. By the end of the day, we'll have enough to fill the hold. Then we'll take off, probably tomorrow."

"That soon?" she said. There was no time to plan anything.

"Yeah. So, if there's anything you want to take with you, I suggest you fetch it now. It's nearly dusk—the predators will be out soon." He gestured at the Mother, as though believed she harbored animals more dangerous than his own species.

The Mother was silent. Not a bird chattered. No mammals rustled the undergrowth. Even the insects had quieted.

The birds were roosting in nests hastily built up out of mud and foliage, a task precipitated by instinct. They would huddle inside, a small hole allowing only the barest whisper of air through. Their only task in the coming storm would be to keep that hole open, their one chance to survive.

Mammals, reptiles, and insects were burrowing deep into dens, caves, cracks, and crevices. Water-inhabiting animals were diving deep to wait for it to be over, for the world to be bright and livable again. In the coming hours many would die, but the Mother would live on to give the survivors succor, and they would grow in numbers again in the coming years.

Hain thought of her small shelter in the abandoned city so far away, and wondered if it would be enough to protect her, if she could even make it there in time.

Images of mummified animals caught out in past storms burbled up in her head from the Mother's memories, unbidden. Their bodies were frozen in paroxysms of hypoxia, mouths open wide in strangled gasps.

She was not immune to this. She might not have lungs, but she had to exchange gases like any other living thing. She would share that fate if she couldn't find a safe haven.

The stillness was deadly.

These brutes created the only sounds, but they didn't seem to notice.

"I will go then, to obtain my belongings and return at dawn," Hain said to Keeb, struggling to contain the hysteria that rose inside her.

He frowned and glanced around at all the others, working diligently. Killing, killing, killing. "Do you need an escort?"

"No need," she said. "I know this place well."

Her soft voice was overtaken by a shout. "Keeb! You've got to see this!"

Keeb barely gave Hain another glance before striding toward this newest excitement.

Hain slipped away, the words of the enthusiastic animal carried on the wind to her as she loped through the grove. "It's a damned face! Can you believe it? I whittled it down, careful-like, with a small laser-carver. Look! There's eyes and everything!"

The animals chattered excitedly over the dead member of the Mother. She left them behind.

* * *

Hain ran, darting through bright spots of sunlight whenever possible, to keep her energy up. She hadn't run since the days when her legs were new. It had felt so good then. Freedom was a wonderful thing.

And now she was on the cusp of a new kind of freedom, if she could make it in time.

She'd depleted her short-term sources of energy and was actively consuming starch now. It made her slower and clumsier. She couldn't convert it fast enough to maintain such a breakneck pace.

But she made it to the ship. And just as she reached it, Hain saw the first motes of yellow skimming the wind. They were a haze, coloring the scenery, making it look like the decaying art she'd seen in some of the oldest buildings in the cities. As she tapped out the code to gain entry, a yellow speck landed on her finger. Instinctively, she brushed at it—but it wouldn't wipe away. It held fast to the corky lichen. She thanked the Mother for the symbiont's dense protection.

The keypad beeped and flashed a red warning.

What? In her haste had she keyed in the code incorrectly? She steadied herself by leaning against the side of the ship. Sunlight washed over her. Her stomata gulped CO_2 from the air, cleaving it and recombining it into carbohydrates and ATP energy packets, discarding the wasted oxygen back into the atmosphere.

Suddenly she panicked. Would there even be CO_2 aboard this ship? How foolish that she hadn't looked to see if the gas was stored somewhere on board. She was so preoccupied with drive technology that she hadn't made certain she could survive inside. Then she remembered Do'Vela, and her panic eased slightly. Do'Vela and all of the bacteria in her enclosure could provide Hain with all the CO_2 she needed, as long as she didn't expend a lot of energy.

The wind picked up, and she looked over her shoulder. Visibility was rapidly decreasing. The haze was rolling away from the Mother, filling the air like a slow-moving wall from ground to sky. She had to get inside fast.

A particle landed on skin scraped raw from her earlier escape efforts. Pain screamed in her head upon that tiny contact.

She ignored that and tapped out the sequence again, very carefully.

The keypad flashed red and the portal did not open as it had before.

Her hungry body felt the sunlight begin to go.

She tried again, but somehow they'd locked her out. They didn't want her inside their domain. They wouldn't let that happen twice.

Tiny amber grains pelted her. Pain burrowed into her skin with each contact. She tried to shelter within the small concavity of the portal, but the wind swirled, and the devilish pollen granules found her.

The Mother was meting out her justice. The Mother wanted to survive, too. And she had. She had not only survived, she had thrived. This world was hers now. There wasn't a corner of it that she didn't oversee.

There was nowhere else for Hain to hide. She slipped one leg out of the hollow of the portal, making contact with the ground. Her last, desperate option was to take root and hope to outlast the caustic pollen storm. If she could tap into some water in the soil and keep a fraction of her stomata functional under her lichen armor, she might endure.

She closed her stomata tight, as she did at night, hoping to preserve the integrity of her skin. No point in gas exchange now. The atmosphere was so thick with pollen that the sun had virtually disappeared. The light had gone dull, shadowless, deepest goldenrod. There would be no more photosynthesis for a long while.

The pollen swirled around her like snow. Her flesh burned, pinpricks of agony, wherever it struck.

In the distance she heard roars and yelps of pain. She squinted over her shoulder to see the indistinct shapes of the mammals far down the edge of the glade. They'd blundered out in the wrong place. She couldn't believe their lungs were still functioning—surely the pollen had turned that fragile tissue to a bloody mass.

Her leg stiffened as the transformation began, toes slowly curling into rooted tendrils, her heel gradually growing into a spur to anchor her securely to the spot.

Could she hear the Mother's whisper? Was she closer to knowing the Mother's truths, the Mother's peace?

Hain tried to curl into herself, to shield some part of her body, to protect it from the ravaging particles on the wind. Pollen burned her eyes. She was sticky, oozing precious fluids from broken veins. If she couldn't reach water in the soil, she would desiccate right here in this shallow alcove.

She heard a beep.

Hain opened her eyes to slits and scanned her surroundings. The beasts continued to advance. She could see them more clearly now, their shaggy fur frosted with pollen. How they could endure it, she didn't know.

They'd be angry when they arrived. They'd blame her. They'd tear her limb from limb.

The beep sounded again. She turned, holding up a hand to shield her eyes. The compartment that housed the keypad for entry was still open. She peered into it. The tiny screen next to the keypad was scrolling the words, "Is it you, Hain?"

Hain blinked. She read it three times before she believed it. It was Do'Vela. It had to be.

She wrenched her foot from the soil and crouched in the small hollow of the portal, hurriedly typing, "Yes, I am Hain."

"You wish access? There is something amiss!"

How would Do'Vela know this? Then Hain remembered how Do'Vela rode in others' minds as a mental escape from her despicable confinement.

"Yes! Please!"

A moment went by. Hain put her hand over the crack in the portal. Her foot and leg ached. She tried not to think about what that might mean. She glanced over her shoulder. The animals were almost to the ship. They would not be happy to see her inside. They might punish Do'Vela for giving her entry.

The door mercifully popped inward. The mammals were steps away, staggering and raging, yellow-encrusted berserkers.

She ducked inside and pushed the door shut with a loud metallic crash. She darted to the nearest interface and sent a message: "Change key code."

Do'Vela responded. "Why?"

There was no time. She could hear them outside. She stared at the door. She heard a soft sequence of tones. They were punching in the code on the other side.

The opening mechanism of the door was exposed on her side. Her discarded tool bag still lay just inside the portal. She grabbed blindly in the bag for a tool, came out with a rasp, and jammed it into the mechanism, hoping it would prevent the latch from turning—from both inside and out.

She heard infuriated bellows. The mechanism wriggled, but the rasp held firm.

Hain dashed back to the interface. The word "Why?" still lingered.

Hain hesitated for a second, then sent, "We don't need them."

There was no answer this time. Hain stood there, unsure how to convey the urgency to Do'Vela. The enraged animals could break through the portal at any moment.

She reeked of ozone. Her fingers were sticky with sap. She'd left blotches on the screen. She began to falter. Perhaps she'd doomed herself. She leaned heavily on the console and sent, "I will take care of you. It will be better."

Do'Vela remained silent. Hain moved unsteadily to the portal. The tool was starting to buckle under the strain as the angry animals battered against the door.

She was out of options. She went back to send another plea to Do'Vela, but when she got there, there were already two words on the screen: "I understand." Hain stood there, swaying on uneven legs, her vision swimming as she blinked away the sticky moisture seeping from her burning eyes.

She wasn't sure what Do'Vela had understood, but the side of the ship thundered with the sounds of meaty paws pounding on it. Threats barked and roared at her, though they sounded tinny and far away. The portal rattled.

Then it stopped rattling, went solid as stone.

Another beep.

She turned back to the screen. Words scrolled by. "She is yours. Come to me and together we will fly from this place and be free."

Hain did not hesitate for a moment.

A Word from Jennifer Foehner Wells

I doubt it would be any surprise to anyone who knows me to learn that I love alien stories. I wear my love of science fiction like a badge. From early familial indoctrination with the *Star Wars* and *Star Trek* universes, to later exposure to television shows like the original *Doctor Who*, *Farscape*, and the *Stargate*s, to Bradbury's short stories and books like Wyndham's *Day of the Triffids* and Adam's *Hitchhiker's Guide to the Galaxy,* I developed into someone who craves alien stories with a burning, rabid passion.

Overall, what interested me most were tales of first contact—of misunderstandings and cultural exchanges, the more bizarre the better, and the human (or sentient?) response to them. I wanted to taste new worlds and leave the mundane Earth behind. I wanted to lose myself in mysteries, in foreign ways of thinking, in outlandish but plausible species. I wanted to be tricked into believing in all of the possibilities that I've always known in my heart are just a star away from being real.

When I started writing *Fluency*, my first novel, I wanted to write a "fish out of water" story, with the kinds of characters that I loved, and a mystery revolving around an enigmatic alien and all the issues that would arise in an uncontrolled first-contact situation.

I didn't expect it to do well, as it was my first published effort. I immediately pushed forward, beginning another novel in a completely different setting with new characters. This new novel would be a superhero origin story—again twisting history to fit my own universe's cosmology as I had done in *Fluency*, but with a new spin. It's called *Druid,* and as I write this, it's unfinished.

As I was writing *Druid*, there was one character that bedeviled me—Hain. She was supposed to be a minor character, but I became fixated on her, developing insane amounts of backstory, something I'd never done quite to that extent before. It wouldn't fit in the book, but I couldn't help myself. I promised myself that one day I would write a story about her. She deserved it. She was too intriguing not to.

Well, *Fluency* did do well. I was encouraged to stop work on *Druid* in order to deliver what my readers were demanding—a sequel to *Fluency*. So, with reluctance, I did. (But I'm coming back, dammit!) The success of *Fluency* earned me invitations to opportunities like this anthology—and immediately I realized that here was my chance to write a story about Hain that would be a prequel to *Druid*—and a nice counterpoint too, because "The Grove" is a villain origin story. I hope you've enjoyed it.

If you did, you may also enjoy *Fluency*. For more information on that novel, check out my website, and sign up for my newsletter to be the first to know when I publish something new. Thank you.

Life

by Daniel Arenson

NEON LIGHTS FLICKERED, the last pot of coffee percolated, and even the janitor had gone home when the first photo of an alien life form came in.

Eliana sat alone in the sprawling office, her coffee mug down to dregs, her eyelids heavy. She often stayed late. She liked the silence of the night, the hundreds of monitors gone dark, and the headlights from the highway outside streaming through the windows like beacons from other worlds. While her coworkers spent evenings with spouses, friends, children, safe and warm in cozy houses, Eliana sought her quiet time here. She had always been alone. She had always been a dreamer. The stars had always been her family, her port of call.

"It's here." She sat up in her chair, and tears filled her eyes. "The first photo. It's here."

Her breath shuddered. She could scarcely believe what she saw. Alerts popped up across her monitor. A life form detected. Data streaming in. A photo being downloaded.

Her mug fell from her hand, spilling its last drops of coffee across the desk.

She leaped to her feet.

"Oh stars, it's here. It's downloading."

In only a few minutes, the last bytes of data would arrive—arrive from *out there*—and she would be the first person in the Agency, the first human in history, to gaze upon alien life.

She spun away from her desk. She padded across the carpeting, barefoot, and placed her hands on the windowpane. Outside, the highway stretched through the desert, and above shone the stars, countless, brilliant, the celestial roads of the cosmos.

"I always knew," she whispered, voice trembling. "I always knew you were out there."

As tears streamed down her cheeks, she was a girl again, a girl alone in a very different desert, in a very distant country, climbing up the hill with her father, lying in the darkness, gazing up at the stars, the falling comets, the brilliant moon, the Milky Way the elders claimed was the heavenly path of chariots. The war had taken her father, and her life had taken her here to the Agency, but the stars remained forever above her, forever inside her, forever a dream of finding a better world. Of finding wisdom up there. Of finding hope.

She blinked the tears from her eyes. For so many years, the others had mocked her, pitied her—the woman with no family of her own, no house but her trailer in the valley, no life but her search for other life, for life above.

But it was worth it, she thought, fresh tears budding. *I've found that life. I've found the hope and wisdom I've always sought—up there. In the stars.*

Behind her, her computer dinged.

The data had downloaded.

The photo was here. The first photo of alien life.

Shakily, Eliana returned to her office chair, sat down, and leaned forward. The file blinked; she just had to click. She just had to open it. She just had to look.

And yet she hesitated.

How would one process such a thing? How could one prepare to see such a monumental sight, such a fundamental discovery, the culmination of one's dreams in an image? Would her brain process it at once, or would the photo sink in slowly, breath by breath? Perhaps she should wait until tomorrow. Perhaps she should wait until her coworkers returned, to look with them, to—

She realized she was panting. She took a deep, shaky breath.

Just click, Eliana, she told herself. *Just look... and the universe will open up before you, full of light and wisdom, full of welcome and comfort.*

Again her tears fell. Perhaps all the hatred she had felt, all the loneliness—the fire that had taken her parents, the flight across the sea, the life in darkness, the unbearable loneliness of stargazing—perhaps it would all fade. Perhaps the eyes of the alien would gaze upon her through the monitor, telling her it was all right. That she was safe. That they had always been watching, that the cosmos was not cold and dark and barren but warm, full of life, full of love for her.

Her hand trembled on the mouse.

She clicked the file open.

And she looked.

And it looked at her.

It's... it's...

Her breath caught. Her fingers shook. Her reflection stared back at her from the monitor, superimposed over *it*, staring back at her, gasping, pale.

Oh stars.

She screamed and placed her palms against the monitor. But she couldn't tear her eyes away. Her cry echoed, her voice hoarse, torn.

"So ugly," she whispered. "So ugly..."

She fell to the floor. She curled up. She wept.

She wanted to rise, to smash the monitor, to run, to jump out the window, to die. To die. To stop seeing. To gouge out her eyes.

So ugly...

She lay on the floor, hugging her knees, and sobbed.

* * *

Joe was sitting at his desk, reading an old western paperback, when he heard the scream.

He leaped to his feet, keys jangling at his belt, and began to run.

That was Eliana screaming, he thought.

He had been working night security at the Agency for ten years now—ten years of long, quiet nights, of escaping the unforgiving neon light into worlds of cowboys, sultry saloons, and the sweeping landscapes of eras long gone. The hours were long, the job dreary and dull, but in his books, Joe could become a hero—a younger, stronger man, battling bandits and saving damsels.

Tonight he would have to be a true hero.

His ample belly wobbled before him as he raced down the hall. Sweat dampened his uniform, and he was breathing raggedly by the time he reached the office doors.

"Eliana?" he called, wheezing. "Eliana, are you all right?"

His heart pounded as if trying to escape his rib cage. His shirt slipped out from his pants, and sweat dripped into his eyes, stinging. He stumbled into the office, wishing the Agency had given him a gun, a baton, at least a transmitter to call for help.

Oh God, don't let it be an intruder. Don't let me die. Please, God, I have a daughter. I have a daughter.

The office spread before him, hundreds of monitors dark and lifeless. He saw nobody. One neon light flickered, and the headlights from the highway outside streamed across the walls like ghosts.

"Eliana!" he called again, heart thumping.

He heard no reply.

Oh God. She's dead. Somebody killed her. Somebody is here, in the shadows, waiting.

Joe wanted to turn around and flee. He wasn't a hero. He wasn't a cowboy like in his books. He was just Joe Benkowski, fifty-six years old, a hundred pounds overweight, a single father whose daughter was getting married next month.

I have to run.

He took a deep breath.

No.

Eliana needed him. She was like another daughter to him. The others who worked here, the most brilliant minds in the country, rarely spoke to him: a few distracted hellos when he came into work, some years a Christmas card or two. But Eliana had always truly cared about him. She always stayed late after the others left, and often she spoke to him, asked him about his daughter, even borrowed some of his paperbacks and talked to him about their stories.

Eliana needs me. And I'm going to save her.

Mustering courage he didn't know was in him, Joe stepped deeper into the office, feeling a little like a cowboy stepping into a rough saloon.

"Eliana!"

Still he heard no reply. He walked between the desks, the lights buzzing above, the highway humming outside. Rows of monitors stretched ahead on their desks, all of them dark but one. That one monitor cast an eerie, pale light, like the moon.

Joe walked closer, his heartbeat increasing. His fingers tingled—that tingle his doctors had warned him about. Sweat trickled down his back.

"Eliana?" he whispered.

He gasped.

He leaped forward.

She lay on the floor, curled into a ball.

"Eliana, my God! Can you hear me?" He knelt beside her. "Are you all right?"

She panted. Her eyes were rimmed with red, and tears streamed down her cheeks. Those eyes flicked toward him, and she gasped, scurried back, and covered her face. She shook wildly.

"What happened?" he asked. He needed help. He needed to call an ambulance. With trembling fingers, he reached for his cell phone, only for the device to slip from his sweaty hand. He cursed.

Eliana whispered.

Joe caught his breath, leaning down to listen. "What is it, Eliana? What do you need?"

"So…" she whispered, "… so ugly."

Joe's heart felt ready to crack. His lungs felt ready to collapse. So ugly? What did she mean? Did she mean him? Herself?

The glow of the monitor fell upon him, and Joe felt something. Felt eyes staring. Felt himself being watched. From the corner of his eye, he glimpsed something, a presence, a swirl of color, eyes staring.

Slowly, he raised his eyes and looked at the image on the monitor.

And Joe Benkowski began to scream.

He collapsed onto the floor, agony stabbing his chest, knowing that this was it, the long-awaited heart attack the doctors had warned of, and Joe didn't care, didn't want to live. He whispered through stiff lips.

"So ugly."

He closed his eyes and never wanted to open them again.

* * *

Dr. Robert Jensen's dented Corolla clunked along the highway, sounding like it might collapse at any moment, sending hubcaps and fenders flying into the desert. Even the radio sounded like some dying old beast, struggling to cough out "Moonshine Blues" by Bootstrap and the Shoeshine Kid before fading to static coughs.

"Goddamn piece of junk." Jensen grunted and stubbed his cigarette into the ashtray.

He was still miles away from the Agency. Miles away from that hub of scientists in the desert. Apparently, a bunch of them had finally gone completely mad—as if searching for alien life wasn't mad enough. And when your alien hunters become catatonic, who do you call? Dr. Robert Jensen, of course—the closest, cheapest psychiatrist around.

The desert spread all around Jensen's car. The sun beat down, gleaming off the distant road, creating mirages of water he'd never reach. Nothing but that tarmac ahead, the dirt and rocks beyond, the cruel sun above. Heat and light and emptiness. Perhaps that's all that remained of his life.

"That and this damned car."

Jensen sighed. His wife had left him little more in the divorce. The house was hers. The kids were hers. The comfy Lexus with those lovely leather seats—hers. All Jensen had left was this clunker, this desert, and his work.

"You'd think as a shrink, I could figure out how to hold a marriage together."

He reached for another cigarette. Two other things the divorce had left him with: a two-packs-a-day habit and a propensity to talk to himself.

Jensen adjusted the car mirror and stared at himself. If nothing else, he still had some good looks. At age forty-four, he stubbornly clung to a certain rugged handsomeness, he thought. A craggy, tanned face. Graying temples. With the cigarette between his lips, he thought he could be featured on one of the highway billboards, riding a horse somewhere in Montana and advertising his smokes.

He coughed out a smoky laugh. As if the brand he smoked these days had money for advertising. He couldn't even afford the good stuff anymore, just these cheap sticks that left his throat burning and would probably kill his good looks even before they killed his lungs.

He was tapping the radio again, trying to revive it, when he saw the Agency ahead.

The complex sprawled across the desert. It would have looked like any other office plaza if not for the massive radio dishes that rose behind it, dwarfing even the three-story buildings before them. The great white ears of humanity, pointing ever into space.

"And those ears picked up something." Jensen puffed on his cigarette. "Something they shouldn't have eavesdropped on."

He rolled the clunker into the parking lot, surprised that it had made it this far. He parked, stepped out, and stretched.

His joints creaked. The sun still blazed down, white and blinding, but Jensen shaded his eyes with his palm and gazed skyward.

They said they found something up there. A shiver ran through him. *Something that's terrifying them more than a divorce or rattling cough.*

Jensen grunted. Aliens? He didn't believe in aliens. The isolation out here was getting to people, that was all. Hell, if he'd spent so long out here in the desert, he'd be imagining alien friends too. Jensen already felt this place seeping into him, this... this *emptiness* here in the desert, those damn dishes that kept staring up into the sky. It was enough to drive anyone mad, let alone some kooky scientists who spent their lives stargazing and dreaming of little green men.

Jensen cracked his neck and walked toward the main building. Perhaps he'd even find a kooky scientist who also happened to be female, single, and looking for companionship with a rugged psychiatrist who might just look a little like a billboard Marlboro Man. It had been too long since Jensen had spent time with a woman.

Perhaps I'm lonely too. Perhaps I too am isolated.

He shook his head, banishing the thoughts. Today he would be a professional. Last he had heard, fifteen men and women had lost their minds in this place. He would have to treat them, to cure them. Their sanity—and his wallet—depended on it.

He flicked down his cigarette butt and stepped into the front lobby. Rather than a receptionist, a white haired, harried-looking man in rumpled slacks greeted Jensen. The man held an ornate cane, its head carved into the shape of a planet. His button-down shirt still showed the folds from its original plastic packaging.

"Doctor Jensen?" the old man said, rushing forth.

Jensen nodded. "The same."

The man clasped his hand in a sweaty grip and shook it wildly, clinging to Jensen like a drowning man to a rope. "Thank goodness you're here. I'm Dr. Sullivan, chief of the Agency. We've spoken on the phone." He turned around. "Come, follow. Let's find a place to talk."

The old scientist turned and began to walk down a corridor, his cane rapping. Jensen followed. They passed by the glass walls of several offices. Within, men and women huddled together. Some whispered. Some merely stared at their feet. Jensen didn't need his doctorate in psychiatry to sense the nervousness in the air, the fear. Oddly, he was reminded of his long walks through mental institutions; this felt more like a place of madness and terror than science.

God above, what did they find up there?

Dr. Sullivan led him into a small, cluttered office. Hundreds of books covered the shelves, a blend of science and science fiction. Scribbly drawings of unicorns and houses—presumably the masterpieces of Sullivan's grandchildren—plastered the walls around a poster of the various constellations. In stark contrast to the crowded shelves and walls was Sullivan's desk: it was spotless, dustless, empty but for a single sheet of blank paper.

"Sit down, please," Sullivan said, gesturing toward a chair.

Jensen sat down uneasily, and Sullivan took the seat across the desk, joints creaking. Jensen stared at the paper on the desktop. He could vaguely make out splotches of color showing through from the opposite side. An upside-down photo, he surmised.

"Is this it?" he asked, reaching for it.

Sullivan gasped. The man looked as if Jensen had just tried to pat a ravenous wolverine with gravy-coated fingers. The old scientist slammed his palm down onto Jensen's hand, nearly crushing his joints.

"Do not lift it!" The scientist's lips trembled. His white hair stood on end. "Do not look! That photo…" Sweat beaded on Sullivan's brow. "It *does* things. It… Dr. Jensen, please, remove your hand from this photo while we speak."

Jensen shook his head in wonder at the scientist's reaction, but he grunted and obeyed, placing his hand back in his lap. Sullivan leaned back, shaken and pale.

"Dr. Sullivan," Jensen said, using his calmest voice, "surely a piece of paper cannot harm me."

Sullivan pulled a handkerchief from his pocket and dabbed his brow. "You don't understand, Dr. Jensen. This is the first photograph ever taken of an alien life form."

Jensen nodded. "So I've heard. I'd quite like to see it."

"As would I." Sullivan gulped. "As did fourteen of my top scientists, the world's leading astrobiologists. As did our night security man. All fifteen are now catatonic. They cannot even tell me what they've seen. When they're not weeping or screaming, all they can utter is: 'So ugly.'"

Jensen raised an eyebrow. "So E.T. isn't the best-looking alien in the galaxy."

"It's more than that, Doctor!" Sullivan gripped his cane and rose to his feet. "Whatever is in this photo—and I have dared not look myself—is so hideous, so monstrous, so terrifying, that all who see it go mad. My dear friend Eliana, our top scientist, has lived through warfare and poverty, has seen things in her childhood you or I cannot imagine, and she overcame them. But since looking at this photo, all she can do is curl up in her hospital bed, repeating the same two words over and over, the same words they all say: 'So ugly.'" Sullivan shuddered. "We went searching for an alien. We found a monster."

Jensen felt that nervousness, that icy hand that had been trailing down his spine all day, finally grip his heart and squeeze. Cold sweat trickled down his back.

He swallowed the lump in his throat.

Calm down, he told himself. *You're a professional. You're a psychiatrist. You don't get spooked by this cosmological mumbo jumbo.*

Jensen rose to his feet and began to pace the cluttered office. He clasped his hands behind his back to hide their tremor. "Dr. Sullivan, what you have here must be some kind of optical illusion. Have you ever seen those optical illusions online, the ones that seem to swirl around, make you see colors that aren't there, make solid lines bend? Those happen because our brains don't know how to process every visual signal sent through our eyes." He stared at the upside-down photo on the desk. "What you have here must be an optical illusion so powerful, so vivid, that it traumatizes the brain."

"Dr. Jensen!" Sullivan's eyes widened. "You don't understand! This photo was taken by a rover sent to planet Kepler-62e in the Lyra constellation. The first planet where we detected clear signals of life. Our probe was programmed to focus on a living creature—an alien life form—and send us photographic evidence of its existence. This probe wasn't pointing at some... some book of optical illusions! There is a life form in this photo. A life form so hideous, so ugly, that its sheer monstrosity is enough to traumatize even the most robust minds."

Jensen licked his dry lips. He needed another cigarette. "A photo of a monster..."

The old scientist sank back into his seat, and tears filled his eyes. "You must help them, Dr. Jensen. You must help them tell us what they saw. You must help us all. Oh God... I've spent my life searching for this life form, Doctor. My life's work, here in this photo, and..." He covered his eyes, and tears trailed down his cheeks. "And now they're in the hospital, gone mad. Catatonic. Because of me." He looked up with pleading eyes. "Can you help us?"

Jensen had seen hard cases in his day, but now he felt more shaken than he had felt in years. He sat down again and stared at the paper.

"Dr. Sullivan," he said softly. "I have some experience dealing with trauma. I've helped veterans who've seen war. I've helped genocide survivors, people who've witnessed the very depths of human evil, find new meaning in their lives. I've treated survivors of abuse, of torture, and many have made much progress in their healing." He stared up from the paper at the old scientist. "With every patient, I work to fully understand what hurt them. To listen to their stories, even the most painful details. To help your people, I must understand what scared them. I must look at this photo."

Sullivan gaped. His cheeks lost whatever color had remained in them.

He looks as if I just asked him to run me over with his car, Jensen thought.

"Dr. Jensen!" Sullivan covered his mouth, struggling to speak. "I cannot allow this! I... by God, first speak to the patients. First see how they tremble. Hear how they whisper of the ugliness. Whatever's in this photo would crush you! Haunt you!"

Jensen's knees were shaking now, and his heart pounded, but he forced himself to smile thinly.

These hermits have spent too many years in the desert, looking up to the sky, expecting to find a cute little Ewok. When they finally saw something unsettling, it fried their minds. But I've dealt with trauma. I'm hardened.

He thought back to his most difficult cases. The victim of an acid attack. A survivor of torture. Refugees of war and carnage. He, Dr. Jensen, had not spent his life staring up at beautiful stars. He had spent his life staring ugliness in the face. He would stare at some ugliness again.

"All my life," Jensen said, voice strained, "I've never shied away from terror. Not when it can help my patients."

Before Sullivan could react, Jensen reached across the table, lifted the photo, and stared.

* * *

As the old scientist gasped, Jensen examined the photograph in his hands—the first photograph of an alien life form.

He narrowed his eyes.

His breath died.

My God…

Tears filled Jensen's eyes, and his lips trembled.

It's beautiful.

It seemed unfair to call this an "alien life form." The term seemed too pedestrian. This was no mere creature. This was… a *being*. A deity. A paragon of purity.

Tears flowed down Jensen's cheeks.

The being in the photo seemed woven of starlight, of pure color, of colors Jensen hadn't even known existed. Eyes stared at him, endlessly wide, endlessly deep, endlessly knowing. They were the eyes of the cosmos. The eyes of angels, of gods, of souls. The being's face was the face of heaven, of wonder, of wisdom, painted with brushes dipped in liquid beauty.

An angel, Jensen thought, weeping. *They photographed an angel.*

She was the sky itself. She was the light of the stars, the dust of space, the soft embrace of night. She was a goddess. She was love. She was purity. She was the song of space, music taken form, solid and liquid, light and darkness, life. *She was life.* She was evolution stretched into heaven, a being of nirvana, a shining star pulsing, beaming out, knowing all. She was perfection.

With a strangled yelp, Jensen noticed his own fingers holding the paper.

Old, wrinkled fingers. The knuckles hairy. The joints knobby. They were profane things. They were an insult. They were blasphemous. They sullied this perfect being with their wretchedness.

Jensen screamed and dropped the photo to the floor, daring not defile it any further with his impurity.

With the photo gone, Jensen found himself staring at the most monstrous, disgusting, impure creature he had ever seen.

The beast sat across the desk from him, clutching a cane, dressed in a wrinkly shirt.

It's Dr. Sullivan, Jensen realized. And he was hideous. The old man's face was a network of wrinkles, pores, blemishes, an oily patch of filth. His hair was a ragged mat, revealing bits of dry scalp. Next to the being Jensen had seen—that angel, that goddess—the old scientist seemed no better than an ape, primordial, grunting.

"Dr. Jensen!" the ape said. "Dr. Jensen, are you all right? Can you hear me?"

All right? Jensen laughed bitterly. *How dare this ape speak to him? How dare humans, these beings barely more evolved than worms, learn to speak? How dare they gaze at the wonder of the stars?*

We're not ready! Jensen wanted to scream. *We're not evolved! We're apes! We're nothing but apes. Filthy, sweaty, disgusting, reeking, leaking, spitting, foul. Impure. Impure.*

Jensen struggled to his feet and stumbled toward the back of the room. When he leaned against the window, he caught sight of his reflection.

He looked at his face, a face he had once thought handsome—what a fool he had been!

Look at yourself! Look! Look at the creature you are!

Thinning, graying hair. A leathery face, his skin nothing but pores and wrinkles hiding the pus and rot beneath. His nose hiding hairs. His eyes bloodshot. His teeth yellow. How had he—he, a creature so base—ever dared to gaze upon the angel? How had he dared to lay eyes on something so perfect, so pure?

We're nothing but animals, he realized, trembling, sobbing. *We're nothing but sacks of meat, hairy, sweaty, hiding ourselves underneath clothes, cosmetics, our own vanity. We're so ugly.*

"Dr. Jensen!" Sullivan cried, shaking him with those hairy old hands. "Dr. Jensen, can you hear me?"

Jensen spun around, gazed once more at the white-haired ape, and then collapsed to the floor. He curled up and covered his eyes, never wanting to stare at another human, never able to look upon this impure world again.

"So ugly..." he whispered, tasting his tears. "So ugly."

* * *

Dr. Sullivan stood above the trembling, weeping man on the floor.

Another victim. Sullivan's hands shook. *Another lost soul.*

He grabbed his coat off the wall and, squinting, tossed it onto the floor, hiding the photo that lay there. Then he turned back to Dr. Jensen and knelt, his joints creaking.

"Dr. Jensen! Dr. Jensen, can you hear me?" He touched the doctor's shoulder, and the man yelped and cowered. "Dr. Jensen!" Sullivan's voice dropped to a whisper. "What did you see?"

The psychiatrist would not reply, only lie curled up, catatonic. Shell-shocked. Just like the rest of them. Just like Eliana. Just like Sullivan's dearest friends, all those he had doomed to madness.

"What have I done?" Sullivan whispered.

He turned toward the window and stared outside at his life's work: satellite dishes the size of football fields, buildings housing the world's brightest minds, and a clear, vast sky above... a sky Sullivan had always sought to understand, to explore, to scour for life, for a sign that mankind was not alone.

"We found that life," he whispered. "And we must never find it again."

He would cancel the exploration program today. He would shut down all communications with the rover, delete all its software and files, erase all records that it had ever existed, that the cursed planet had ever been found.

"No one will ever see the photo again." His voice shook. "I will never hurt anyone again."

Sullivan pulled his lighter from his pocket. Screwing his eyes shut, he knelt and rummaged under his coat until he found the photograph. He straightened, eyes still shut, and lit his lighter.

With trembling hands, he brought fire and paper together.

A Word from Daniel Arenson

"Life" is a story about what we might see when we view an alien life form… and how it might change the way we see ourselves.

Most of my novels are in the epic fantasy genre. Four of my trilogies—*Dawn of Dragon*, *Song of Dragons*, *Dragonlore*, and *The Dragon War*—are set in Requiem, a world where humans can turn into dragons. I'm also the author of *Moth*, a series about a world torn in two—one half always in sunlight, the other always dark.

If you'd like to read more of my science fiction, feel free to grab a copy of *Alien Hunters*, my first science fiction novel. It's available in all the ebook stores: Amazon, Barnes & Noble, Kobo, and so on.

Or, join my mailing list and receive a free ebook as a gift: DanielArenson.com/MailingList

Thank you for reading, and I hope we meet again between the pages of another book.

Second Suicide

by Hugh Howey

I WONDER, SOMETIMES, if this is not me. Holding a tentacle up in front of the mirror, turning my eyestalk and studying these webbed ears, these bright green eyes with their space-black slits, I become convinced they belong to some other. It is a morning contemplation that, much like the gas from breakfast, eventually passes by mid-afternoon. But when I rise, I feel it is in another's body. My brain is discombobulated from sleep, and I sense some deep gap between my soul and my form. I think on this while on the toilet, until my bunkmate, Kur, slaps the bathroom door with his tentacle.

"Always in a rush to shit," I shout through the door, "but never in a hurry to be first from bed."

Kur pauses in his protestations, possibly to consider this contradiction. "It is your smelly ass that wakes me," he finally explains.

I flush and pop the door. Somewhere, our spaceship home will turn my waste into a meal. I like to pretend it will all go to

Kur. Outside, we jostle in the tight confines of our bunkroom as he takes my place in the crapper.

"What day is it?" he asks, farting. Most of our conversations are through this door. Once our shifts begin, we don't see each other. Kur works in Gunnery, and I moved up to Intelligence ages ago, after the conquest of the Dupliene Empire. The new job came with a superiority complex, but, alas, not a larger bunk.

"It's Second Monday," I tell him. We are practicing our Native. Kur and I are both assigned to Sector 2 landfall. He will be shooting at the very crowds I have studied, and on this planet they have seven days to a cycle instead of twelve. Such confusions are likely why I awake feeling like some other. You settle in the skin of an alien race, and by the time you feel at home there, they are no more.

Kur flushes. "Not day of the week. What day 'til planetfall?"

I hear the sink run as he washes his tentacle. Kur's personal hygiene makes up for much else.

"It's eight days to planetfall," I tell him. "Near enough that you should know."

He cracks the door. His bottoms are still undone. "I dreamed today was the day," he says. "Very confusing. I was mowing down the pink cunts when your foul emanations stirred me." He screws his eyestalks together, suppressing a laugh or a bout of gas. "Explains the cannon fire in my dreams," he says.

He laughs and farts and laughs some more.

I am reminded of my own nightmares. They usually come right after a conquest. In these dreams, it is suddenly the day of the next planetfall, and I don't know my assignments. I don't know the language or my targets or the geography. I haven't had these dreams in a long time, though. I feel prepared. I know this planet Earth twice as well as I have any other. I am as ready for this invasion as I have ever been.

While Kur finishes dressing himself, I tap the grimy terminal on the wall. A light in the top corner is flashing, twice long and one short: a message for me.

* * *

To: Second Rank Intelligence Liaison Hyk
From: Sector 2 Supervisor Ter

Bad news, Hyk. Mil from Telecoms Sector 1 has killed herself again. As this is the second offense in a span of twelve sleeps, Mil has been reassigned to Gunner Crew 2, Squad 8. Due to some shuffling in landing parties, we need you to clean out your desk and report to Sector 1. We apologize for any inconvenience. See Supervisor Bix when you arrive.

-Ter

Do not reply to this message. All commands are my own and do not reflect the commands of my Supervisors.

Planetfall in eight sleeps and counting. Have a happy invasion!

* * *

"Fuck me," I say.

"Seriously?" Kur asks. He flashes his fangs and points to his bottoms. "I just got the last button done."

"I've been reassigned."

Kur's joke hits my brainstump a moment later, too late for a retort. He shoulders me aside to study the terminal for himself.

"A new bunkmate," he says. "A girl. Maybe this one will sex me."

"I will miss you, too," I say. It is a half-truth. But my feelings are raw that Kur seems not sad at all. Part of me expects him to grieve.

"I wonder if she's cute," Kur says. He is making his bunk before breakfast, a feat I have never witnessed. He says her name aloud: "Mil." Almost as if he is tasting the sound of it. Tasting her.

"I think she must be deranged is what," I say. "Two suicides in a cycle. How much do suicides cost these days?"

"Two thousand credits," Kur says. "Squadmate of mine had to pay recently. Cut his neck shaving with a butcher's knife. Swears up and down it was an accident." He turns and shrugs his tentacle as if to say: *No damn way it was an accident.*

"Well, glad I'm not getting this roommate," I say. "She'll probably kill herself in the crapper while you sleep."

Kur laughs. "You're jealous. And I'm not the one with eight days to learn a Sector."

This only now occurs to me. Sector 1. That's the continent known as Asia in native. A large landmass, heavily populated. I pray the languages there are mere dialects of Sector 2's. Hate to waste my vocab.

I also mull the four thousand credits this Mil from Telecoms now owes for the two suicides. That's a lot of cred. All of that in a lump sum would be nice. It takes five thousand credits to buy a settlement slot these days. I could own a small plot of land on one of these worlds we conquer. Watch the fleet sail on without me.

Such are my thoughts as I pile my belongings onto my bed and knot the corners of the sheets. Everything I own can be lifted with two tentacles. Kur describes in lurid detail a girl he has yet to meet while I double-check that my locker is empty and I have everything. I find myself imagining this Mil dangling by her own tentacle from the overhead vent—and then I see Kur sexing her like this, and I need out of that room. Maybe he is right about me being jealous.

Opening the door and setting my sack in the hall, I turn to my mate of the last three invasions. Who knows when I'll see him again?

Kur has a tentacle out. He is looking at me awkwardly and plaintively, as if this goodbye has come just as suddenly for him. I am overwhelmed by this unexpected display of affection, this need to touch before I leave the ship, this first and final embrace.

"Hey—" he says, his eyestalks moist. "About that fifty you owe me—"

* * *

The transfer shuttle is waiting for me. The pilot seems impatient and undocks before I get to my seat. As he pulls away from my home of a dozen lifetimes, I peer through the porthole and gaze longingly at the great hull of the ship, searching for familiar black streaks and pockmarks from our shared journey through space. This far from our target star, the hull is nearly as dark as the cosmos, her battle wounds impossible to find. My face is to the glass, and it is as though an old friend refuses to look back. Suddenly, it is not the shuttle peeling away from my ship. It is my ship withdrawing from me.

I remember when she was built. It was in orbit above Odeon, thousands of years ago during a resupply lull. It was the last time I was transferred. Those thousands of years now feel like hundreds. I try to remember a time before this ship, but those days are dulled by the vast expanse of time. It often seems as though we were born together—like the ship is my womb but the two of us share the same mother.

I brush the glass with a tentacle as I gaze at her, and I hunt for the marks of wear upon my own flesh. I search for reminders from my years as a Gunner—but those scars must be on another tentacle. It was so long ago. Or maybe I am remembering old scars that are gone now, washed clean when last I died. It is a shame to lose them. With them go my memories of how they occurred. Those reminders should be a part of me, just as I was part of that ship. But now its steel plates fall away and lose detail, until my old home is just a wedge of pale gray among hundreds of such wedges.

I turn in my seat. Past the pilot I can see my new home, a similar craft, practically identical. And beyond that, a disc of illumination brighter than the neighboring stars—the planet that all the fleet has its pointy bits aimed at.

The pilot docks, lazily and with loud, jarring clangs. I thank him as I enter the airlock. Onboard the new ship—with some struggle and crappy directions—I find my bunk. My mate is not there. On shift, no doubt. I leave my things on the stained and bare mattress of the upper bunk, wondering idly if this is where the girl of the second suicide slept, or if perhaps my new bunkmate has been waiting for this day to claim the lower. The suicide girl probably passed me in another shuttle, is at this very moment surveying my empty bed. Or lying in it. Or she is dangling by a tentacle from my old air vent.

I can't stop thinking on the suicides. As I wend my way down foreign corridors, placing a tentacle here and there on the unfamiliar pipes and plates that squeeze in around me, I wonder what madness in some strange woman brought me here. Not that I haven't killed myself, but that was a very long while ago, after my second or third invasion. I remember waking up in the same body the next morning—same but newer and still smelling of the vats—and realizing the futility of it all. My Supervisor at the time—Yim, I believe—sat me down and explained that bodies weren't cheap and to cut that shit out. I soon realized that taking a blaster to my own head was no different than falling in battle, just more expensive. It took centuries to work off that debt, what with the interest. It only takes once to know the headache is not worth it, that the numbness is not worth it. Going to sleep at night is a more useful and less costly way to not-exist for some short while.

Unless… maybe this girl in my old bunk is so far in debt that more of it is hardly felt. Maybe she enjoys the waking. Maybe she loves learning to use her tentacles again. I remember that, the deadness in my suckers after reviving. Like I'd slept on them wrong. That is not a feeling I crave enough to kill myself for. But there are those much crazier than I.

Eight days to planetfall, and here I am lost on another's ship and thinking on nonsense. This will be one of those invasions where I am useless, standing on the sidelines and watching, no time to adequately prepare. I'm comfortable with that. No one can blame me. The late transfer is not my fault.

I pass a woman in the corridor and notice the way her stalks follow mine. Hey, maybe a new ship will be good for me. Maybe my bunkmate is lousy at gambling. I can get used to this life, as I have so many others. This is what I tell myself, that I can be happy in this skin of mine. For what other choice is there?

* * *

I find Supervisor Bix in the Sector 1 command hall, near the front of the ship. A terminal tech points him out through the glass. There are three men and two women bent over a table that glows with a land map. Stretching my stalk, I can see

Sector 1 and part of Sector 2. I watch these supervisors argue, can hear their muffled annoyance through the glass, and I see that things operate similarly here as everywhere else—with very little grease and a lot of grind.

The more I watch, though, the more I note the added stress among Bix's superiors, those men and women wearing emblems of High Command. I don't know these commanders personally (nor anyone of their rank—I report to those who report to them) but I can clearly see the tension in their tentacles, in the twitch of their stalks, and I do not envy them their jobs.

The display screen is centered on the fat land of my new sector. I see great swaths of blue, and then the coast of my old sector at the very edge of the map. The men and women inside the room seem nervous. Tentacles are waving, and I can hear shouts through the thick glass. Eight days to planetfall, and this must be the stress of ultimate responsibility. Why any ship jockeys to lead these incursions is beyond me. Surely it is best to be number two.

Cycles ago, after selecting Earth as a target and assigning sectors, there was a pissing match between my ship and this one over who had final rank. This happens when you study a planet long enough. You see its history through the lens of your sector, and you feel rightly that your target is the most crucial. With Sector 2, I would have landed on a long continent pinched in the middle like a woman sucking in her gut. Sparsely populated, but my supervisor liked to point out that the wealth per life-form was high and that their military spending outpaced all other sectors. But invasions are about bodies in the end, and no one can compete with Sector 1.

Heh. Funny how quickly I adopt the other side's arguments now that I'm here. Part of me always thought they had it right. Or so I tell myself. The homesickness is draining away as I wait for Supervisor Bix to finish his meeting. I imagine that he requested me personally. He must have studied my files. My chest inflates with the sudden pride of a new home, a new position, new people to know and impress. It is like a new body, but I get to keep the scars.

I make eyestalks with one of the receptionists in the waiting room. She smiles, and I can see her neck splotch in embarrassment. "Here to see Supervisor Bix," I say, tucking a tentacle into my waistband. "I work in Intelligence."

The receptionist opens her mouth to reply when Bix comes out, trailing his superiors. I introduce myself and offer a tentacle, which Bix declines. He seems confused. And then his eyestalks straighten with awareness. "From Sector 2," he says.

"That's right." I puff out my gut. "Liaison Hyk. Intelligence, Sector 2."

Bix waves a tentacle. "No, no. You've been moved to Gunner. Go see Yut for your assignment, I'm busy."

The air is out of me. I look to the receptionist, who diverts her stalk. "Ship's Gunner?" I ask with all the hope I can muster.

"Ground Gunner," Bix says. "See Yut."

"But I'm a man of learning," I complain.

Someone snickers, and I see that I'm a walking cliché.

"I haven't been a Gunner in lifetimes," I add. "I'll last five minutes down there."

"Then you'll wake up here and be sent right back in," Bix says. "I suggest you die heroically, so the body doesn't cost you."

"But why was I transferred?" I ask. "Was there something in my files—?"

Bix swivels his eyestalks toward me. "You're on this ship to get someone else off it," he says. "Nothing more. You can show us what you're made of"—I catch him looking at another officer with something like worry—" the next go-around."

With this, Bix and these other men and women of high station lumber off on their tentacles. The receptionist looks at me with pity for the barest of moments, and then turns back to her work, leaving me to show myself out.

* * *

Gunnery is in the rear of the ship, where all the other little ships are kept. It's far enough to take a shuttle, which allows me to sit in sullen silence. I watch the stars go by. I pick out my old ship among the fleet. At least, I think it's mine. I wonder if my bodies are still on that ship. If the shuttle loses pressure and I die right now, where will I wake up? And what would be the last thing I remembered? It's been a while since I saved my thoughts. I'll have to do that soon.

The constellations are strange from this point in space, but I can pick out a few stars we've visited. I have small souvenirs from a few. There are others that exist only in the history books. Like Celiad, where we learned the secret of the vats. Or ancient Osh, where our ancestors learned how to store the memories of man into machine.

Our current gun tech came from Aye-Stad, which I visited countless cycles ago. Our ships are from Rael. And thanks to the K'Bk, we no longer have disease, but I remember how such things as plagues used to work. The races I study still employ their immune systems, and the parallels between those systems and us as a race are striking. For we have become what Earthlings would call white blood cells. We remove foreign bodies from the cosmos. And every one leaves an imprint, a bauble of tech or a new idea, all of which we neatly coil into our lives, into our molecular structure. We are an immune system, and we are immune to death. This last, alas, is our curse.

As the shuttle takes us aft, I gaze through the cockpit past the pilot, and I imagine Second Fleet off in the distance, those ships out there identical to our own. Second Fleet trails us dutifully in case something awful happens. A backup full of backups. With my sudden demotion, I wonder what it would be like to wake up there, in the wake of my former home, with true mortality within tentacle's reach.

Thinking of tentacles makes me realize mine have slimed up with thoughts of Gunnery. It has been a long time since I landed on a planet with the first wave. Surely this is temporary, this demotion. Didn't Bix say so? It is simply because of the short time until planetfall. It is because of that silly woman with her second suicide. She is being punished, and so they punish us both. It should have been Kur sent here, a true Gunner.

When was the last time I fought with a first wave? Memories of bright and colorful worlds swirl together. The one thing in common is the brown mud on my boots. Slogging through battlefields. Noticing details like how the insides of sentient things have much in common: the same blood that colors red in the air, the sacs for breathing, the sacs for pumping blood through tubes, the tendrils for turning thoughts into things.

The dead and these worlds, they blur together like all colors into a dull brown. All I remember in the end is that I did my job, shooting so I would not be shot. All I remember in the beginning is the fear of death.

This is something you get over. You live with the fear until you die for the first time, and then you realize death isn't the end. Not when you have another body waiting in a vat with a backup of your recent recollections. It is painful, though, both the death and the rebirth. Painful and expensive. Both are deterrents meant to keep us on our guard. That's my theory, anyway. That they add the rebirth pain on purpose so you avoid dying the way a tentacle avoids a fire.

I no longer fear death, but still I try not to draw her attention. I like this me, however imperfectly it fits. I like my small scars, even if I can't recall where I got them. I search my tentacle for an old wound as the shuttle banks around the ass of my new ship, but some scars are memories that have faded, and some memories go with scars that no longer exist.

A glimmer of stars beyond my porthole distracts me from these sentimental thoughts. I think I can see Second Fleet, those little pinpricks among pinpricks, back there where true immortality lies. Though I fear a return to Gunnery, I know I will go into battle invulnerable. Our fleet is invincible when planetfall comes. We march through civilizations the way a child splashes through puddles, for in the distance lies our safety valve. One day, of course, we will face a surprisingly resilient foe. Or we will drop our guards because a thousand conquered worlds have left us bored with victory. Someone will vanquish us, but we will awaken in bright new ships, and we will show this foe that we do not die so easily.

Bah. Listen to me. An hour back in Gunnery, and I am giving speeches meant to clench loins and rush boys into battle. Already pretending to be brave. When what I really need is a strong drink and to meet those among my new bunkmates who gamble recklessly.

* * *

To: Third Rank Gunner Hyk
From: First Rank Gunner Kur

You've only been gone two days, and I can still nose your stink in the bathroom! I have other insults prepared, but now is not the time for banter. I need a favor. You know your old bunk? I'm sleeping in it. Why? Because I'm sexing my new bunkmate every night! You are envious, I know. Of her! Ha!

Only one problem: She's crazier than a hogtied rampus-mare. I've stopped her from killing herself two more times, and all she does is sit around, slack-jawed and oozing on herself. I'm worried if she manages to kill herself again they won't bring her back. Or worse: that they'll bring you back!

Har. Anyway, lend me a tentacle and I'll forget about the fifty you owe me. Can you find out what's eating at my sex-mate? I'd like to know before we hit the ground. Handing this beautiful creature a gun feels like a bad idea.

Fuck off, Kur

* * *

It is six days to planetfall, and instead of working on my aim with the new and improved double-barreled GAW13s, here I am in the smelly hall of records digging through files. I am looking for a girl who I'm not even sexing on behalf of a former bunkmate who little loves me. My mother would say the suckers on my tentacles have grown soft, and she would be right. Look at how little a fight I put up with the demotion to Gunnery. I would think myself spineless were it not for the invasion of Hemput III, where I got a damn fine look at my backbones before the lights went fully out.

I find the suicide girl's records by looking up her bunk. Easy to do since I sleep in the thing. Mil. I do like that name.

And so of course I imagine Kur sexing her. My brain loves torturing the rest of me.

I start a ship-to-ship file transfer to Kur's terminal so he can pry on his own. Aware that Mil might be the one checking the terminal, I come up with an innocuous header for the message: *Hey, Fart-Sac — The report you wanted.* While the computer does its job, I scan the file for myself. I remember my transfer orders saying Mil was in Telecoms. Now I read that she was a Terminal Technician in the radio wing. Gad, I would kill myself too! But now our suicide girl has brains, and Kur is sexing her even more. I resolve to get out tonight and meet someone. Why was not Kur transferred instead of me?

Speaking of transfer, the ship-to-ship is taking forever. Less than an Earth cycle to planetfall, and the networks are as packed as a mess hall on garbum night. I decide to send myself a copy on the intership network, just in case. Besides, I have nothing to read. Sector 1's written language is nothing like Sector 2's. If you planted a bomb in Sector 2's language and scattered the remains on a terminal screen, you would have Sector 1's language. It's no wonder this planet is always at war. My language instructor once said: *No two people have ever battled that read each other's poetry,* and I believe that. It's why we in Intelligence are told to avoid poetry at all costs. Learn, but do not empathize.

That should apply here as well, as I read up on Mil. I tell myself I'm doing a bunkmate a favor, but the truth is that I'm in love with a woman I have never met. A woman my former friend is most likely sexing at this very moment. A woman who seems to hate her life as much as I hate mine.

* * *

Second Squad, Gunner Troop 5, Sector 1 plays cards with some fucked-up rules. Quks are wild, but only if you have a five-tentacled Kik in your hand. And in a run, you can skip a number if all the cards on both sides are the same gender. They call this the "missing buck" play. What I'm missing is thirty-five credits, and it isn't because of any difference in skill. It's because I can't keep these blasted rules straight.

"Two pair," Urj says. He's bluffing, and I wait for the player to his left to call him on it, but a card is drawn instead. This squad will have me broke before they get me killed.

"Urj says you were a Liaison Officer."

It takes me a moment to realize I'm being spoken to. I'm trying to determine if my Quk is wild or not.

"Yes," I tell the brawny woman across from me. Rov is her name. Hard to keep all the new eyestalks straight. "I worked in Intelligence on Warship 2."

"Warship 2," someone says with something like sympathy.

I take a sip of my bitter drink.

"Lot of transfers all of a sudden," Urj, our squad leader, says. He aims a tentacle at Rov. "You were in accounting, right?"

Rov waves in the affirmative.

"And I was in water reclamation until two weeks ago," Bek says. We're all waiting on him to play, but he doesn't seem to be in a hurry. He has one tentacle curled protectively around an enviable pile of credits.

"I thought you all had been together a long time," I say. I feel less like the new guy. It makes being down thirty-five creds even harder to bear. Unless these are ship-wide rules.

"Nah, they're throwing everyone to Gunnery for this one," Urj says. "Heard it from Sergeant Tul. Said it's 'All-Tentacles' this go-'round."

I think back to the argument Bix and his superiors were having when I reported for duty. Seemed tense, but I figure the pressure is always greater on Warship 1. Taking the lead into battle is a heavy responsibility. Performances are judged against prior conquests, and there is a lot of open space between worlds in which to measure one another.

"So what's this world like?" Rov asks. "If you were a Liaison Officer, you must've done a lot of reading up on the natives. You fluent?"

"Not for our landing sector," I admit.

Rov looks disappointed.

"But I know quite a bit about the planet in general. From studying Sector 2."

Urj squares his cards and rests them by his remaining credits. A chair squeaks as the player to my right settles back. All eyestalks are looking at me, and I realize these Gunners aren't curious so much as worried. We've had a few All-Tentacle raids in the past. Last time, Warship 5 was lost in orbit, taking all the vats onboard with it. A replacement ship had to be called up from the trailing fleet. Until everyone could be sorted and new bodies grown, there were men and women walking around on their last sets of lives.

"They write about us a lot," I tell my squadmates. I can see their tentacles stiffen. Except for Bek, who ties three of his limbs into knots of worry. "I don't mean *us*, exactly. I mean… their culture is full of doomsday musings. Raids from space are a particularly popular trope."

"All races are full of doomsday musings," Bek says. He looks to the others, is trying to comfort them more than himself. "We have our own stories of all this coming to an end. It's fear of final death."

"This is worse than most," I say. "I can only really speak for Sector 2, but they think on little else. They spend more of their money on warfare than any other thing. We submitted a report to the Command Committee about this a while back—"

"Must be your report that has me back in Gunner," Rov says, her accusation flying across the table.

"And him too, don't forget," Bek points out, waving a tentacle at me.

"Hey, what's wrong with Gunner?" asks Urj, who has obviously never been anything but.

"Pipe down," someone shouts from a bunk room down the hall. Sounds like the sergeant. A hush settles, and eyestalks swivel guiltily toward the door. Someone makes a move at a pile of credits, but a tentacle slaps the thievery away.

"Tul heard from High Command that the Warships are to be kept in low atmo," Urj says quietly. He is Squad Commander, and to report out of chain is a great sin. Somehow, the hush deepens. The game is forgotten, even the thirty-five that I'm in the hole.

"Reboot and reload?" Gha, a Gunner, asks.

Urj nods.

"What's that mean?" Bek asks, and I am thankful. I grow tiresome of admitting my ignorance on these things.

"It means there are more of us in the vats, and those bodies may be needed as well."

"Fast as they can grow us," Gha says, "they'll send us down."

Everyone looks at me like I'm responsible for this mess. But what do I know? It's been ages since I took a life or gave one up. There have been occasional worlds that we passed by because they were deemed too dangerous to take on. There have been worlds we conquered with a single warship. Then there are worlds like these that worry the stalks of those much higher in rank than I'll ever be. So many types of worlds, and I've studied them all.

* * *

Instead of spending my free time greasing the outdated gear I've been assigned or going over the tactics in my squad manual, I sit in my bunk in the days before planetfall reading about Mil, my absent bunkmate. This is what I call her: my absent bunkmate. We share our bunks, hers and mine, just not at the same time. She is sexed where I used to sleep, while I suffer the dreadful slobbering snores of her old roommate, Lum. I wonder at times, woken at night by the awful noise of Lum sleeping, if the mystery of Mil's suicides is not right there, one bunk below me.

Mil's files are full of a vague strangeness, but nothing I can put my sucker on, either for myself or for Kur. Lots of messages are gone—the original ordering is intact, but some numbers are skipped. Reminds me of the "missing buck" play my squad inanely ascribes to.

Quite a few messages are to and from a secretary at High Command, saying that Mil's reports are being passed along. The actual reports are not among her files, however. There is one partial report quoted, describing a missing signal of some sort. I wonder if one of our advanced scout ships has been taken out. It is from these ships that all my intel came. Does Earth have warning of our arrival? Wouldn't be the first time. And it would explain the All-Tentacles and the consternation among the higher-ups.

I think of the long-range scans of Earth I used to study. It was evident that fighting had taken place recently and might still be going on. Not unusual on planets we raid, and this planet's inhabitants are an especially warlike people. If they stopped that fighting and trained their guns toward us, that would be very much not-good. The problem with hitting an aggressive race isn't just their honed skills, but their state of readiness.

Maybe I'm reading too much into Mil's records, but with so many bodies being thrown into Gunner, it is time to consider that we are being lowered like a skink into boiling water. Maybe Mil was suggesting we bypass this planet entirely, and High Command is having none of such talk from a radio tech. Perhaps they deleted her suggestions in case she turns out to be right.

But why the suicides? It's not just that suicides are expensive, it's that the chances of offing oneself twice in a single cycle are low. Whatever is ailing someone is not likely to be present when they are brought back.

When my new bunkmate Lum returns from her station duties, I set the terminal aside and broach the touchy subject.

"Hey, Lum," I say.

My bunkmate is eating a gurd. With her mouth full, she raises her stalks questioningly.

"Did you… notice anything strange about Mil before she… well, before either of her suicides?"

"Mmm," Lum says. She swallows and starts taking off her work clothes. I haven't been able to tell if she is coming on to me, but I knot my tentacles that she isn't.

"Yeah," she says. "She was very different the days before. Both times."

"How so?" I ask.

Lum throws her clothes into the chute and steps into the crapper to run the shower. "She got real calm," she says. Steam starts rising in the crapper. I've scalded myself twice showering after Lum's lava blasts.

"You mean, she wasn't usually calm?"

"Her normal state was to raise hell," Lum says. She sticks her head out of the crapper, but I notice a tentacle wrapping around the edge of the door. She is dying to shut the conversation off and get in the shower. "The reason Lum offed herself was because of her demotions. She was in High Command a few raids ago. Got bumped down, and she's been getting bumped down ever since. Causes too much trouble."

Lum screws up her eyestalks. "*Speaks her mind,*" she says, as if this is a great sin.

"Seems weird," I say. "Two suicides in a cycle. Taking on that much debt."

Lum eyes the shower. The steam is, blessedly, cloaking her lower half.

"You ever done it?" I ask. "Ever... you know."

"No," she says, smiling. She looks down at herself. "I'm all original. And I'm wasting water. You wanna come in? I can tell you about my crazy ex-bunkmate and you can scrub the barnacles off my back."

"I'm good," I say. "Just curious is all."

Lum seems, if anything, relieved. I can't get a bead on her. "Suit yourself." She starts to pull the door shut, then sticks her head out one last time. Considers something. I'm waiting.

"You were in Intelligence," she says.

"Still am," I say. "Gunner is just this one time."

"And other races, they do it too? Off themselves?"

"A lot," I say.

"But it's final death for them," Lum says.

"Yeah. That's the point," I say. "They do it when they get depressed." Here, I'm drawing more from my own experiences than any of my studies. I remember feeling like I wanted to sleep for a long time. Forever, if I could.

The steam is filling our bunkroom. I feel sweat gathering on my back. Lum studies me for a painfully long while.

"I don't think Mil was depressed," she finally says. "I think she was... satisfied. Content, maybe. Or resigned. Or maybe..."

"Maybe what?"

"Or maybe she was scared out of her senses, and she couldn't get anyone to pay attention. So she finally gave up."

* * *

The next morning, I find what may be a clue. It is discovered by my sensitive back: a lump in my mattress or a spring bent out of shape. This is two mornings in a row with an ache in my spines (my mother would, again, call me soft of tentacle). I tear the sheets off my mattress in search of the answer.

All the springs are in fine shape, but running a tentacle across the mattress, I feel a lump. A very hard lump with sharp corners. It turns out to be a small data drive sewn into the fabric of the mattress. This is most curious. I wouldn't think my beloved Mil would be into sexing vids, which is all I have ever used these for. The drive is locked. I try to access it with the wall terminal, but it refuses my tentacle. Coded to Mil's secretions, unless it belongs to someone else.

One mystery is solved, and that's the second suicide. Even with Mil's memories restored to some prior, stable state, she would have found the drive and accessed some reminder. She had left a note to herself before the first deed, and upon discovering it, gave a repeat performance. Maybe her superiors knew she had left some memory behind, and so they sent her to another ship. To my bunk. Where she is being sexed by Kur.

The only problem with my brilliant theory is that Kur says she's still trying to hang herself. But that could be explained by the sexing! I chuckle to myself. I will have to tell Kur that one. I bring up my messages on the terminal to pass this joke along and to tell him about the data drive, when I see a message waiting in my inbox from him, saying that he has thwarted another attempt on her life.

Why does my heart go out to her? Why am I not disturbed? And what if she kills herself yet again and they are out of bodies for her in the vats here? They might bring her back as a man, and now it is too late and I already love her.

Listen to me. A cycle ago, I was dreaming of saving enough for a plot of land and a settlement pass, of making a permanent home on some ball of mud. Now I am worried over a woman with a career of demotions and a pile of debt.

I study the locked drive, this lone token of hers. It was sewn into the top of the mattress, almost as if designed to gouge a spine and annoy the resting. Like it was meant to be found. Maybe it wasn't planted for her at all—but for me.

Two days to planetfall, and a radio tech's madness consumes me. I should be worried about my own skin. A bad death means more debt I can ill afford. But it's difficult to stop being a Liaison Officer. I am trained to dig and to study and to know a soul before we destroy them. Now I find myself curious about a soul intent on destroying herself.

* * *

It is download day, one day before planetfall. After mess, we file by rank down to the vats and hold our tentacles very still in the tight confines of the scanner. Annual copies were taken in my old line of work, but they were treated casually—few people fall over dead at their research terminals. This time, I don't move a muscle. I try not to think any stray thoughts. I have a very good feeling that this copy will be needed.

Will I wake up with my current sense of dread intact? Will my first thought be, upon my rebirth, *please don't let me die tomorrow?* What a strange life. It is only strange to me because I have studied so many races who only know final death. Their one life is all, and this causes some among them to guard it until it cannot breathe. Others flail and spend it recklessly. And what do *we* do? We grow bored of it.

Before I joined the fleet, I remember thinking that we were conquerors of worlds. But we are conquerors of death. How many copies of ourselves have we left behind? How many will be enough? The scanner clicks and whirs around my head, recording these disjointed musings of mine, the hollow in the pit of my soul, and what is really eating at me becomes clear:

I do not dread dying tomorrow as much as I loathe the thought of taking lives with my own tentacles. I have studied for too long, read too much poetry, perhaps. I am used to making planetfall with the last of the landing parties, the crafts full of advisors and record-keepers and relic-takers. I land once the bloated bodies of all a world's poets have already been turned beneath the soil.

So this I dread. And what else? The repetition. The waking up to do it all over again. Death becomes no more than sleep. And even if I put a bullet to this brain, and the next, and the next, swift enough to test the staying power of the vats, there will always be another of me in Second Fleet, and finally I will tire of this as well.

The scanner records these worst of my thoughts. And then the whirring and grinding falls still. Ah, how I wish I could fall still as well. Into some meditative, or more permanent, silent state.

And with this, the mystery of Mil's second suicide is solved. It is so obvious, I feel like slapping myself with my own tentacles. I squirm from the scanner. As the next Gunner takes my place, I badger the scanner technician to look something up for me on his terminal. He is annoyed, but I have all the charm of a Liaison Officer. All I need is a date. I need to know when Mil performed her last routine backup. I tell him it is a matter of life and death. Of life and debt. And he relents.

The date is near enough that I know that I am right, but I rush back to my bunkroom and pull up Mil's records to be sure. And yes, her backup was soon after the missing messages but just before her first attempt. Whatever she knows, it doesn't look bad to a technician on her scans. It is not a black fog of depression, no bright colors of mental imbalance. Just a piece of knowledge, cleverly hidden away.

I fish the locked data drive out of my pocket and study this mystery. If only I had another day or two, I would get to the bottom of this. As it is, the why of it all will have to wait until after Earth. I just hope when I die in the morning, that I'll be able to piece these more recent epiphanies together again.

* * *

It is planetfall, and as our attack craft soars down through the atmosphere toward this green and blue and white target of ours, my thoughts drift to a heat-tech I met once. I don't remember his name, it was so long ago. He came to the bunkroom Kur and I shared when the thermostat was out. It was so cold in our room that our piss froze and crinkled before it hit the toilet. While he was working to fix the unit, the heat-tech complained that he was always cold, which I had never thought of before. Strange to think of a person who fixes heaters never being warm. But of course. He only works where the heat is broken. He must be cold all the time.

I am thinking this on the day of planetfall, because lately I have only seen our conquests in ruin. The planets are already smoking from the orbital bombardment and the armies of Gunners by the time we Liaisons ever get mud on our boots. The power grids are out; satellites blown to bolts; fires raging. Others stay behind and build an empire; they will see the place whole. But not me. I am like the heat-tech, forever cold. I am the conqueror who never glimpses what he has won. I only see these worlds in their cultural writings from deep space, and then I see them battered and broken.

These are my thoughts as the shuttle touches down and sways on its struts. The Gunners around me loosen their harnesses as the rear hatch lowers. There is gunfire from a squad that got here first. There is the scream of something heavy plummeting through thick atmosphere. Sergeant Tul yells for us to *"move, move,"* and we do.

I am third off the ship, and my tentacles are moist with fear. My GAW13 kicks as I fire. Tanks rumble and drones and fighter craft swirl overhead, a maelstrom of missiles exploding, fountains of dirt erupting, my first glimpse of real-life humans taking shelter, taking aim.

I have studied them so long that they feel intimate and familiar. I know them. I launch a volley into a small squad, and one of the humans is ripped in two. Our shuttle is taking fire and screams as it pulls away, lifting up to gather more bodies as they spill from orbiting vats. The resistance is stiffer than we were promised. A grenade takes out Urj, and one of his dismembered tentacles tangles around my ankle. Sergeant Tul is yelling at us to take cover. There is a mound of metal nearby, some kind of bunker half-covered with dirt that a few Gunners huddle behind. Bullets pepper its side. I fire into the humans until my gun overheats and then dive into the bunker. The last thing I see overhead is the flash of a new sun, a blinding ball of light, as one of our warships and all of its vats wink out of existence.

There is much yelling. Radios bark back and forth. I check my gun and my tentacles, make sure all is in place, and then I see what I am hiding inside of, this makeshift bunker. It is familiar. It is the ruin of one of our ships, a troop shuttle, but something is not right—

Bullets ping off the hull, and I can hear the natives of Sector 1 yelling and coordinating. A Gunner from another squad has taken shelter with us. Her radio barks, and she yells at Tul, "War Two is down!"

I think of Kur. Our home. Our bunkroom. Now that ship is a hailstorm of bolts plummeting through the high clouds and scattering across this ball of mud.

Inside the busted troop shuttle where we've taken shelter, tall grasses are swaying, waving at me, trying to signal some warning. Rov stands by the gaping hole in the shuttle's skin, scanning the sky, her armored bulk blotting out my view of the carnage beyond. I am going to die a cowardly, expensive death, I realize.

"War One has taken a hit!" Rov shouts.

Flashes of light stab in around her, another brightening of the sky. A moment later, there is a deep grumble that I feel in my bones, a noise like the belly growl of a hungry god.

Closer by, a bomb explodes, a sharp crack followed by the howls of my kin. I hear alien craft buzzing overhead, filling the sky with the piercing shrieks of their passing, and with the whistle of loosed munitions.

All is background noise. I am watching the tall grasses wave and wave. Their feathery blades are growing up through the destroyed hull of one of our ships. There is rust here and there, cables chewed by local varmints, all the signs of that universal destroyer: Time. The scars he leaves are everywhere I look.

I hold a tentacle in front of my visor and study it. Where are my scars? Where are the physical artifacts of wounds I remember suffering? Has it really been so long? I search for an old injury that I have been hunting for and have been unable to find for a cycle now. The last thing I remember is waking in my bunk, feeling like someone else. I remember a last glimpse of my ship, dimmed and showing no pockmark, no wear of war.

Another bomb erupts in the distance. More of my people dying. And I think of the stress I witnessed among High

Command on my warship. I think of the way things have been falling apart—so many people thrown to Gunner. There is a girl who will not stop killing herself, a girl who knows something, a fragment of a report about a missing signal from another ship.

There is a helmet by my feet, half-buried in the dirt of planet Earth. Tul is yelling for us to fight, and I am trying to remember a poem I once knew. The words are not with me. All around us are the signs of an invasion that did not succeed. And I know a sudden truth with all the fierceness of a hot blast—I know this as bullets zing by my helmet and bombs rage closer and closer:

We are the second fleet.
We are the reserve.
All that's left.
And hell has come for us at last.

A Word from Hugh Howey

"Second Suicide" was a story that wouldn't leave me alone. I wrote the first draft over a year ago. Other projects got in the way, so that rough draft sat on my computer (and swirled around in my head) for a very long time. It all started with this idea that we believe in one of two extremes: Either we have this one life, or we will live for an eternity. While these seem like the two possibilities before us, there's a more interesting case: What if we only got one second chance? And tragically, what if we only realized it once it was too late?

In order to inspire myself to live a full life with a positive impact on my surroundings, I've chosen to live as if this is the only life I'll ever have. But what about this instead: What if I did this all before, but I screwed up everything I tried, hurt those around me, and lived a truly wasted and despicable life? I know that sounds horrible, but what if this is my second chance, a chance to do more with my life, to be a better person? Should we wait on a near-death experience to show us what a gift this is and to turn things around? Or can we just pretend?

A Word from the Editor

It has been my privilege to work with Samuel Peralta and the many talented authors who have contributed to the first three installments in the *Future Chronicles* series of science fiction anthologies.

As a reader, I have always loved short stories—but as every reader knows, the risk when diving in to any short story collection is that sometimes the stories included are hit-or-miss. A few "gems," a few "duds," and you hope that the good outweighs the bad.

What we have aimed to do with the *Future Chronicles* is to create a place where a reader can reliably expect quality storytelling from start to finish. No duds, no afterthoughts. True, not every story will be your cup of tea—and this is inevitable in any anthology with a variety of styles and topics. But our goal is for every single story to convey *quality*. What we hope—and what we have been delighted to observe thus far in reading the reviews of the prior *Chronicles* anthologies—is that *every* story will be *some* reader's favorite.

Although I will step aside from editing the upcoming installments in the *Future Chronicles* (due to other commitments), I can assure you that the series will remain in excellent hands. Samuel Peralta will continue to coordinate the contributing writers, and the talented Ellen Campbell will take over editing duties. The authors lined up for the upcoming *AI Chronicles* and *Dragon Chronicles* are top-notch, and I'm looking forward to reading what they come up with. I hope you are too.

David Gatewood

A Note to Readers

Thank you so much for reading *The Alien Chronicles*. If you enjoyed these stories, please consider these other anthologies edited by David Gatewood:

The Robot Chronicles
The Telepath Chronicles
Synchronic: 13 Tales of Time Travel

Finally, before you go, could we ask of you a very small favor?

Would you write a short review at the site where you purchased the book?

Reviews are make-or-break for authors. A book with no reviews is, simply put, a book with no future sales. This is because a review is more than just a message to other potential buyers: it's also a key factor driving the book's visibility in the first place. More reviews (and more positive reviews) make a book more likely to be featured in bookseller lists (such as

Amazon's "also viewed" and "also bought" lists) and more likely to be featured in bookseller promotions. Reviews don't need to be long or eloquent; a single sentence is all it takes. In today's publishing world, the success (or failure) of a book is truly in the reader's hands.

So please, write a review. Tell a friend. Share us on Facebook. Maybe even write a Tweet (140 characters is all we ask). You'd be doing us a great service.

Thank you.